HER DREAMS WERE JUST AROUND THE CORNER...

Her eyes tracked to the end of the pedestrian street and latched onto a man who came around the corner wearing a navy pinstriped suit.

Her heart immediately started pounding.

His hair was thick, curly, and ink black. He had golden skin, which she fantasized came from sunbathing on his yacht in Saint-Tropez. Black designer sunglasses hid his eyes, but his bone structure would rival that of a Greek god.

When he flashed a dashing smile and called out a greeting to her waiter, she pressed her hand to her chest, where her pulse was galloping. He was as a local, and an affable one at that.

As he turned the next corner and disappeared from sight, she slumped in her chair. She was out of breath and trembling. She couldn't even lift her coffee cup right now. My, oh, my...

Mr. Pinstripes was like no other man she'd ever seen. He certainly bore no resemblance to any of the Joe Schmoes she'd dated back in Nowheresville. Not that it mattered—she didn't have a shot with a man like him.

PRAISE FOR AVA MILES' NOVELS

SEE WHAT ALL THE BUZZ IS ABOUT...

"Ava's story is witty and charming."

BARBARA FREETHY #1 *NYT*
BESTSELLING AUTHOR

"If you like Nora Roberts type books, this is a must-read."

READERS' FAVORITE

"If ever there was a contemporary romance that rated a 10 on a scale of 1 to 5 for me, this one is it!"

THE ROMANCE REVIEWS

"I could not stop flipping the pages. I can't wait to read the next book in this series."

FRESH FICTION

"I've read Susan Mallery and Debbie Macomber... but never have I been so moved as by the books Ava Miles writes."

BOOKTALK WITH EILEEN

"Ava Miles is fast becoming one of my favorite light contemporary romance writers."

TOME TENDER

OTHER AVA TITLES TO BINGE

The Paris Roommates

Your dreams are around the corner…

The Paris Roommates: Thea

The Paris Roommates: Dean

———

The Unexpected Prince Charming Series

Love with a kiss of the Irish…

Beside Golden Irish Fields

Beneath Pearly Irish Skies

Through Crimson Irish Light

After Indigo Irish Nights

Beyond Rosy Irish Twilight

Over Verdant Irish Hills

Against Ebony Irish Seas

———

The Merriams Series

Chock full of family and happily ever afters…

Wild Irish Rose

Love Among Lavender

Valley of Stars

Sunflower Alley

A Forever of Orange Blossoms

A Breath of Jasmine

The Dare Valley Series

Awash in small town fabulousness…

Nora Roberts Land

French Roast

The Grand Opening

The Holiday Serenade

The Town Square

The Park of Sunset Dreams

The Perfect Ingredient

The Bridge to a Better Life

The Calendar of New Beginnings

Home Sweet Love

The Moonlight Serenade

The Sky of Endless Blue

Daring Brides

Daring Declarations

———

Dare Valley Meets Paris Billionaire Mini-Series

Small town charm meets big city romance…

The Billionaire's Gamble

The Billionaire's Secret

The Billionaire's Courtship

The Billionaire's Return

Dare Valley Meets Paris Compilation

———

The Once Upon a Dare Series

Falling in love is a contact sport…

The Gate to Everything

———

Non-Fiction

The Happiness Corner: Reflections So Far

The Post-Covid Wellness Playbook

———

Cookbooks

Home Baked Happiness Cookbook

Country Heaven Cookbook

———

The Lost Guides to Living Your Best Life Series

Reclaim Your Superpowers

Courage Is Your Superpower

Expression Is Your Superpower

Peace Is Your Superpower

Confidence Is Your Superpower

Happiness Is Your Superpower

———

Children's Books

The Chocolate Garden: A Magical Tale

THE PARIS ROOMMATES

AVA MILES

www.avamiles.com
Ava Miles

To my ultimate roommates…you know who you are.

ACKNOWLEDGMENTS

To Patrick for his generosity in answering questions about restaurants in France and what would truly happen in Nanine's case. The conversation was hair-raising. I should have had wine.

To my beloved café and restaurant staff and chefs who have become friends and family. You make every encounter a magical feast of friendship, connection, and cuisine.

To my dear friends at Simone Pérèle, Virginie and Natalie, and for my other makeover helpers—Benedikt, Angélik, and so many more. Thea wasn't the only one who benefitted, and for that, we are eternally grateful.

To my baking teachers, especially the charming chef at *Le Cordon Bleu*, who made the experience transcendent with humor and intensity.

ABOUT PARIS...

Ernest Hemingway once wrote: "If you are lucky enough to have lived in Paris as a young man {or woman}, then wherever you go for the rest of your life it stays with you, for Paris is a moveable feast."

So if you're looking to create a delicious life for yourself, when she calls you home, you don't hesitate.

You go.

A MOTHER'S WISH

Food is comfort. Food is home. Food is love.

In the hardest times of my life—and there have been many—I've turned to food for succor. Is it any wonder? With the right ingredients, you can create anything. There's magic in that.

So it shouldn't be a surprise that when my dear husband died ten years ago, I turned my focus to my restaurant.

Only it wasn't enough. I could still feel the empty space my dear Bernard had left all around me. The spot in my kitchen where he'd lean against the wall, his arms folded, that gleam in his cognac-colored eyes as he watched me cook for our guests. The boxy chair where he'd sit and go over the week's paperwork, muttering as he ran his hands through his thick gray hair. His rumpled side of our bed. The corner of my heart that beat for him.

My restaurant, Nanine's, was missing its main ingredient: love.

Was it any wonder I sought something to bring some spice back into my life? To fill the silence that echoed throughout my space and my heart, because even my magical chandelier had stopped chiming its whimsical notes, bereft as I was.

And so I contacted the Sorbonne and *Le Cordon Bleu* to place an ad: *Restaurant positions open in exchange for room and board. One-year term. Contact Nanine Laurent.*

Of all the applicants, and there were many, I chose six lovely young people from the United States. I picked them because I liked the feel of them and the complexity of their diverse characters. What I didn't know was that I was putting together one of the grandest menus I've ever created.

Because it became apparent to me very quickly that that was what they were: a feast. Each of them a course in the most delicious dinner you could imagine.

Thea: First Course, the *apéritif*, the little bites designed to set the purpose for the entire meal. She was from the middle of Nowheresville, USA, as she called it, and yet she wanted to passionately bake croissant and baguette, as if she had a French soul. In her personal life, she prefers to take small steps, but those she takes capture one's attention.

Dean: Second Course, the *entrée*, the appetizer created to be the entry point into the meal, the best of which feels like a dream when it caresses your taste buds. He has so many ideas swirling in his head that he's still mastering what he truly wants to share on the grand stage of life.

Brooke: Third Course, the *plat*, the main course invented with flourish to leave its signature in one's memory for years to come. She's always wanted to be driving the show, making a grand impression, but that makes her unable to sometimes enjoy the little things that fulfill one's heart.

Sawyer: Fourth Course, the salad, a refined tradition few today understand or give its due, which cleanses the palate for more inspiration to come. He's a throwback to a bygone era whose complexity lies under the surface, an artist at heart afraid to unleash his own brilliance.

Madison: Fifth Course, the cheese plate, another part of the meal not everyone finds suitable or pleasing, but which can change the digestion of the meal. She embodies so many brilliant strong flavors that she often cultivates a barrier to others, not believing everyone wants her or understands her.

Kyle: Sixth Course, the dessert, which is an indulgence and a delicious treat all its own, especially when it is savored and not rushed. He's the classic golden boy, appearing too perfect at times, all the while hiding the rich layers he holds inside himself.

What I have never told them is that I was the fish course, the only course served either before the main course or becoming one itself depending on the depth of its flavor and ingredients. You see, I was adrift at sea myself, delicate in flavor, unable to hold my own place in the feast of life, the current taking me where it would.

Yet for that one magical year, we all grew more confident in what we brought to one another's lives. We all learned that people could become family even though they are not related by blood.

But then our time together ended. We went back to our respective lives, changed, yes, and while we remained in touch, the inroads we'd made in becoming the perfect feast began to slip away.

I did not realize how much of an echo of my old self I'd become, rather like the shell of a cicada, a ghost of my youth —the young woman who was brave and unstoppable even in the midst of great betrayal and challenge.

Now such betrayal and challenge has darkened my door yet again, threatening everything I hold dear. For the second time, I have called upon my Courses. This time because they are family.

And so the Courses are coming back to help me, and we will once again create the perfect feast together.

I hope.

CHAPTER
ONE

Paris was a city full of what could have beens.

What could have been if ten years ago she'd stayed instead of returning to her hometown of Nowheresville, USA? What could have been if she'd gone for it instead of playing it safe?

There was no way of knowing, but this time Thea Rogers was determined to have it all.

Even if she was a sour mixture of exhaustion, worry, and fear sitting awkwardly alone at her favorite old haunt, Café Fitzy, decked out in wrinkled travel clothes and glaringly white tennis shoes with her outdated blue suitcase jammed next to her tiny corner table.

The August sun was beating down on her, keeping her skin damp with sweat, a constant state since she'd landed at CDG airport and taken the maze-like public transportation nightmare jammed with other grumpy, rumpled passengers. After the plane from Des Moines, Iowa, to Chicago and then on to Paris, she'd had to navigate who-knew-how-many Métro transits to make it to the heart of Saint-Germain.

The hour and a half transit had been a nightmare, and

dragging her suitcase while needing to pee had been agony, until she'd broken down and stopped at her old favorite café for a coffee so she could use the bathroom. If the waiter ever gave her the time of day and took her order. She didn't see Antoine, the owner, who used to be a friend, and her chest grew tight. She could have used a friendly face right now.

Maybe it was the jet lag, lack of sleep, or the worry coiled up inside of her, but she was so sensitive, she swore everyone was staring at her as she sat there. The chic Parisian women smoking gracefully as they conversed in sultry French had their eyebrows raised her way, as if they were hoping she would leave. She could all hear them thinking that she was taking up space. Totally gauche. A rutabaga in a sea of exotic fruits.

If only they knew she'd once lived in this neighborhood and thought of it as her own. Forget that she'd arrived in a purple jumper with a white shirt boasting a Peter Pan collar. Because she'd thought it was coolest thing she could arrive in Paris wearing.

For that one magical year, she'd stretched her wings, but they'd been made of spun sugar, and she'd let them dissolve after returning home, where she'd slid into a routine that was as regular as it was boring.

Then, two days ago, her best friend and former roommate from Paris had called her. She'd been at the bakery where she worked, putting freshly proofed croissants in the oven.

Brooke hadn't wasted time with any preliminaries.

"Thea!" she'd cried, her voice charged with emotion. "Nanine was rushed to the hospital after a heart attack."

The bread pan had slipped from her hand, falling to the floor.

"The doctor called me for her. She wants all of us to come if we can and stay at the house together again. You're the first of our Paris roommates I've called. I'm leaving as soon as I can arrange it with my editor."

Her roommates' faces flashed in her mind. Brooke, the go-getter. Dean, the dreamer. Sawyer, the thinker. Madison, the rebel. And Kyle, the golden boy. From the beginning, they'd been the most unlikely of friends, so different from each other in just about every way anyone could be. But their connection was proof friendship could be found in anyone, anywhere.

"I'll take off from the bakery and leave as soon as I can."

But it hadn't been that easy.

Fate had followed through with another kick in the pants —despite her years of service, her boss had refused to grant her any of the vacation she was owed, pushing her to do something she'd never imagined: quitting her job. On the spot.

The very thought of it had her sucking in air and moaning, "Oh God," making the two Parisian women who would never find themselves in a life crisis from the looks of them give her a haughty glare.

She wasn't the kind of woman who made abrupt decisions. She dreamed of owning her own bakery someday, and quitting a successful job ran counter to pursuing that dream.

But this was family. Nanine! The mother of her heart.

After quitting, she'd jumped on the first flight to Paris she could find, draining what little savings she had. Her parents had tried to talk her out of it, of course. *Thea, but you've worked there ever since you got your fancy degree in Paris. The Snyder family has been so good to you. Everyone loves you there. Don't be rash. You're not thinking straight.*

She'd tried to explain. *The bakery hasn't been the same since Patty died two years ago and Fred took over. He never lets me have time off. All I do is work.*

They hadn't listened, of course. Her people were farmers and had married early. They'd never traveled out of the Midwest—never wanted to, especially not to a faraway place like Paris. They hadn't understood why she'd worked every job she could find to save money to train as a baker instead of living and working on the family farm, and now they didn't understand why her long-time job wasn't enough.

Feeling a little faint from heat and dehydration, she signaled to the waiter as he swept in to refill the wineglasses of the two chic women two tables over. He didn't spare her a glance, and she wanted to slide under the table in shame. She'd bet F. Scott Fitzgerald had never had a problem getting a drink here when he was reportedly writing *The Great Gatsby* in the right corner table beside the mahogany bar.

She supposed she could leave, but that would also be gauche since she'd already used the bathroom. Rule number one of Paris: when you had to use the bathroom, you got a beverage to pay for the privilege.

He was making her wait because he didn't think she belonged, and that wasn't right. This was her old stomping ground, and Antoine's place. Old Thea might have slunk away with her tail between her legs, but the new Thea she wanted to be would stand her ground.

She dug into her carry-on for her old recipe journal. If she kept herself occupied, she might feel less awkward. The sight of the dancing breads made her run her fingers over the front cover. When she'd packed, she'd spontaneously rifled through her hope chest for the perfume Nanine had given her as a gift years before, and she'd found her old spiral-bound journal under it. She'd brought it with her to Paris ten years ago, thinking to fill it with recipes, but instead, she'd filled it with her dreams after realizing it was too corny for *Le Cordon Bleu*.

As she'd lifted it out of the chest, a scrap of paper had fallen out. The glue she'd used to adhere it to the page must have given out. Much like she had on some of her dreams. The fortune cookie slip was from one of her last meals in Paris with her roommates and its message still gave her goosebumps.

The friendships you make will last a lifetime.

She hadn't known then how true that was, but she and her roommates had stayed in touch and seen each other when they could. Of course, certain people were closer with each other, like she and Brooke, and everyone had stayed in touch with Nanine. She was the rock, the anchor, the woman who had given each of them something special.

Returning to Paris and bringing her old journal was like coming full circle. The whole book was chock-full of her dreams of running her own bakery and becoming more confident, along with memories of her roommates and their time together with Nanine. She still remembered the moment she'd tucked it and her perfume away. Her mother had called her *fancy* for wearing perfume to Sunday dinner. She'd cried when she'd gotten back to her apartment, missing Paris and her roommates and Nanine.

Well, that half-life she'd been living was over. She was back and she could resurrect her dreams like she had her old journal. She turned to the first page and read what she'd written on the note card ten years ago.

Recipe for: *A Delicious Life*

Date: August 24

Prep time: One Year

Ingredients: Studying & working hard, Patience, Confidence, Openness, Friendship, Humor

Hard-to-find ingredients: see Confidence above, Mastering the French language, New look

Notes: This is your chance. When you work hard, good things happen. This year is your ticket to better things. Getting a degree at Le Cordon Bleu will help you own your own bakery someday. Listen to your teachers. Try and put yourself out there more. Don't be weird. Maybe learn a few tips on how to dress better.

Every successful recipe starts with finding the best ingredients and following the directions.

She stared at the last part. She *hadn't* followed all the directions once she'd gotten home. She'd settled back into her old life, one where every day tasted like oatmeal. Sure, she'd gotten a great job as a baker at a renowned family-owned bakery. Sure, she'd kept her friendships with Nanine and her roommates alive. But she hadn't kept up the whole *put yourself out there* part. She still didn't fit in where she'd been born and raised, and she'd gone back to hiding in plain sight.

The truth was, the prospect of turning thirty in October had made her take out a magnifying glass to examine the state of her life. As Nanine liked to say, milestones had a way of making one examine one's journey so far. She turned to the first entry she'd written on the plane—the one she couldn't even bring herself to put in the first person because that would make it too real.

Recipe for: *PATHETIC*

Date: NOW

Notes: Thea Rogers works like a dog.

She rarely dates.

If she has a day off, she's either at her parents' farm helping out or curled up alone on her couch bingeing shows about other people having lives.

Nothing in her life is exceptional except for being a baker.

Life is passing Thea Rogers by.

And if she continues on this track, she's going to end up alone, with nothing but bread and croissants to keep her company, which will probably make her fat.

Conclusion: Thea Rogers is sick of herself and her life.

Cure: Thea Rogers needs a life makeover. Bad.

She wanted to cover the words with her hands to make them less overwhelming, but maybe she needed the reminder. Her boring but reliable life was gone. It felt freeing but terrifying, and now that she was here in Paris, she had no idea what she was going to do with herself beyond offering some comfort to Nanine. Nausea steamrolled her, so she sucked in several slow breaths of Parisian air. The faint scent of freshly baked bread helped her straighten her spine.

Being back here with no return ticket was a curveball, no doubt. But it could also be a gift—a chance to reinvent herself and her life. In Paris, where everything had changed for her once before. It could happen again.

She grabbed a pen as a phrase came to mind and wrote it on the next blank page in her journal.

Recipe for: *Living Life to the Fullest*

That would be her new recipe, she decided, especially since Nanine's heart attack had shown her just how short life could be. She was going to use her time here to become the person she really wanted to be, the one she'd originally written about. Not the boring play-it-safe nice girl from Nowheresville she'd returned to being.

Because here was a truth that both terrified and thrilled her: she planned on staying. She had a terrific résumé, didn't she? And she'd brought her essential tools of the trade so she could give a potential employer a demo of her abilities: her sourdough starter named Doughreen (God, she was such a geek), her broken-in pastry cloth, and her well-washed pink apron with a croissant and heart on its lapel.

Once Nanine was back on her feet, Thea would find a job. Yep, absolutely, she thought, nodding to a pigeon who stopped in front of her, hoping for food. He looked a little starved like she was, so she nudged a bread crumb on the ground his way. Bread has a way of making you feel better, she wanted to tell him.

Thea heard her phone trill in her purse, prompting the pigeon to fly off. She cringed as the two Parisian women glared at her for her *faux pas*. She jumped up immediately, almost knocking the table over, and darted across the pedestrian street to take the call. Digging through her remaining snacks in her purse, she pulled out her phone. Brooke!

"Hi there! I'm at Café Fitzy's trying to get a coffee. Where are you?"

"Hey, sweetie! I'm running a little late. I had an interview with one of the hottest new fashion designers in Paris when I arrived. I set it up at the last minute because I got here before everyone else and couldn't bear the thought of sitting alone in Nanine's. I'm so glad you stopped at Fitzy's."

Thea caught a dagger-eyed look from a waiter when he came out and gestured pointedly to her luggage. "I had to pee, but I might never get a coffee. I reek of tourist."

"Typical, but you can turn that around. Look the waiter in the eye and say, 'Excuse me, sir. Is Antoine here today?'"

Then Brooke repeated it in perfect French. Thea couldn't imagine pulling that off. Her French sounded like a dying tractor engine coated in rust. "Maybe I should just leave money for a coffee on the table."

"You just arrived in Paris for the first time in eight years. Follow my directions! You'll get your coffee."

Her journal's helpful hint about following directions came to mind, and for the first time since before she'd heard the news about Nanine, she felt her mouth twitch. Brooke loved to boss people around, and Thea sometimes liked it. It felt like her friend was the rudder in her boat. She'd need Brooke's help now more than ever to become the Thea she wanted to be.

"Okay, Brooke. I'll try."

"And pump Antoine for information about Nanine. The

doctor said she refuses to talk to anyone until we're all here and together. I'm scared, Thea."

Suddenly she could use that comforting bread crumb on the ground herself. "We all are."

"Yeah." Silence hung over the line for a moment before she pressed, "How are you *really*? You must be going out of your mind about quitting your job."

Her stomach quivered, but she decided to give a spunky comeback. Spunky comebacks were for girls trying to turn their lives around, weren't they? "This is the best thing that could have happened to me. Not that I wanted Nanine to ever—"

"Oh, Thea, I know that. But are you seriously telling me you haven't cried? I know you. Not once?"

She worried her lip. "Well, I did run through a pack of tissues on the plane, but then I started watching all my feel-good Paris movies. Worked like a charm." Mostly.

"How many movies are we talking?" Brooke asked suspiciously.

"I started with *French Kiss*, then went on to *Julie & Julia* before ending with the movie that kicked off my love for everything France."

"*Sabrina*." Brooke sighed heavily. "Oh, Thea. I don't want you to worry, okay? You won't have rent, staying at Nanine's. What did you do about your apartment?"

Oh, that. Her nausea rolled back like a freight train. "I told Mrs. Randall everything. She's too nice to hold me to my lease. I only have to pay rent until she finds a new tenant. I worked like a dog to pack up my personal belongings before I left. I didn't have much since I was never home. My parents agreed to store my stuff at the farm." That had gone over like a lead balloon, along with them agreeing to keep her car until she could arrange to sell it.

She'd even dropped some boxes off at the Salvation Army on her way to the airport, things she never wanted to wear again, things her mother had given her. Black old lady shoes in her giant size of eleven and ugly print dresses that made her like look she could star in *Little House on the Prairie*. Her mother had always had a fondness for the show and hoped Thea could turn out like Half-Pint. Her school photos wearing floral print flannel dresses with her hair in braids would haunt her for the rest of her life.

"Out with the old and in with the new!" Brooke's enthusiasm was a soothing balm. "Thea, I'll cover anything you need. That asshole you worked for didn't appreciate you, and I'm glad you quit. I'm so proud of you."

She couldn't blame jet lag for her tears this time. It was those words—she'd rarely heard them from her parents. "You're the best. Did you know that?"

"Tell that to my ex. Ugh. Did I tell you he's dating this hot new Brazilian model named Plumonia? My editor asked if I was going to be able to still report on what she wears during fashion week."

Brooke was a style editor for *TRENDS*, which meant it really would be part of her job. Sighing, she added, "I had to bite my tongue so I wouldn't ask, but seriously, what kind of name is Plumonia?"

"Sounds like pneumonia to me."

"She's nineteen, by the way. *Nineteen!*"

Which meant their age difference was eighteen years. Now it was Thea's turn to cheerlead. "I never liked Adam. You're better off without him."

"That's what I've told myself every day for the past four months since I changed my ringtone to Beyoncé's 'Best Thing I Never Had' to help me remember. Hey! You need a new ringtone."

She'd ignore the fact that she wouldn't be using her U.S. phone in Paris because the fees were too expensive. Going back to using an international calling card had its advantages. One of them being that she wouldn't have to call her parents for a while. When she'd first come to Paris, they'd gone six to eight weeks at a time without talking, and since they still didn't have a computer, email was out of the question. "I'll think about it."

"All right, Thea," her friend said. "I'll see you in forty. Don't get into trouble. You're not in Kansas anymore, Dorothy."

She groaned. "*Dorothea* is my name, and jokes about me being from Kansas aren't funny. Iowa is an entirely different state."

Brooke's snort had her smiling again. "Sorry, you know I love you, but we New Yorkers don't care about the middle states. I'll see you soon. The others will start rolling in shortly. Dean could beat me, in fact, but that depends on traffic. The Second is a nightmare. I've never seen so many tourists around the Louvre in August."

"Wait!" Thea cried out as a new thought struck her. "You didn't tell everyone else about me quitting, did you? Nanine should be our focus right now."

"My car is here, sweetie. Gotta go."

The call ended. Thea worried her lip. She didn't want her other roommates to know about her issues just yet. They'd always considered her a little sister, the nice small-town girl who needed looking after. Okay, some of that had been true when she'd arrived fresh-faced with only two years of high school French to carry her along.

She'd been so unprepared then, and maybe she wasn't much better off now. But she didn't want her roommates' pity, and she sure as heck didn't want anyone to think her problems were on par with Nanine's heart attack.

Thea dropped her phone back into her purse, her spirits better after talking to Brooke. Her friend had more confidence in her little finger than Thea had in her entire body. Such confidence could be catching. That was an ingredient she desperately needed for herself.

She headed back to her table, already looking forward to her café. Brooke was right. She had to have it. A coffee in Paris was not a regular event. Sawyer used to say a single cup was filled with existential meaning, decadent pleasure, and toe-curling comfort. But that was Sawyer for you, always thinking deeper than the rest of them.

As she watched for her waiter to reappear, she opened her recipe book to the photo of her and her roommates at Christmastime ten years ago. They were all drinking champagne at Café Fitzy's after opening presents. Brooke's short bob still looked stylish even though she'd been blond back then. Dean was making a funny face for the camera. Sawyer had on his very studious-looking glasses and was trying not to laugh. Madison wasn't smiling, but her golden eyes were bright with happiness. And Kyle was as beautiful as ever, being the golden boy he was, and he had his arm wrapped around Thea. Then there was Nanine, sitting in the middle of the group, her elegant long gray hair trailing down her shoulders.

Thea's heart warmed. That was still the best Christmas she'd ever had. She touched the photo. Soon she was going to be back with them all.

Coming back here was one of the best decisions of your life, Thea Rogers.

Then Antoine stepped outside and her chest welled with nostalgia. He was here! He held a pack of cigarettes in his weathered hand and walked across the cobbled pedestrian street to where she'd just been standing, lighting one and taking a deep drag. His oblong face had a pronounced chin and an insouciant straight nose that worked with his usual tourist-directed scowl. The sun-kissed lines around his dark eyes were a stark marker of his joys and sorrows while his hair was almost pure white now, making him even more distinguished. She'd known him when it was silver, and while he had a few more age lines, he was very much the same.

"Antoine!" She broke into a smile and waved like an American before she caught her *faux pas*. The French did not wave.

He took another drag on his cigarette and stared at her with narrowed eyes. Then he blinked, as if coming out of a dream, and darted over after letting an unsteady cyclist ride by. "First Course!" he called enthusiastically in French, leaning over and kissing both her cheeks in greeting as he stubbed out the cigarette in the ashtray on the small table.

She winced. "Yes, it's me, First Course," she answered in French and wanted to crawl into a hole at how she sounded. "Thea."

"Thea! You're here to help our lovely Nanine, yes?" he asked, again in French, as his face grew shadowed. "Everyone in the neighborhood has been so worried."

"Yes, I hope to." She switched to English. "You know how she is. My other former roommates are arriving soon as well."

"All six courses back in Paris," Antoine said, his dark eyes showing a telltale wetness before pointing to the photo she had out. "You are cataloguing memories, I see. I remember the night. Nanine had given you each a special gift of fragrance, I believe. You could smell the love between all of you in the air."

Thea fought back her own tears. "It was a beautiful night. Antoine, the news about Nanine was such a shock. She's always been so healthy."

"Maybe her heart gave so much, it finally couldn't give any more," Antoine muttered. "Always a big heart for everyone, Nanine. Especially lately."

She made a conversational sound before asking, "What happened lately, Antoine?"

He shook his head. "I would not feel right, talking about Nanine's business. She is better telling you."

If there was one thing about the French Thea appreciated, it was that they valued others' privacy. And yet Brooke would want her to push. "We are all friends, are we not?" she asked badly in French, hoping to be more persuasive. "It would help us—"

"*Oui*, but you must be thirsty, Thea." The change to English as much as the shift in subject was as good as a period at the end of a sentence. "*Café crème*? Croissant?"

She nodded vigorously. Antoine called out in rapid French to the waiter who had stopped his serving and was openly listening to their conversation. He darted inside after Antoine sent him off with a flick of his hand.

Antoine gave a Gallic shrug. "He thought you were a tourist. Welcome home, First Course. Tell Nanine her first café back at Fitzy's will be on me."

Clearly she wasn't cut out to be Sherlock. She hoped Brooke wouldn't be upset. "I will, Antoine, and thank you."

His smile was a little watery as he went inside. She dashed at her own tears and told herself to hold it together. The waiter finally arrived with her coffee and croissant with a brief smile. Progress, Thea thought, as she ripped open two brown sugars and poured them into her café, stirring slowly to maintain the light-as-air foam on top. She closed her eyes and took a sip. The sweet blend of roasted coffee and rich milk saturated her senses, and for a moment, there was peace.

Everything seemed possible. Even her own transformation.

Not that she expected her renewed recipe for a delicious life to be a cakewalk. More like making bread. She would need new ingredients to come together for herself, ones she'd have to mix and incorporate until she found the perfect dough. Then she'd have to let it all sit, rise, and take shape. Fire had a way of sealing everything together, and there *was* fire inside her—her drive, her passion. When she got the right recipe, she knew she'd come out a masterpiece.

A masterpiece, huh? The Paris air is making you delusional, Thea Rogers.

No one could call her a masterpiece right now. She fingered the baggy tan T-shirt over her wrinkled black cotton drawstring pants and eyed her giant tennis shoes. Should she change before seeing Brooke? Her friend would be dripping style like always, all the way down to her fashionable heels. Thea tucked her feet together under the table in shame. Wearing a size eleven was the bane of her existence, especially in Paris where the steps on most stairs ran more to a size seven shoe.

She glanced in the café's glass windows and caught her reflection. Her brown hair was overdue for a cut and hung in a shaggy mess down her back. Because when did she have time for a haircut? Usually she put it in a ponytail.

Back home, she looked like everyone else. The one-length plain Jane hairstyle wasn't supposed to stand out. Neither were her boring, neutral clothes.

Her mother said she was a late bloomer. That was stopping now.

She signaled to the waiter for her bill when he appeared. As she was opening her purse for her money, her journal fell to the ground and another slip of paper danced in the air before falling to the ground. She bent down to pick it up and read the phrase she'd cut out of one of Brooke's old fashion magazines.

Your dreams are just around the corner.

Emotion rolled through her, and her eyes tracked to the end of the pedestrian street as she tucked the paper back into her journal. Her eyes latched onto a man who came around the corner wearing a navy pinstriped suit.

Her heart immediately started pounding.

Suddenly all she could feel was a rumbling throughout her entire body, as if a Métro train were passing underground. She grabbed the table's edge to steady herself as she watched him come closer.

His hair was thick, curly, and ink black. He had golden

skin, which she fantasized came from sunbathing on his yacht in Saint-Tropez. Black designer sunglasses hid his eyes, but his bone structure would rival that of a Greek god.

When he flashed a dashing smile and called out a greeting to her waiter, she pressed her hand to her chest, where her pulse was galloping. He was as a local, and an affable one at that.

As he turned the next corner and disappeared from sight, she slumped in her chair. She was out of breath and trembling. She couldn't even lift her coffee cup right now. *My, oh, my…*

Mr. Pinstripes was like no other man she'd ever seen. He certainly bore no resemblance to any of the Joe Schmoes she'd dated back in Nowheresville. She tried to catch her breath as she told herself she was being stupid. She didn't have a shot with a man like him.

She gulped more oxygen, but her nerves were wired from Mr. Pinstripes. Perhaps his pheromones had some insane effect on the opposite sex. Glancing around, she eyed other women at the café. None of *them* seemed to have noticed him. If she hadn't known any better, she would have sworn she was dreaming. Then she thought back to the message that had slipped out of her journal. It had to be a coincidence, right?

She finished her café and allowed her body to settle down. Then she checked her phone again. Nothing more from Brooke, but Dean had texted her. She couldn't wait to see him. He was like a Ferris wheel, always fun but forever turning in a circle, barely stopping.

She clicked on his text. *Hey sweetie! Heading straight to Nanine's. Probably fifteen minutes out. Can't wait to see you.*

Heartened, she decided to head over to Nanine's herself. The walk would do her pheromone-crazed body good, right? She would be the first one to welcome Dean, and Brooke would arrive soon as well. She would have loved to have had someone waiting for her. Plus, she could take care of Doughreen. Her starter needed to go into the cooler, stat.

And maybe she'd run into Mr. Pinstripes again. There was no harm in looking, was there?

When the waiter finally appeared, he said, "Antoine says it's on the house."

Her eyes grew wet again. "Tell him thank you," she said as she didn't see the older man hovering in the doorway.

He gave a little incline of his jaunty chin as she eased out of her chair and grabbed the handle of her suitcase, taking off down the sidewalk as a quartet of tourists on rented bicycles angled by.

The way to Nanine's was familiar, but her eyes took in the new bar around the corner called Speakeasy with its crisp navy awning. She'd bet Mr. Pinstripes frequented the joint, and her heart rate spiked again at the thought.

Her luggage wheel caught on the sidewalk as her attention wavered before she dragged it along. La Maison de l'Entrecôte emitted the familiar scent of grilled steak, green pepper from its succulent sauce, and frites in the air as she passed. A new tea salon called Old Hong Kong had her wanting to cross its threshold simply because of the name. Besides loving tea, she'd never been to Hong Kong but had always been curious about it. Heck, she'd never been to anywhere but France and Canada.

More bucket list items, Thea.

Next door, The Little Black Dress Shop ironically displayed a slinky one-shoulder dress in *blue*. She stopped short. Holy moly, it was gorgeous. Something she'd wear on a date with a man like Mr. Pinstripes in her fantasy world.

She rolled her eyes at herself and kept going. Walking on Paris' golden streets was like wrapping herself up in bright, shiny wrapping paper tied up with a big red bow. Her excitement spiked as she neared Nanine's restaurant and her old home. Picking up her pace, she turned the next corner and stopped cold. *"Oh, my gosh!"*

The burgundy awning was gone, the one that had sported the simple but somehow comforting sign reading *Nanine's*. The menu placard on the wall by the double doors was missing, and the curtains were gone. The windows looked grim and dusty, as if the building had been abandoned for years.

Her stomach started to burn. What had happened? Nanine hadn't mentioned any changes when Thea had spoken to her last month.

She rushed across the street to look inside.

The restaurant was gutted, the tables gone, the walls torn open. And was that exposed wire hanging out? Had there been a fire? Her hand flew to her mouth.

Was this why Nanine had had a heart attack?

She stood breathing harshly. Brooke and Dean were going to freak when they saw this. Everyone was. "Okay," she assured herself. "We'll figure it out."

Unsteady, Thea headed to the alley. She had to get inside. Reaching the back of the restaurant, she tucked her luggage out of sight. Nanine had always kept a spare key taped below an old loose brick under the back steps. Thea found it and tore the tape back, grasping the brass key. She prayed Nanine had fixed the lock. The key was notorious for being difficult, something the older woman had intentionally not fixed as she found it a satisfying battle of wills on occasion—something to get the blood pumping.

She faced the old lock. *Here we go.* She inserted the key. It stuck like it always had. "Oh, come on," she pleaded softly. She pressed the key harder and heard the metal scrape. Then it finally turned.

As she walked inside, her knees went weak with relief. The kitchen was exactly as it had been—except covered in dust, she quickly realized as she scanned the stainless steel prep counters and let her eyes wander over to the industrial range and ovens.

Nanine's famous chandelier gave a faint jangle of its crystal, almost like a weak pulse. Thea's gaze traveled across the room to where it hung in the small hallway leading to the dining room. Nanine had kept the small chandelier in the kitchen because the former owner had said it had a personality all its own, like many unexplainable things in Paris. The crystals served as a weathervane of sorts for the restaurant's atmosphere.

She coughed as dust reached her nose, and when she inhaled, she could have sworn she smelled roast chicken. Nanine was known for her roasted chicken laced with butter and herbs de Provence. Just like that, her mind flashed back to sitting at the large wooden farm table in the kitchen with her roommates, all of them laughing and drinking wine while stealing bites of chicken and roasted potatoes as Nanine smiled from ear to ear at the head of the table.

The kitchen was eerily quiet except for the sound of the antique Horloge on the wall. Nanine had hung it there because it had a second hand that new staff could watch for time-sensitive sauces like béarnaise or hollandaise.

She knew she was putting off going to the front of the restaurant. But she couldn't make her feet move in that direction. Dean and Brooke would both be arriving soon, she assured herself, and they would all face that disaster together. She could distract herself by taking care of Doughreen. She silenced any thoughts about her being a coward as she went back for her luggage and dragged it back to Nanine's walk-in cooler.

"Doughreen, you're going to be so happy here," she told her starter after unzipping her suitcase on the floor. Her airtight plastic container was perspiring in the Ziploc bag, but Thea gave a moment of thanks that Doughreen hadn't exploded like her bottle of shampoo.

She set it aside with a grimace and then shot to her feet when she heard staccato-like footsteps in the kitchen. Dean! The crystals in Nanine's famous chandelier gave a sudden clang as she raced toward the back door.

Only to be faced with three men in police uniforms scowling at her with their feet braced, as if ready to take down a dangerous intruder. It took her a second to realize who the intruder was.

Her.

CHAPTER
TWO

Dean Harris didn't just love Paris—he adored it like a young kid adored his older brother.

As his taxi raced across the bridge to turn onto Rue Saint-Germain, he caught sight of the Eiffel Tower on the right. He soaked it all in as they turned left into his old neighborhood.

The city was still as gorgeous as she was worldly, and back when he was a cocky twenty-year-old, she'd taught him how much he didn't know about life—and how much he wanted to experience.

He'd always teased Nanine that Paris was more than a multicourse meal—it was a weeklong feast, a veritable bacchanal. She'd retaliated by calling him the Second Course, the appetizer, the entry point into the meal. And that had kicked off her ascribing meal-related nicknames to all his roommates.

In her sage-like way, she'd had him pegged from the moment he'd arrived in a chambray shirt and designer jeans he'd gotten at a consignment store. He *was* only interested in whetting his appetite before moving on to the next great thing. Funny thing: he'd made a career out of it in tech in his hometown of San Francisco. He'd sold his creation—an early app for high-end restaurants to deliver their delicious meals to foodies like him—for millions and then became an angel investor, mentoring tech start-ups so they could be acquired in one to three years for life-changing money.

He thrived on new ideas, people, and places. But tech wasn't like it used to be. Entitled tech babies were more common than the original visionaries, and everyone was looking for a *get rich quick* scheme. He was juiced to be back in the one place that had never disappointed, even though bad news had beckoned him there.

Paris had captured his heart ten years ago hook, line and sinker, and the time he'd spent completing a year abroad at the Sorbonne Business School had been his happiest. The city herself wasn't the only reason. There had been his five incredible roommates, friends he was eager to reconnect with.

And Nanine herself.

Seeing her advertisement on a bulletin board for international students had been a pivotal moment in his life—although he hadn't known its full significance then. He simply had the compulsion to apply. Following that gut instinct had changed his life.

Nanine needed them now, and when Brooke had shattered his easygoing life with the call about Nanine's heart attack two days ago, he'd shifted his entire world to come to Paris to help get her back on her feet.

Like the city herself, Nanine had been his teacher as much as a mother figure. There was no one he owed more, and while she'd never look on it like that, he was a man who paid his debts.

Then there was Thea…

According to Brooke, the Paris roommates' little sister had quit her job to come help Nanine. Not that he was supposed to admit he knew that. Thea hadn't wanted to eclipse Nanine's situation, rightfully so, and totally in keeping with the sweetheart she was. She'd soon find out that they had her back too. Didn't he help douches achieve their dreams every day? How much harder would he work for the people he loved?

He hadn't seen Thea in person since her visit to Manhattan to see Brooke two years ago, a visit he'd decided to spontaneously fly out for. They'd talked on birthdays and at Christmas and kept in touch on social media. He appreciated her continued outreach, something he wished he was better at. If he couldn't see or touch something, he had a hard time giving it his continued attention.

Except not with Nanine. She'd been everything his parents had never managed to be: supportive and serious. Staying in touch with her through phone calls every four to six months had been unique for him—unique and grounding—and she'd continued to give him advice when he'd asked for it. But mostly, they'd laughed over each other's mundane stories, like a young tourist not knowing what a Cornish hen was to how Dean had gotten back someone else's leopard-print boxers instead of his own from a new laundry service. Those conversations kept things real. And Dean liked real. There was so much fake crap in San Francisco, and he was so over it.

As the taxi passed the eye-catching shops on Rue Saint-Germain, he smiled. This time in Paris was going to be a breath of fresh air once they figured out a plan to help Nanine and Thea get back on their proverbial feet. He could manage his clients from here for a while after taking a couple of weeks of vacation. Right now, he didn't have a clue how long he'd need to stay, but he was more than okay with that.

Arriving on the familiar street, he fumbled with his money clip as he glanced out the window. The restaurant's awning was gone, and the building looked condemned given the grimy windows. What the—

Then he noticed the empty police cruiser parked halfway

on the sidewalk blocking the alley. Thea was supposed to be in there!

"Keep the change," he muttered in French, shoving euros at the driver. "Just put my bags on the sidewalk."

He burst out of the car and jogged across the street, forcing a tall man on a motorized scooter to veer to miss him. He raced down the alley to the kitchen entrance, circumventing the police car. The door was wide open. He could hear Thea trying to speak in a mix of English and French, and a man's aggressive rapid-fire reply.

Rushing inside, he skidded to a stop as three police officers swung around to face him, all business. Nanine's chandelier gave a loud clang before going silent. He held up his hands as he looked at Thea. She was pale.

"You okay?" he asked, his palms turning sweaty.

"They're saying I'm a thief," she said in a clogged voice, looking like an overemotional kid in the principal's office. "I think."

"*A thief?*" He took a breath, formulating his thoughts in French. "Hello, I'm a friend of Nanine Laurent—like this woman here. I think there has been a mistake."

The one in charge, Crew Cut, shot off another rapid response that Dean only half understood, something about a break-in, while the other two officers—Thin Lips and Scar Brow—fingered their police belts, which he noticed held guns. Terrific. Green lights were visible on their bulletproof vests. He realized they were recording the incident as he eased slowly across the dirty kitchen to stand next to Thea, putting a comforting arm around her.

She was trembling. "I told them I have a key, but they aren't listening and I can't communicate…"

"We'll take care of it." He turned to the head officer. "Can I show you a picture of us with the owner?" He nearly cringed. God, his accent was *merde*.

"I already tried to show them," Thea bemoaned. "They

say Nanine takes photos with many customers. They want to know why I'm in the restaurant when it's obviously closed, and Nanine is in the hospital."

So whoever had called the police knew about that, huh? "Let me—"

Crew Cut interrupted him from saying more, shooting off more hostile French. He was going to have to turn this around and quick. He didn't want to have to call Nanine in the hospital. That would definitely raise her blood pressure.

"Didn't expect to get arrested on my first day back in Paris," he joked, rubbing Thea's spine. "You?"

She didn't laugh. Only bit her lip like the nice, law-abiding girl she was. Hell, Thea wouldn't even drive past a stop sign in the middle of the night in a ghost town in California. Not that French cops would care about that.

"I have photos of us upstairs in Nanine's home," he began, giving them his signature charming smile. "Here, let me show you."

They watched his every move, and when he held out his phone, Crew Cut had Thin Lips step forward. After glancing at the picture, he scoffed in a very French way. "This was ages ago. You look like a little kid. That explains nothing."

"*Well…* What do we have here?" came a contralto-like voice in liquid French.

Brooke Adams breezed into the kitchen in *haute couture*—a black Dior business suit accessorized with a pink Chanel bag and black Louboutins—and tilted her head to the side. The chandelier seemed to purr. Brooke oozed class. Even an inanimate object could see that.

She flashed her very captivating smile, the kind that had fashion people spilling their *couture* guts to her. "*Dites-moi ce qui se passe.*"

He tried not to grin at the polite command. Brooke had always known how to make an entrance, and she sure as hell knew how to dress someone down when necessary. He'd always admired how effortless it was for her. Some women oozed sex. Brooke oozed authority.

Crew Cut started first, followed by Thin Lips. Scar Brow might have gotten his tongue cut out on an undercover mission since he still hadn't once spoken. Dean noted the two officers weren't talking as fast now, mumbling about recent problems at Nanine's. That had him thinking back to the missing awning.

What the hell was going on?

Brooke removed a pack of Gitanes from her purse along with the gold lighter from her father, likely worth more than their monthly salaries combined, and lit the cancer stick without looking at them. She only smoked in Paris, he knew, and often when she wanted her way. This was a prop in her show, but still, he tried not to inhale.

She breathed in a full puff before blowing it out in a commanding trail straight out of a black-and-white gangster classic with James Cagney. Then she shrugged. Damn, but she was still a master at the indelible French shrug, the slightest lift of the shoulder made to convey a classy nonchalance.

Crew Cut shot off a rebuke about smoking in the restaurant. Thea coughed, punctuating his point. Dean sent little sister a pleading look.

Brooke only took another puff before responding in flawless French, "The people you see before you are Nanine's adopted family. We've come back to take care of her and will be staying upstairs in her home. All of this has already been very stressful. *You're not helping.* Would you like me to call the doctor at the hospital and have him vouch for us? Perhaps Antoine at Café Fitzy? Or are the Paris police eager to cause Nanine Laurent more health issues?"

Dean bit the inside of his cheek. Damn, but he still had something to learn from Brooke. No doubt about it—this trip to Paris was just what he needed. He felt more alive than he had in forever, which was kinda weird given the circum-stances. Only made it more right in his mind.

Crew Cut made a rude gesture before saying, "I am just to believe you?"

Brooke blew another trail of smoke into the air and uttered one crisply punctuated word: "*Oui.*"

More than any of them, Brooke had taken to French like a duck to water since she'd started taking French classes in second grade. She dripped French from her soul.

Crew Cut and Thin Lips seemed to know it. Nodding to Scar Brow, they all detoured to the door.

Brooke took another draw from her Gitanes before saying, "Thank you for checking on the restaurant, officers. You never know who might be out there."

She gave them another pointed smile as she flicked cigarette ash like a pro into a nearby ashtray used by the kitchen staff on breaks. They nodded, and Crew Cut wished her a good day. Male egos had been assuaged. No one was going to jail on their first day in town. Dean considered it a win, especially for Thea. The last thing she needed after the two punch of hearing about Nanine and quitting her job was to get thrown in jail.

Dean thought he could have toughed it out. How bad could French jail be? Didn't all the books and movies show the prisoners drinking brandy and playing cards with the guards? He could handle that.

When the officers' footsteps had faded from the alley, Dean let his grin fly. "Damn, Brooke. That was hot. Why didn't we ever hook up?" he joked to lighten the mood.

She stubbed out her half-smoked cigarette and dropped her purse on the grimy stainless steel counter. "Yuck, that's dirty. I'm glad to see you haven't lost your funny bone, Dean. Now shut up and hug me. Both of you."

They all came together, and Dean wrapped them up in his arms. They both felt small compared to his six-one frame. He finally became aware that Brooke was trembling like Thea. Not her usual.

He angled her back and tipped up her chin. Her cat-shaped green eyes were unusually sad. The dyed caramel hair was different than the natural blond she'd worn when they were roommates. Blond didn't garner respect, she'd told him when they'd had lunch in New York a few years ago. But there wasn't a strand out of place in her slick blunt bob, and she was still picture perfect. "Hey, Third Course. You okay?"

"No," Brooke whispered harshly. "The minute I landed in Paris, I wanted to cry, and I hate that. That's why I scheduled a meeting before coming here. I was afraid I'd lose it if I came here directly. Then I saw the front and the police car. Thea, where the fuck is the awning for the restaurant? Did Antoine say anything?"

"No, he was too discreet to say," Thea said, leaning against Dean's shoulder.

"Sometimes I wish the French were more gossipy," Brooke said with a sigh. "Not that I thought everything was just peachy or anything. Nanine had the doctor call me and ask us all to come, after all."

"We knew it had to be bad." Dean rested his chin on the top of Brooke's head, his gut tense with worry. "Nanine never asks for anything."

"We'll get to the bottom of it." Brooke caressed Thea's face. "You okay, sweetie? The last thing I expected was to find the cops here."

"They wouldn't listen to me, and my French is so rusty... I couldn't keep up. I tried to switch to English but they didn't speak it."

He rubbed Thea's back. Rusty was a spot-on description for his French too. He hadn't spoken the language consistently since his last visit to Paris two years ago to see Nanine and grab some mental space. "Your French will kick back in time. Getting my brain back in gear usually takes a week when I'm going back and forth between French and English."

"A week would be a miracle," Thea moaned. "I haven't spoken it since my last trip here. Eight years. I hate that helpless feeling of not being able to communicate again. Especially to men carrying guns."

"Just do what I do in those moments." Dean tightened his arm around her. "Use your charm."

"Yeah, they were totally falling for your charm when I arrived," Brooke said dryly. "Someone in the neighborhood must have called them."

"Thea has hardened criminal written all over her," Dean teased.

Brooke gave him a gentle shove. "Things are worse here than we imagined. Do you think the awning was stolen?"

"Maybe." Dean didn't like that thought at all. Paris had always felt so safe to him, but he knew the city was changing. Nanine had shared her concerns about growing crime, rubbish in the streets, and graffiti. He supposed he would see it for himself soon enough.

"It's not just the awning," Thea said haltingly. "I looked in the windows, but I couldn't make myself go into the front alone."

"Good plan." Dean pushed back his nerves. "We'll face it together."

"I'll call the doctor and arrange for us to visit Nanine tonight when everyone gets in," Brooke said, walking to the back door. "We need to get to the bottom of things. But before we face the boogie monster, let's be practical. Dean, my bags and yours are out front. Be a dear and grab them, will you? My drivers couldn't wait with traffic."

She'd always been the queen of overpacking but *drivers* sounded ominous. They both knew there was no elevator, and the stairs were a narrow, circular engineering of physical treachery. If he capitulated this early, she'd have him jumping through her every hoop.

He decided to prevaricate. "My back has been twitchy, Brooke. You should wait until Kyle gets here. With his bulk, he can probably heft all your suitcases upstairs in a single trip."

"Thank you for confirming that chivalry is dead, darling," Brooke drawled.

"I can help you with your bags, Brooke," Thea said brightly. "Dean, I have some ibuprofen in my purse if you need it."

"Let's definitely go get you some ibuprofen," Brooke said, taking his arm and leading him after Thea. "That'll set you right up."

She was going to call his bluff.

They followed Thea to the walk-in cooler. Dean stopped short alongside Brooke, staring at Thea's open suitcase lying on the dusty floor. Gray-cast big-girl panties were lying on top.

He cringed. Jesus. The thought of Thea and those panties were going to short out his brain.

Brooke charged forward as Thea attempted to slam the bag closed. "Thea, these are grandma panties. Why do you have these?"

Dean almost walked out of the room, but he didn't want to hurt Thea, who was now blushing to her roots. Instead, he averted his eyes.

"My mom bought them for me for Christmas, and I couldn't throw them out." She finally slapped the suitcase closed. "It's not like we have *fancy* French lingerie, as my mom calls it, in Nowheresville."

Oh shit. Here it was. His first opportunity to help Thea. But panties…

He fell into his comfortable clothing of problem solving. "Of course you don't. You're in Paris now, the lingerie capital of the world. The question is: do you want to keep wearing these?" Damn, but he wanted to slap himself on the back. He was going to win Best Guy of the Year at this rate.

Only Thea couldn't meet their eyes. "No. I wish…"

"What do you wish?" Dean asked softly.

"I wish my mom would stop buying me the same things she wears." Her inhale was as good as a sharp cry in the quiet kitchen. "And I wish I wasn't the ninny who wears them because I'm afraid she'll notice if I don't."

"You didn't want to hurt her feelings," Dean said, his own insides shrink-wrapping. His parents sucked, but they didn't buy him matching outfits. And how would Thea's mom know what underwear she was wearing? "Do you remember how we helped you find things to wear when we were room-mates back in the day?"

She'd come to Paris dressed like some small-town farm girl in that purple jumper with the white collar. On her first day at culinary school, she'd arrived at Nanine's in tears after someone made fun of her clothes.

Dean hadn't been surprised. Mean kids were a global phenomenon.

"We'll do it again," Brooke said briskly, rising slowly. "You told me you wanted a makeover. Thea, what happened to the things I sent you from Paris for Christmas?"

"I looked weird wearing them. People talked about me. So I stopped. But I brought a few. See." She was valiantly gesturing to her suitcase, vulnerability in her eyes.

"People really suck," Brooke said, catching his eye as he nodded in agreement. "Well, we're going to turn this around. Don't you worry."

Thea picked up her purse and pulled out a bottle of ibuprofen, handing it to him. He managed a poker face. He was relieved when she distracted Brooke by holding up her old recipe book with the cute dancing breads, the same one she'd always had out ten years ago. She used to cut things out of Brooke's old fashion magazines and glue them in her journal. He didn't do vision boards himself, but he understood the value of them. He storyboarded with companies to help them create a vision for their future, saying *You gotta see it to believe it.*

"I brought my old journal with me. I mean business this time."

He believed her. "Good for you." Was this when he was supposed to mention he knew about her quitting?

Brooke elbowed him, as if reading his mind. "Go take your painkillers, darling."

He rolled his eyes before tucking the bottle in his sports jacket pocket. "You should probably see to your luggage, *babe.* Crime is up, you know."

"Oh my God!" Thea cried out, abandoning her bag and running to the back door. "I hope they're still there."

"You don't seem very concerned," Dean mused as Brooke met his gaze.

"I've learned a new bit of wisdom. Everything can be replaced."

Well, shit. Was this part of her post-breakup funk after Adam? He wasn't sure he was supposed to mention that either. Or commiserate. He'd gotten dumped for not being serious enough three years ago after trying a more committed relationship for a change. With a brainy graduate from Stanford with great legs working in venture capital. Stupidest decision of his life. Then he'd stepped back into stupid by agreeing to help a woman he'd dated with her start-up because she'd turned on his brain *and* his body, a rarity. He'd just finished his contract with her, thank God.

The silence grew. Was she going to say something? "So…"

"Thea is still as sweet as ever, but I can't have her hefting my bags," Brooke interrupted, walking off toward the back entrance. "And don't make a joke about us procrastinating about the monster up front. I can't take it."

So he'd tease her about the bags instead. Because he wasn't skipping off to the front either.

"Just how many suitcases did you bring, Brooke?" he asked as he followed.

"Eight."

"Eight!" Now his back was twitching for real. How was she going to put all that stuff in her small bedroom on the Girls' Floor? Of course, she'd always been the queen of decorating. But still.

"Don't say a word, Dean," she warned.

That tone prodded his internal smartass. "A word."

She looked him up and down. "Funny. And don't think I don't know you're lying about your back."

He didn't believe it was unmanly to lie in the face of eight suitcases given those stairs. Knowing Brooke, she would figure out a way to get her bags to her room. He made a show of stretching. "My trainer says I need to be careful."

She gave an indelible snort. "I'll bet he did."

They shared a smile, and then they engaged in another hug. When she didn't move away from the embrace, he knew for sure she wasn't in top shape. Her father had suffered a heart attack a year ago, and that was likely on her mind too.

It was okay that she was struggling. He was too. They all were, probably.

Brooke rubbed her cheek against his chest. "Damn, but you still smell delicious. Nanine set you up for life, didn't she?"

The memory made his throat thicken with emotion. Nanine had taken him and his roommates to *Le Bon Marché* and helped them pick out their signature scents as a Christmas present.

He'd stuck with his choice—*L'Homme* by Yves Saint Laurent—a miracle for him since he loved to change things up. Its understated yet diverse masculinity of warm fragrance notes like citrus, basil, and bergamot appealed to him. But he was too self-aware not to know the other reason. Nanine had helped him select it, saying it was perfect for him. *He* was warm, relaxed, and outwardly subtle despite the complexity inside him. Praise he'd never forgotten. Praise he wanted to live up to.

He sniffed Brooke when she angled her neck to the side. "You're not rank or anything. Thea and Madison will be relieved since you're sharing the Girls' Floor again."

She laughed, and some of the sadness faded from her green eyes. "You never change in the best way."

In some ways, neither did Brooke. She wore the same scent as Nanine—Chanel No. 5, the perfume that had revolutionized the way women wore perfume. As the dreamer and visionary of the group, he respected the sea change Coco Chanel had brought in wanting to create a scent for the modern woman.

Her story embodied his ideal. His aspiration. He hoped to discover his next "it concept," powerful enough to change an industry and subsequently the world, in Paris while helping Nanine and Thea find their way.

His idea was here. Waiting. He could feel it.

CHAPTER
THREE

S he was going to fall apart.

Brooke excused herself from Dean by saying she needed to use the bathroom, asking if he could watch her bags for a second with Thea. Every last one was accounted for, as well as Dean's single bag. His face had turned serious, but he'd nodded and left her alone. He was more observant than he wanted people to know.

She had to force her legs up the narrow stairs to the Girls' Floor, where she stayed every time she was in Paris. For her, it was a second home. She came to Paris for fashion frequently, and while she could have bought her own place, there was nowhere she'd rather stay than with Nanine. But today, she could find little comfort in its familiarity.

Before learning Nanine had entered the hospital, she'd already had the worst year of her life. Her father's heart attack had occurred last September. Then Adam had broken things off with her four months ago after a two-year relationship she'd thought was heading to marriage. Now Nanine, her adopted mother, was sick, and Thea, her adopted sister, needed help too.

She clutched the top of the staircase railing. She told

herself to be relieved to see the old furniture on their floor was intact. The velvet green couch and mahogany book-shelves looked like they could use a good dusting. She stopped her mind from veering to the dust covering Nanine's usually immaculate prep counters downstairs.

She should make a list of what needed to be done, like getting a professional cleaner in. God, she was too exhausted to start it, and that said something.

She detoured to the hallway. Her room was the last one on the right, and she waited until she closed the door to lean her head back and shut her eyes. This place, while small, had always been her refuge, one she'd decorated herself with Nanine's blessing. She hoped that feeling wouldn't be lost with whatever was going on.

No, it wouldn't be. She wouldn't allow it.

She pulled out her phone to check her messages. She'd called the hospital upon arriving to leave a message for Nanine that she couldn't wait to see her. Part of her hoped Nanine would call and tell them what the hell was going on.

Her dad had left her a voicemail, and she pulled it up and listened. *Hi, princess. Hope you arrived safe. Just wanted you to know I sent Nanine some flowers after you told me which hospital she was in. Call me when you have a chance. I need to talk to you.*

Her legs went rubbery. Had something happened to him? The doctors said everything was going so well. She immediately dialed him up.

"I'm glad you called," he began. "I know you have a lot of moving pieces right now. Are any of your roommates in yet?"

"Thea and Dean are here with me. Daddy, are you okay?"

"Yes, of course. What? Did I scare you by asking for you to call me back like that? I'm sorry, princess. I wanted to say a few things to you is all. I didn't feel it could wait."

She started tapping her fingernails together. Right now? Seriously? When she had so much on her plate? "All right. I'm listening."

"No one knows better than me how much you love Nanine. She was there for you from that first horrible moment when your mother showed up with her new family at Nanine's restaurant, when we were both in Paris for spring break."

How could she forget? She still dreamed about that night, and in every dream her mother ignored her presence, just as she had that night, flanked by her two new perfect stepdaughters. Brooke and her father had just begun their second course when they'd arrived. She'd been thrown into a whirlwind of fear and happiness upon seeing her mother, but the woman hadn't so much as greeted her. She had looked over—once—but her new husband had put his hand over hers, pulling her gaze away, and she hadn't glanced back.

Even after all these years, Brooke still couldn't understand how a mother could do that to an eleven-year-old girl. Thank God she'd gone to live with her dad after her parents' divorce. Her mom's new husband already had children and didn't want her around, her mother had told her. Like that made her actions A-okay.

"Nanine turned one of the worst nights of my life into one of the best."

"Mine too. I'll never forget how she marched over and told them that her staff had made a mistake. That the table was already reserved, and there was no room for them."

Brooke knew the rest of the story from her father since she'd been crying behind the restaurant, which was where Nanine had found her and embraced her ever so softly as she'd sobbed through an explanation. True to form, her asshole stepfather had argued with Nanine over the "error," prompting her to tell them they were not welcome in her restaurant. Ever.

When Brooke had finally come back to the table, her mother and her new family were gone. A waiter had appeared immediately with lemon sorbet out of order on the menu. There was love and sweetness in that silver dish, and it had cooled Brooke's enraged heart.

To this day, to Brooke's knowledge, Nanine had never been so short with anyone. That night, she had become Brooke's champion.

"Daddy, I'm so scared for her. She's never been sick. Not a day."

"That makes her recovery more encouraging, Brooke. I speak from experience after all the doctor appointments I've been through this year for my heart. Plus, she has you, and that was the best medicine I had."

She swiped as tears ran down her face. "Thanks, Daddy."

"Brooke, the way Nanine has taken to you has been a bright spot in our lives, one I feel indebted to her for. The year you stayed with her in Paris, working at her restaurant and learning more from her, has made you the woman you are. That's something a single father couldn't be more grateful for."

"That year was filled with some of the best decisions in my life."

When Bernard had died, Brooke had decided to study a year in Paris at the International Fashion Academy to be closer to Nanine and round out her career path at NYU. One night, Nanine had mentioned one of the ways she planned to combat her grief—by opening her home to six foreign exchange students, three boys and three girls—in exchange for working in the restaurant. Brooke had asked if Nanine would consider her, saying the chance to work in the front of the house with clients would help her career. A stretch for sure. She'd known Nanine had been surprised, but she'd readily agreed.

That decision had enriched her life in a way she hadn't expected. Her roommates had become cherished friends, and they'd faced all the highs and lows of growing up during that year.

"Which is a good reminder for you, given how tough this year has been," her daddy said. "I don't know about the others, but from what you said, you and Thea need each other as much as Nanine needs you."

Her daddy had embraced Brooke's bond with Thea. Maybe it was because of Thea's sweetness, but Brooke thought of her as a little sister. Still, Thea was a caretaker, and she took care of Brooke too. One time, during her master's degree, Brooke had mentioned to Thea that she felt overwhelmed, only to receive a special package in the mail. Her friend had baked and sent her favorite cake—a *Gâteau au chocolat*—to her.

"Thea is going to be all right, Daddy. Don't worry, I'll see to it."

"I never had a doubt."

But maybe Brooke was the one who needed a little more help this time. Thea might look up to Brooke, but she looked to Thea for a fresh perspective on life. Thea had said she wanted to change things, and she'd resurrected her old recipe book to help.

When it came to her own life, Brooke didn't know where to start.

"I think this time in Paris is going to be good for you, princess. Being back with all your old roommates. Being with Nanine. I know her heart attack has probably brought up some bad memories of when I had mine, but I wanted to remind you that the doctors say I haven't been this healthy in years. Which is why I don't want you worrying about me."

Was he kidding? She still checked to make sure he'd picked up his heart medication. "I worry because I love you."

"We have that in common, which is why I decided to call you and give you my two cents. I think you should stay in Paris for the foreseeable future. The breakup with Adam was bad, and you haven't been happy in Manhattan. Paris has always been different for you. The magazine will agree to let you work from there, I have no doubt."

She'd already had that idea brewing in the back of her mind, along with a way to expand her role in its culture and lifestyle section. She hadn't told a soul, but she was tired of writing about perfect nineteen- to twenty-three-year-old women who only wore clothes for a living. Maybe it was because she was turning thirty, but she was bored with it all. Fashion had started for her because of the rich fabrics and the textures that led to *haute couture*. Over time, she'd gotten pigeon-holed at the magazine by her own success. "Are you a mind reader now?"

He laughed. "Maybe it's my pacemaker. And I'm going to make you worry even less by telling you that I'm thinking of retiring and moving to Paris. That way you can keep your eyes on both me and Nanine without exhausting yourself. And you won't feel guilty about not being in two places at once."

Her eyes burned as she pressed them closed tightly. "Oh, Daddy…"

"Princess, I'd do anything in the world to make things easier on you. You know that."

"I do," she whispered. "I didn't expect this."

"I'll start looking for apartments, but I'm thinking I'll make the move around Christmas. Until then, I want you to focus on helping Nanine and Thea and getting reacquainted with your old roommates. But this is also a chance for you to figure out what you want for yourself. Make the most of it, princess."

Her throat was raw from emotion. "I love you, Daddy. You have no idea what this news means to me."

"Yes, I do, Brooke, which is why I called when the sky was falling." She could hear the smile in his voice. "I'll talk to you later, princess."

"Bye, Daddy."

She walked to the double windows and opened them a crack, pulling out a cigarette with shaking hands. Thea and Dean were standing on the street beside her luggage, chatting companionably, their bodies turned away from Nanine's restaurant. She knew she had to handle her bags shortly, but she could use a moment.

Her daddy had seen what she'd been trying so hard to hide with makeup and couture. She didn't feel much like herself right now. Adam walking out had ruined her confidence, and him picking up with a nineteen-year-old Brazilian model hadn't helped. If she were being honest, she was probably as timid and hesitant as Thea on the inside right now.

She needed her friends. As much as Nanine did. And Daddy had just given her the blank slate she hadn't realized she needed.

She took a long pull from her cigarette. What lay ahead was not going to be easy for Nanine, especially in light of whatever had happened with the restaurant. She knew the difficulties that were coming from dealing with her father's heart attack and recovery. She exhaled another long trail of smoke, preparing a mental to-do list for her two favorite people—Nanine and Thea. They would be the main event while she took a back seat to give herself some time to heal.

First things first: she needed to buy Nanine aspirin and a blood pressure cuff from the pharmacy. Thea needed a hair appointment with Tony Karam and a private lingerie appointment with her friends at Simone Pérèle.

Focusing on someone else's life was so much easier than trying to fix your own.

47

CHAPTER
FOUR

Thea watched in awe as Brooke sauntered across the narrow street with three gorgeous servers trailing behind her.

While she had been happy to stay with the luggage, she'd grown uncomfortable standing there alone. First Brooke had walked off to find assistance, and then Dean had left to take a call from a client who didn't understand what a vacation meant. People had stared at her as they walked past, and to her mind, plenty of them found her wanting. She didn't like being reminded of all the things she wanted to change about herself. She was a boring line of nothing from head to toe.

"You found help," Thea called out.

"*Bien sûr*," Brooke said as she reached her. "I knew I could hire someone from Café Fitzy, although Antoine was only happy to let them help after I told him about the police debacle. He was so tight-lipped I couldn't get anything out of him about Nanine. By the way, the police did stop in there to ask if we were legit. Come on. We'll grab your bag on the way up."

She forced a smile. "Already done."

Brooke sighed exasperatedly. "Thea, please tell me you

didn't heft your suitcase to our floor while I was out finding people to help with that."

Dean had told her he'd take care of it himself when he went back in, putting his pointer finger to his lips and whispering, "Our secret. I'll make sure to put your ibuprofen back in your purse too."

Call her gullible. She'd believed him about his back. But she couldn't begrudge him. Brooke was known for traveling with a full wardrobe, being in fashion and all. Somehow she always managed to fit it all into her room, however big or small the space, which made Thea think of Mary Poppins and her unending tapestry bag. Brooke attributed it to mad packing skills.

The men greeted her and then picked the bags up as if it was an honor to do so. Classic Brooke. As she watched her friend lead them to the restaurant like the Pied Piper, the gentle breeze carrying Brooke's sultry French, she shook her head in chagrined fondness. Something—a presence—made her look over her shoulder. A man with thick black hair was walking on the sidewalk toward her wearing a blue pinstriped suit...

Mr. Pinstripes!

Her heart began to pound in her chest. He had on the same dark sunglasses as earlier.

As he drew closer, she froze. Was that a smile on his face? No, it wasn't possible. A man like that couldn't be smiling at *her*. As he neared, she moved aside to give him room, only to bump into the stone wall behind her. Oh crap!

Her whole body was seized by the flight impulse. Without thinking, she dashed across the street, almost colliding with a tall blond woman on a scooter. She could swear she heard a masculine voice call out something in French. Probably him, telling her to be more careful.

Thea Rogers, the klutz in the house.

Cheeks burning, she jogged back until she was nearly to

the alley. Why did she feel so panicked? Why couldn't she simply move out of the way like a normal person as Mr. Pinstripes passed her on the sidewalk? Maybe nod and say *Bonjour*? Heck, she knew why. She was afraid she'd trip over her two big feet. Hadn't she run into a wall while trying to give him space?

She was ducking into the alley as Brooke emerged from the kitchen, the handsome waiters trailing behind her, all three with classically seductive French smiles. She handed them each fifty euros with a throaty *Merci*. All of them suggested she swing by for a café later. To that, she gave a flirtatious response in French.

Thea didn't think *but of course* sounded the same in English. Heck, she could never utter that line in French and sound like Brooke. Something to work on. She should add that to her journal. After her debacle with Mr. Pinstripes, she clearly had a lot of work to do.

She went inside as Brooke continued the flirtation. Back in the kitchen, she dug the spiral-bound book out of her purse. Her cheeks were still hot. Heavens!

She debated writing something about noticing men more, something she didn't do. Before now, she'd never come across a guy who gave her the kind of buzz they talked about in the movies and on TV. But Mr. Pinstripes had.

Oh, who was she kidding? He'd never be interested in someone like her. Even if he *did* want her, she wouldn't have a clue what to do with a yummy man like that.

Yummy, really?

Yeah, like yummy chocolate croissants fresh out of the oven.

Okay, she might not know what to do with him, but she wanted to…

Her gaze traveled to the chandelier, which had made an almost plaintive tinkle, but she still wasn't ready to check out the front of the restaurant. Better to distract herself by focusing on her journal. Exploring the front was something they could all do together once the others arrived, like pulling off a bandage.

She retrieved her green pen and put it to the side of her mouth—a color she'd chosen to signify spring and renewal—and gathered her thoughts after turning to a fresh page. What would make a man like Mr. Pinstripes notice her? What did she need to do to deserve a man like that? She stared at the fresh page for a moment and then started scribbling.

Recipe for: *Attracting a Man Like Mr. Pinstripes*

Directions

1. Speak French like Brooke. Okay, maybe master a few phrases with a seductive, non-rusty-nail accent.

2. Find my glamour bone (every woman has one, according to *Cosmo*). Maybe it's like the funny bone? I have one of those.

3. Buy new clothes and shoes. Something that makes my feet look smaller. Please God, let those shoes exist!

4. Cut hair into a more classic look. Could I pull off Julia Ormond's short, sexy cut in *Sabrina*? How great would that be?

5. Have someone do my eyebrows. Don't be a 'fraidy cat. Sure, that time in Des Moines was horrible when that woman ripped off part of your brows. Don't think about them being numb for weeks or how the shape made you look like a Vulcan from *Star Trek*.

She paused for a moment and studied the page. Then she started writing again in the notes section at the bottom.

Apparently I'm not just listing but talking myself through my fears. That's okay. It's a journal. Brooke will know someone for a haircut and brows. Can I afford it? Oh, just do it and move on to the next idea on the list.

She rested the pen against her cheek, thinking about what else she wanted, but the image of bumping into the wall and then running across the street to flee Mr. Pinstripes—the most gorgeous man on earth—kept playing over and over again in her head like a horror movie. She was going to be so embarrassed when she saw him again, and she would. He clearly lived in the neighborhood. Heck, she'd already seen him twice in one day!

Only one phrase crossed her mind. It was so depressing, she almost gave up then and there and accepted a life of boredom and neutrals. But then she bit her lip and found the courage to put it on paper under the others.

6. Fix everything...

Gosh! Was that how she really felt? Yeah, she realized as her eyes teared up. She wanted... No, she *needed* to change a whole bunch of things about herself.

Bread and pastry, she knew. Bread and pastry, she loved. She was a maestro in that realm. Was that why she'd so rarely left it and the safety of the bakery?

Yeah, it was.

People could call her Queen Baker in the streets, and she would accept their accolades. She'd collect the roses they'd throw at her feet, but she couldn't convince herself that she was deserving of any other kind of praise. Definitely not said Big Bird feet. And she knew why it was so hard for her. She'd been raised to believe you could compliment someone for their work and their character, but anything else was vanity. That kind of praise would ruin a person, her parents thought.

And yet, what was wrong with her wanting to look pretty? Or to be complimented by other people every once in a while?

Her biggest secret wish was to shrink her feet. People got nose jobs and boob jobs, but if it were her, Thea would get a foot job so she could have cute little feet and wear sexy shoes like Brooke.

Not happening.

Depressed, she shoved pen and book back in her purse. Small steps led to bigger changes. She hadn't even written down *Find A Job* on her list yet, and she wouldn't. Too much pressure.

Brooke reentered the kitchen. "Who's going to carry Nanine up the stairs if Dean's back is bad?"

Thea's brows slammed together. Brooke knew Dean was lying and was going to rake her over the coals to get the truth. Crap. "I thought doctors wanted patients to take the stairs."

Brooke folded her arms across her chest, all business now. "Not if they feel faint and fall down said stairs."

"I only read it online." She fought a sigh and then decided to go and make them *café crèmes*. The milk in the walk-in was still good, so she went into it and grabbed the container.

Brooke trailed after her as she headed over to Nanine's coffee machine. The door leading to the front was to its right, and all Thea could think of was how much she feared pushing open that door.

"We really need to go see what happened here," she whispered.

Nanine's chandelier gave a weak murmur, and they both stopped short, tears filling their eyes before Brooke looked off, her mouth tight. "When Dean comes back. Right now, part of me wishes he wouldn't. I don't want to go in there."

"Me either."

"So back to Nanine," Brooke said as Thea ran through the familiar motions of making coffee. "My dad couldn't climb the stairs by himself until two weeks after his heart attack. He only had one flight while Nanine has three death-defying ones. Of course, we could move her to our floor, but she'd hate that."

Thea laid her hand on Brooke's arm as the coffee machine

purred. "I know this is hard since you've already been through something with your dad, but it's going to be different with Nanine. Please don't kill me for saying so, okay? It's just...you've always taken care of your father, and he's relied on you." She'd even taken a month off from work to take care of her dad after his heart attack.

Brooke's mouth pursed before she said, "Guilty. Classic abandoned single child syndrome overcompensating for the other parent."

Thea knew a potential emotional disaster had been averted. "Nanine is the toughest woman I've ever met except for you and Madison."

"Thanks." She put her hand on Thea's shoulder before letting go. "Sorry, I'm a little tense." Seemingly distracted, she wandered over to the big mahogany table where they'd all eaten oodles of exquisite food during breaks or family meals.

Thea brought their cafés over. "We're all going to be tense. I imagine Nanine might even have a bad moment here and there. Let's be extra kind with each other."

"I said this about Dean earlier, but you never change in the best way too, Thea."

"I was just thinking the same about you, Brooke. I'm glad we're here. Together."

She reached for her friend's hand and squeezed it. Brooke's eyes started to shine—a rarity since Brooke wasn't a crier—which made Thea well up too.

Brooke gave her hand one last squeeze and then reached for her café, fingering the handle of her coffee cup. She hid it well, but Thea knew she was trying to cover up the trembling of her fingers.

They drank their coffee in silence to the sound of the Horloge ticking.

"Okay, I'm toughening up." Brooke pushed her coffee aside. "I can't wait anymore. Let's go face the monster."

This was why she was Third Course. "What about Dean?"

Brooke inclined her head to the closed door separating the kitchen from the front of the house. "He'll come running when we scream."

"Let's do it."

Thea hastily downed her coffee and followed her friend, only to ram straight into Brooke's back when she stopped dead after opening the door.

"*Holy shit!*" Brooke hissed out as the chandelier's crystals gave an answering clank. "It's gutted!"

"What—"

Thea rose onto her toes when Brooke didn't move. She cried out in shock upon seeing the empty restaurant. It looked even worse than it had through the window. The walls had literally been sawed open, and wire lay like clumps of seaweed on the floor. "*Oh, my God!*"

Brooke took a few steps inside and flung her hand out. "No wonder Nanine had a heart attack. Who could have done this? Criminals?"

Thea wished she could go back in time and stop herself from entering. The sight of Nanine's beloved restaurant torn open and stripped of its beauty broke her heart. Her eyes tracked to the far wall beside the front door. "Brooke, Nanine's wall of honor is gone."

It had been devoted to all of the famous patrons who'd given her photos or keepsakes and artists who'd drawn something special for her to hang. There'd been photos of Ryan Gosling, Meryl Streep, Chevy Chase, Andy Warhol, and so many more.

Her friend's gasp was pained. "Oh, God, I can't believe this!"

She wanted to sink to the dirty floor and cry. "Neither can I."

"I'm getting Dean."

Thea stayed where she was as Brooke stomped over to the back stairs, making the crystals clang again. She heard Brooke yell Dean's name twice at the top of her lungs. So out of character.

Thea closed her eyes to try and halt the horror coursing through her. Tears trickled down her face. How were they going to make things right for Nanine when the spirit of her restaurant was gone?

"You were supposed to wait for me," Dean was saying as he and Brooke reentered the front. *"What the fuck!"*

"Yeah, exactly," Brooke said as the chandelier clanged again.

"Who did this?" Dean spat out, stalking into the space.

"You don't think Nanine sold the restaurant, do you?" Thea whispered, making fists at her sides. "And they're opening another one here in its place?"

"Gutting it like this could kick off a renovation," Dean conceded as he ran a hand through his thick sandy hair, leaving spiky puffs in its wake.

"But why would she sell?" Brooke lashed out. "She loves this place. Every inch of it has a part of her heart. I'm calling the doctor right now. I can't wait to talk to her about this."

Dean snagged her arm before she could leave the room. "She said she won't talk to us until we're all here. I want answers too, but everyone will be here in a few hours. Let's start off as a unit, Brooke. For us and Nanine. She just had a heart attack, for Christ's sake."

Brooke turned her back to them and took a couple deep breaths. "I know that, dammit!"

"We know you do." Thea put her hand lightly on Brooke's tense shoulder. "We're all here together at her request. We have to remember that. She gets to call the shots."

"Besides," Dean said, nudging her playfully, as was his way, "do you really want to get on Madison's bad side this early?"

Thea appreciated his attempt at humor. Madison Garcia was Fifth Course—cheese—sometimes a little too strong for everyone's taste. Certainly a course Thea hadn't appreciated until coming to France, and it had taken her even longer to fully understand and appreciate Madison. She was the rebel and wore bad girl on her sleeve with unapologetic pride. Thea now knew she'd only been protecting herself after growing up in a tough Miami neighborhood with a mostly absent father after her mother split.

Madison and Brooke had that in common, and their antecedents had created strong personalities. They butted heads on occasion. Thea was the middle child, always negotiating peace between the two of them.

"I don't want issues with anyone." Brooke worried her lip as Nanine's famous chandelier gave an answering shake. "Nanine has enough to deal with." She glanced at Dean. "You and Kyle had better play nice too."

"I love Kyle like a brother," he said, but his eyes narrowed as the chandelier mocked him with a clatter. "Damn, but I forgot how eerie Nanine's chandelier is. It's like a Ouija board."

Thea cleared her throat. If she didn't like Kyle so much, he'd probably make her sick. Everything seemed to come easily to him. He'd been the high school football star before blowing out his knee as a senior. Heck, he'd even been the prom king.

If they'd gone to high school together, they wouldn't have been friends. But as roommates in Paris, a million miles from their hometowns, they'd hit it off. He loved her like a younger sister. She supposed they all did.

But Dean and Kyle were like Brooke and Madison. Strong personalities when it came to what mattered to them. Kyle couldn't stand Dean's habit of hopping from one thing to another, and Dean, who'd had a more difficult childhood, envied what he saw as Kyle's time on easy street. True, Kyle's parents had refused to bankroll his trip to Paris, and he'd had to sell his car before coming, but he'd grown up insanely wealthy with all the privileges attached to it. It was going to be interesting to see how their dynamic had changed. Dean had acquired a golden touch in tech, which had made him a millionaire, while Kyle remained the boy born with a silver spoon in his mouth—something he'd translated into a restaurant empire.

Brooke's phone rang, playing "La Vie en Rose." Gasping, she exclaimed, "That's Nanine's ringtone!"

As she raced back into the kitchen to answer, the chandelier gave a melodic jingle. Thea and Dean hurried in after her, arriving as she picked up. "*Allo*, Nanine."

Her eyes closed for a moment before she said in French, "Wait a moment. I'm putting you on speaker so Thea and Dean can hear your voice."

"Hello, my loves," Nanine said in French, her voice carrying an unusual roughness Thea attributed to fatigue. "When I heard the police had almost arrested you, I decided I couldn't wait for your visit."

"It was me," Thea responded in English. "I couldn't talk fast enough in French yet."

"No one can ever speak fast enough with a police officer, but I am glad they did not arrest you," Nanine replied in English, probably for Thea's sake.

"Us too," Dean said, choosing English. "How are you, sweetheart?"

"Oh, it's another spa day here." She gave a raspy chuckle.

"Here too," Dean shot back, but his teasing tone was rough.

"It's good to hear your voices," Nanine said hoarsely.

Dean's hand came to rest on Thea's back, and she realized he was embracing them yet again. It only felt natural, with Nanine on the other side of their call, hurting. Brooke bit her lip, and Thea knew she was fighting off an emotional storm.

"We've noticed some changes at the restaurant," Dean

began after clearing his throat. "Anything you want to tell us? Even a hint? You know I love previews."

"I can only tell the story once, and after that, I will never speak of it again."

The words were harsh and filled with pain, and Thea had to brush away more tears.

She heard Dean take a fortifying breath before saying, "All right. Whatever you want. Is there anything we can bring you?"

Nanine's breath turned shallow. "Besides a carving knife? No, nothing but your beautiful selves and perhaps my perfume and lipstick. Maybe a note from another doctor saying I can leave this place tomorrow. Dean, would you forge one for your dear Nanine?"

"Do you still keep your stationery upstairs in your writing desk?"

Her weak chuckle was enough to unleash Thea's tears.

"We will consider forgery and perhaps a prison break if my doctor continues to be unreasonable. I will see you soon. The story, you see…"

When she said no more, Thea returned her gaze to her friends. Brooke had her eyes fixed downward, every muscle tense. Dean's jaw was working.

"Whatever it is, Nanine, we'll fix it," Thea said, hating the quiver in her voice.

"Of course we will," Brooke said harshly.

"Damn right." Dean rubbed Thea's back in comfort. "Get some rest, Nanine. We'll see you soon."

The line went dead, and they all stared at the phone.

"Jesus," Dean breathed out. "*I can only tell the story once, and after that, I will never speak of it again.* I don't know what to say."

"She's never talked that way." Thea rubbed her eyes. "Not ever."

"She's never had a heart attack before after her restaurant

was gutted," Brooke said with heat, her phone clenched in her hand. Then she shook her head. "God, I'm sorry. I'm in a terrible mood now. I'm going upstairs to find what Nanine asked for."

She stomped out again, her heels so thunderous Thea imagined Brooke might leave marks on the floor. The chandelier matched her tune with a staccato clang.

Dean shook himself. "I feel like I'm twenty again, watching Brooke stomp off in her first snit. That time I think it was over the group's decision to not go to a new club in Pigale."

Thea knew a diversion when she heard it. She jumped for the lifeline. "No, it was *L'Arc*. I remember because I couldn't afford it."

"Neither could I. Not even Kyle would spring for it."

She nodded. They used to vote on outings, and the ritzy places hadn't held a majority. "The place in Pigale was later. I forget why we voted it down."

"Probably had a crazy cover charge." He cleared his throat. "Okay, let's close the door to this shitshow and grab a coffee while we wait for the others. Unless you want to unpack?"

She shook her head. She couldn't leave him when he was feeling this way, and truthfully, she didn't want to be alone either. "No, let's sit." She would allow herself a third coffee because she was jet-lagged and it was Paris, and many times one or even two just wasn't enough.

They were sipping their coffees when the sound of Brooke's heels returned. She reentered the room with a makeup bag in hand. "Madison and Sawyer found each other in baggage claim since his plane was delayed leaving Baltimore and arrived late. Seems Kyle is picking them up. He caught a seat on the private jet of a friend who was heading to London for business and then flew the rest of the way here."

"Talk about a nice friend," Thea said, blinking in shock.

"Posh," Dean said, shaking his head. "We sure he's staying here and not the Ritz?"

"He's staying here," Thea told him. "He wants to be with all of us and Nanine, of course."

Brooke crossed her arms and glared at Dean. "Come on. Don't start this. He's always been mega-rich. And now you are too."

"Not at that level." His eyes were hot. "Yet."

"Get over it, Dean," Brooke fired back.

Thea grew tense. "He's still Kyle."

"With the hot, nubile fiancée and the perfect life," Dean continued with a roll of his eyes.

Brooke socked him, making the chandelier clang sharply. "Stop that right now. I can't bear it if we start fighting. I'm barely holding it together as it is."

Thea glanced between the two of them helplessly before Dean held up his hands. "I'm stopping. Guess I'm in a bad mood too. Call me when they get here. I'm going to do some work."

After he left, Thea pretended to pick at a hangnail to cover her worry. "You need anything, Brooke?"

"No. I'm going back upstairs to close my eyes for a few minutes and breathe."

"You still using meditation and breathwork to manage your anxiety?" Thea asked, knowing how tough the last year had been on her friend.

"Yes, and when that doesn't work, I do a kickboxing class. After my breakup with Adam, I sometimes do a morning and evening class. Why don't you come unpack too? We've got a lot ahead of us. Especially once everyone else arrives."

Thea gazed at the door to the front of the restaurant. Soon they would find out what calamity had befallen Nanine's restaurant.

A story Nanine would only tell once…

God help them.

61

CHAPTER
FIVE

Being back in Paris was surreal, especially under the circumstances.

Only something dire would make Nanine ask for all six of her former Paris roommates to drop everything. Madison was having to work extra hard to compartmentalize her worry.

She was working to compartmentalize the slick car Kyle had picked them up in too. "I still can't believe you decided to drive here, Kyle," she said, hoping to poke at him so he'd poke back and keep her mind from conjuring up the worst-case scenarios it had been churning out ever since she left Miami. "Clearly, you've lost your mind. But not your golden boy looks. Shame they never impressed me."

Sawyer muttered, "Here we go again," from the back.

Kyle slid her a knowing look. "You going to bitch about my ride? This is a Maserati GranTurismo Convertible. It's sweet."

She let out a feral grin, grateful he'd taken the bait. "You're going to come off as one of those rich tourists who speed through the Parisian streets playing out their *Fast and*

Furious fantasies. I've had enough of those jackasses in Miami to last a lifetime."

There was another inaudible mutter from Sawyer in the back, but Madison could feel the walls surrounding her emotions snap back into place.

"Just don't wear a white Speedo and gold chains and nothing else while driving, okay?" She tapped her boot to his floorboard. "I can tolerate that outfit in a city with a beach scene, but not in Paris. Just warning you. I might snap and take you out with my cleaver."

"Violence doesn't solve anything."

She nearly smiled. Dr. Sawyer Jackson, the college prof, was in the house, quoting philosophy like he had since she'd first met him ten years ago.

"But it feels *so* good," Madison shot back.

Kyle grunted. "I'd like to see you take me."

Which only made her smile widen. "You still good back there, Sawyer?"

The usually quiet Sawyer had started huffing about the lack of leg room in the back seat as they zipped down the A1.

Kyle had picked them up outside baggage claim with his usual aplomb—Nanine couldn't have found a better nickname for him than Sixth Course, dessert, since he loved to indulge—posing for photos as tourists and horndogs dug out their phones to capture his hot ride.

Of course, she'd insisted on sitting in the back since she was three inches shorter than Sawyer's five-ten frame. The front of the car had plenty of room, even for Kyle, who was six-four. Sawyer wouldn't hear of it, however, being that rarest of breeds: an honest-to-goodness gentleman. Only, now she was hearing his frequent huffs, mumbles, and sighs and starting to feel a little guilty. As if they didn't have bigger things on their minds.

Her compartmentalization shattered again.

Nanine.

Madison loved that woman, and she didn't love very many people. Maybe six, she realized: Nanine and her old roommates. Dammit, she used words like *love* more sparingly than truffles during truffle season. She hated emotional roller coasters, too, and from everything she knew so far, they were in for it.

Thea had quit her job to come, but they weren't supposed to talk about that yet. Little sister was adrift, and since she reminded Madison of Dorothy in *The Wizard of Oz*, something they'd always teased her about, she was fighting off that overwhelming feeling that they were driving into a storm.

"Turn right at the next off-ramp," she told Kyle as Google Maps talked her through the directions to Saint-Germain. "Rouen, Périphérique O, etc. Then merge onto Boulevard Périphérique."

He glanced her way, wearing his classic aviator Ray-Ban sunglasses. "I'm surprised you need navigation, Madison. You never got lost in Paris when we lived here."

Was that supposed to be a dig to help her regain control? They all knew her well enough to know that's what she needed to feel better. "Growing up in a bad neighborhood with no street signs will do that to a girl."

Riddled with drugs and crime, her neighborhood had had sidewalks covered in enough broken glass to prevent bicycles from being utilized. Everything there had a short shelf life, businesses coming and going. The only way to create something beautiful in Miami was to have it be momentary. Otherwise, someone would try to steal it, deface it, or destroy it. Choosing to be a chef had seemed like a smart choice in the face of that life truth.

Yet, she'd stayed.

Coming back to Paris was her chance to lop off her roots if she wanted—with her favorite cleaver. She hadn't quit her job yet—that would be too much, too fast—but she was going to think about it. Right now, being on leave was all she could handle.

Her dad's face flashed in her mind, taunting her. Her box for him had so many cracks she didn't think there was enough adhesive to put it back together. What was he thinking, hooking up with a woman younger than Madison? Worse, they were having a kid. When he couldn't even hold down a regular job. He knew he was a failure as a father. He said so all the time to excuse himself for his behavior toward her.

Madison had lost the final thread of respect she'd had for her father, who had sunk to so many lows as a parent, she was surprised he hadn't been inducted into the Deadbeat Dad Hall of Fame.

"Madison has always had maps in her head," Sawyer said from the back seat after she gave Kyle another directive from Google. "I swear she could have led an ancient army back in the day through unexplored lands like Mongolia or the Sahara."

"Dr. Jackson strikes again," Kyle drawled in his thick Texas accent that sometimes grated on her nerves.

"Madison, can you move your seat up any more?" Sawyer asked softly.

Angling around in her leather seat so she could see him, she said, "We can stop, and I'll switch with you."

He shook his curly black head and waved a hand at the traffic beside them. "Nah. I'll make it."

Sawyer Jackson was not a tough guy. She loved that about him. His gold-rimmed glasses gave him a scholarly air he didn't have to fake. Nanine called him Fourth Course—the salad that came after the meal, which was unique to the French and had a long history that was more and more forgotten in these rapid-paced modern times.

To look at him, he wasn't substantial, but like a classic French salad, there was brilliance and complexity if you paid attention. He understood and appreciated things most people didn't, and that made him pretty special in Madison's book.

While she and Sawyer were both of mixed parentage, their upbringings couldn't have been more different. His mom was Asian and his dad Black, both of them successful employees for Xerox, brainiacs who'd met on scholarship at Harvard Business School. He'd grown up in the Washington D.C. suburbs, where he now taught art history at the University of Maryland. This was after Georgetown, the Sorbonne, and a doctorate from Columbia University.

Madison's mom was white, and her dad Colombian American. Neither had graduated from high school or held down a regular job—although God knew where her mother was now. She'd left when Madison was thirteen.

Madison had lived in the hood in Liberty City and worked three jobs as a preteen, forming a work ethic and a savings account that had helped her attend *Le Cordon Bleu* in Paris after falling in love with French cuisine watching Jacques Pépin on PBS. The first episode she'd seen had captured her heart with its *fines herbes omelet*, which her twelve-year-old self could pull off with their grocery budget and a few fast grabs from overgrown herb gardens as she walked to school.

After that, she'd learned how to cook simple, inexpensive dishes that tasted delicious, which had brought out a lighter version of her usually sullen, unemployed father. Food had become her everything, forming an impenetrable bubble that kept her going and filled up her mind with dreams of special dishes.

She'd barely made it through high school, and she didn't care. They hadn't taught her anything useful for *her* life. What the hell good was British literature or European history when the refrigerator was empty?

She glanced at Kyle. On the surface, he couldn't be more different than her. His silver spoon was so polished it could compete with his reflective Ray-Bans. His life seemed charmed, and to Madison, who'd never seemed to have much luck, he was a mystery.

But she also admired him, even if he was wearing a tailored gray suit jacket and pants with an open white shirt that likely cost more than her monthly rent. She knew he was capable of working hard too—had seen it when he'd worked side by side with them at Nanine's restaurant, having sold his Porsche so he could make the trip his parents had refused to fund.

His car... Okay, now she understood the Maserati. Total overcompensation. She did the same with food. There was always more than enough food in her house because growing up she'd gone hungry.

Who'd have thought she and Golden Boy would have anything in common?

"Kyle," she said, setting her phone on her jean-clad thigh, "take the exit toward Porte Maillot. Keep right at the fork, and then follow the signs until we merge onto Rue Gustave Charpenter."

"I know it from there," Kyle said, shifting into second and zipping to the left when the Peugeot in front of him braked hard. "Thanks, Madison."

Don't be kind to me! I can't take it. "Whatever."

Kyle cleared his throat. "Anyone want to talk about how they're feeling about Nanine?"

"No," Madison answered immediately while Sawyer said, "Yeah," at the same time.

"What about Thea?" Kyle asked, his ash brown brows winging up over the curve of his sunglasses.

She didn't bother to repeat herself—she didn't believe in it. If someone didn't hear you the first time, they didn't want to hear you.

Sawyer remained quiet.

"Anything else you want to ask, Kyle?" she drawled badly.

His mouth twitched. "You are still the biggest badass I have ever met, and I love you for it. So don't take this the wrong way. But you really need to get in touch with your feminine side."

She gave him the bird, which made him laugh. "Let me remind you again about my cleaver and assure you I know how to use it. Don't confuse me with Thea, Kyle."

Dead silence reigned in the car before Kyle said, "I'm sorry. I retract that. I was short-sighted in thinking you wouldn't be carrying your chef knives with you. I wouldn't want you sweet. I was just suggesting we discuss why we've dropped everything and come to Paris at Nanine's command."

Madison wanted to bang her head against the dashboard. "Can't we wait until we're together to do that? Don't take this wrong, but I only want to get heavy once."

"You are such a guy," Kyle drawled, "but again, that's why we love you."

She didn't point out he'd just implied something else. She could never win this argument. Their conversation reminded her of her situation at the restaurant she'd just taken leave from—Le Fleur in the heart of the Miami Design District. They had one Michelin star, a star they'd received after she'd started working there. She was a damn good chef, and everyone knew it.

Only their GM was a small-dick Latino who didn't like women outshining him, and he enjoyed making her life hell. He saw her as a threat to a grand illustrious male kitchen tradition just because she had tits. Why didn't it come down to her being damned good at what she did? If it weren't for the head chef, Marcel Fournier, she would have left sooner.

Now she had some decisions to make. She could join a Michelin-starred place here in Paris and cut all ties to Miami once and for all, like Thea seemed to have done with her hometown. God knew, she was more than tired of Miami's dating pool. If she never got propositioned by another old guy with a hairy gut smothered in gold jewelry, she'd die a happy woman.

"Anyone want to talk about work?" Kyle asked.

"Not much to tell," Madison lied.

Sawyer chuckled from the back. "Talkative as ever, Garcia."

"*Some* people could learn from me." She inclined her thumb toward Kyle. "When did you become Chatty Cathy? You have things you're dying to share?"

His mouth twisted, and for a moment she wondered if he wasn't as chill as he was pretending. He rubbed his freshly shaven face. Who came off a trans-Atlantic flight clean shaven? Kyle Taylor, that's who.

"Me? Not a thing. Only, Madison… Could you dig my phone out of my pocket and turn it to silent mode? It's been vibrating nonstop for a while now."

She couldn't pass up the dig. "Why? Is it turning you on?"

His head whipped to stare at her. "Jesus, where is your mind?"

"Hey, I went there too," Sawyer called out from the back in solidarity.

"Then both of your minds are in the gutter. I'm just distracted. I should have turned it to silent."

"No kidding! Don't take this the wrong way, Kyle, but I'm not comfortable slipping my hand in your pants. I mean, I haven't seen you in three years. No offense."

Sawyer chuckled from the back seat.

Kyle sighed. "I've missed you too. I wish we all lived closer sometimes."

She gaped at him. Was he being serious? Seeing each other at the occasional reunion, texting or calling on special occasions, and liking each other's Facebook posts was one thing, but did he really think someone like her would fit into his daily life? She'd seen *The Breakfast Club*—she knew the cool, rich kid didn't regularly hang out with anyone from the other side of the tracks. "It's just the way it is," she cautiously said.

"I agree with Kyle," Sawyer said softly. "I'm glad we'll have this time together even if I hate that it's because Nanine is suffering."

Suffering. That was a word only Sawyer would use. She didn't want to think about Nanine suffering. She and Nanine talked faithfully once a month, always on Monday—the day they both shared off, being in the same business. That call was sacred to Madison, and it was clear Nanine felt the same way.

How was Nanine going to be when they saw her? Sick-looking? Distressed? Madison saw old, sick people all the time in Miami, and she didn't like thinking Nanine would be like them. There'd always been something ageless about their friend.

Kyle squirmed in his fancy leather seat. "Can you please grit your teeth and turn off my phone? I'm not kidding. It's distracting."

"Ask Sawyer."

"No way." He glanced in the rearview mirror. "No offense, but I don't want your hands in my pants either."

"I would never cross a line like that," Sawyer promised in a professional tone.

Madison started laughing, and Kyle joined in as a car darted in front of them, causing him to brake.

"Okay, I'm going in." She winced as she fitted her hand in his pants pocket. "You so owe me."

When she slid his phone out and held it up, she blinked at all the text messages on the display. They were from the same person: Paisley—Kyle's gorgeous fiancée. "Does Paisley usually text you nonstop like this?"

He shifted harder than usual when he changed lanes, scowling now. "She wasn't happy about me taking off."

"Taking off?" Madison dropped his phone in the console. "It's Nanine!"

"Yeah. Not everybody gets that. They didn't understand ten years ago either, remember?"

Sawyer leaned forward, inverting his legs in the cramped space. "Who else other than Paisley? Your parents?"

"Yeah, and my business partners. Friends. You know…"

"So *everybody*," Sawyer said dryly. "That's cold, man. There's a human being you love who needs help."

"Should I call them all bad names, Kyle?" Madison asked, trying to steer Sawyer away from the suffering comments. "I'm crazy good at that. I've found it relieves anger and tension. With my last jerk boyfriend, I think I called him some derivative of asshole for about ten minutes at the end. I felt great after. I could teach you a few."

Kyle laughed with strain. "Maybe later. First we need to focus on Nanine. Then Thea. We're in the home stretch now."

Sure enough, they arrived a short time later, Kyle coming to a stop illegally in a no-parking zone. The first thing Madison noticed was the front of the restaurant.

"The awning's gone!" Kyle gestured rudely. "What the hell?"

"Thea texted me a little while ago to say there'd been some big changes," Sawyer said quietly. "I didn't think I should say anything since you didn't want to talk about things, Madison."

"I would have talked about *that*." She swung out of the car and clicked the seat forward so Sawyer could crawl out.

Kyle came around the car after slamming his door, and the three of them stood there in silence. Where were the curtains, and why were the windows filthy?

Then they heard a yell, and Thea rushed out with her usual wide smile on her sweet face and hugged everyone with so much sincerity even Madison's heart turned into a warming oven. Brooke and Dean joined them, although they were more subdued, and suddenly there was a love fest on the street. Damn, but it *was* good to see everyone. Still, her cred needed establishing up front.

"Okay, I've had my hug quotient for the year." Madison pointed aggressively at the restaurant. "What in the hell is going on?"

Thea, Brooke, and Dean shared a look before Brooke walked to the front door. "We've been dying for you to arrive. We need to get to the hospital stat so Nanine can tell us the whole story."

"How bad is it?" Sawyer asked as he followed her to the door, Madison and Kyle behind him.

"See for yourself," Brooke said, opening it.

"What the fuck!" Sawyer shouted as he cleared the door.

Dr. Sawyer Jackson had the cleanest mouth of any guy she'd ever met, and he knew Nanine didn't allow the f-word inside her place. Nanine's famous chandelier gave a decided clang like a cowbell, echoing his sentiment, and Madison took a deep breath and stepped inside in her black canvas high-tops.

"Shit. Shit. Shit." Her mind spun. "It's gutted."

"Fuck me," Kyle said when he arrived beside her. "Who did this?"

"Nanine didn't want to say anything until we were all here," Brooke said brusquely. "Sorry to be pushy, but we really do need to go to the hospital right now. Nanine said she wouldn't tell us what happened until we were all here. Dean, grab their bags."

"Funny, Brooke," Madison heard him reply over the roar in her head.

She wasn't one for nostalgia, but her cherished Nanine's was gone. Ripped out. Like her heart felt right now. Nanine's place was supposed to last forever, dammit. She'd always counted on that.

Kyle put his hand on her shoulder. She realized he was

shaky too. Yeah, her gut was flip-flopping like a fresh-caught fish.

"Let's go," she said in a voice she didn't recognize.

Their reunion could wait. She needed to know who to use her cleaver on.

CHAPTER
SIX

Nanine Laurent resented holding court from a hospital bed with her very existence hanging in the balance.

Of course, the vibrant flowers helped, bouquets from friends and colleagues and her beloved Courses.

She angled back into the ghastly plastic hospital pillows and drew herself into a regal posture, folding the edges of the white sheet as crisply as a napkin at her restaurant. *Her restaurant.* The very thought of Nanine's gave her pain, and she gasped as its tentacles shot through her. She'd learned not to bite her lip, for it would bleed. Her monitors beeped, and she took calming breaths until they quieted.

Her heart may have been *attacked*, as they doctors called it, but the stress that had caused her episode was far from over.

She straightened her shoulders again, determined not to show the Courses how weak she felt. In the past, she'd been bone-tired after cooking for nearly twenty hours a day, but she'd never experienced anything like her current state.

How could she have? Nothing had ever broken her heart like recent events, not even her first tragic love affair. Worse than the weakness, she hadn't stopped herself from berating herself for her stupidity. That kept her fire going—at herself, where it belonged—and pushed off the drowning feelings of loss and defeat.

Nanine Laurent was not defeated, and she would never be.

As a Frenchwoman, she took her vows seriously, and this one she would have made with blood, if she'd had a paring knife on hand. Hospitals were wise not to keep sharp implements around for patients with dark thoughts or questions of honor.

A nurse named Anais, professional but deeply kind, opened the door with a smile. "Your Courses are here, Nanine. Again, the doctor wanted me to remind you we're keeping the visit to five minutes."

She forced herself not to frown. Having never been sick, she had little experience with people in healthcare, but she'd quickly discovered they were like some of the wealthier patrons who came to her restaurant. They liked to give orders and feel in charge. She was beginning to play their game her way. The strategy had always carried her through difficult patches in her life.

"Thank you, Anais. Let them in."

Brooke appeared first, charging to her side with the makeup bag and pressing it into her hand. They were alike in many ways, and she cupped the younger woman's face as they pressed their cheeks together. "My beautiful Third Course."

When Brooke stepped back, Thea approached her next, her softhearted one. "First Course. I'm so glad your boss gave you the time off. I was worried he might not."

Her crestfallen look conveyed there was a story there, and a bad one to be sure. She felt another heart pang. Well, whatever it was, they would take care of it.

"Come," she said, "we must greet each other quickly. I have much to tell you, and the nurse is going to be difficult."

"We can save hugs for later," Nanine heard Madison say.

"Speak for yourself," Kyle answered as Dean and Sawyer also muttered their disagreement under their breath.

She smiled at Madison after kissing the men. She stood in front of the now closed door dressed in a snug black T-shirt and black jeans, arms crossed over the chest she'd always been embarrassed about.

"Madison, kindly lock the door so the nurse won't bother us. It's time to tell you what happened. At least what I know."

Thea linked hands with Brooke and then Dean, Nanine noted as she opened the bag and drew out her precious Chanel No. 5. She spritzed her pulse points, inhaling the familiar confidence in the scent. Kyle and Sawyer cleared their throats and took up positions in front of the windows filled with vases stuffed with yellow lilies.

She decided to add a few patches of color and definition to her face quickly. As a working woman, she'd always been able to do her makeup in seconds. Opening the small mirror, she went for a splash of powder, the marked definition of a brown eye pencil, and a hint of rose on her lips. Satisfied she looked less ghastly, she faced them all again and put the bag at her side.

"You will be shocked by what I'm about to tell you," she said in English, as Thea and a few others might be a little rusty and tired from their flights, "but if you'll let me say my piece without interrupting, it will go better, I think."

She raised her head a little higher and looked each of them in the eyes before continuing.

"As you know, my daughter, Adrienne, and I have not been on the best of terms since her childhood. She didn't understand why I didn't marry a man and stay home like other mothers. She never understood my love for the restaurant. And she resented not knowing her father, who has always vehemently denied her very existence. I did not know how much she blamed me for it until recently."

Her stupidity had caused some of those events as well, but she'd forgiven herself for her mistakes long ago. A leading chef who taught at *Le Cordon Bleu* in Paris had seduced her when she was a student, telling her he was secretly divorcing his wife. She'd foolishly fallen in love with him, and when she got pregnant around her graduation, she'd chosen to have the child. The father, Chef Auguste Dassault, had acted much like all seducers in history. He'd told her he wanted nothing to do with her or the child and had forbidden her from telling anyone of their affair or the child. He was not secretly divorcing his wife, of course.

Except their "secret" liaison had been known by others at *Le Cordon Bleu*, and secrets that juicy tend to spill out. Auguste had changed his tactics and branded her a slut and schemer to everyone in the culinary industry.

She'd applied at restaurant after restaurant, a humiliating experience, until she finally came to a one Michelin-star restaurant named *L'Étoile Éclatante*. The head chef hadn't only given her a job. He'd offered to help her find a good woman to help raise her baby. His motivation had shocked her—Auguste had seduced Chef Louis Champion's wife in culinary school and left her in tatters as well.

She'd taken the chance Louis had given her and helped him garner his second Michelin star before striking out on her own at Nanine's after Adrienne began secondary school. She'd thought her daughter would understand with age and time why she had wanted a career, but Adrienne refused to see things her way. Even the love Bernard had wanted to shower on her child had been refused. Four years later, at eighteen, she'd left home and they'd barely spoken to each other since.

"I know many say it," she said, pressing her hands flat on

the mattress to keep her composure, "but I did the best I could as a single parent. I don't deny I wish things had been different. But they were what they were then, and there's no changing them."

Nanine wished for water, but she could indulge her thirst later. "Adrienne and I had not spoken for many years, as you know, when she suddenly arrived on my doorstep on Bastille Day a month ago. She was married again—this was her third husband, Jeremy, whom I disliked as much as the earlier ones."

She watched as Madison scowled, and she found strength in her anger. Fifth Course had the most fire, and Nanine needed that fire as she shared her stupidity.

Clearing her throat, she found her voice again. "I said nothing to any of you because I knew you would have strong feelings, and I wanted time to turn our estrangement around. Jeremy was looking for a job and had no experience. Honestly, I don't think I would have taken them in, only… there was Chloe, my grandchild, whom I hadn't known about. I fell in love with her on sight."

As she'd expected, everyone had a strong reaction to the news. Brooke gasped and groped for her hand, which she squeezed hard. Sawyer wandered from the window to the other side of her bed and laid a strong hand on her shoulder. Dean stared at the ceiling, fighting emotion, while Kyle turned to look out the window. Madison's mouth was a flat line, and then she lived up to her course by saying, "That bitch. She knew that would get you."

A few people gave a strangled laugh, but it helped return balance to the room.

"Sorry for the language, Nanine," Madison said, holding up her hand in peace.

"No, you're accurate about what my daughter has become." She looked heavenward to push back her own tears.

"I do not know her anymore. It's a horrible thing for a mother to admit—to herself or anyone. I've lived with the weight of having failed Adrienne for a long time, but with Chloe, I thought I was being given another chance. You don't know this yet, but you'll do anything for your child. The same is true for your grandchild."

Her mouth lifted into a smile, but it slipped away as Chloe's face came to mind. Curly brown hair. Round face. Button nose. Pain streaked through her chest. Her *belle* Chloe.

"She was a quiet little girl when we first met. She'd just turned two, but I found the way to her heart. I would put a treat in her little hands—anything from a sliced carrot to a macaron—and she would smile at me and skip around my kitchen as she ate. I love her with my whole being, and now she is lost to me forever."

Those tears she'd forbidden herself welled in her eyes. She pursed her mouth to keep them from falling. She had to look away from a few of the boys and girls, who had tears falling for her. Brooke. Thea. Sawyer. Even Dean. Madison's eyes blazed, though, and a muscle ticked in Kyle's jaw. The silence in the room was the kind one observed at a funeral, which she hated.

She gave herself a moment. "I brought them into my home. They stayed on the Boys' Floor. I gave Jeremy a job, which he was poor at, as I expected. He didn't really want to work, especially at the restaurant. I knew I was being used, but I reasoned he couldn't do much damage. He wasn't given any real duties, and my staff continued to run things like always under my direction."

She rubbed her nose, which was dripping like a leaky faucet. Sawyer pulled out his cloth handkerchief, something he'd begun using in Paris. After dabbing at her nose, she tucked the cloth in her palm, careful of her IVs.

"I didn't realize Jeremy had planned the whole thing

79

before he'd arrived in Paris. Adrienne denied it, of course, when I discovered... But I'm getting ahead of myself. They had told me they'd like some time alone together, so I went off to Bretagne with little Chloe. I considered myself the luckiest of women to have time alone with my granddaughter."

The next part was the most difficult, and she looked at the monitors, imploring her heart not to aggravate them. "I did not realize that Jeremy would take the opportunity to ruin my restaurant while I was gone. It is only because one of my neighbors called me after seeing Jeremy and some other men take down my awning and start removing things from my restaurant that more damage was not done."

"Jesus, no," Kyle said as the others muttered under their breath.

"After not being able to reach my daughter or Jeremy on the phone, I returned immediately. I arrived in time to stop the workers before they took down my beloved chandelier and removed items from the kitchen and the cave. I marched into my restaurant—*my restaurant*—and I found what you discovered earlier today. He'd taken away everything I'd created in the front. Everything I'd worked like a dog to establish. Everything from the irreplaceable signed photos and artwork from patrons to the dinnerware, serving utensils, and furniture. Even my antique Limoges soup tureens."

Even now she could taste her fury. She took a breath as emotion colored her Courses' faces, from white to green to red. Ghastly colors, all.

"We had a horrible argument, Jeremy and I, with my daughter watching. In front of their own Chloe, who started crying. It was...awful."

She could still hear her granddaughter's sobs, but the worst part was that Adrienne didn't stop spewing hatred at her long enough to comfort her own daughter. That more than anything kept her awake at night. Her granddaughter was being raised under conditions no child should have to endure.

"Jeremy said he had proof that I had authorized the sale of these items," she continued, a metallic taste in her mouth where she'd bitten her cheek in fury. "Then he waved a paper in front of me which had my name and address on it. Adrienne said maybe I was getting old and had forgotten what I'd done. Me! Nanine Laurent, who never forgets one ingredient in my entire kitchen. I realized I had been scammed. That is the word, yes?"

Brooke nodded slowly before letting go of her hand. Nanine watched as she stalked to the window, but she resisted the temptation to check on the others. She had to finish the story.

"That was when I had the pain in my heart and collapsed. One of the workers called for an ambulance. That is what made them flee, in the end. I had not thought to call the police. Adrienne is my daughter, after all. All the way home in the car, I had hoped it was some kind of misunderstanding."

Madison swore under her breath again, and Nanine gathered Fifth Course's fire into her. She would need it now.

"I accept my responsibility for what happened. I should not have invited Jeremy into my home when I did not trust him. I had hoped in doing so I could make him feel useful and help Adrienne and Chloe. I'm sorry to say this, but many men need to feel useful."

She had to clear her throat again, but it didn't assuage the knife she felt lodged within it. "On paper, it looks as though I intentionally sold the furnishings of my restaurant to another restaurant owner. Obviously a forgery."

More swear words from Madison, and Kyle joined in as well. Her own heart was beating like an angry drum in her chest. She needed to finish her story. Then she would never speak of it again.

A quiet knock sounded at the door. Everyone turned their heads.

Madison set her weight against the door, her dangerous side visible in the slits of her golden eyes. "Keep going, Nanine. I'm not letting anyone in."

She nodded. "I still do not know the full extent of the damage Jeremy did, but my lawyer is looking into it."

The monitors beeped, and Thea rushed toward her along with Sawyer and Kyle.

"I'm fine," she assured them, waving them off.

"But Nanine—" Thea protested.

"No! I had a heart attack because they broke my heart." She had to pause after that dramatic outburst. "I've never been sick a day in my whole life. With all of you around me, I will heal from this. Like I did after my Bernard died—and my daughter didn't even show up for the funeral."

Another harsh mutter from Madison, which stopped the memory of her daughter's harsh words when she'd called to tell her of Bernard's death. *You loved Bernard more than me.*

"There is much to address," she continued, "and with my infernal weakness, I knew I needed your help—all of you— getting my restaurant back on its feet and to sort things out. I know you have other commitments in your lives—"

"Don't be silly," Brooke said in a raised voice taut with emotion.

"We'll stay as long as you need us," Dean said with a firm nod of his sandy head. "Right, guys?"

The others nodded, and if she didn't hurt so badly, she would have smiled.

Madison straightened and cracked her knuckles. "Where are Jeremy and Adrienne now?"

"They cleaned out their meager belongings after the workmen called the ambulance."

She could still remember the young man kneeling over her, while her own daughter thought only of herself. Afterward, he sat and held her hand. She wondered if she would ever learn who he was so she could thank him.

"I'm hoping you will work with my lawyer," she rushed on as another knock sounded on the door. "His name is Jean Luc Mercier. He's a long-time customer who lives on my block. He will be coming by the restaurant. I want you to meet with him. Especially you, Kyle, with your restaurant investment and management experience. You'll know where to look for more damage." She was sure it was there, waiting under the surface like the garbage tourists tossed into the Seine.

"Done," he said crisply. "What else? Will you press charges?"

She blew out a long breath this time. "With my name on the papers, forged or not, it is unclear whether I can. I have not been able to spend much time on such matters with Jean Luc. My doctor wants me to be free of stress and has limited my visits and calls. He's an idiot. How could I not be stressed?"

Thea came over and took her hand. "We'll help you. Whatever it takes."

She patted First Course's hand. "Thank you. I know you will. Dean, you're good with start-ups. It seems I'm starting over in some ways. I'm sure there are better ways we can do things in the front, including on the technology side for reservations. Adrienne accused me of being as old and tired as Nanine's herself. Well, if I must redo the restaurant, I'm going to do it with a new vision and dare the Michelin people to deny me my star."

"Damn right," Madison said, and the others nodded in unison.

That goal had yet to be reached, and right now, it had never seemed farther away. But if Nanine had to lasso that star and pull it to her, she would, because that was what someone did when they wanted their dream to come true.

She felt new fire spread in her belly, as bright and warming as her Crêpes Suzette after she lit a match to the Grand Marnier sauce. "Sawyer, I want Nanine's *ambiance* to embody your specialty: an Impressionist painting."

He tilted his head to the side, his dark eyes intent behind his gold-rimmed glasses. "Do you have a painting in mind?"

"I cannot remember where I saw it or its name, but I see beautiful women in long dresses from Le Belle Epoque, painted in apricots, golds, and creams with a touch of green and red. Think Renoir. Think Icart. With a modern feel. Banquettes and tables. Lush curtains, of course. Draw me up some designs. Your artist's heart will guide you."

He shook his head. "Perhaps, but I'll do my best work for you, Nanine."

"I know you will, *mon cher*. Brooke. I need new fabrics to accompany the design: curtains, tablecloths, and napkins. Not damask. They cost a fortune to launder. Some kind of new fabric that looks exquisite. We can finalize the colors later. Can you find me samples?"

Brooke tapped her French-manicured fingernail on her thigh. "Of course. And I'll make sure to find you deals on what you select. At cost, hopefully. Maybe I can even find a sponsor. For the dishes and flatware too. I'll do my best."

Brooke could negotiate like a Turk in the Spice Market. "Good. I'm counting on that. Madison." She looked over to where Fifth Course was standing. "I love Jacques, my sous chef, but he is too soft for what lies ahead. A new Nanine's will need a new menu. I want you to act as the *chef de cuisine* in my absence and start developing ideas for our new menu. Find me some old classic recipes no one is making anymore. I want to showcase ingredients like the black figs of Caromb and cherries of Venasque. I want *our* take of old and new French cuisine to be unforgettable. Let your brilliance shine forth, Fifth Course."

"*Oui, Chef,*" Madison said in the way of formal kitchen staff.

Both the nature of her response and how quickly she'd made it brought tears to Nanine's eyes and down her cheeks. She brushed them aside. "Thea, I want you to work with Madison on desserts and pastry and breads."

"*Oui, Chef,*" Thea said. Nanine caught her blush of embarrassment over her tongue-tied French, but she persevered, haltingly adding, "I brought my sourdough starter."

"Of course you did, as breadmaking is part of your soul," Nanine said softly in French before switching back to English. "Use mine as well. In fact, take some from each, and let our magic mingle. I can't wait to see the bread we'll make together."

Thea wiped at tears and nodded.

The knocking on the door renewed, heavy and insistent. It sounded like a man's hand this time. "My doctor is likely trying to force his way in here. Lastly, Kyle— This is the hardest for me to say out loud, least of all ask."

He walked to her side and took her hand, careful of those damn tubes they'd covered her in. "Just say it."

She swallowed. "I'm going to need help raising the capital for the renovation. Jean Luc does not believe my insurance will cover what was taken from me."

His green eyes filled with fire. "I've got you covered, Nanine. Don't give it another thought."

"Thank you," she said, forgetting her rule about not biting her lips. "It's a bitter pill to be taken advantage of. Stolen from. To have everything you've worked for suddenly disappear as if it had never existed. This was Adrienne's way of punishing me, and she could have not served a colder dish."

That wasn't the worst of it, though. Losing her grandchild had been the worst pain of all. She'd never forget the way Adrienne screamed at her, accusing her of ruining everything even as she lay on the floor, fighting for breath. Chloe had sobbed the entire time, and it had been impossible to go to her, to comfort her.

"Children, I don't know all that Jeremy did or with whom he did it, but I want you to remain watchful. My confidence has been shaken. It's not like the old days where I believe in the goodness of all people, even my estranged daughter."

No, the old days were gone.

CHAPTER
SEVEN

Kyle couldn't fight the urge to speed all the way back to Nanine's, bruising his hand on the gearshift and testing the brakes.

He clenched the wheel, trying to contain his rage. Someone had stolen from Nanine. Put her in a hospital bed. Reduced her to tears. He was tempted to find that bastard Jeremy and beat him to a pulp. Him, their so-called golden boy.

He slammed on the brakes when the light turned red on Saint-Germain Boulevard. Madison braced her hand against the dashboard, and Thea knocked into the back of his chair.

"We all want to smash things right now," Madison said softly in the rarest of voices—a tone imploring for calm.

He glanced in the rearview mirror. Thea was looking out the window as pedestrians crossed *en masse*, brushing aside tears. Like she didn't have enough on her plate. He hadn't even had time to say anything to her yet. Then he remembered Brooke telling him not to mention the job situation until Thea officially told them. Shit. What a mess.

"I'm sorry." And his tone was heartfelt. "I'll slow down."

When the light changed, he pressed the pedal as if he were pushing a baby carriage.

"A few deep breaths sometimes helps me," Thea offered from the back.

He realized he was barely breathing at all. But God… His entire chest might as well have been wrapped in zip ties. He managed a shallow inhale and took care to get them safely back to Nanine's. The taxi the others had taken had beaten him. They stood waiting outside the restaurant.

Kyle parked in front again and swung out of the car, deciding he would risk a ticket or a tow. Later he'd find an underground garage close by. He hadn't thought through the whole *having a car in Paris* thing, or he would have been prepared. He'd just promised himself he'd never be without one again after selling his Porsche to come to Paris ten years ago. He'd thought it poetic justice to have the most expensive ride he could rent. Blah, blah, blah. He was such a jerk sometimes.

"We're contemplating drinking lots of the wine Nanine's daughter and her asshole criminal husband didn't steal," Brooke said over-brightly, dressed in *haute couture* from head to toe like always. "My treat. We're unanimous. How do you vote?"

Just like that, they were back to their old dynamic, to what had been. "I like the idea of keeping money coming into the restaurant, even if it's only as a bar bill. Good energy."

"Agreed," Dean said, coming over and standing beside him.

"Dinner is on me," Madison said, kicking at the sidewalk.

"I can't eat anything that reminds me of Nanine's right now," Sawyer said harshly, shoving his hands into his pants pockets.

"So pizza?" Brooke suggested.

"Pizza is like old times," Thea said emphatically. "I'll be right back."

Kyle watched as she hurried off toward the alley. "We should change the locks. I'm guessing Jeremy and Adrienne had a key."

"I need to check her computer," Dean said with a glower. "Although I'm worried about that forgery. Sounds like a professional scam."

"Yeah, that's what it sounded like to me too." Sawyer held up his phone. "Both items are already on the list I made in the taxi. We should also go through Nanine's belongings, especially her jewelry."

"I'll do it," Brooke said tightly.

"We have to assume they would have stolen anything easy," Sawyer said harshly. "Fuckers."

Kyle walked over and gave Sawyer a man hug. "I like this fierce side of you, Dr. Jackson. So unacademic. We've got a lot to do if we're going to pull off a full renovation. I need to make some calls. Looks like we're going to need to be here longer than I thought, so I'd better call Paisley first."

He headed to the back door of the kitchen and stopped short when he heard Thea crying from the adjoining bathroom. Shit. He swallowed thickly, the raw sound putting him in touch with a pain he didn't want to feel. Anger was better. The hurt over seeing Nanine like she'd been, stark and white and scared in her hospital bed, and hearing that story could cut him apart if he let it. Thea had a story too, he realized, and she was hurting as well. He couldn't leave her alone, so he walked to the white bathroom door and knocked softly.

"Hey! It's Kyle. Come out here."

"I'm crying!" She sounded aggrieved. "Like always."

A small smile broke over his mouth. "That's why you're a sweetheart. You care about others deeply. Come on. I want to comfort you." Jeez, did that sound awkward?

The door cracked open. Her face was wet with tears, her brown hair plastered to the sides of her face. "You do?"

Even he surprised himself sometimes. "Yeah. I'm upset

too."

"But you never cry."

"You remembered." His throat burned, and he found himself telling her why, something he hadn't done when they were roommates so long ago. "When I was a kid, my dad got out his belt if I cried. Seemed smart to stop."

More tears welled up and fell from her brown eyes. "Oh, Kyle. You can cry with me. I promise I won't tell anyone."

He drew her close. It meant something to him that she'd offered him that freedom, but he still wouldn't cry. He was like some of the wells in Texas. Once they dried up, they were dry forever.

She cried against his chest while he patted her back. God, he didn't know what to do. Most of the women he spent time with weren't criers, at least not around him. "You want to talk?"

"Not yet." She finally raised her head and touched his face. "You're a good man, Kyle Taylor. Thanks for that."

He tapped her nose like an older brother. "You're welcome, First Course. I'm going to arrange to stay here longer. We're going to get all of this fixed up for Nanine, you just wait and see. You okay if I go make some calls?"

"Yes, I feel better now." She gave a watery smile. "It helps to imagine Madison punching Jeremy in the mouth if he dares to show his face here."

She wouldn't be the only one taking a swing. "You and Sawyer are showing new stripes. I like it."

He found he could laugh as he walked off. Who would have guessed he'd be capable of it on one of the worst days of his life? Heading up to his old haunt on the Boys' Floor, he wasn't laughing anymore. He was out of breath after climbing three treacherous flights of Parisian stairs!

Jesus. He worked out six days a week at the gym. So much for being in shape.

But he was heartened to see that the furniture was still

there. Nanine had mentioned her relations had stayed on this floor, but there was no sign of them. He only saw the messy sprawl of Dean's things, which he never managed to contain in his room. Hell. It was going to be weird, living with everyone again. They were adults now. He'd just have to get used to having roommates again for a while.

When he pulled out his phone, some internal compass of horror had his entire body going eerily still. He had one hundred and sixty text messages, all from Paisley. No wonder Madison had expressed alarm when he'd asked her to turn his phone to silent. His call list registered seventy-two missed calls and thirteen voicemails from her as well. They joked about her being high-maintenance, but he wasn't laughing this time.

She'd hidden his passport when he'd told her about the trip and refused to reveal its hiding place, forcing him to pay a mint to get an expedited one before his trip, which was what had prompted him to investigate a private flight to make up for lost time. He was still seething with anger about it, but as he scanned the first few texts, he stopped in disgust.

How could Paisley be all about herself when the woman who'd become another mother to him—more caring than any of his blood relatives—was in the hospital? Maybe he was emotionally stunted, but no one had captured his heart like Nanine. He only felt this protective of her, and maybe Thea, what with her sweetness and hometown innocence. Then there were the rest of his Paris roommates. They couldn't be more different from him, but he never questioned that they would have his back when push came to shove. He'd trusted all of them, even as a jaded kid of twenty when he'd arrived in Paris.

He was even more jaded now, having turned thirty last month. Disillusioned. Disgusted. He was surrounded with people who played games and only looked out for them-selves. His fiancée included, he was ashamed to admit.

What does that say about me?

Paisley hadn't seemed super high-maintenance in the beginning. She'd taken care of little things, like making them a picnic. He'd drive out to the countryside, and they'd pull over and eat under an old mesquite tree on a freshly pressed designer tablecloth.

But everything had changed after he'd proposed to her four months ago, after a year of dating. They didn't have sex as much—only twice a week since she usually had some excuse. He didn't know if that was normal, and he had too much male pride to ask anyone.

The other signs were equally alarming. She'd practically moved into his house and taken over, even starting to redecorate it, saying it needed a woman's touch. Worse, he'd caught Paisley dressing down a Hispanic caterer she'd hired for an engagement party she hadn't run past him. Her tirade had reeked of racism. He'd been raised in a racist household, and he'd hated it. He'd never understood why one person would judge another based on the color of their skin or their sexual orientation.

When he'd asked Paisley about it, she'd said, "You need to keep on top of people like that."

He'd known it was all wrong—he'd felt it in his gut ever since he put that three-carat engagement ring on her finger— but he'd held out hope that the woman he'd fallen for would return. Everyone had told him he was getting older. He'd heard over and over again that it was time to get married, be an adult, start a family. Paisley was supposed to be that next step. But the hissy fit she'd thrown when he'd told her he was urgently needed in Paris had only made his gut churn more.

Is this how they were going to be for the rest of their lives?

He didn't have any models of happy marriages, but Nanine had talked about her relationship with Bernard. Her musings and photos had knit a story of a couple who'd had both a loving familiarity and a passionate connection. A part of him wasn't sure such a bond was possible for him. But he didn't want the kind of relationship Paisley was showing him right now. That was for damn sure.

He paced for a solid minute before gathering up enough courage to call back his fiancée. His own fiancée, for God's sake.

"It's about time," she began in an ear-grating drawl. "Where in the *hell* have you been, Kyle? You landed hours ago."

Paisley was a good Southern Baptist, and she didn't typically use words like *hell*. He gripped his phone. "The minute I arrived at the restaurant, we left for the hospital to see Nanine."

"When are you coming home?" she asked petulantly.

Not one word about Nanine's health.

He'd hoped for something different, but he had to admit he hadn't expected it.

Every person in his life back in Austin had always tried to stop him from coming to Paris. Why was that? How could they not understand how much he loved it here? How free he felt.

"I'm going to be here longer than I thought, Paisley. The situation is worse than I could have imagined. Nanine's situation is dire, and Thea needs some help too."

"What about me? *I* need you here. We all do. Jim called and said he couldn't reach you. They have a client they want you to meet."

He ground his teeth. His three business associates were just as self-centered as his fiancée, although Alan was usually the most reasonable. They'd made a ton of money together, but he didn't enjoy their company anymore. They didn't discuss anything except business, the women in their lives, and of course, football. They were carbon copies of his parents, only with different careers. His oil-rich family had originally objected to him working in hospitality. Funny how making a ton of money shut some people up, his parents included.

"Paisley, I know this time apart will be tough, but I need to be here."

"No, you don't. Let your old roommates help. Come back right now, Kyle. I mean it. We have a wedding to plan."

"The wedding is a year off." Paisley wouldn't contemplate having the reception anywhere except at The Estates, a highly exclusive resort outside Austin. She was already showing signs of being a Bridezilla.

"Kyle, I'm telling you. This is unacceptable."

He didn't know who had taught her that phrase, but she used it with everyone from the doorman to her own fiancé when she wasn't getting her way. He lowered his phone to his side, his throat burning with anger.

He couldn't take this anymore.

He thought of Thea. Is this how she'd felt with her boss? Pushed to the edge? Well, if she could walk away, so could he.

This was so unacceptable.

He lifted the phone and pressed it to his ear. "Paisley, I hate to do it like this over the phone, but you haven't left me any choice. I'm not going to marry a woman who doesn't understand how important Nanine and this situation is to me. We're done. Move your things out of my house and leave the key with my parents. The engagement is off. *We're off.*"

"But—"

He clicked off. The phone immediately started ringing again. She wasn't going to stop. Pulling up her contact information, he took the nuclear option and blocked her.

The zip ties around his chest seemed to fall away. He could suddenly breathe, and with it, a storm of emotion rose in his chest, overwhelming him.

Then he lowered himself to the floor.

But he didn't cry.

CHAPTER
EIGHT

The first rule among roommates was simple: secrets were hard to keep.

Even after all these years, Thea knew Kyle enough to sense something was wrong. She ventured up the uneven stairs slowly—sideways due to her big feet. When she reached the Boys' Floor, she wandered past the salon with its blue velvet couch and ottomans to the hallway, glad to see nothing was missing.

She still couldn't take in the deliberate cruelty of someone ruining another person's life like that. And to use a child to do it... Thea didn't understand that kind of selfishness, and she prayed she never would.

Padding down the hallway, she noted Kyle's bedroom door was open a crack. Arriving at the doorway, she saw him sitting on the floor, holding his head in his hands with his forehead pressed to his knees.

She froze, not knowing what to do. He'd told her he never cried, and she knew he had his pride. She wasn't sure he'd want comfort. Wouldn't he have sought one of them out if he had? He didn't look up, so she retreated quietly and headed back downstairs, her heart heavy.

Sawyer was in the kitchen, arranging wine bottles on the counter. The trap door to the cave below the restaurant was open, the treacherous stairs visible in the soft light.

"I chose two reds—a lovely Côtes du Rhône and a Bordeaux—and two whites—"

"A Sancerre and a Chablis like always," she finished, crossing and putting her hand on his back, hoping happy memories could wash away some of their sadness. "We were all blown away by Chablis when we first arrived. I still remember Nanine's horror at hearing it was a cheap box wine in the States."

"She was like, 'what eez zis box wine?'" Sawyer laughed a moment before sobering. "She's going to be here, dammit, drinking with us, as soon as you can say 'Rip van Winkle.' Where's Kyle?"

What should she tell him? "He needed a moment."

"We need some champagne too, Sawyer," Brooke said as she breezed in, the chandelier clinking in time with the sound of her heels. "I'm not letting anything ruin our homecoming. We're toasting Nanine getting out of that horrible, smelly hospital—like she'd want us to."

"Damn straight," Sawyer said with a heartbreaking smile. "You know, I checked out the chandelier, and the workers stripped the screws holding it in place. Remember how we used to wonder whether there was a ghost using it as an instrument to communicate from the other world? Maybe it was true, and the spirit goaded them into stripping the screws. Hard to remove it after that."

"That story always creeped me out," Thea admitted. "But I like the idea of the magic of Paris keeping bad people from doing bad things."

"Me too," Brooke admitted, "although the ghost clearly fell down on the job and should be playing a funeral dirge given the circumstances. That's why we need to start with champagne. Nanine says you *always* drink champagne in low times. I'd suggest Bérèche. Maybe Tarlant or Benoit Déhu."

"Yes, my queen," Sawyer said with a mock bow.

Brooke shot him an amused look. The joke was an old one, another relic of old times. "Thea, where's Kyle?"

"Coming," she said, managing a smile. "He needed a moment."

"Understandable. I'm resisting the urge to buy paint and spray it all over the walls. We'll have to remodel anyway. I've always wanted to do graffiti."

"Really?" Thea asked. "I'd be terrified of being caught."

"Inner bad girl," Sawyer mused. "Hot."

"Or it's the result of a repressed childhood," Brooke said dryly. "Speaking of… I still can't believe Adrienne would do this."

"To use her own daughter to hook Nanine…" Sawyer shook his head. "That's stone-cold."

"I feel horrible for Nanine." Thea blew out another breath as her emotions went haywire. "She loves her granddaughter so much, and now she's lost forever."

"Not forever perhaps," Sawyer said in his philosophical way. "She might come around when she's older…after she's learned the truth about her parents. God, that's depressing. I'm headed back down the stairs for more liquor. Were they always this treacherous or have I gotten old?"

"Both," Brooke quipped with a smirk. "It's because we're turning thirty in a few months."

"Don't remind me of the Big Bitch."

Thea had never heard it called that. "But you still look good, Sawyer. You too, Brooke."

"Thanks, Thea." Brooke slid her a smile. "Sawyer, grab those bottles. We haven't caught up yet, but that's going to change. We're about to play an old game. Divulge or Drink."

Thea winced. Some played Truth or Dare. Brooke had

97

decided on a different name. As Third Course, she liked to put her own spin on things.

Sawyer made a show of putting his foot on the first step. "I'll bring a bottle of brandy up with the champagne then. Gonna be a long night, and we should end on a *digestif* French style."

"And calvados," Brooke called as he disappeared. "Dean and Madison love it—or they did. God, what a day. You okay, Thea? Were you crying?"

Caught already. "Yes, but is that surprising? You always say I cry over everything, even Christmas movies."

"It's perfectly acceptable to cry during *It's a Wonderful Life*, but *Elf* is another matter."

She couldn't help the smile. "I swear you had tears in your eyes when Will Farrell's character and his dad reunited." The two of them had watched it on their first Christmas together, two years after they'd met, something her parents hadn't liked one bit. You were supposed to spend the holiday with your family, her mother had complained. Not in New York, no matter how magical Central Park had looked with snow falling.

"I could never cry for a character named Buddy," Brooke said, walking over to the server's station and grabbing a waiter's corkscrew. "But if you need to watch *Elf* or any of your other favorites as we get you back on track, I'll do it."

She got totally choked up. "What about *Anne of Green Gables*?"

Brooke took a fortifying breath. "Even that."

She wiped a tear. "That's love."

"Word," she said as she began opening the wine with her usual efficiency. "We'll have to drink from the bottle since all the glassware is gone. I still can't… Never mind."

After opening the last bottle, she tipped the Chablis to her lips and drank deeply before holding it out to Thea.

In high school, Thea hadn't gone to the parking lots where

her other classmates went to get drunk. She'd never understood why someone would plan a Friday night around getting trashed. Not that there was much good French wine around in Nowheresville, of course. Somehow drinking from the bottle in Paris seemed different, though—it seemed like a *must-do*.

Her new mantra came to mind: live life to the fullest. Maybe she should make that into a new recipe card.

"Yum." She took the wine and drank deeply as well. The acid of the grapes filled her tongue, followed by a delightful medley of flowers and yeast. They were some of the ingredients that filled her soul, she realized. It was the aroma of her sourdough starter—the aroma of life. She knew how to create that. She was good at it. It gave her hope that she'd be able to figure out how to be good at living life too.

"Why does wine always taste better in Paris?" Brooke asked, taking the bottle back.

"Because this place is fucking awesome," Kyle said, appearing in the kitchen.

"Language." Brooke rolled her eyes. "We're going to have to start complying with Nanine's house rules."

"No swearing, no smoking, no fraternizing, and no guest sleepovers," Thea recited and then winced as Brooke confessed, "I smoked from the window earlier and am still feeling guilty."

"Life is a series of accommodations," Kyle said bitterly, holding his hand out. "Give it over."

As upset as he'd been upstairs, Thea gave him a surreptitious glance as he drank. His usually perfect ash brown hair was out of order and the entire cut of his body was tense with anger. Crossing to him, she laid her head against his side in comfort. He hugged her with his free arm and took another swig before handing the bottle back to Brooke.

Sawyer's head appeared at the top of the stairs. "Get these, will you?"

Brooke took the champagne bottles from him, and he ducked back downstairs before returning with two digestifs. Kyle grabbed the calvados and uncorked it, taking another drink. Thea's worry radar went sky high.

"Easy, sweetie," Brooke said, unwrapping the foil and wire from the champagne bottle and popping the cork with a whisper before putting her thumb over the top to contain the gasses from escaping, something Nanine had taught them all. "It's Divulge or Drink night."

Kyle's color looked off under his golden tan. "Terrific, although I suppose it'll be a good crash course in catching up, seeing as we're roommates again."

"I'm really happy about that," Thea said softly.

Kyle kissed the top of her head. "Me too, but Dean already threw his sh—stuff all over our floor."

"Then you and I are going to have to do what we used to and shove it in a corner or hide it from him," Sawyer said with a wicked grin.

"I'm not hiding it," Kyle said with an edge in his voice. "I hate that being done to me. But we'll need to have some parameters about living together again. I'm thirty now, and I have less tolerance for bullshit."

"You were tolerant at twenty?" Brooke asked with a raised brow.

"Some ground rules make sense to me," Sawyer said, then started to count on his fingers. "Kindness, understanding—"

"No loud music after eleven goes on my list," Brooke added.

Sawyer snorted. "We sound like we're kids again. We're adults now. Surely we can do better."

"*Surely,*" Brooke said as she took a drink from the champagne bottle.

"There's always the Ritz if we can't take it," Kyle joked, although it sounded half-hearted to Thea.

"Yeah," Brooke responded, "but while it has incredible

room service, we wouldn't all be together, and I really want to be. As much as Nanine does."

"It must have been a really tough year," Kyle said, his gaze directed at Brooke. "I'm sorry I didn't do more than call when I heard the news about your dad—or Adam for that matter. I should have flown out, but I guess I didn't know what more to say."

"I probably couldn't have talked about it." Brooke drank from the champagne bottle again. "I'm still not sure what to say."

Even to Thea, Brooke hadn't said much, focusing more on how she was keeping busy as opposed to how she was feeling about everything. Her usual.

"How about 'it sucks'?" Sawyer's dark eyes were somber. "That's a start."

Brooke looked away, her neck moving with emotion. "It sucks. Really hard."

"Yeah," Sawyer said, crossing and kissing her cheek tenderly. "We should eat, especially with the booze and emotion flowing. When is the pizza coming?"

"Soon, I expect." Brooke looked at her gold designer watch. "Thea, can you see if they left Nanine's dish set, flatware, and napkins in her apartment?"

Kyle leveled her a look. "Madison would have asked for them to include plastic flatware and napkins, knowing her."

"Do you want to eat in Nanine's apartment?" Thea asked softly.

They all turned and looked at her, the emotion on their faces visible.

"I can't do Nanine's tonight," Sawyer said quietly.

"Let's eat in the freak show," Brooke said with a tight smile. "We need to face the beast so we can tame it."

"Imagining how incredible it's going to be when we finish renovating will be good for morale," Sawyer added.

"Good idea," Kyle said, grabbing two bottles and heading

to the front. "Let's get this party started." He tipped the bottle to his lips again before disappearing from sight.

"He's hurting," Thea found herself saying.

Brooke picked up the champagne and started after Kyle. "We all are."

"Is it just me or is Brooke softer than she used to be?" Sawyer asked.

"And *you're* swearing now," Thea said with the glimmer of a smile.

"Yeah. College students do that to you. So does the pursuit of tenure and professorial greatness. Too bad I'll have to reform my ways for Nanine."

She crossed and kissed his cheek. "I'm glad you're here, Sawyer."

"I'm happy to see you too. What brought us back is the most mendacious bit of Shakespearean treachery, but we're together. We'll help Nanine dig her way out of this, and it's pretty clear we're all going to help each other too. Sounds like it's been tough for some of us lately."

She glanced sharply at him, but he was already tucking bottles against his lean frame. Did he know about her quitting her job? Brooke would find a way to get her to admit it in Drink and Divulge. She was sure of it. Truthfully, she'd be glad for everyone to know.

She grabbed the remaining bottle and entered the front of the house, only to find Dean and Madison laying eight pizza boxes on the dusty floor. Brooke was sitting on a pillow from God knows where, but that was Brooke. Industrious. Sawyer patted the floor beside him, and she sank down onto the hardwood. Her fingerprints made impressions on the floor, and maybe it was Sawyer's influence, but she thought it showed how much they were already making their mark on what had happened.

"I think we should start a trend with the no-glasses approach," Madison said, holding out her hand. "Sawyer, I need some Bordeaux to wash my mouth out from this whole horrible business."

"Let's talk turkey for a minute," Kyle said, taking another pull from the calvados. "Nanine's going to need investors who will be silent, supportive partners. I want your thoughts, but from my experience, it's going to cost around three hundred thousand to make this restaurant into what she wants. Of course some things we can't replace, but we can't think about that. We have to start fresh, or it will kill us—and her."

"I agree," Madison said, gesturing to the space. "Onward and upward, but we need to consider that Paris prices could run higher, especially with all the permits required."

"Yeah," Sawyer said, "I read about a remodel of an Art Deco bathroom in the Second costing like three hundred thousand alone."

"Jesus," Dean said before shuddering. "Thank God she got back before that asshole could touch the kitchen."

"Yes, thank God," Thea said quietly as Madison passed around the takeout table settings. Once she was done, Brooke got the pizzas circulating.

Kyle plucked a slice from the box and balanced it on his knee as he looked around. "Sawyer, I know we need to create a vision—your job—but I also want us to start lining up contractors who can do quality work on time. The longer she's closed, the more money she loses. She'll want to keep paying the staff, of course."

"She probably has to according to French law," Brooke said, closing her pizza sandwich style like an Italian. "The lawyer will know more on this subject."

"We'll talk to him." Kyle bit into the pizza. "Nice choice, Madison. Okay, here's how I'm thinking. I don't want to bring in outsiders to fund the restoration. Most of them would want to put their own stamp on it."

"Been there, done that," Madison said with an edge as she reached for more Bordeaux. "It bites, and I wasn't the owner."

"Yeah." Kyle lifted his shoulder. "I'm going to personally invest. If anyone wants to join in—doesn't matter how much —tell me. We keep this in the family."

Thea rubbed her eyes as her emotions welled. "Nanine would like that, except I'm not in a place to help right now. Crap, I'm crying again."

Madison shot her a really kind smile, which only made her want to cry more. "That's your MO, Thea, so cry away. Hey, how did you pay for your last-minute flight over? My ticket was insane. And no offense, but it's a sin to the gourmet gods how badly bakers get paid."

Everyone turned to stare at her, and Brooke cursed. "I should have thought about your ticket, Thea."

"People who grow up with money don't," Dean put in before clearing his throat. "No offense. Thea, you should have said something. I would have sent you the funds."

A few other people muttered their agreement, making her vision blur. "I have a roommates trip fund I save for." Although it had only covered half of it.

"It probably wiped out what little savings you had," Brooke continued, making her cheeks flush. "I'm covering it."

"Not if I beat you to it," Dean said, sending Thea a wink.

Her cheeks were burning now. "That's very nice of all of you, but can we talk about this later and get back to Nanine? Madison, you were saying…"

Madison gave her warm look before turning back to Kyle. "Okay, I'm in. I know it's not much, but I can probably do ten thousand without having my savings go haywire. Every girl needs a rainy day fund. And Thea, I'm investing one of my thousands in your name. You should be a part of this."

She pressed a hand to her mouth to stifle more crying. From the concerned looks she was getting, she knew everyone was already aware of her situation. Brooke must have told them, which was actually a relief, since it saved her from doing so. "Oh, gosh, you don't have to but thank you."

"Hell, Madison," Sawyer said, blowing out a long breath, "you're going to make me cry acting like that. Are we really talking money like *this*? Helping each other instead of talking about who has what and from where. This is pretty adult of us. I remember when money was a *thang*."

No names were mentioned, but Dean shrugged. "Maybe some of us were assholes back then."

"Back then?" Brooke scoffed.

"Fine," Dean agreed. "I deserve that. Can we move on like Thea said? I can put in whatever's needed money-wise. And let me just say this one thing: damn but it feels good to be able to say that. I like this idea, Kyle."

Brooke took a deep draw from the champagne bottle. "Okay, since we're being adult… I can do whatever is needed too. Kyle?"

They shared a long look. "We'll split the remainder between us three. Good?"

"Perfect," Brooke said as Dean nodded crisply.

"Everyone pick up a bottle." Madison raised hers. "It's time to toast to all this adultness and partnership."

Thea ended up with the Chablis. Lifting it, she smiled at all her old roommates. She wished Nanine could see them now.

"To being business partners," Kyle said, and everyone leaned forward to click their bottles together.

Thea drank and wiped her mouth with a paper napkin. She really needed a slice of pizza, but her mind was on the invisible cat being out of the bag. "By the way… Yes, I quit my job to come here because my boss wouldn't give me time off."

Dean's bottle clattered when he set it down dramatically. "*You quit*? I didn't know that."

"Stop," Brooke said with an eye roll. "She's onto us. Or me. I *had* to tell them, sweetie."

Sawyer grabbed her shoulders, his eyes intense behind his gold-rimmed glasses. "You're an angel, Thea, but Nanine wouldn't have wanted you to lose your job."

His steady gaze helped her share the total truth. "I know, but I wanted to… Leaving was easier than I'd expected. What happened with Nanine forced me to make a change, something I'd been starting to think about. Turning thirty in October is really making me see things in a new light."

"Yeah, it has a way of doing that, doesn't it?" Kyle answered.

"I'm not…happy," Thea confessed. "I feel like life is passing me by."

"I hit that wall before I turned thirty in June." Dean's face seemed to fall like an undercooked soufflé, and then he was scooting toward her and pulling her against his side. "I'm here for Nanine, but I need something new. I know I'll find it here. Because—"

"You were the happiest here," she finished for him. "Me too. Only there was so much I didn't do. I was too scared. Maybe I wasn't brave enough."

"You were plenty brave, Thea," Madison said, inclining her chin. "You came to Paris on your own when you'd barely traveled in the U.S.—and with beginner French no less. In some ways, you were braver than any of us."

"I agree," Brooke echoed as the others nodded.

"Thanks for saying that." She took Sawyer's hand and looked at her other roommates. "I've missed you guys."

"If we're doing Divulge or Drink," Kyle said, taking a long draw from his bottle, "I'm next. I just broke things off with Paisley."

"*What?*" Brooke and Sawyer cried out.

Now Thea understood why he'd been so upset.

"Good for you." Madison lifted her bottle in his direction. "You deserve better. She didn't treat you good."

"She did in the beginning," Kyle objected, dangling the bottle between his hands and staring at it contemplatively.

"You okay?" Dean asked.

"Yeah. Maybe. I don't know. I've never called off an engagement."

Brooke made an anguished sound. "As someone who is still processing a bad breakup, my only advice is to find an outlet or you'll explode."

"From everything Nanine didn't say when I asked about your breakup, I'm convinced Adam is an incurable asshole," Madison said, leaning forward.

"You asked about my breakup?" Brooke sounded shocked.

"Of course I did." She grimaced as she tucked her long legs more firmly under her. "Look, I told you when we were leaving here all those years ago that I don't do the *keep in touch* thing well. Yeah, we meet up, and I try texting and doing the social media thing once in a blue moon, but with my hours—"

"I think you did pretty good," Sawyer interrupted. "I probably didn't do as much as I could have either. How about we all just let that go and be here now?"

"I'm good with that," Madison said as others nodded. "I should probably admit that I'm rethinking things myself."

Brooke's eyes narrowed. "Such as… Drink and Divulge is on you now, Fifth Course."

Heat flashed in Madison's golden eyes. "Terrific. Here it is in a nutshell. My GM has it out for me even though Chef loves me. I'm sick of little limp-dick guys messing with my life. My father included. He's having a baby with a woman younger than me, by the way, which means he'll be asking me for money like always."

"Jesus, Madison," Kyle said with a whistle. "You're still giving him money? That must have—"

"Made me want to disappear off the face of the earth?" She shook her head, making the long bangs over her forehead bounce. "Kidding. But yeah, I want to knock him senseless for being so stupid, but you can't teach an old dog new tricks. I should have cut him off a long time ago, and it pisses me off that he asks for just enough to make me feel bad if I don't give it to him."

Thea couldn't believe anyone could manipulate Madison like that. "I guess you understand Nanine pretty well then," she told her.

Madison nodded. "It's my half sister I feel bad for now. My dad is no better a man than he was when I was growing up. And no better than the worthless losers who have paraded through my life. Then I wonder: what's wrong with me? Why do I go for guys who are no better than him?"

"I take exception to that," Sawyer said, but his gaze was compassionate. "So your dating life pretty much stinks too, huh?"

Thea reached for her bottle and drank deeply as silence filled the room. She wondered if Madison was going to respond.

She took her time before she said, "I'm tired of the whole scene in Miami. Half-ass dating. Disappearing acts. Stupid excuses. Lies. And cheating."

"You deserve better than that, Madison," Sawyer said in a quiet tone. "We all do, but hell, maybe it's my turn. After I turned the Big Bitch this February, there's more pressure from my parents—hell, even from fellow faculty members—to check off the big life moments. Like settling down and shit."

"Like you're on the clock," Kyle said, his jaw locking.

"Exactly!" Sawyer pushed his glasses up the bridge of his nose. "Even some of my so-called friends have started dropping hints about me being old enough to get married and start a family. Like they have. Like it's something I owe to the world. I've barely started my career, and I certainly haven't found the love of my life yet. That's a pretty big decision if you ask me."

"Amen!" Thea blurted out like the total geek she was. "I mean, I think it's a pretty important thing. Not that I date much or anything."

"I don't understand what the hurry is," Sawyer continued. "It's not like you can go out and buy a soulmate like they're a freaking flat-screen TV."

Brooke started laughing, and soon Thea and the others joined in.

"God, but I love you, Sawyer," Brooke said at last.

"You *can* 'buy' yourself a soulmate," Madison said with snark in her voice. "Trust me. I live in Miami."

"We know what you both mean," Thea said, taking another sip from her bottle. "So what is everyone planning? You know what I'm doing. I'm here for the duration, and once we help Nanine, I'll need to find a job."

"I'll go," Sawyer said, raising his hand. "I decided to take a sabbatical in Paris for the semester. The university knows about Nanine, of course, and they arranged for my teaching assistant to take over my classes with supervision. I'm required to write a journal-worthy article in my time here—piece of cake—but now I'm wondering if I should take off the whole year. I mean, the situation with Nanine suggests a long timeframe, right?"

A whole year? Thea's mind spun. Was that how long it would take for the restaurant to bounce back?

"I've only done a total renovation in Miami once," Madison said, "and it was a shit show. I'm guessing I'm going to have to leave Miami in the dust to help here. That's something I'm willing to do. In fact, this is the kind of *line in the sand* moment I needed. I can get a job here too—after we create Nanine's new menu. Paris will look great on my résumé. Also, listen up, because I feel like it needs to be said. I'm not counting on having a job at Nanine's after it reopens."

"Me either!" Thea blurted out.

"She has her current staff and the way she likes to do things," Madison said after catching her eye. "Those decisions should stay with her and her alone."

"Agreed," Kyle interjected. "But…would you be open to an offer given your qualifications? You too, Thea."

They shared a look before nodding. Smiles touched their roommates' faces before Madison leaned forward and swept her hand around. "Kyle, what's your gut tell you on how long it will take to redecorate this place? Forget the likelihood that this guy pulled off more shit that's lurking in the shadows."

Thea's stomach gripped at that thought.

"Did anyone notice how they removed the copper wire?" Kyle's brow knit. "That's why they opened the walls. With the electrical too, I'd say three to four months. Optimistically. Very optimistically."

"I agree," Brooke added, "although I'm not sure Nanine realizes it yet."

"She knows what it's going to take," Sawyer said softly. "That's why she asked us to come."

Silence reigned for a moment until Brooke cleared her throat. "Right. Contractors have schedules and so do suppliers. And we're dealing with the French. Even with inducements, they do things on their own time."

That put the restaurant opening around the holidays. Thea worried about waiting so long to find a paying job. Oh, heavens, she would think about that later. "Is there no way for things to go faster?"

"We can try," Kyle said, sending an encouraging wink her way, "but the world over, contractors and suppliers have you by the balls. Especially when you want things done right. Upstairs, I arranged for a four-month absence with one of my business partners after I broke things off with Paisley."

"But you might not want to go back to the city where your ex-fiancée lives, especially since she already has a phone stalking problem," Madison said with a knowing look.

"She's a phone stalker?" Brooke asked, frowning.

Thea felt sick to her stomach suddenly. Who treated someone they loved like that?

"Not anymore," Kyle added mysteriously.

"I can work from here too," Dean broke in, scratching the stubble on his jaw. "I've been downsizing my client list because I'm tired of dealing with entitled tech babies."

"Well, I'm tired of New York and my old life," Brooke said, taking another sip. "So I'm staying as well. Lucky for me that Paris is the fashion capital of the world, and Milan is only a short distance away. My editor will be in heaven. Besides, this scare with Nanine has made me want to be closer to her. And my dad just told me he plans on retiring here."

"How's he doing?" Dean asked quietly.

"He's in the best shape he's been in since he was forty, probably, which makes it easier."

"I'm glad he's doing so great," Sawyer said.

"Me too," she replied with overbright eyes.

"It seems this time is going to be good for all of us," Thea said, looking around the circle. "Beyond the obvious job hunt —after Nanine is taken care of, of course—I need some help with my old recipe book for a delicious life. I hate thinking I might actually look like Dorothy from *The Wizard of Oz.*"

She watched as a few people fought smiles, but it was Dean who predictably said, "Where's your little dog?"

"Enough," Brooke said with a finger pointed in his direction. "I'm already on your head-to-toe Paris makeover. We're starting right away. Nanine wouldn't want you to put it off."

"You're already beautiful," Sawyer said, squeezing her hand. "You just don't see it yet."

"Bravo, Thea." Madison lifted her bottle. "You're finally going to stop hiding. About time."

"Jesus, do you always have to be *that* direct?" Dean winced. "Don't let her hurt your feelings."

Funny how she remembered having this exact exchange years ago, on another occasion when Madison had tried to get real with her.

No one got real with her in Nowheresville. She'd missed it, to be honest.

"She didn't offend me." Thea extended her bottle to Madison and clinked it before taking a sip. "She's right. I'm putting First Course behind me."

"There's nothing wrong with being First Course." Sawyer patted her hand. "It holds an important place in the meal. Done well, it captures one's attention and sets the entire theme for the evening. That's what you do, Thea, with your smile and your kindness. I mean, you're like the most delicious fougasse bread to start. Not the stale peanuts some places serve."

She leaned over and half hugged him. "You're the best, Dr. Jackson."

"He really is," Dean said with a grin. "If I were a girl, I'd totally go for him."

They all started laughing. Then they took a hearty drink and sat in silence for a moment. Thea found herself doing what Sawyer had said she was good at: smiling at everyone—and they were all smiling back.

A wave of belonging came over her, and she wanted to tuck it somewhere safe inside herself for when she needed it.

The Paris roommates were back.

CHAPTER
NINE

Dean woke up with a smile as Miles Davis' "Seven Steps to Heaven" softly filtered through the walls of his bedroom.

Sawyer had always been an early riser, and he loved the blues. Dean never listened to them on his own, but they seemed to fit the mood in Paris. Rain was falling softly outside. Man, he'd always loved this city in the rain. The air turned fresh and the water seemed to wash away a layer of secrets, revealing something new and bright.

God, he was starting to sound like Sawyer already and they'd only just arrived.

He rolled out of his queen bed, an adjustment he'd have to get used to again. Much like his limited closet space and the shared bathroom. But his head was remarkably clear after their late night, which was a win. Then again, he never got drunk in Paris. Perhaps it was that indescribable magic in the air or maybe it was the good company and laughter. He hadn't laughed that much in ages, and they'd all commented on how special it was, given Nanine was in the hospital. As Thea had commented, though, she would have wanted to hear the sound of their friendship blending with the occasional tinkle of her famous chandelier.

Tugging on some dinosaur boxers, he padded across the high-ceilinged room and opened the door. It squeaked, calling forth a slew of memories. When he entered the parlor, Sawyer looked over.

"Nice shorts. I especially like the T-Rex over your junk."

"My last girlfriend thought it was pretty funny."

Sawyer sat up on the couch, definitely not dressed for class this morning. He had on a black T-shirt and shorts and was drawing in pencil on a large art pad. "Seeing anyone now?"

"No. The women I keep meeting all seem the same. Blond, not always natural. Into yoga and Rumi but wouldn't know who Voltaire or Sartre was if their life depended on it. Something you couldn't take since you love those guys so much."

"Sad souls for sure," Sawyer commented with a laugh.

"Place hasn't changed much, huh?" Dean refrained from adding he was grateful to see it hadn't been combed over by Adrienne and her husband. They still needed to go through the place with a fine-tooth comb, but at least the upper levels hadn't been cleaned out like downstairs.

"Feels good to be back. Lots of good memories here."

Yeah, there were. Dean wandered around the room, smiling at the frescoed ceiling that was a relic from this place's past as a hotel. After the hotel closed, the first level had been turned into a restaurant while the other three floors were each converted into three-bedroom apartments with galley kitchens. When the apartments had come up for sale, Nanine's husband had snapped them up, wanting to own the entire building. She still talked about what a gift that had been.

She sometimes rented the apartments if she met someone she liked, but mostly she kept them to herself, letting the Courses and other friends stay when they came to Paris. Dean knew Brooke had spent the most time there. But he'd also made frequent visits along with some of the others.

The Boys' Floor, as Nanine liked to call it, still had a blue velvet couch and long white curtains tied to the sides of the floor-to-ceiling double windows. Sawyer had the windows open, making the scene absolutely sleepy. Rain and all, Dean couldn't have been welcomed with a more perfect Paris morning, and he crossed to drink it in deeply.

"Word to the wise. I already tripped the breaker in the bathroom trying to shave while recharging my phone. I forgot how bad the electrical situation is. You must have hit the hay hard. I heard you sawing logs through the wall."

Dean looked over his shoulder at his friend as the patter of rain bouncing off the wrought-iron balcony touched his skin. "I consider that a win. I already miss my California King."

"We're lucky it's not a double bed like the girls have."

Nanine had bought queen beds ten years ago, knowing the guys would need more leg room. He couldn't imagine a full bed at any age or for any kind of sex, honestly, but it was Nanine's home. Not that she allowed sex in her home—another house rule. He'd have to think about that when he found someone he wanted to roll around in the sheets with. Then again, he'd gotten to a point in his life where he could afford a really nice hotel room. He grinned.

"Why are you grinning?" Sawyer asked, studying him.

"I'm thinking about hotel sex in Paris."

"Nice. And here I was, thinking about buying art supplies."

"Art over sex? You really are a sick puppy, Dr. Jackson. Kyle still asleep?"

"Yeah, I think he had trouble catching Zs after we left the girls." Sawyer set his pad on the rosewood coffee table next to Nanine's worn copy of Christine de Pizan's *The Book of the City of Ladies*, or *Le Livre de la Cité des Dames*.

"She still has these books, huh?" Dean asked, picking up

Voltaire's *Candide*. He'd never read any of them, although they were some of Nanine's favorites. He was too impatient to read a novel. Too many words. Too much time. God, he was so Second Course.

Sawyer picked up *Fables* by Jean de la Fontaine. "Like most people, if you want to know about Nanine, all you have to do is look at her books. We have one of the first women-centric novels in France, a book of fables I consider better than the Brothers Grimm, and a banned book about an optimist's descent into disillusionment with the system. God, I miss Nanine. This morning I was kicking myself for letting two years go by since I last visited her in Paris. Where does the time go?"

"Some black hole, I think," Dean said ruefully, sitting down in the ottoman to the right of the couch. "So… Kyle's breakup came out of nowhere."

"Yeah. I didn't like what I knew about Paisley—not that any of us met her—but it's still got to hurt."

"Breakups suck. That's why I don't do them anymore." Dean plucked the art pad off the coffee table and studied the sketches. Sawyer was already working on designs for the restaurant, not that he was surprised. "This is really good, Sawyer. I like the idea of the individual panels to give the walls more structure and interest. Damn, but the curtains look like a woman's skirt when the wind moves them."

Sawyer chuckled ruefully. "Nanine will love that. Everything starts with the design, so I'm going to put my head down and come up with more ideas. I thought the panels might be close to what Nanine had in mind. Some simple plaster or molding definition. Maybe a few antique mirrors to add a sense of space."

Dean set the pad aside and kicked back in the chair. "Art Nouveau light fixtures will make a huge difference. Maybe even globe pedestal lights. Too bad we don't have an outside ceiling where we could do stained glass."

God, they probably needed to have a longer talk about the budget.

"That feels too dated to me." Sawyer took off his glasses and polished them with the edge of his T-shirt. "We could do some murals. I thought I'd go to the Musée d'Orsay and get inspired. Then I'm going to have to get some pastels at Sennelier. I want to work in color."

"But clearly you're still drawing since you have a pad and pencil with you?" he asked with a knowing look. "Your parents haven't beaten it out of you, even after your infamous negotiation to come to Paris for a year to study art."

"They gave me a year to make it as an artist, and I didn't. So I got serious with life, just like they asked me to. They were right."

"Were they? You chose to teach art history, so you obviously still have the art bug." No way Dean was going to let him off the hook that easy. "A year was bullshit. You make it when you make it. Obviously you can't quit it."

Sawyer half laughed. "Every hack brings their art supplies to Paris and draws."

"I think I remember Jack in *Titanic* doing that." Only his friend was no hack, and this was an old argument. "And don't think I'm done with this topic."

"I am," Sawyer said with a jerk of his chin.

Fine. Later. "Well, I need to get my thinking cap on about the tech side. I'll check into the best reservation systems and price them. Something simple." And later, he would check Nanine's computer to look for further problems, a necessary task which nonetheless made his gut nervous. That fake signature must have come from somewhere, right? What else had it been affixed to?

"Yeah, better keep it simple or Nanine will simply unplug it."

His heart got tugged by an image of her doing just that. Man, he wanted her back on her feet, shrugging at them and using her hands when she talked and kissing them on both cheeks, her perfume lingering in the air. "I don't want to contemplate suggesting she have a website, but…"

Sawyer positioned his glasses firmly on his face with an ease as smooth as the blues he had playing. "She's old school, but I think she might be open to the idea now. The only problem is finding someone to manage it long term."

Once they left…

He didn't want to think about that right now.

"Yeah, someone is going to have to update it," he acknowledged. "*About Nanine's* will be constant, but not the menu. I can put the reservation system online too, but a website's only useful if it's being used."

They turned their heads when they heard a door squeak. Kyle emerged in navy boxers, scratching his stubble. "God, I forgot where I was for a moment. Then I rolled over, and I woke up with my shoulder hurting like it used to back in the day. Clearly my mattress is still made of stones. Coffee?"

Dean suppressed a chuckle. Kyle had never been a morning person, jet lag or not, but given his breakup, Dean wouldn't tease him. "We haven't ventured downstairs yet."

"I'm going," Kyle said, heading to the front door. "Thea will be in the kitchen. She makes the best coffee."

"We're not dressed," Sawyer protested. "And Dean has a T-Rex on his junk."

"Bring the smelling salts." Kyle gave a chortle before disappearing.

They followed him down the death-defying spiral stairs in their bare feet. Paris stairs sucked when you wore a size twelve. They smelled coffee as they reached the bottom floor. Someone was humming. Thea. Then she let out a scream.

"Kyle! Holy cow. You scared me."

When Dean reached the kitchen, Thea was clutching her heart, standing in front of a counter covered in flour, wearing a cute little pink apron with a croissant wearing a beret. "Don't scare the woman making treats," he told Kyle.

"Noted." Kyle walked over and lifted the white towel covering two bread loaves rising. "What do we have here?"

She moved so swiftly her ponytail swung as she lifted his hand away, replacing the towel with the care of a young mother covering her baby. "Apricot and walnut and a plain honey wheat."

"God bless you." Kyle went in for a hug, but Thea carefully edged away.

"Sawyer said we should have gotten dressed." Dean laughed. "Like my dinosaur? *Are* you going to faint?"

"Don't tease her," Sawyer cautioned.

Thea's blush popped up on her peaches-and-cream cheeks, making her look like the proverbial girl next door. "Don't be silly. I'm just not used to bare chests in my kitchen."

"I love it," Brooke said, breezing in dressed like a flame in red yoga pants and a tank top. "Looking good, boys. Dean, I especially love your dinosaurs. Sawyer, will you take your shirt off so I can compliment your chest too?"

Her grin was all flirty, and Sawyer primly grabbed his shirt and held it in place. "Only my woman gets to see the goods."

"Do you have a woman?" Brooke darted over and made a playful grab for his shirt.

Sawyer stepped back and used Thea as a human shield, which made her giggle. "I'd been seeing someone for a few months."

"I can hear the 'but' coming a mile away." Dean walked over to the coffee machine to start the ball rolling there, hoping Thea would join him. She *did* make the best coffee. He thanked the coffee gods that Jeremy and the workers he'd brought in hadn't gotten to this machine or the cups.

Sure enough, Thea took over the task. But something felt like it was missing, and he realized why. Nanine was supposed to be puttering around this kitchen. How was she this morning? She would be having a hospital breakfast. Could she even drink coffee, her favorite, after a heart attack? Brooke would know, but it would be a downer if he asked. They would find all this out when Nanine came home. The doctor hadn't shared a schedule for her release yet, although he'd chastised them for keeping Nanine too long when they'd finally unlocked her door last night.

"Talk, Sawyer," Brooke ordered and hopped onto one of the stainless steel counters. "Who is she?"

"She's a graduate student—not one of mine—and getting her PhD in English literature. We met at a poetry reading."

Dean almost rolled his eyes. He couldn't imagine attending a poetry reading, least of all meeting a girl at one. "Is her prose stronger than her passion?"

"Crude, Dean," Brooke said with narrowed eyes. "Don't listen to him."

"Well…" Sawyer rubbed his jaw. "He's mostly right. She's nice. We have a lot in common. Just not…"

"So hot you think you might die only to discover you're reborn," Thea said softly.

Everyone turned to look at her.

She blushed again. "It was in a movie."

"Oh, Thea," Brooke said after crossing her arms. "If you *ever* feel like that with anyone, grab him. I don't think I ever have. And I thought I'd marry Adam. But let's change the subject. Sawyer. Keep going."

"There's not much to tell. She's great, which I told her when I also shared that I was going to Paris for Nanine and taking a sabbatical, which she was totally cool with. She clearly wasn't my soulmate."

The room seemed to sag with heaviness. Kyle was looking down at his feet, and Dean thought he heard him mutter, "Fuck soulmates."

"Easier to buy a flat-screen TV instead," Dean quipped,

picking up two coffee cups and acting like he was prepared to juggle them.

"Stop that," Thea cried, grabbing them from his hands. "We don't have much glassware as it is. I'm making the coffee."

"Good." He kissed her cheek, which had her blushing again. "You have magic coffee hands."

"Quit sticking your Tarzan chest in her face." Brooke grabbed his arm and pulled him away from her. "She's going to burn the milk."

"It's fine." Thea turned her back and forged on with her work. She was like a coffee trailblazer, he decided as the chandelier gave a delicate murmur. The kind of person who climbed a cloud-forest mountain to procure the best coffee in the world. She'd find the secret blend that would ignite coffee drinkers around the world and change everything. The coffee market. People who—

"Earth to Dean," Brooke called, snapping her fingers. "Move, Mr. Dinosaur. Thea needs space."

His fantasy fell flat, but the idea wasn't his "It" idea anyway. Except his creativity was flowing, and that was something. His inspiration had been DOA in San Francisco recently.

"I'm going." He danced out of the way and settled back against a counter. The coffee machine seemed to purr under Thea's hands. He decided to reduce her embarrassment in a way that wouldn't require him to climb back upstairs and grabbed a staff apron from where Nanine kept them, putting it over his neck and tying it at the waist. "Better?" he asked, modeling it, making his roommates laugh.

"I know I'm happy not to be looking at your goods anymore." Kyle laughed before gesturing to the ceiling. "Madison in bed?

Brooke nodded. "You know her. She's always been a late riser."

"She works late nights," Thea said, defending her. "All bakers are morning people. Here, Dean."

He took the cup she was offering him. "In Paris, caffeine is another food group." Closing his eyes for a moment, he took a sip and savored the rush of flavor in his mouth. "Damn, Thea."

"Thanks." She smiled brightly. "Who's next?"

"Kyle started the quest for caffeine," Sawyer said with a pointed glance at Dean. "Any word on Nanine?"

"I called the hospital first thing this morning to inquire about her release." Brooke twisted at the waist, like she was stretching her back. "The doctor explained that all of the beeps from her heart machine during our visit gave him serious concern. He's running more tests and keeping her at least two more days. His voice was very disapproving."

Dean set his café down, his diaphragm tightening. "Is it normal for them to keep someone so long?"

Brooke gave a half-hearted shrug. "The range for a hospital stay depends on the doctor's determination of the patient's healing. Nanine is still stressed to the gills."

"Is he worried she might have another heart attack?" Thea asked, passing a café to Kyle, who kissed her cheek but kept his eyes on Brooke.

"I don't know," she said, tapping her fingernails together like old times, the left thumbnail over the right one.

"That's a little scary," Sawyer said, calling out the white elephant in the room. "Hell, are we even asking the right question? Is the restaurant going to be too much for her? Should she retire?"

"Don't you dare say that!" Brooke's raised voice stopped everyone short. "Don't even think it. She's going to be fine. And she'll retire when she wants—which she's always said would be when she didn't have a heart for food anymore. Which would mean she's dead."

The passionate outburst rocked the kitchen and had

Brooke putting her face in her hands before saying hoarsely, "Thea, I have a few appointments for you to consider. When you finish making the coffee, come find me upstairs."

She left the room in a blur of red.

"I'm going to…follow her," Thea said, her face tight with tension as she left the room.

Sawyer scratched his skull under his mass of black curls. "I had to ask the question."

Kyle slapped him gently on the back. "Asking questions is who you are. Making the restaurant great is what Nanine wants. So it's what we'll do. We take it one day at a time."

Dean couldn't agree more. He and Kyle were in pretty solid accord so far, so he decided to take a chance. "If *you* need anything, you tell us. I'm probably going to go for a run later. You're welcome to join."

Kyle peered at him over his coffee cup as he drank. "Thanks. I got depressed as hell when I got winded climbing those stairs. I didn't realize I was that out of shape."

Dean started laughing. "It's Paris stairs—and I sucked wind too. You're fine."

"Shall we hug now?" Sawyer smirked. "I think we're having a moment. Only you should know… *I* wasn't out of breath."

Kyle set his coffee down and looked at him. Dean understood his intent as surely as if they'd last lived together yesterday, not a decade ago.

Sawyer started backing out of the kitchen. "Don't you do it!"

"You make a snarky comment like that, and we've gotta pants you, Dr. Jackson. Those are the rules," Kyle said, lunging toward him.

Dean didn't go all out, and neither did Kyle, but Sawyer certainly ran from the kitchen with a howl. They heard him pounding up the steps.

Kyle lifted his coffee and saluted Dean. "He should be out of breath now."

They both started laughing.

"It's good to see you, man," Dean finally said.

Kyle inclined his chin. "You too."

Then they leaned back against the counter and drank their coffee in their bare feet like old times.

CHAPTER
TEN

Propped against the headboard of her bed, Thea stared at the recipe card she'd just started.

Recipe for: *Living Life to the Fullest*

Date: NOW

Prep time: ??? Could take up to ten years

Ingredients: Wine with friends, Baking, Mr. Pinstripes???

Hard-to-find ingredients: Self-confidence

Notes: THIS IS HARD!

She sighed and tossed her pen aside. It was like looking at a delicious recipe so complicated to make you never tried. You just dreamed about making it. Or worse, you watched someone else on TV prepare it and told yourself it was enough.

Brooke still hadn't come out of her room, and there was no peep from the boys, so she headed back down the stairs.

The kitchen was quiet as she walked to open the back door. The Paris sun warmed her face, and she closed her eyes for a moment before crossing to check her bread rising on the counter. Her loaves had doubled in size and were ready for baking. Fantastic. She could use some bread comfort herself, and clearly so could the others.

Turning the oven on after mentally calculating the temperature in Celsius, she decided it was time to marry Doughreen and Nanine's sourdough starters. Her palms grew damp as she headed to the walk-in cooler and faced the starter Nanine had begun when she was a newly graduated chef at eighteen. Reverently pulling the plastic container off the shelf, she walked like an acolyte back to the stainless steel shelf and told herself not to trip over her big feet. Or freak about Nanine's starter representing *four decades* of magic.

Returning to the cooler, she laughed at herself. "Sorry, Doughreen. It's not that I don't love you. It's just an honor to be handling Nanine's starter. She—no, he—had to go first. You think it's a he too, right? Not that Nanine would ever name her starter. We're special."

Special in the head, she thought, as she placed Doughreen next to Nanine's starter. Should she call him something secretly? She gently pried off his lid and lowered her face to inhale his scent. A *mélange* of yeast and apples with a *soupçon* of the mystery of life.

She loved the definition of *mélange*—mixture didn't sound nearly as profound—in baking chemistry: the physical combination of two or more substances in which the identities are retained. Her baking instructor at *Le Cordon Bleu*, a master baker who'd won numerous national French baking competitions, couldn't speak enough about the *mélange*.

"Don't you smell simply gorgeous? Better than any man's cologne if you ask me. Do you want a name? I mean, you're about to make a baby starter with my girl, Doughreen. Shouldn't we be on a first-name basis?"

She stared at the starter with its delicate bubbles, trying to decide what he looked like. He was strong like Nanine. With a big heart. An image of Nanine lying in the hospital bed flashed in her mind. She breathed deeply, sadness and love a powerful *mélange* inside her, before she refocused on her task.

"Silence, eh? Oh, I get it. You're one of those mysterious men. Well, you are French, after all. The men here are so much more mysterious than the ones where I'm from. No mystery whatsoever. Well, I need to call you something bread-like and French then. How about Leonardough? Léonard means lion, I think. Let's feed you a little, shall we?"

She would need to feed him anyway after she took some of his mass away to combine with her girl. Doughreen too. Oh, this was going to be a bright spot in her day! Finding a new plastic container in the pantry was her first job, and then she dug a few large spoons from the utensil tray and decided a quarter cup of each starter would be a good place to start to make their baby. As she tenderly inserted her spoon into Nanine's delicate starter, she felt her heart expand inside her chest. He was perfect.

"Don't you feel wonderful?" she exclaimed, extracting a quarter cup from him into the new baby container. "I bet you rise for Nanine like something special. And, just between us, I'll bet you rise for me too."

After adding Doughreen to the mixture for the baby, she measured out some flour and gently stirred the creation together. The chandelier's crystals tinkled with her ministrations, sounding like Christmas music and the fall of snowflakes.

"Aren't you two going to make sweet, sweet love together? Doughreen, be nice to Leonardough, and you— mysterious man—you be sweet to her. She's a little shy, but once she gets to know you, she'll give you everything she is and more."

"Do you always talk to your bread starters like they are lovers?"

She jumped in place and spun around, the spoon clattering to the ground, and with it, a poof of flour rising into the air. She gasped at the man standing just inside the back door to the kitchen.

Mr. Pinstripes!

The floor under her feet seemed to tremble as her heart rate surged in her chest. "What are you—"

"I am deeply sorry for frightening you, but you were a marvel to watch in action," he said in that same fluid, sexy voice.

The chandelier chimed delicately, seeming to purr in response to his presence. The air around her felt charged as he walked toward her with complete ease. He was clad in another blue pinstriped suit with a white shirt and scarlet silk tie. A lock of ink-black hair had fallen onto his forehead, but it was the smile on his face that had Thea's heart making repeated attempts to leap out of her chest.

"Let me introduce myself," he said in English again with a hand to his heart. "I am Jean Luc Mercier. Nanine's lawyer."

The earth opened under her. She remembered Nanine telling them his name. "You've got to be kidding."

He lifted his shoulder in that classic French way, his smile widening with amusement. "I sometimes have existential questions about who I really am—as do we all—but yes, I am Jean Luc. And you are Thea. Who is not from Kansas, although your friends joke that you are. We meet at last. *Enchanté.*"

She put her hand to her forehead as the shock lingered. "I'm sorry. I must be jet-lagged. Umm... How do you know about me?"

When he settled himself against the opposite stainless steel counter, Thea's mouth went dry. His masculinity was like a giant rainstorm to her senses, washing her in a desire she'd never thought possible. He had long legs and a strong broad chest, and holy moly, did he smell good. Maybe even better than freshly baked bread!

"Nanine is not just my client but a friend, and she's told

me a lot about her dear Courses, as she calls you. She speaks of you, Thea, with unique affection, saying you are the kindest woman she has ever met. High praise, I think. There is a photo of you in her salon. You were making bread as you are now."

She knew the photo. Her old boss had hired a photographer to take photos for their website. "Nanine...asked me to send it for Christmas one year."

"Three years ago, if I recall." His smile seemed to brighten as he held her gaze. "Your beauty and passion have always intrigued me. I am delighted to see that you are even more radiant in person, Thea who is not from Kansas."

She felt an answering smile flicker on her lips.

"But I must ask again... Do you always speak to your bread starter as you would a lover?"

Her brain went blank. "I'm sorry. What?"

He chuckled, dark and luscious. "Never mind. We French speak of love as often as we can. Watching you work... Your passion is evident. I can see why you are such an acclaimed baker. I hope to have the opportunity to sample your *pâtisserie*. It would be an honor."

"I don't know that I would go that far. We all needed some comfort, and bread is that and more." She swallowed thickly. An honor? *Wowza.* It would be an honor to have something from her hands in his gorgeous mouth. She'd start a page in her journal just for that. *Recipe for: What I Want to Feed Jean Luc.*

She shook herself out of that daydream. "When we saw Nanine in the hospital yesterday, she mentioned that you know about everything."

His blue eyes darkened. "Yes. I am here to help, now that you are all settled in. I came by yesterday, but you...seemed in a hurry to cross the street."

So he *had* been calling out to her as she ran away. Her face flushed with heat. "I didn't know you were trying to talk to me," she managed in a rush.

"I could have handled it better," he said smoothly. "How is Nanine? I have only spoken to her on the phone. Her doctor is being very cautious, as is only right with her condition."

His tender gaze calmed her beating heart, and suddenly she wasn't nervous anymore. She felt…comforted by his presence and compassion. "She's… I don't know what to say. I mean, she's in the hospital after the worst kind of betrayal. She's determined to get the restaurant back in shape. She's always been the boldest and bravest woman I know."

And yet, Nanine was also scared. That much was evident, but no one had commented on it last night as they'd eaten pizza and talked. What good did it do to state something so shocking?

"She's an incredible woman, and I'm honored to have her as both a friend and a client. Have you heard when she will be coming home?"

"Brooke said the doctor wants her to stay for at least a couple of more days." She tried to smile and failed. "We have our orders to renovate the restaurant, though. All six of us. My friends will be eager to meet you, Jean Luc."

His name was uttered in a soft French accent that shocked her ears. His blue eyes brightened again. The chandelier's crystals tinkled as if stirred from a gentle breeze. And when he smiled, she had to struggle to remember what they'd been talking about.

Right. The others. "Kyle especially will want to talk to you."

"The one from Austin with the big Texas accent who creates successful restaurants."

She nodded, her mouth going dry as Jean Luc took a step closer, his gaze holding her in place.

"I'm eager to discuss business as well, but first, I have something I must ask you."

She pointed to herself. "Me? Sure. Fire away."

His smile turned practically rakish. "I love that John Wayne talk you Americans favor."

"He was born in a town right outside Des Moines where I...lived."

God, was she really talking about John Wayne's birthplace?

"I didn't know that and I find it equally interesting you are from a town which is French for *of the monks.*"

She'd lived in a town named after monks! How had she not put that together before? Gosh, is that why she'd practically lived like a monk herself? Plain. Sexless. Way too freaking nice.

"I apologize for distracting you with my observation." He tilted his head to the side, making his dark lashes even sexier. "I find I have many concerning you. Thea... I was wondering if you would be willing to join me for dinner."

She jerked back. "*What?*"

He gestured with a graceful hand. "I know Nanine will need you, of course, and you and your roommates have only just arrived. But I would very much like the opportunity to spend time with you and get to know you better. That is how you Americans say it, yes?"

Get to know her better? Her heart began another jailbreak from her chest. No, he couldn't be...

She studied him, trying to understand. But he only watched her with quiet grace laced with masculine intensity —the perfect *mélange*, her brain decided. Then her synapses began barraging her with one word, as if it were snowflakes hitting her in the face during a blizzard.

Date. Date. Date.

She couldn't breathe suddenly. "Sorry. What are you trying to say?"

He took another step toward her until he was standing directly in front of her. A rueful smile flickered over his perfect mouth. "Perhaps I said it badly. English is not the language of my heart. You know French, yes?"

She bobbed her head. "I'm very rusty."

"I will speak slowly then." His eyes found hers, conveying another meaning straight from his heart to hers, before he said, "*Passe un soir avec moi,*" in the most seductive voice she could imagine. "*Va dinez avec moi.*"

Her knees turned weak, and she had to rest her elbows on the counter to keep herself from sliding to the floor.

"You understand me now, no?" he asked in French.

She nodded as slowly as he'd spoken, still spellbound. "*Oui.*"

Her accent didn't sound like her at all. She sounded sexy and French and mysterious—like she'd written on her recipe card.

"You are blushing."

Her hands flew to her face. "Oh my goodness!"

"It is charming." Another step put him close enough for her to feel his body heat. "You also have flour on your nose— if you will let me."

She watched in slow motion as he lifted his golden-skinned hand and brushed the right side of her face in the lightest of caresses. Her breath shuddered out, making his eyes darken as they gazed into hers.

No one had *ever* touched her like that. No one had ever looked at her like that. She had to be dreaming.

Then he gave another rueful smile and said, "But there is one thing you should know before you either shatter my heart or fill me with the anticipation of your company."

His scent filled the air around her. "What is that?" she managed to say in that same raspy voice she didn't recognize.

"I am the one who called the police on you yesterday."

CHAPTER
ELEVEN

"*Y*ou called the police?" Thea asked, shocked.

"My neighbor saw a woman with brown hair at the back door. Given the past incident, she flew over to talk to me. The door was open when Madame Bessault dragged me to my window, and given Nanine's recent situation with her daughter, who also has brown hair, I felt it necessary to call the police. I am sorry if my actions distressed you. Again, allow me to make up for it."

He wanted to make up for it? Was that his reason for inviting her to dinner?

"Thea, who is this man and what does he want to make up for?" Madison asked, suddenly appearing in the kitchen wearing her usual black jeans and black T-shirt and narrowed, suspicious eyes.

Mr. Pinstripes gave her one last earnest look before smoothly crossing to Madison and holding out his hand. "You are Madison Garcia, the incredible chef in Miami whom Nanine speaks so highly of."

Madison crossed her arms, tucking her hands against her sides. "Keep going."

His mouth twitched. "I am Nanine's lawyer, Jean Luc

Mercier, and I'm afraid I was apologizing to Thea for calling the police yesterday. I was also attempting to ask her out for a romantic dinner."

"This can't be happening," Thea breathed out loud, her knees going weak at the confirmation.

Mr. Pinstripes smiled rakishly at her before returning his gaze to Madison. "What you Americans call a date."

"Right, since the French don't date." Madison nodded thoughtfully. "So you're a different kind of Frenchman, huh?"

He laughed. "Nanine said you were disarmingly forthright. I mentioned my wish to ask Thea on a date so there are no secrets in the kitchen. My mother likes to say secrets in the kitchen make the food turn sour."

"I like the sentiment," Madison said with a nod. "I can see why Nanine has you as her lawyer. How about you show yourself into the front of the house while I grab the others? You didn't just come here to ask our Thea on a date. Right?"

"*Oui.*" He turned back to look at Thea and smiled softly. "We can talk about your decision later if that pleases you."

With that, he strode out of the kitchen. Thea leaned against the counter and touched her now burning cheeks. "*If that pleases me?* Oh, my God!"

"You never say 'God.' Put your head between your legs before you faint. You weren't sure what to say, right? I figured I'd give you a little breathing room. Thea, your face could flambée a crème brûlée."

She bent over at the waist, her heartbeat loud in her ears.

A date! He wanted a date. With *her*.

"I know it's ridiculous. It's just… Mr. Pinstripes showed up, and I'd totally noticed him yesterday."

"Mr. Pinstripes, huh?"

She could hear the humor in Madison's voice. "That's what I called him before I knew his real name. Anyway, he came in here and said Nanine's talked about me and he wants to bring me to dinner. I thought I'd heard him wrong, but then he said I was beautiful. And radiant! Which is so not true. I mean, that's the craziest thing I've ever heard. I didn't have any time to recover before he told me about calling the police yesterday. Honestly, you could have knocked me over with a feather."

"That *was* quite a surprise," Madison agreed. "So you like him, huh?"

She was going to need ice for her cheeks at this rate. "What's not to like? He's gorgeous. But there's no way he's being serious. I mean, he's French and elegant. And look at me."

Madison raised her up slowly and looked her straight in the eye. "Thea, am I a bullshitter?"

"No," she sputtered. "You always say what's on your mind."

"So listen to me… When a man Nanine trusts tells you that you're beautiful and he wants to go out with you for a romantic dinner, he's for real."

"But—"

"No buts." She shook her gently. "Nanine would kill him otherwise. Also, you're underselling yourself. Like usual. You are beautiful in a very innocent way. Not like some ho in South Beach in a neon thong bikini." Her mouth tipped up. "You were supposed to laugh. Okay. Let me start again. Do you have any idea how cute you are in that pink apron with your hair up? You're like a guy's Suzy Homemaker fantasy come to life."

She looked down at herself. Her big feet in her white tennis shoes seemed to mock her. "I am not. I have—"

"I could go get Kyle to back me," she threatened. "Or Dean."

She let out a laugh. "Don't you dare. I know where Nanine keeps her cleaver."

"I always bring my own." Madison nudged her shoulder gently. "That's the spunk I've missed. You're nice until you get pushed around a little. Come on, let's go find the others and talk to Mr. Pinstripes. Unless you'd like to make him a café while I get them and tell him you want to go out on this *rendezvous.*"

Gosh, those words made her usually reliable knees weak. Again. "But Nanine—"

"Would want this." She nudged her again. "The question is: do you?"

Madison didn't wait for her answer, and moments later, Thea was once again alone in the kitchen. Pressing her hands to her cheeks again, she reminded herself this was exactly what she wanted. She pulled out her journal from the bottom shelf where she'd tucked it away earlier and opened it. Taking her pen, she amended what she had.

> **Recipe for:** *Living Life to the Fullest*
> **Date: NOW**
> **Prep time: ??? Could take up to ten years**
> **Ingredients: Wine with friends, Baking, ~~Mr.~~ ~~Pinstripes???~~ Mr. Pinstripes!!!**
> **Hard-to-find ingredients: Self-confidence, Courage**
> **Notes: THIS IS HARD! Sometimes a pep talk from friends is all you need to get started, and you won't find happily ever after if you say no to the prince.**

Truth was, she'd never met a potential prince before. A couple of other chefs in training had asked her out when she'd been at *Le Cordon Blue*, but she'd played it safe then, only agreeing to coffee, saying she wanted to focus on her studies and her work at the restaurant. And hanging out with her roommates.

The truth is she'd been scared of what came *after* coffee. She'd waited until she was twenty-four to sleep with a guy, and it hadn't been the experience she'd dreamed about. She'd tried it again at twenty-six, but she'd felt hollow afterward.

No rockets had flared. She'd been embarrassed by her body and what he'd tried to do to her.

She hadn't gone there again since, and that was her deepest secret of all. And for a woman who had no secrets, the fact that she had one was telling.

Sawyer was right. It wasn't easy to find your soulmate. She'd wanted to find hers and *then* have sex. Only…

He hadn't shown up, and she'd been getting older. Finally she'd told herself she needed to have the experience. She'd figured maybe she was reaching too high. But dammit, she wanted to find a guy who liked her and made her weak in the knees…

Mr. Pinstripes did, and he was standing in the restaurant waiting for her answer.

She started walking, bypassing the coffee machine, and flung open the doors. He looked up from reading something on his phone and smiled at her again in that sexy, tender way of his.

Her knees went soft, but she didn't slow down. She stopped in front of him and said, "I'd love to go out with you."

His smile widened, and then he was taking her hand, caressing the back of it in a luscious, sensual way that had her breath going haywire. "You have made me a very happy man, Thea. How about tomorrow night?"

Nerve endings she hadn't known existed sprung to life, shooting sparks up her arms as he made another sexy sweep over her hand. "That would be great."

She heard footsteps behind her and started to yank her hand away. Jean Luc held her gaze as he caressed the length of her fingers before releasing her. Her knees quivered along with something in her belly.

Madison appeared at her side and swung a companiable arm around her. "Everything settled here?" she asked in that bold way of hers.

Thea bobbed her head as Jean Luc gave another flirtatious smile before saying, "*Oui.*"

"Good. Because the others are coming and things are about to get real."

They gathered back in the kitchen, where Thea made everyone coffee. Once they were all sitting around the table with their drinks, Madison took the lead with introductions. Of course, Jean Luc knew everyone from Nanine's descriptions. They hadn't expected that.

"Nanine's briefed us," Kyle began after Madison gave a slight nod. "Why don't you tell us a bit about the current legal situation and what you're thinking?"

"Can I say something first?" Dean interjected. "I checked Nanine's computer. Someone was on it. I would suspect Jeremy, not Adrienne. He cleared the history of his searches, and it doesn't show any suspicious emails sent from her account, but you can't clear the timestamp for use. Someone was on her computer when she was on vacation, and since she wasn't here…"

"It had to be Jeremy," Jean Luc concluded darkly. "It's as we feared. Thankfully, her bank accounts are intact, and I have informed the bank to add a second verification process for transactions."

Thea watched as Mr. Pinstripes—no, Jean Luc—leaned his elbows on the table and turned completely serious.

"Without seeing the document Jeremy waved in front of Nanine, it's hard to determine what exactly they did. But it sounds like Jeremy forged her signature. I do not know who the workers were employed by. The neighbors I have spoken with—especially the one who called Nanine—only remember a white moving truck. No company logo. The bigger concern is what else Jeremy might have done. In France, once you sign something, you are bound to the contract—even if it is a forgery, which is impossible to prove. It's called scamming."

"And identity theft," Kyle uttered in a savage tone. "It's

fraud. Criminal."

"Under French law," Jean Luc said, "once a deal is signed, it's over. Different than in the United States."

"And Jeremy being an employee only complicates matters, right?" Kyle pressed.

"Yes," Jean Luc answered. "But let us not go there, as you say, unless we need to. Right now, we know they have stolen items from Nanine's restaurant. Have you discovered anything else missing? Nanine said you were checking."

Thea turned to look at Brooke, who said, "I went through her apartment and her jewelry box. She doesn't have much. But I didn't notice anything missing."

"Because that would have been a more clear-cut crime." Jean Luc shook his head. "We are dealing with a professional. I fear we will have to wait to see what else comes forward. But we should pray this is it."

"Are you trying to find Jeremy?" Madison asked. "Have you talked to the police?"

"I have spoken with our local gendarmes, but they agree that Nanine's signature makes things *compliqué*. I have not located Adrienne and Jeremy yet on my own. When Nanine is back home, we can see if she would like to pursue additional ways of finding them."

"What are those?" Thea asked.

His mouth lifted before he responded. "I know some police officers who would look into the matter quietly. We could also hire a private investigator. Mine is very good. But still, I am not sure what good it would do. Under French law, there is no crime, sadly."

"Fuckers," Sawyer muttered savagely. "So we're just supposed to sit back and wait? What in the hell happened to justice in this country? Voltaire said: *the sentiment of justice is so natural, and so universally acquired by all mankind, that it seems to be independent of all law, all party, all religion."*

Jean Luc's mouth curved. "Voltaire also said, *if you want*

good laws, burn those you have and make new ones. I fear that is the situation we have before us."

"Shit," Kyle breathed.

"Sawyer, I believe you've met your match," Dean said, trying to lighten the mood and failing.

She sent him an encouraging smile, but there was no ignoring the mood now. Everyone was quiet. She eyed her roommates. None of them liked what they'd heard.

"I figured France wasn't any different when it came to legal battles being a bitch," Kyle finally said after a long silence. "Excuse my French."

"'Bitch' isn't French," Madison said dryly. "Sounds like we'll have to play wait and see. Fine. *Our* best plan is to get the restaurant up and running."

"I agree," Brooke said, tapping her fingernails together. "She wants to open Nanine's, so we do that. She *needs* to open it."

"And her health?" Jean Luc asked in a quiet voice. "Will she be ready for its demands?"

It was the same question Sawyer had asked earlier—the one that had cleared the kitchen—but this time everyone just turned more solemn.

"We have a few months of renovation." Dean gestured to the space. "She'll have some time to recover and then decide."

"Good," Jean Luc said, picking up his café finally and taking a sip. "If there are any new developments before Nanine is out of the hospital, let me know."

He reached inside his suit jacket and extracted a thin gold case filled with business cards. Sliding one onto the table, he gestured to the number at the bottom.

"This is my office phone. I've added my cell as well. Call anytime."

"Thank you," Kyle said, tapping the card. "We appreciate you taking care of Nanine."

"It's an honor," Jean Luc said, "but like I told Thea, I hope you do not hold it against me for calling the police yesterday. My neighbor thought it was Nanine's daughter reentering the premises."

Everyone turned to look at her. "It's all good now," she said lamely.

"I'm glad her neighbor is looking out for her," Brooke said.

"Paris may be a large city, but the neighborhoods are small communities, like you know. We take care of each other." He stood and bowed slightly. "It's been a pleasure to meet all of you. Thea, might I speak with you for a moment?"

Her cheeks started to burn as she rose, aware her roommates were staring. Then Jean Luc put his hand to the small of her back, sending lightning through her entire body. The chandelier whispered sound, the tinkling as soft as distant sleigh bells.

She heard Madison quip, "He probably wants a bread recipe."

Their restrained laughter might make her expire, except she was probably going to expire from Jean Luc's touch first. He led her to the back door and then followed behind her, shutting it firmly.

He gave her a slow appraisal, his gorgeous lips forming another rakish smile. "Now… About our evening together tomorrow."

Our evening together. Her heart thumped in her chest. "Yes?"

"Can I pick you up here at eight?"

She nodded, her heart beating madly.

"*Parfait.*"

Yes, it really was perfect.

When he leaned in and kissed both her cheeks, lingering over the time-honored gesture with his powerful *mélange* of tenderness and masculine intent, she had to put her hand on his arm to keep from sinking to the ground.

He took her hand gently, a mere caress across the palm, before stepping back and gazing pensively at her. "The hours will pass slowly until I see you again. Of that I am certain. *À bientôt*, Thea."

"*À bientôt*, Jean Luc," she answered in that confident voice she still didn't recognize as her own.

He smiled at her one more time before walking away. Her knees were weak, but there was a warm, luscious feeling spreading through her body, almost like when she soaked in a bubble bath at the end of a long week at the bakery. She had her hand pressed to her heart when Brooke blew the back door open, the others huddled in the doorway.

She jumped. "Oh my God! Were you *listening?*"

"Madison told us you'd said 'God,' but I didn't believe it." Dean pointed at her. "The sky has fallen. And so has our little Thea."

Brooke strutted toward her. "You have a date! And with Nanine's gorgeous lawyer. Tell, tell."

She crossed her feet over each other, mortified to the bone. "There's nothing to tell really." It was only the biggest moment of her life.

"He told her she's beautiful," Madison said in an unusually sweet voice.

"She *is* beautiful," Sawyer affirmed.

"I told her she's especially looking like *the girl next door* fantasy today in her little apron with her hair up," Madison teased. "I added that I thought Dean and Kyle would like that look."

Dean laughed before he made a face. "Guilty. Appears Jean Luc does too."

"He has great taste," Brooke said matter-of-factly. "So we have a lot to squeeze in, don't we, crew? Nanine wants a new look for her restaurant, and Thea needs a Paris makeover. Who's going to help?"

Everyone raised their hands.

CHAPTER
TWELVE

Operation Thea started an hour later, after she'd finished baking her bread.

Because, priorities. Heaven help her, Brooke had shoved her into the deep end—to a lingerie appointment at Simone Pérèle.

At least Dean hadn't been allowed to join them—Brooke had voted him down, citing another uncharacteristic uttering of *Oh my God* by Thea as reason enough for his exclusion.

Brooke and Madison had both come, however, possibly because Madison would chase her if she tried to run away. Until today, Thea hadn't known there were different levels of mortification, but she was already at DEFCON 5. The artfully decorated window displayed brightly colored lace teddies and silky robes she couldn't possibly pull off. Her feet dragged as her friends herded her into the store.

"Don't you think this is premature?" she whispered. "I'm just having a date."

"You wear lingerie for yourself, not a man," Brooke said, taking her by the arm gently.

"That's never been how it's worked for me," Madison shot back from her place on Thea's other side.

"And I thought you said you wanted this," Brooke continued, ignoring Madison's joke. "Wearing lingerie is about radiating confidence from the inside out. Like Nanine taught us. What's closest to your skin? Lingerie. Now smile. This is going to be fun. Nanine and I both love the women who work here."

"Meaning Nanine buys her panties here, Thea, so you should be good."

"Madison. Enough." Brooke flashed a glamorous smile and charged forward with a warm *Bonjour*. She kissed both cheeks of the two chic women in black who'd greeted them and then made the introductions in French, slowly, likely for Thea's benefit. "Renée and Emmy, this is our focus today. Her name is Thea, and she has a *rendezvous* with one of the dreamiest men I've laid eyes on in Paris in ages."

"Do not trust him, Thea," Renée said with a twinkle in her blue eyes. "French men start off all romantic—"

"But it ends, as do the love words and all other grand gestures, as if they were ripped from their very souls," Emmy finished, nudging her colleague knowingly.

"Nanine approves of this one," Brooke added with emphasis after a beat.

"That changes everything!" Renée looked Thea up and down like she was a prize cow at the Iowa State Fair. "Nanine is *never* wrong. How is she?"

While Brooke filled them in, Madison led Thea over to the display. "Don't let Brooke push you around. You don't have to go from wearing white underwear to going all Mata Hari. We both work in the kitchen. Comfortable is key for day, but you might branch out into something a little sexier for nighttime. If you want."

At this rate, Thea couldn't begin to imagine a sexy nighttime. Other people did that. On TV.

"Maybe one set," Madison continued as wild laughter echoed behind them. "Because Brooke might be right about wearing it for you, but it's hot when a man you want looks at you across the table, and you know he's wondering what you have on underneath your clothes."

Thea gulped. Is that what Mr. Pinstripes' masculine intent meant? "I'm so out of my league. Maybe I—"

Madison faced her, a dark angel of truth in all black. "You've gotta want the change, Thea. You say you do. How bad?"

Her throat clogged. "Bad," she whispered.

"Then sometimes you've got to take the training wheels off the bike and ride like mad down the proverbial hill. You think I wasn't scared spitless my first day after we got a Michelin star? But I wanted it. Got it?"

"Got it." She hesitantly reached her hand out toward the lacy yellow bra with blue flowers. "I do like this one." Then she turned the price tag over and winced. This would be the most expensive bra she'd ever bought.

"Sexy yet sweet. Just like you."

"If you start mentioning that Suzy Homemaker fantasy again—"

"Brooke, we have our first set," Madison called out.

She looked up from where they were huddled at the main counter. "Excellent. We're conferring here on styles."

"Shouldn't I be in on that?" Thea whispered.

"She's in fashion. Let her do her thing."

She was still gazing at the display when Brooke turned her around, the lingerie duo beside her. "What size do you think?" Brooke asked.

"I'm a 34B," Thea answered.

"*Non, pas* 90B," Renée's crisp declaration was followed up by her hands coming up around the sides of Thea's breasts with brisk efficiency. "85C."

"I concur," Emmy said in French.

That sounded huge. She looked down for a moment to see before whispering, "What is that in the U.S.?"

"It's a 32C, Thea," Brooke told her.

"You are disturbed," Renée said, "so we will speak of the things of your heart. You are a baker, Brooke tells us, but trained in pastry as well. What is your favorite pastry?"

She sputtered to keep up in French. "A rhubarb tart."

"Why?" Renée asked, her delicate blond brows scrunched together in concentration.

"Because it's got bite, and it takes a special balance to bring the fruit into balance."

Renée nudged Emmy. "She's a romantic deep down who likes to take her time. If your man is lucky enough to gain access to your bed, he will be well satisfied, I think."

OMG. Her brain shorted out. They got all of that from her rhubarb tart?

"Listen to Frenchwomen, Thea, as they always know," Brooke said, "but we're embarrassing her."

"I told you we needed to take it easy," Madison said with a glare. "Her crème brûlée cheeks are back."

"She needs to claim her sensual self," Brooke said, tapping her fingernails together. "Right, Thea?"

She bobbed her head briskly yet again. When she got back home, she was going to add to her *Living Life to the Fullest* recipe card. She was starting to realize lingerie was definitely an essential ingredient.

"I think you might like this set, yes?" Renée asked, pulling her thoughts back to the display as she selected a bra with indigo, pink, and black lace designed to resemble vine-ripened grapes.

The grapes were as breathtaking as the blue flowers on the yellow bra she loved. The beauty had her melting on the inside. Who knew bras could be like works of art? "Yes, I like that very much," she answered thickly in French.

"Good." Renée smiled for the first time. "Let's get to work then."

Brooke and Emmy joined Renée in pulling down more

styles. More than Thea could ever imagine buying on her current without-a-job budget.

Madison steered her toward the sleeping attire. "You're still mostly a cotton PJ wearer, aren't you? And fleece robes?"

"It gets cold in Iowa," she said defensively as she stroked a pretty navy tank top in a rich cotton with lace at the hem. "The wind chill can go below zero. Sometimes even a cow's udders can freeze."

Madison blinked at her.

Then they both burst into laughter.

"Good thing you're not a cow." Madison followed up with a *moo* sound.

"We shouldn't laugh. It's really painful for the cows."

"Stop horsing around," Brooke called, pointing toward a set of stairs leading downward that she started toward herself. "It's time to start your fitting. Let's go."

Fitting? Emmy handed Renée her selections, and the young blonde swept past them with her arms filled with bright bits of lace and satin.

"That's all for me?" she gasped.

"Aren't you the lucky one?" Madison teased.

The distinctive sound of champagne popping from the floor beneath them had her looking at Emmy, who answered, "Only champagne for our best clients."

That would be Brooke. Not her. She couldn't buy more than one set, two if it was on sale or something.

"You like this navy sleep set, right?" Madison held it up next to her face to refocus her.

Her brain was already calculating the costs. "It's pretty, but I'm only going to get a couple of bras." And even that was a stretch.

"Okay, First Course," Madison said, nudging her gently toward the stairs. "Let's go have some champagne."

Downstairs, there were more product displays, and to the right, two changing rooms. Brooke stood by a tall table next to the stairs, an elegant flute of champagne in her hand. The bottle and a few filled glasses waited on a silver tray in a sitting area. This place had couches?

"Grab your glass," Brooke ordered, "and let's toast while Renée gets you set up."

Thea handed a glass to Madison before grabbing her own.

"To sprouting new wings," Brooke said with a smile.

Thea's heart sped up, but this time she took a deep breath. This was her *live life to the fullest* moment and she knew it. "To sprouting new wings."

They all drank, and then Madison said, "She's going to be the sexiest bird in the sky with this underwear. Come on, Thea, let's see the goods."

Mortified, she took another sip and headed over to the elegant changing room. Once inside, Renée snapped the curtain closed behind her. Alone, Thea eyed the treasures arranged for her. Where to start? The yellow one with flowers, she decided. When she finally clasped the back, she eyed herself in the mirror. She didn't look at herself much, certainly not in her underwear. Too weird. But the bra was pretty. She felt…special. Like she was a newly decorated white cake with yellow buttercream frosting and blue marzipan flowers.

"Are you ready?" Brooke called.

Ready for what? "I'm just trying them on."

The curtain moved, and Brooke's head popped in. "Oh, that's lovely. Madison, come see."

They were going to look? "Oh, my God."

"She swore again," Madison observed as she ducked her head in.

"Don't worry, Thea," Brooke told her. "No one's coming down the stairs with Emmy standing watch on the top floor with the other customers."

"I adore the style on her," Renée said in French, sweeping *into* the changing room. "Let's check the size."

Before Thea could react, the woman tugged on her straps

and measured her again with her hands in a professional way. Thea was sure she was still blushing, but Renée wasn't being weird. Thea was the one feeling weird.

"It suits you, I think," Renée said with a firm shake of the head. "Sexy and sweet."

"I was just thinking it's like frosting on a cake."

"I'd eat you," Madison joked.

"Me too," Brooke said as she sipped her champagne. "Keep trying things on. I'll grab your glass."

The curtain didn't close after that, although she turned her back when she changed into the multicolored vine one. Everyone oohed and aahed along with her. From there, she changed into a series of bralettes, so comfy even Madison decided she was going to check them out. In black, of course.

"Underwire is the devil," Madison spat.

"You could live in New York, Madison, wearing all black like that." Brooke fingered the rim of her glass. "I love coming to Paris because I can wear other colors. Fashion is so much more expansive here."

Expansive. Right. *She was a bird.*

Thea continued the lingerie tour. Most of the styles worked, but she grew increasingly nervous. Renée was spending so much time and effort on her. How was she going to admit she could only afford two of them after trying so many pieces on?

When Renée thrust yet another bra into the changing room, Thea almost panicked. But the silky caramel bra was so pretty, she found herself taking it from the woman's hands. When she tried it on, she stopped short in the mirror and stared at herself.

"Wow, Thea," Brooke said, lounging in the doorway with Madison.

"What she said," Madison echoed. "Girl, look at you!"

Maybe she was getting used to seeing herself like this, but she *did* look pretty. Maybe even a little sexy. Mind blown.

Renée tugged her straps up and fitted the bra in that efficient way of hers. "This one. Yes. If you will let me?"

Before she knew it, Renée had taken her ponytail down and was briskly spreading her hair out in waves around her shoulders with her usual proficiency.

"Do you see how sexy you look like this? I think we have found the bra to create the perfect harmony for you. What do you think?"

She looked in the mirror. She didn't recognize herself with her hair falling softly onto her skin.

But. That. Was. Her.

"The caramel silk compliments the natural highlights in her hair and skin," Renée added. "Your man will be on his knees should he ever see you like this."

"*Oui*," Brooke said softy.

"How do you feel, Thea?" Madison asked. "Because that's what matters."

"Pretty," she whispered reverently, staring at herself.

"Good." Renée left the room. "Then our job is finished."

The curtain closed, and she was alone again. With her burgeoning self. The one she was really starting to like. She was taking shape—like one of her artisan breads. She touched the straps reverently. These were the nicest bras she'd ever tried on. Now she had to make a hard decision.

She knew she wanted the yellow one. She looked longingly at the vine-colored one. It was either this one or the caramel one. But how could she forget the way she'd looked in the latter? She'd seen a new side of herself. She *had* to choose it, but it was hard to set the other aside. Maybe she could come back for it after she found a job. Yes, that's what she'd tell them.

Opening the curtain, she found Brooke and Madison talking quietly beside the champagne. They looked over as she joined them.

"All done?" Brooke asked.

"Yes." She made herself smile. "I'm going to take the yellow and the caramel bras right now, and then come back for the vine one when I have a job."

"Told you," Madison said with a curve of her dark brows.

"What about matching panties?" Brooke was tapping her fingernails together again.

There was no way she could afford those. But how would they look with her granny panties? Horrible! "Next time maybe."

Brooke breezed past her and brought out the vine one as well as another green one she'd looked lovely in. "Thea, it just so happens that you have five fairy godmothers who would all like to help fund your makeover."

She frantically shook her head. "But you can't... You don't have to."

"If you need to, think of it as a trade for all the bread and pastry you're going to be making for us," Madison said, putting her hands on her hips.

"I don't—"

"Dean has already been posting pics of himself in *bread bliss* today," Madison said, interrupting Brooke. "God help us. But you get my point."

"I don't want her thinking it's a trade," Brooke said with a frown. "Thea, we have a lot ahead of us. Hair. Eyebrows. Shoes. Clothes."

"I should have thought about the cost." She very much wanted to cry, but she forced it back. "I don't mind baking bread for the next century, but I'm not sure it'll be enough."

Brooke didn't smile. That was why Thea loved her.

"I *need* to contribute," she pleaded when Brooke remained silent.

She tapped her fingernails together again. "You *need* to be a good receiver."

"Like you are?" Madison scoffed.

151

"I didn't say I was perfect." Brooke bit her lip. "Can't you accept this stuff as early thirtieth birthday presents?"

She shook her head slowly. "Bread and other treats. The best I can make."

Brooke sighed. "Fine. Come on. Let's find you some panties. Because there is no way you're matching these with granny panties on my watch."

Thank God Brooke was a mind reader sometimes.

"She could go commando down low," Madison teased, inflaming Thea's cheeks.

"I'd never!"

"Enough!" Brooke said. "Do you like thongs or shorties?"

Had she ever worn those? She followed Brooke back up the stairs. Soon, matching underwear were spread out over the main table. They were gorgeous. Every single pair.

"Now I understand 'The Thong Song,'" she breathed out.

That had Madison bursting into laughter again. When Brooke hummed a few bars of the song for Renée and Emmy, they joined in.

"I didn't mean for it to be funny," she protested.

"We know you didn't." Madison swung her arm around her. "That's why we love you."

CHAPTER
THIRTEEN

I f there was one thing Brooke appreciated about Paris, it was the effort people put into making their spaces beautiful.

Even in Manhattan, shopkeepers didn't change their window displays or décor as much as business owners did here. When they walked into the salon called The Green Room to get Thea's brows done, she had to smile at Thea's wide-eyed expression, followed by her exclamation, "Everything is green!"

"Maybe they have a Kermit obsession," Madison joked.

"The green is meant to convey optimism," Brooke informed them as she said hello to the receptionist, whom she knew from her own visits.

"Or wealth," Madison shot back. "People who have money like to be reminded of it, even subliminally."

Thea looked between them, as if waiting to see if Brooke would fire back a response. But this was an old battle, Madison being from the streets, as she called it, and Brooke being from a penthouse.

Even after ten years, Madison still didn't realize how much Brooke hated the superficiality and exclusivity that so often went with fashion. That was why she respected Blanche, who was a wonder with brows. Sure, models were her canvas, but she opened her studio to anyone who wanted to come in. Not everything in beauty and fashion was accessible to everyone.

That's why Brooke loved creating décor. All you needed was an interesting fabric, paint, and accessories. The Green Room was memorable for its bold statement, for being a piece of livable art. If she hadn't gotten a job in fashion, she might have worked as an interior designer. But she'd thought she could make a bigger mark in fashion, describing fabrics and textures in a way no one else did.

"Maybe I'll do an article on this salon," Brooke said, "and their concept. Ah, here's Blanche."

It had always struck Brooke as funny that the woman's name meant white when she was working in an ocean of green. She greeted her longtime friend the Parisian way before turning to introduce her companions.

As always, Blanche was eager to get started and linked arms conspiratorially with Thea as she rattled off her ideas in rapid French.

"You'd better translate," Madison broke in as they followed the two women to Blanche's station. "Thea freaks when the French is that fast."

"Never fear," Brooke said with a grin. "Blanche will begin to speak in English after she works her ideas out in French. It's her way."

The moment Thea was sitting in the oversized green chair, Blanche said, "You have beautiful features: the curve of your eyes and brows, the angle of your cheekbones, and the line of your nose. They all make my job so easy."

Thea stared in wonderment at the tall, gorgeous woman. Brooke made demurring sounds while Madison pursed her lips, clearly as surprised as Thea was. Brooke could all but hear them thinking: *didn't women usually look for flaws in other women?*

That was what made Blanche unique. She saw the beauty in everyone. Her fingertips were gentle as she examined Thea's face from all angles before gently plucking at her brows for what only seemed like a few minutes. Brooke sent Thea reassuring smiles, but then Blanche turned Thea around to the mirror.

Brooke could see the art of her work. There was no serious arch to Thea's brows or a super thin trail near the edge of her eyes like she'd had before. The lines were in harmony and her eyes looked bigger.

"*Parfait,*" Blanche exclaimed.

"*Oui,*" Brooke murmured.

"As subtle as peeling a carrot," Madison said, shaking her head. "Blanche, I might let you take a crack at me."

Blanche laughed heartily. "It would be a pleasure, Madison. Thea, your brows are so natural you do not need to do anything more. You are lucky."

As she looked at her friends, she smiled grandly. "Yes, I am. What's next?"

"She's getting into the spirit of things," Brooke said, nudging Madison. "So are you, it seems."

"Except I'm not the one with the hot date," Madison said as they left the salon and caught a cab. "But I am hungry. Do we have time before Thea's next appointment?"

"Hair," Brooke said, checking her phone. "I talked Tony into working over his lunch hour. We can stop and grab some sandwiches. He likes the lobster rolls from a place in Saint-Germain."

Madison rolled her eyes. "What is Paris coming to? Okay, I can swing that. Thea?"

"I've never had one," she answered honestly.

"Another first." Brooke hugged her arm. "I know I never stop being inspired here."

"I got inspired by a new dish I made in a dream last night," Madison said, kicking out her black canvas high-tops. "Thea, what's the blackest bread you can make?"

Brooke watched as she put a finger to her lips, clearly thinking. "Probably a rye bread with espresso and cocoa powders and molasses."

Madison made a humming sound. "Good toasted, I bet. Aromatic too. Okay, when we get back to the restaurant, I want to walk you through what I'm thinking. You up for baking a batch of that bread when we get home?"

"I can't imagine a better way to end today," Thea replied.

"Who says we're finishing with breadmaking?" Brooke asked. "We have a lot to cram in. I'm going to call the lobster place and get them started on our order."

"It's the New Yorker in her," Madison joked, except she was right.

Fifteen minutes later, they had three brown paper bags stuffed with food and were heading to the second arrondissement. As they neared the golden stones and soaring glass pyramid of the Louvre, Thea's face went all soft. "It's still so beautiful."

Brooke was a little more jaded about this area. It was tourist central.

"You couldn't pay me to go to the Louvre again," Madison said, shuddering. "I have *never* been in one place with so many people."

Brooke laughed. "A private showing is best. And yes, I have had one. If you're nice to me, maybe I'll make you my plus one for a fashion event."

"So long as you understand I'm only interested in a one-night stand," Madison deadpanned.

Thea gasped, and then they all started laughing.

When their driver stopped on a quiet side street not far from the Palais-Royal Gardens, Thea looked at Brooke. "Is this the right place? I don't see a salon."

Brooke knew her smile was that of a Cheshire cat. "That's the point. Tony doesn't have a storefront. He's invitation only, and before Madison gets all huffy about exclusivity, he only takes people whose spirit he likes."

"Still exclusive," Madison pointed out.

Brooke fought back the eye roll. "Thea, I told him he'd adore you."

They exited the car and Brooke pressed a button with the number 7. No name. Tony liked his privacy.

Thea started backing away. "I can't possibly afford this," she whispered as a discreet buzzer sounded and the door clicked.

Brooke grabbed her arm gently and pushed open the door. "The Fairy Godmother Account has you covered, remember?"

"I'm going to have to make a ton of bread," Thea muttered before trailing off as she caught sight of the courtyard.

Brooke felt her shoulders unwind. The sound of a burbling fountain captured her attention as her eyes soaked in the potted trees spilling with ripening oranges and lemons. Other ornamental pots overflowed with flowering rosemary, tea roses, and fuchsias. Heaven.

"It's gorgeous," Thea breathed out. "A hidden paradise."

"Paris is cool like that," Madison said, tilting her head back and letting the sun stream over her as she closed her eyes. "You'd never know this was here. So different from Miami's in-your-face luxury."

Yeah, she wasn't a fan of Magic City. "I'm going to take a few pictures and text them to Nanine. She adores her plants." Brooke added it to her mental list to make sure she watered Nanine's when she got home.

"Her doctor wasn't letting her use her phone," Thea reminded her.

Tension flooded back into Brooke's body. "She'll see them at some point. Let's go."

She led them to the matte black door to the right of the garden and opened it, bringing them into another wonderland. Art Deco furnishings filled the space with black wallpaper on one wall decorated with a design of thin gold vertical lines. Another wall was solid red. A teal-green couch seemed to lounge in the middle with a modern art painting above it depicting a woman's hair dripping to the floor with gold shot through it.

Brooke had called Tony the minute she'd seen the painting by the sensational artist KATHIA in a private gallery showing last year and told him he should check it out. He'd bought it on the spot. She'd celebrated by opening a bottle of champagne for herself, knowing it was going to be a signature piece.

"Wow," Thea whispered, proving Brooke right.

Tony rose from a plush white chair in the corner. His thick black hair fell in long waves to his shoulders and worked well with his tall but lean frame. He studied Thea with his rich brown eyes, his presence quiet but compelling like always. He was the one who'd listened to Brooke when she'd told him she wanted to go darker with her hair color because being a natural blonde meant people didn't always take her seriously enough. Then he'd made it happen with a kindness and proficiency she'd never seen from anyone else in hair.

"You like my space?" he asked in English.

Thea nodded slowly.

"I have your friend to thank for the beautiful painting."

Both of her friends gaped at her. She only shrugged.

"You must be Thea. I am Tony, and today we are going to make magic together. Are you ready?"

"I think so," she answered shyly, like Dorothy in *The Wizard of Oz* they teased her about.

"Don't think." He crossed to her and held out his hands, not looking at anyone but her. "Just feel. You can trust me."

When Thea took his hands without hesitation, Brooke wanted to cheer. Even Madison glanced over sharply.

"Thank you for seeing me," her little sister said with a bright smile. "Brooke says you don't do everyone."

His mouth tipped up in a smile. He leaned toward Brooke without releasing Thea's hands and kissed both her cheeks. "Hello, my love. And you must be Madison. Now, *you* I would not do."

Brooke smothered a laugh.

Madison cocked her hip in her total bad girl persona. "No?"

"You wouldn't let me make magic with you." He laughed dryly. "Come, let's eat quickly while I tell you what I'm thinking."

Brooke started digging out the sandwiches. Tony sat cross-legged on the floor and gestured for Thea to sit beside him.

"I can see you have an image in your mind." He thanked Brooke as she handed him a lobster roll.

"I've always liked the haircut Julia Ormond gets in *Sabrina*," she answered as Madison passed her a lobster roll and sat down on her other side.

He took a large bite of his sandwich and chewed thoughtfully before saying, "I can do that haircut, of course. But not for you."

She looked oddly deflated.

"It would be the completely wrong look for you." He wiped his hands and took a lock of her hair, tugging it gently. "You have an understated natural beauty. You fear being seen."

Bingo, Brooke wanted shout.

"Today we are going to coax out that natural beauty and, if you want, a more confident version of you. How does that sound?"

She looked down at her sandwich. "You make it sound easy."

"Life is as easy as you make it. Take me. When I started in hair, I was in a maelstrom of drama cutting ten to twelve people's hair a day in a cramped soulless space this size with eight other hairdressers. I decided to stop the madness. Now I am here. Alone. Happy. Only being with clients I want, who want to be here with me. Do you understand what I am saying?"

She nodded slowly. "I do. I'm…trying to do things differently too, but I've just begun."

He smiled, a beautifully engaging expression that seemed to fill his whole face. "You're ready to make magic then. But I knew that the minute I watched you look at my haven. You have something precious inside you, something others have lost and wish to regain. Innocence. Awe. In this world where we are so self-focused and so cynical, you still see the beauty of life and share it in your smile and the light in your eyes. I hope you know how special that is. How special you are."

Tears popped into Brooke's eyes along with Thea's. "She really doesn't know," Brooke said softly.

Thea dragged in a breath. "I'm not used to people talking about me like that. I mean, it's been a nonstop day of it, from the lingerie ladies to the eyebrow person I just saw. But usually…"

"A great artist sees beneath the surface and speaks honestly," Tony said. "It is up to you to believe them. Finish your lunch, and then we'll begin."

Madison stretched out her legs and polished off the last bite of her lobster roll. "Brooke, I just have one question. When did you start amassing a rolodex full of makeover shamans?"

"*Makeover shamans*?" Brooke started laughing.

"Every shaman I've met is way too serious," Tony said, rising and posing like he was being painted for a portrait. "You can call me a makeover maestro."

They all laughed at that.

But Thea wasn't laughing when he started to wash her hair. Brooke understood. Tony's hands were otherworldly.

"You like it, yes?"

"You have magic hands," Thea managed. "If that's not weird to say."

"So I've been told—in my salon and outside."

"Outside too, huh?" Madison leaned against the adjoining wall. "There's a shock. You men…"

He only chuckled before saying, "She's tough, isn't she? Fact is, I adore strong women like Madison."

Madison's eyes flickered up, and for a moment Brooke watched them stare at each other before Madison averted her gaze. She knew her friend would not like to be seen in such a way.

"Word, Tony," Brooke said richly. "Your taste in women has also gotten you into trouble, if you don't mind me reminding you."

"No, that trouble was all mine and my impulsive romantic heart. I just can't seem to look before I leap when it comes to love. Ah, *c'est la vie*. Love *is* the greatest force inside us. If we stop seeking it out, we stop our very selves."

Brooke appreciated Tony's wisdom, but she still couldn't imagine putting herself out there again. Not after Adam. The jerk.

"Come," Tony added after a quiet pause, "let's rinse your hair and we'll be ready to start."

Brooke was eager to watch this transformation. Soon Thea was sitting in front of the full-length gold-rimmed mirror, smiling. Maybe it was all the love talk, but Madison said she was going to use the time to look up some more recipes for the new menu in the garden.

"I'm really excited about this now," Thea told Tony softly.

"As you should be," he answered with a smile before picking up a pair of scissors. Then he combed her wet hair with one hand, his fingers sweeping through the locks, muttering, "Yes, I know. Exactly."

Then he started lifting strands of her hair and cutting it in a way Brooke had never seen another stylist do. Almost like he was spearing each strand on the diagonal. Every person who'd cut her hair had usually done it straight across. Hence her old, sharp blunt cuts. But now her hair didn't have an edge, and she loved it.

"I think we will leave your length here for now, resting on your heart," he murmured and then brought out another product, which he massaged into her hair, before beginning the blow dry.

Brooke thought it was too bad Madison was still out of the room. Thea's hair wasn't shorter, she noted. It wasn't even significantly more layered. It was...elevated. She didn't know any other word for it.

"Do you see the more confident version of you?" Tony muttered. "Smile, Thea, and feel your heart."

She looked at herself and gasped.

Brooke knew what she was seeing. It was still Thea. But beyond the sweet and innocent look she'd always had was a quiet something she couldn't name. Little sister had an understated sexiness.

"I can't believe it," Thea breathed out.

"Believe it." Tony put his hands on her shoulders. "You were ready to be beautiful."

Brooke charged out to find Madison, and when she stepped into the salon, her mouth dropped open. *"Holy shit! Thea! What happened to you, girl?"*

Brooke nudged her. "I knew Tony was brilliant—"

"Blessed by the hair gods," Tony said, blowing himself a kiss in the mirror.

Madison charged over and spun Thea around. "You're you, but...posh."

"Elegant," Tony added, combing her hair again with his fingers.

"I love it!" Brooke exclaimed. "What about you?"

Tony's hand fell away. Thea's hair resembled a water fountain of highlights and texture now in a way it hadn't before. "It's beautiful. I feel…beautiful. I hadn't really felt beautiful until today."

Brooke knew why. Her damn parents had never used that word for her, or even pretty. Thea had tried to defend them in the past, saying they were practical and hardworking, the kind of people who didn't show off. Except that was crap. They'd never supported Thea's dreams, not even when she'd clearly shown them how important coming to Paris was to her with all the odd jobs she'd taken to afford the trip. Brooke was still in awe of all the babysitting, car and windows washing, and cake and breadmaking.

But the single worst thing Thea had told her that they'd said was the zinger right before she'd left for Paris without their blessing: *the flower which stands out above all the rest will be the first to be cut down.*

As far as Brooke was concerned, fate could stick both her and Thea's mothers in a paper bag and shake them until… They got some basic human kindness in them.

Madison leaned in and whispered, "What's wrong with you all the sudden? You look like you could spew fire."

"I was thinking about how much I hate Thea's parents," she responded.

"Nearly all of us are from a bunch of jerks," Madison answered practically. "Even our golden boy. You're lucky your dad is a stand-up guy. You might be the only person with a parent who isn't a pecker."

That had Brooke bursting out laughing. "God, you're the best, Madison."

"You're both the best," Thea said, her heart in her eyes.

"Just a warning. When old doubts rise up, I'm going to lean on you guys to help me remember how I feel today."

Brooke went over and touched her hair. "Self-improvement takes a village, sweetie, and there are no shortcuts. And since I know your background, I'm going to add this. There's nothing wrong with being beautiful. In fact, every woman should be able to see herself that way."

Wasn't that what fashion and the beauty industry sold? It was too bad they didn't always deliver it.

Tony swept off the cape as he helped her from the chair. "Enjoy letting others see your beauty, Thea, inside and out. I know I am grateful for my view today."

She hugged him. "Thank you, Tony."

He kissed both her cheeks. "It was a pleasure. Come again, Thea. Anytime."

Madison turned her toward the mirror again. "Our little sister is growing up. Wait until the guys see. Nanine too. And Mr. Pinstripes."

She touched the ends of her hair, which rested over her heart, making Brooke ask the question. "After all this, do you think you're ready for him, Thea?"

Her smile conveyed that and more as she said with a new confidence, "Yes, I'm ready for him."

Brooke wanted to cheer. Her work today was done.

CHAPTER
FOURTEEN

A shadow fell over Sawyer Jackson as he finished the final touches on what he thought was his best sketch of the restaurant's new look.

He ignored this person as he had the dozen or so others. Art gawkers were out in force this afternoon. He continued to soften the edges in his drawing as his feet dangled over the quay's stones on which he was sitting, the Seine rushing by in all her mystery.

Since his first trip to Paris when he was twelve for what his parents had termed self-improvement vacations—something they'd read about in a book—he'd loved this quiet spot across from Sennelier, a Paris bastion for art supplies. He'd come to this very place every day he was in town. With a lone willow dancing to the river's subtle music at the far end, this place was a perpetual source of comfort and inspiration.

God, he needed both. The pressure in his chest had been unbearable since he'd been given his monumental task from Nanine. You'd think he would be used to the pressure. He'd had it all his life. His parents had pushed him to excel starting at the age of two when they enrolled him in an elite preschool specializing in languages, art, and music. Still in diapers, he'd been able to say hello and count to ten in not just the prereq-uisite five languages but ten. Plus, he had been able to play simple melodies on five instruments.

Hell, people had been gawking at the freak show of Sawyer Jackson since he was a kid genius. No wonder he'd grown tired of it. Only he hadn't been genius enough to become the celebrated artist he'd hoped when he'd cut that edgy deal with his parents. Sure, he'd had to pay for the trip himself—hence his work at Nanine's—but he'd *craved* their approval. Back then, he'd burned with an unquenchable thirst to become an artist. He hadn't been able to pull it off.

It remained the only thing he'd ever wanted but failed at.

The Universe must be laughing at him. Because here he was again, Sawyer Jackson, sitting along the Seine, shading the apricot color Nanine had wanted at the edge of the room he'd drawn. But he couldn't shut off his inner critic. He'd theorized it was why he'd never become a brilliant artist and never would. Nothing he did was ever perfect enough, another parental legacy implanted in his brain.

"Is your work for sale?" a deep baritone voice finally asked in French.

Sawyer lifted his pastel and made a slashing motion of dismissal. "*Non.*"

"It really is quite good," the man persisted. "You have talent, but then again, I'd already heard from Nanine that you're a frustrated artist trapped in invisible professor robes."

He looked up sharply at that.

Jean Luc Mercier was standing over him.

Paris really *was* a small town. "We don't wear robes anymore, and you can't be a frustrated artist when you have nothing to say. Regurgitating other people's ideas about art is what art professors do."

"*It is difficult to free fools from the chains they revere.*" The dark-haired man tilted his head to the side, studying him after delivering that Voltaire bombshell. "I don't believe you regurgitate anything, but then again, my opinion hardly matters. I will say, however, that your drawing of Nanine's reimagined restaurant captures her special classic atmosphere while modernizing the space in a very compelling way."

Pressure eased under his ribs. That was exactly what he'd been going for. He didn't want to let her down. Hell, he didn't want to let anyone down—even when it meant giving in a little himself. "Thanks for the vote of confidence, but Nanine's thoughts are the only ones that matter here. What are you doing out this way?"

He gestured to the spot on the ground next to Sawyer. "May I?"

"Of course," he replied, but he couldn't help but be a little surprised. Mr. Pinstripes—hell, he shouldn't keep calling him by Thea's nickname—was wearing superexpensive threads. Sawyer didn't mind getting dirty, but he was wearing casual clothes.

"It's the Parisian way to walk, as you know, and this is my favorite route after I eat lunch before returning to work."

Lunch?

"Jesus, what time is it?"

Jean Luc checked his watch—a mega-expensive Swiss timepiece. "It's a quarter after two."

"*Merde.* I lost track of time." He dug out his phone and winced at the texts, most of which were from Brooke keeping him apprised of Operation Thea's locations.

"Good artists always become lost in their art," Jean Luc said with a classically elegant French smirk.

"You're not just a lawyer, are you?" Sawyer asked, as if the man's habit for quoting French philosophers weren't indication enough.

"I have a French soul. While I love the law, I also love beauty, art, and culture. Reason."

A French answer if ever he'd heard one. Truthfully, it resounded with Sawyer too. Still, Sawyer felt the need to press this guy. To make sure he was good enough for Thea. Dean and Kyle—and maybe Madison—would want to buy him a drink afterward for his due diligence. "And women?"

Jean Luc's affable expression faded, and in his suddenly flinty eyes, Sawyer could see the lawyer. "You are wondering if I will treat Thea well? I suppose it is to your character to ask, and from one man of honor to another, I will answer you."

Right. To question a Frenchman's honor was to ask for a fight. Sawyer had stepped into serious *merde*, but it was Thea they were talking about. He'd do that and more for her.

"I do enjoy women. They are wonderful beings of intellect and imagination—and their bodies are designed to be worshipped and given pleasure. But if you're asking the very American question of whether I am a 'player,' then no, I am not. I feel like Proust in this regard: *The real voyage of discovery consists not in seeking new landscapes, but in having new eyes.* Do you understand?"

Quality over quantity. He was the same way. "Good. Thea's like a little sister to us and she's led a pretty sheltered life."

"It is her naturalness and kindness that attracts me."

"She thinks she's too kind sometimes," Sawyer pointed out to see what he would say.

"Is that possible?" Jean Luc sighed. "Forgive me. I am tired of women who have more regard for their image than their humanity, and if I never again see a pout on a woman's face, I will live out my life as a contented man."

Satisfied, Sawyer bit the inside of his cheek. "Come on. You have to admit a Frenchwoman's pout is totally sexy."

Jean Luc's mouth twitched. "Perhaps, but after my last relationship ended, I am cured of its temptations."

"That bad, huh?"

The man inclined his head crisply. "When you have a true

French soul, you feel things deeply, and to complicate the matter, I am also half-Italian."

"Which means you'd howl at the moon over love," Sawyer said before he winced. "Sorry, I get carried away sometimes."

He only tilted his head again and nodded. "Accurate though. It gives people the power to injure you. The ruthless ones don't regard that characteristic with empathy, and that's when love affairs turn tragic, I'm afraid."

Well, hell, Sawyer understood what it was like to be hurt by someone's ruthlessness, although he hadn't gotten that treatment from any women he'd dated. It had been from his mother. "Thea wouldn't hurt you, but that's not the only reason to ask her out."

Jean Luc's eyes grew flinty again. "*You* undervalue your friend's beauty and allure."

If anything, his affront was reassuring. "I don't. I just wanted to make sure you didn't and weren't only interested in her because she was nice. She's so much more than that."

The man made a rude sound. "You are a good champion, Dr. Jackson. For both Thea and Nanine. I will leave you to your non-artistic pursuits."

He rose, and Sawyer fought a chuckle at the man's rebuke. Back in the day, they might have dueled at sunrise over such ripostes. He was so glad the practice was out of favor. Sawyer Jackson would have gotten creamed by his opponent and lived a short, tragic life. So French.

"If I change my mind about selling the painting, I'll let you know," he called out, feeling like they'd reached a new level of kinship.

Jean Luc waved a dismissive hand. "Frame it and hang it in the new Nanine's. Patrons will be in awe of the prototype for the new look. *Bonne journée*, Dr. Jackson."

Ah, that damned formality of the French. It saturated their language. You could know someone for years and still refer to them in the proper grammatical tense, not the informal tense reserved for chummy friends. But as a professor, he appreciated the language's complexity and the history. He wondered for a moment if he should switch to Italian to be cheeky, but he decided he didn't need to sweep the board. "It's Sawyer."

"So you say," the man said as he walked away.

Sawyer chuckled softly. Jean Luc was holding out on becoming chummy. Point taken. He glanced at his texts and grimaced. He'd told Brooke to keep him updated since he'd planned to meet up with them. Now she was on a rampage, so he sucked up the courage to call her.

"Where are you? I've been calling and texting to keep you abreast of Operation Thea with no answer."

He eased the phone from his ear at the volume of her pique. "I was working on my design for Nanine's, and I lost track of time."

"You close to being done?"

Glancing at the drawing, he felt his hands itch to continue. To scrap it and start again. Nothing he ever did felt finished. *Are you sure it's as great as it can be, Sawyer?* He didn't just hear his mother's voice saying the words. The sentiment had been carved into his very skin. Perfectionism was the bane of his existence. His Achilles' heel keeping him from reaching his true potential with the one thing he'd always loved.

"I had someone offer to buy it, so take that for what it's worth."

"That's not surprising, but do you think it captures Nanine's vision?"

His insides trembled from the pressure. "She's the only one who will know."

"Dammit, Sawyer. I love you but set aside your mommy issues for once. *Is it done?*"

He stared at the drawing. The colors were both soft and bold—a contrast Nanine had asked for—and the lines were sweeping and feminine. He could fuss with the lines, but it would only muddy them. "Yeah, it's pretty good."

"Wonderful! Take a breath, Sawyer."

How did she know he needed the reminder? He no longer had panic attacks like he used to in high school, but sometimes he stopped breathing. He inhaled shallowly as a trio of tourists clattered over the cobblestones behind him on their ugly green rental bikes. The offensive sound refocused him.

"Want to hear some good news?" she asked softly.

"Yeah," he managed, sipping in the air and the smell of dank river water. "Operation Thea went well?"

"*Superb*. Thea had two moments where she felt beautiful."

He rather liked that Brooke said it that way. "That's what counts."

"Yeah. It really got me. Wait until you see her."

"Can't wait."

"And on the business front... I have four interested parties on the fabric side already."

He didn't ask how she'd managed to do that and help with Thea's makeover. Brooke was a multitasker, so much so it had always puzzled him that she'd taken to the French like she had, what with their incredible culture of living in the moment and finding contentment in most things in life. Balance, he imagined. She'd explode if she kept going like she did. He would too, he imagined.

"That's great, Brooke. By the way, I ran into Mr. Pinstripes —Jean Luc—and made sure he wasn't going to play with Thea's heartstrings. He checks out."

"Nice! All right, you're forgiven for losing track of time. We're going to a couple of boutiques to buy her some clothes. I'll send you our next stop if you still want to meet up."

"Aren't I one of her Fairy Godfathers? On my way."

He clicked off the phone and noted another shadow falling over him. Looking over his shoulder, he eyed the gray-haired woman wearing green capris and a white T-shirt.

"That's stunning!" She had a crisp British accent. "Is it for sale?"

His mood crashed as a spark of hope flared inside him. *Was* he good enough? He snapped the pad shut to hold back the age-old allure. It was like the serpent's whisper in the Garden of Eden. "No."

"Are you represented by a gallery?" She edged closer. "I love art. That's why I come to Paris. I'm Ivy Banks—"

He hastily stood and brushed past her. "It's not for sale, Ivy."

He was halfway to the stairs when he realized what he hadn't said.

He hadn't told her he wasn't an artist.

CHAPTER
FIFTEEN

Operation Thea had become one of the best days of Thea's life.

With her friends draping her in one piece of beautiful clothing after another at the first boutique, she felt like a princess. Madison had gone back to Nanine's to work on recipes, but Sawyer had just arrived. He melted her heart by framing her face in his hands and saying, "You've never been more beautiful. You're glowing, Thea. It looks good on you."

"It feels good." She kissed his cheek. "Brooke said you've finished the drawing. Can I see it?"

He suddenly looked sick. "I'd rather show Nanine first. Her opinion matters the most. You know how I get."

"I know," she said, wishing she knew what an Operation Sawyer looked like.

The boutique bell rang. They both turned, only to see Dean and Kyle stroll in.

"Holy shit, Thea!" Dean threw open his arms, almost knocking over a clothing display. "You look terrific. I love the hair."

"Me too," Kyle said, tipping her chin up when he reached her. "You look happy."

She hugged him. "I am! By the way, you have bread on command for the rest of your lives for helping me out with the Fairy Godmother Fund."

All of the guys frowned at her.

"That's not what this is all about," Kyle said, putting his hand on her arm.

"Don't piss me off," Sawyer added.

"I agree with them on principle, but I'll take the bread," Dean exclaimed with a wide grin. "We're going to have to keep buying you things, though. Rack it up."

Her heart was going to fly out of her chest from all this kindness. "I couldn't possibly do that!"

"Good one, Harris." Sawyer gave Dean a high five. "*Rack it up*. And I'll allow for the gendered use of godmother in this case."

"But I *am* interested in seeing what kind of lingerie the Fairy Godmother Fund bought." Dean pointed to the Simone Pérèle bag at her feet. "Gimme."

Her face heated. "Don't you dare!"

He started walking toward it. "Only a peek."

"Leave her alone, Dean," Kyle warned.

"Is nothing sacred?" Sawyer huffed.

"She's seen *me* in my underwear." Dean's mouth was twitching, but Thea couldn't tell if he was just joking or meant to follow through. She could totally see him pulling out her undies and holding them up to the light like he was examining diamonds or something.

"Rest assured, hers don't have dinosaurs on them," came Sawyer's response. "Step away from the lingerie, or I'm telling Madison to come back with her cleaver."

"Brutal, Doc," Kyle said, fighting a smile. "Thea, give me your shopping bag. I'll keep it from Dean's grubby hands."

She snatched it off the floor as Dean made a half-hearted play for it.

"I concede defeat," Dean said as Thea thrust the bag at Kyle. "But at least share what colors you picked. Tell me you used the fund for a sexy red bra."

She was going to die right there.

"What about black?" Dean pressed.

"You'd better go to the changing room," Sawyer told her. "He's not going to stop."

"Can I help that I'm curious? I'm not into her, so it's not weird."

"You're kidding, right?" Kyle gave him a slight push like guys do.

"Thea!" Brooke called from the lower level where the changing room was located. "Enough horsing around with the guys. Come try things on."

With a final glance at Dean, she flew down the stairs and fell into a marvelous adventure of modeling one outfit after another. When Brooke finally allowed the guys to come down, Dean whistled at regular intervals, Sawyer nodded his appreciation, and Kyle gave his brotherly approval.

Brooke, of course, pulled on her clothes to make sure they fit to perfection. A couple of times, she even had to show her how to wear a certain dress that had a sash threaded through the fabric. She was going to so suck at doing that herself. Then she realized she'd be around Brooke for the foreseeable future. Her friend would help her.

When it came time to choose, she told Brooke she would do two shirts, two pairs of pants, and two dresses. Brooke looked at the guys, who shook their heads in tandem. Her Fairy Godmothers insisted on buying all of the clothes she'd secretly wanted. The money thing still bothered her even as she kissed them all on the cheeks and told them she was grateful and would bake them thousands of loaves of bread, which they told her to stop saying in unison. She got objections from everyone but Dean, who ordered her famous chocolate bread while the others punched him playfully as he gave pretend howls of pain.

Two boutiques later, the men were calling for a drink and a snack. Thea agreed. They'd done plenty of shopping. Brooke texted Madison an invitation to join them.

When they arrived at a hip brasserie that stayed open all day, Thea noticed the shoe store across the way. She'd secretly been hoping to come across a display like this one, because she needed new shoes to go with her new clothes—tennis shoes wouldn't cut it. It would be like putting frosting on plain white bread.

And in the window was the cutest pair of navy heels with white polka dots. It was instant love. Wouldn't those shoes make her big feet look cute?

"Brooke," she whispered. "I see shoes that I like."

Her friend looked up from checking her email on her phone. "You do? I'd been trying to figure out a targeted shoe-op, knowing how much you hate shopping for them. Let's go."

"We'll be right back," Thea told the guys, who were talking to the hostess about an outside table for six. They each held several shopping bags.

Madison was exiting a car as they crossed the street. "Hey! You're going the wrong way."

"Thea's got the shoe bug," Brooke called back. "How many recipes did you work on while we shopped for clothes?"

"Three, but I'm not happy with them. I need to find some old cookbooks. Like super old. I've exhausted Nanine's copy of *Larousse Gastronomique*. Damn but I love that book. It's been my cooking bible since I went to *Le Cordon Bleu*, but I want more. Do you think the library would have any?"

"I have no idea," Brooke said as they walked to the store. "We can check."

Thea was barely hearing them. The shoes were shining in the window display, a whisper of hope.

"They'd suit you," Madison said when she reached them. "Come on. Let's go inside."

Thea looked down at her feet. Suddenly she was scared. Shoe shopping had never worked out for her. Stores, both retail and online, rarely carried her size in capital C Cute shoes. When she'd come across a so-called "cute" shoe and not the more common sneaker or basketball shoes—apparently shoe manufacturers thought you must play sports if you had big feet—she looked like one of Santa's elves in drag. They never looked right on her, and finding shoes that fit her arch were even harder. Returning shoes from online shopping was a job in and of itself. Those size six, seven, and eight girls had all the luck. Thea Rogers was cursed with bad shoe karma.

Brooke opened the door and took her arm gently. The pencil-thin brown-haired woman behind the counter had what Brooke called resting bitch face. Her *bonjour* was crisp and unfriendly. Thea instantly tensed up.

Brooke sailed ahead. "*Bon jour, madame.*"

Thea listened as her friend asked for the shoes Thea had admired in the window in her size in French—a forty-two.

The number eleven was bad enough, but *forty-two* sounded downright grotesque on the number scale. Like she had an overweight foot. She looked down at her feet. It was like she was wearing binoculars now. *Big bird feet*, she could hear old classmates jeer.

"It's impossible," the storekeeper answered dramatically in French, gesturing to Thea's feet.

Madison swore under her breath.

"Let's just go," Thea whispered, tucking one foot over the other in a hopeless attempt to hide them from view.

Brooke looked back at the clerk, her green eyes blazing

fire, and shot back a rapid-fire comment in French—her tone was so terse that the storekeeper turned silent.

For five seconds.

"No store can accommodate her size, madam," she finally responded in stone-cold French. "Perhaps a store in Germany. In the Alps. I believe some of the mountain women have feet that size."

The invisible whip of the woman's words crashed over Thea. Was it that obvious she had Germanic roots from the mountains? She wanted to die.

"What did you say?" Madison shot back in hostile French.

"Madison," Brooke said quietly in a hard tone in English. "I'll handle this."

Thea hunched her shoulders, staring at the floor. She should have known better. There were never pretty shoes for her.

Madison's gentle hand guided her to the front door, and the bell clanged in her ears as they exited.

"That bitch." Her friend's black high-tops slapped the sidewalk as they walked away. "Don't you dare let that woman ruin your day, Thea."

"I just want to go home." She embraced the numbness rising within her. She just wanted to crawl into her bed and curl up with a book and forget this had ever happened. She'd been stupid to dream it could be different—to think she could be elegant and beautiful.

"What's wrong?" Dean asked, jogging toward them.

Madison told him. Thea heard the story through the dark glass surrounding her. It didn't jar her to hear Dean swearing, to see him heading toward the store. Brooke met him on the sidewalk as she let herself out, her cheeks a red boil.

Thea herself couldn't summon any anger. She was too numb. She'd been here before. The dreaded days of back-to-school shopping swam through her head. Her mother dragging her to store after store, hoping they would find something. Settling for ugly white basketball high-tops at the athletic store, the only shoe in her size. Shoes the kids at school made fun of. Big Bird Rogers, they would jeer.

Operation Thea couldn't change reality. She was still a freak with big feet.

Why had she thought Paris would be any different?

CHAPTER
SIXTEEN

Operation Thea went on the offensive the next morning.

Dean surveyed the command center they'd set up in the monstrosity that was Nanine's beloved restaurant. They'd moved the kitchen table and chairs to the dining room to give them more space and privacy, all of them arrayed around it.

Thea hadn't come down since yesterday afternoon. He hated to think of her still sealed off in her room, but no one had been able to coax her out. Her hurt had run so deep she'd even declined dinner.

Self-esteem triggers were the worst, and Thea's longtime issues with the size of her feet, which had shaped her identity as a freak of nature in her mind, weren't simple matters, he knew. Everyone had something.

Changing things like hair was easy.

Accepting things one couldn't change and seeing them differently was tougher.

He knew from personal experience. Changing his view of himself as a poor kid who hadn't gotten any breaks growing up was his holy grail quest. Seeing Kyle again had made him realize that self-perception hadn't totally left him. Fun. He'd get right on that after helping Thea through this crisis.

Trouble was in the air. Thea had even mentioned canceling the date with Mr. Pinstripes tonight in the most depressed voice he'd ever heard from her. She'd walled herself off. Shut down.

He got it. He'd done the same every time his father had come home from work and started drinking, shouting at everything in the house, from him and his mother to his worthless Barcalounger and cold dinner.

Past shit sucked ass, and Thea was clearly knee-deep in hers.

Well, they had five people to wield shovels.

He started to dial another shoe store on his list.

"I have two shoe boutiques with six pairs in Thea's size!" Sawyer blurted out, making him pause in his dialing. "The clerk was sweet enough to text me the pics after I told her we were trying to find our girl last-minute shoes for a hot date. I say we pick them up and have Thea try them on. She said we can return them if they don't fit."

"It's nice to know there are decent people in the world," Madison said harshly. "I got another clerk who said finding that shoe size is *pas possible*. Jerk! They don't carry anything over a forty-one."

Dean surveyed the four stores he'd rung so far—all big fat shoe flops. "I got nothing here. I had no idea this was such a problem for girls."

"I've called a few custom shoemakers after I hit dead end after dead end, and they'd all need a few days to complete the order," Kyle said, cracking his neck. "They also need Thea to come in for a measurement."

"My update," Brooke said, tapping her fingernails on the table. "I decided to call a few fashion houses I know and am waiting for some pics on what they have from past shows. Models have big feet."

"*Stop this!*"

Everyone turned. Thea was standing in the doorway wearing tan cotton pants and a black oversized shirt—not her new clothes. Even her new hair and brows couldn't change the gray cast to her face or the defeated cut of her shoulders.

Dean looked at everyone else before raising his hands. "Okay, Thea, we can stop. But that's not what you said you wanted. You said you wanted a Paris makeover as part of your recipe for a delicious life, and I'd like to point out that it was going great until we hit Shoe Bitch yesterday."

"You're missing the point," Thea said, leaning against the doorframe. "It's not her. It's my feet. Why would anyone have my size in stock? I'm a freak. That's why kids used to call me names."

Brooke let out one of her dragon sighs, the kind where fire was forthcoming. "Thea, I love you. So much. And I know you're back in sackcloth because you're crushed. But don't let that bitch make you feel bad about yourself. Do you have any idea how many people have big feet? Tyra Banks wears a size twelve. Oprah wears an eleven—your size. So does Kate Winslet."

"And you know how much you love Kate Winslet's movies," Sawyer added before wincing when everyone looked at him. "Sorry, but she does. Me too for that matter. Don't you think Kate's beautiful, Thea?"

She lifted her shoulder. "Yeah."

Dean watched Brooke dart out of her chair. She was ready to pounce. "And do you know all the horrible things people have said about her body? People are cruel sometimes."

"People fucking suck," Madison said, turning her chair around and straddling it. "Are you really going to let some miserable pouty-faced Frenchwoman mess with you like this?"

"I know I shouldn't." She wiped away a tear as Brooke rubbed her arm. "I've been telling myself that as I lie in bed, not wanting to get up. I was like, 'you're being stupid, Thea. Sticks and stones.' I even tried to write in my journal. But she made me feel ugly—and that really hurts."

Her voice broke, crushing Dean, as she buried her face in her hands.

"Just when I was just starting to feel beautiful and excited about myself and my date with Mr. Pinstripes," she said hoarsely. "Now all I want to do is hide."

"Jean Luc thinks you're beautiful, Thea," Sawyer reminded her softly, making her drop her hands, her eyes glistening with tears. "I swear he was going to duel with me after I grilled him about his interest in you. The dude flat out told me that I was the one who was underplaying your charms if I was questioning his honor."

"That's really sweet, isn't it?" She looked down at the ground. "But I still don't feel good about myself or our date. And that's the worst. It was like…I was flying for the first time, and then I fell smack into the ground."

Dean's throat backed up, and he crossed to her. "Hey! We've all been made fun of for things we're sensitive about. Okay, maybe not Kyle."

"Shut up, Dean." Kyle rose and tucked his hands in his pants. "All right, if we're doing this, let's do it. You think I like being called a pretty boy? Or a dumb jock? When I was in school, I wanted to smash people's faces in for talking like that. But we grow up and get a thicker skin."

"Thea doesn't have a thick skin." Sawyer pushed his glasses up. "Neither do I, really. I've been called egghead. Loser. Teacher's pet. Chocolate milk. Kids can be mean. They grow up to be mean adults—like that shoe bitch—who then create mean kids when they breed, and there's where the world is. But Thea… You can't let it stop you from living your life or being you. Do you know what I did when the so-called cool kids made fun of me?"

She shook her head.

"I used to study harder and visualize how I was going to be a successful adult while they languished with their petty little groups getting nowhere. Because cruelty doesn't get you anywhere in life. Rousseau said: *What wisdom can you find that is greater than kindness?*"

"Nice one, Doc," Dean said, "but we digress. Here's where we are. Operation Thea is continuing because we love you. Yesterday you were glowing. You're going to feel that way again. If it takes a fucking gorgeous pair of shoes, I'll break into a cobbler and hand-tool them myself."

"Or steal them off a fashion model," Kyle added, "although I'd rather offer to buy them. No jail time that way. Unless you're planning on bailing me out."

The first hint of a smile appeared on her face. Victory was in the air.

"We're going to find you pretty shoes," Brooke said with a pointed finger punctuating the air. "You have my word. But what I really want is for you not to feel like a freak. Thea, we all have things we don't like about ourselves."

She scrutinized each of them before saying, "Like what?"

"My nose," Brooke answered. "Kids have said it's a Jew nose and other horrible things I don't want to repeat. Sometimes my nose is all I can see in the mirror. I wish it were cute and perky. Who's next?"

"What about my hair?" Sawyer offered. "You think I like looking like lightning struck me?"

"I thought all professors wanted Einstein hair," Dean quipped. "Okay, me. I don't like my ears. They're already big, and they keep growing. My old man had giant ears filled with ear hair. I'm terrified that will be me—minus the ear hair since I have personal grooming habits. *Kyle?* Anything?"

Kyle shot Dean an annoyed look before saying, "My feet

actually. My dad has hammer toes, and I'm starting to see mine change. I love to go barefoot, whether it's at home or the beach, and I don't want that to go away. Madison?"

She cocked her hip. "I hate being a woman. How's that?"

That brought Dean up short. "*Why?*"

"Because some men want to poke at us or talk shit to us or try to scare us. Since I was a kid, I thought it would be easier to be a boy and a whole hell of a lot safer. What's the worst thing that can happen to a guy? He gets punched. In my neighborhood, a woman is the zebra for the lion. And the size of my tits doesn't help."

Dean's eyes wanted to go there at the reference—it was like primordial code: women and breasts—but he shut it down. He had the impression they were big, but he didn't look at her like that. Never had. "Jesus, Madison. You've never said anything like that. Not even back when we were roommates the first time around."

Kyle walked over to her, his face crestfallen. "I'm going to ask because you talked about wanting to feel safer. Because everyone here cares about you. You don't have to answer if you don't want to or you can tell me to buzz off. Were you raped?"

They all fell silent, but Dean was glad Kyle had had the balls to ask. He hadn't been the only one thinking it.

She worked her mouth for way too long before saying, "No. But it's been really close a few times."

Thea brushed at more tears. "I feel really stupid being this upset about my feet after hearing that. Madison, I'm so sorry."

"Me too," Brooke said quietly.

"Is there anything we can do?" Dean asked, holding out his hand to her before letting it fall to his side.

Madison rubbed her thighs. "I'm fine. Mostly. Kyle's right, you grow a thicker skin each time. Or people like me do. Thea, you and Sawyer get hurt and want to escape.

Growing up, if I did that, it would only have made everything worse."

"Me too," Kyle said. "I learned not to show things bothered me. Some people feed on that in a bad way."

"Yeah," Dean said, remembering his father standing over him, shouting at him. He'd wanted to shout back time and time again, so much he'd bit his cheek hard enough to taste blood. But he knew his father would have hit him, which he'd sometimes done, or turned his fists on his mother. "Sometimes ignoring it or walking away is the best strategy—even when you want to strike back."

"I just keep going," Brooke said. "Because if you stop, that's when all the hurt and shit rises up, waiting to put its claws in you and take you down. God! I thought life was supposed to get easier when we got older."

"Or start to make sense," Sawyer added in despair. "I still don't understand why people are so mean or why there are so many of them in the world."

"Me either," Dean confessed. "But we're not that way."

"We're lucky to have each other," Thea said in a voice that sounded more like herself. "I'm sorry if I seemed ungrateful or overreacted."

"No one knows what you're talking about right now." Dean was glad that put a smile back on her face. "And we *are* lucky to have each other. Now, how about we find our little sister here some shoes and then make sure she's ready for her date tonight?"

"Before we move on to other things, I just want to say one thing." Thea wiped another tear away as a heartbreaking smile broke across her face. "I love you guys. Thanks for being my friends."

Dean pulled her to him and rocked her as everyone walked over and gave in to an uncharacteristic group hug, Madison included.

"We love you too," he said, kissing her cheek. "Come on. Let's finish Operation Thea."

She made a small sound which ended with a chuckle. "Operation Thea is clearly a work in progress."

"Aren't we all, sweetie," he said as everyone nodded, "aren't we all."

CHAPTER
SEVENTEEN

Nanine Laurent decided her best strategy was to check herself out of the hospital.

Her doctor tried to argue with her, but like other bombastic men she'd crossed swords with, he soon gave up under her withering stare. How could anyone else purport to know how she felt? she'd told her doctor as she tapped her chest. Only she knew.

Her tests had come back fine, and he'd done what he could. Now it was up to her. She would take her daily aspirin, but her best medicine was being with her Courses and taking care of her restaurant and whatever other trouble might be lurking in the shadows.

Yes, she would come back for checkups, but sitting any longer in a hospital bed wasn't going to make her feel better. In fact, she might as well put one foot in the grave if she languished there much longer under those rough, worn white sheets.

His clipped *good luck* as he left told her she'd won. Soon she was being discharged, dressed in the slightly wrinkled clothes she'd worn upon arrival. Her only saving grace was the fact that she smelled of Chanel No. 5 and her color was enhanced by her darkly lined brows and lipstick-red lips. More like herself.

When the cab she'd taken from the hospital deposited her in front of her restaurant, she pressed her hand to her aching heart as she beheld its naked frame. The Nanine's she'd created was like her very self: stripped naked of everything it had been and forced to be reborn into something new. She took a moment to gather herself on the sidewalk, closing her eyes and letting the afternoon sunlight wash over her face.

Her father used to say, what more did anyone need than the sunshine, a good meal, and working with one's passion? She could suddenly see the yellow mustard fields he'd walk in Lyon as he hummed an old Edith Piaf song to himself. Brooke would call this visualization, but Nanine's mother had always referred to them more simply as good thoughts, the kind to lift any downtrodden spirit.

A slow smile started on her face as she opened her eyes and beheld her beloved neighborhood. Its familiar sights and smells wrapped around her in love. The faint aroma of baguettes from the patisserie around the corner made her think of Thea. The street was quiet with everyone tucked away in their homes for lunch. Well, everyone save the two female tourists walking toward her wearing New York T-shirts and designer jeans.

"Excuse me?" the younger blonde asked. "Do you speak English?"

She thought about lying, but she needed all the good karma she could take at the moment. "Yes."

"Do you know what happened to Nanine's? I can't find anything online about why it's closed. Have you eaten there? It's one of the best restaurants in Saint-Germain."

Nanine put a finger to her lips. Her father used to say signs came when they were most needed, like the rain did to the fields during dry spells. Funny, how much she'd thought of her father this morning. Perhaps he was walking with her in spirit, knowing she needed his guidance yet again. "It is closed for renovation at the moment, I'm afraid."

"Oh, darn," the brunette tourist replied, reminding her again of Thea and her conservative exclamations. "That's too bad."

"I hear it will be better than ever when it reopens," Nanine told them. "Do you have a favorite dish?"

"The *boeuf bourguignon*," they both blurted out at the same time.

Her heart settled back where it belonged. "That is one of my favorites too. Enjoy your stay in Paris."

The two women waved in that very American way Nanine found charming. Again, she thought of Thea. Brooke said they had kicked off Operation Thea and created a Fairy Godmother Fund. Oh, her Courses. How she loved them.

Head held high, she went around the back to her kitchen to face the music. The door was open, and given the gorgeous day, Nanine could understand why. Latin music painted a sultry atmosphere as she entered her kitchen. Thea and Madison had their backs to her, their aprons knotted around their waists.

"It is good to see you here, my loves," she called out in French, setting off a sweet, nostalgic melody from her prized chandelier.

Thea and Madison swung around. First Course already had a giant smile on her sweetheart face while Madison merely leaned back against the counter, her eyes banked with rare happiness.

Nanine had a moment to take in Thea's new hair and visage before she opened her arms. "Ah, *ma petite*. You look even more beautiful. These changes are right for you, I think."

"Let's not talk about me," her dear girl replied in English, rushing over. "It's so good to see you, Nanine, but why didn't you tell us you were coming home? We would have picked you up."

Thea's embrace was too gentle, too cautious—as if Nanine would break apart. That would not do.

"Nanine wanted to do it on her own, Thea," Madison said, pushing off the counter and sauntering toward them. "It's what independent women do. Right, Nanine?"

"*Exactemente*." She hugged Madison, her pride satisfied because Fifth Course's embrace was the usual combination of affection and love. "I wanted to make it clear from the beginning. I am not an invalid."

"No one thinks that, Nanine," Thea assured her.

Nanine scoffed and raised a brow.

Madison only laughed. "A few people might want to wrap you up in a blanket and ply you with a cup of *thé verveine*."

First Course winced. "Guilty."

"I don't mean just you." Madison pointed to the ceiling. "A couple of others upstairs might test your patience."

"They'll understand the way of it soon enough," she answered, feeling her imperial air return, knowing it was the power from her very own kitchen returning to her.

Madison gave a crisp nod. "Nanine, I was just walking Thea through an idea I had for the menu. Do you want me to run it by you? It's early but I think I'm onto something. Let's see if you agree. Then you should find Sawyer. He thinks he has the design right."

"Of course he's beset with insecurities," Thea said with a sigh. "He never sees how great he is."

Nanine ruffled her new hair and took in her slender brow line. She was still Thea. Only Brooke's helpers had refined her beauty subtly—like a Frenchwoman. "Neither do you. I will find him after you tell me your idea."

"Bread," Madison began, taking a chef's stance with her arms folded behind her back. "Nanine, I've been looking at old recipes, but I've also been reading everything I can on the current Paris restaurant scene. There's a lot of chatter about it not being like it used to be."

"I have read that as well," Nanine said, leaning back against the counter.

"Do you want to sit?" Thea asked with worry lining her face.

She strove for patience, and her chandelier uttered a few notes in solidarity. "No. I want to stand in my kitchen and talk about the new menu."

Madison nodded. "The talk has traction, Nanine, and one item in particular caught my attention. People are saying it's hard to find good bread. In Paris."

She narrowed her eyes. "Though it hurts my Parisian soul to say it, I agree. There are many reasons for this, of course, but it is not right that it should be so. Bread is the soul of this country."

"I agree." Madison crossed her arms over her chest now. "And people come to Paris to eat bread. It's one of the cities where you give yourself permission to indulge. Even those carb-centric maniacs. Nanine, I think we bring it back in a new way and create a menu around it, especially with Thea as our bread guru. We serve perfectly paired artisan breads with the meal. I know it's not traditional, but it's something no one is doing from what I can tell, and it's grounded in French culture."

Nanine watched as Thea folded her arms behind her back and took a wider stance. A chef's stance. Like Madison had done only moments earlier. "We both think it's a powerful theme for the new menu."

"Give me a for instance."

Madison clenched her hands, her intensity palpable. "*Pain d'Epices* with *foie gras* to start. Midnight black bread with *boeuf bourguignon*. French thyme and gruyere bread with *pot-au-feu au veau*. Mushroom tart with roasted tomato basil bread. Fennel chicken with caramelized orange bread. *Côte de boeuf* with fig bread. I haven't settled on the right bread for *canard aux cerises*—maybe a mustard leek bread—"

"I thought those flavors would be great with the duck course," Thea interrupted.

"Lastly," Madison continued after a pause, "I think we have a limited array of stuffed pumpkin for two. We can make it seasonal but something with Toulouse sausages entices me. We'd serve it with a walnut apricot bread. Eye-catching *and* mouthwatering."

"Two characteristics that make an excellent menu, as does the comfort appeal of superb savory artisan breads," Nanine said, letting the ideas simmer around her as though she were the soup bones in a broth pot.

The flavors of each *plat* swirled on her tongue as if summoned, and she closed her eyes to bring each dish to the halls of her mind. Her girls remained quiet as she inhaled deeply, imagining the rich fragrance of the food. A menu must also blend in fragrance, allowing each dish's aroma to harmonize with the others in the dining room. A true chef understood this.

"Perhaps we serve *gougères* as well," Nanine added, seeing herself reaching up onto her mother's counter for a freshly baked savory cheese puff when she was a child. Good memories. The kind she wanted to bring to every menu.

"We thought about *gougères*," Madison said.

"But they have to be served immediately," Thea added, "although I do love them."

"*Soufflés* need to be served immediately too, and yet my staff has always managed it."

Madison lifted a shoulder. "I gave up doing *soufflés* and chocolate lava cakes in my first couple years. The timeframe from oven to plate is tighter than I like. But you know your staff, and it's your menu."

"It is *our* menu this time," she said, putting her hand on Madison's forearm. "And it seems you two have been hard at work, although I expected no less. Your ideas are *superb*. Do you have your draft menu written down?"

"*Oui*, Chef," Madison responded.

Nanine touched her cheek and watched the vulnerability and love spark in Madison's golden eyes. "There is magic in the kitchen again, and I am happy to see it. Thea, tell me more of your thoughts."

She stood a little taller. "I think Madison is onto something. People love bread. Especially here. Make it a small portion, perfectly paired, as you would a *plat* with wine, and you have something very special, something I believe people will be lining up to savor. Especially since we'll use our sourdough starters in some of them."

"What about dessert?" Nanine rubbed her hands together, calling forth her creative fire.

"We didn't get that far yet," Madison said, "but I'll bet Thea has ideas swirling."

"Poached pears with crystallized ginger bread," Thea said after looking at Madison. "Cherries Jubilee with cinnamon swirl bread. Granny Smith apple tart with a chocolate fudgy bread. Nanine, it'll be delicious."

She walked over to the young woman and caressed the back of her head. "Which one, *ma petite*?"

"Oh, all of them!" Thea laughed at herself. "My tummy is already rumbling."

Nanine found her own hunger had returned during their discussion. Then again, she was not shocked by this. Her hunger for life was back, being here where she belonged. With the family she had chosen for herself. "My entire being is dancing with ideas. What about roasted pork with a rhubarb glaze? What bread would we pair it with, Thea?"

Her newly delicate brows slammed together. "Something light. Oh, yes. A lemon poppyseed bread to counterbalance all the richness of the *plat*."

Nanine pursed her lips. "A unique choice. Inspired even. Let's start making the pairings. Can you have three of the dishes and accompanying breads cooked for me to try tomorrow?" It was ambitious, but she knew these women. They would eagerly pull it off with aplomb.

The women exchanged a look before saying, "*Oui*, Chef," with a smile.

"*Excellent*," Nanine said, deciding she would allow herself to sit down now and have a *café crème*. "Madison, would you find Sawyer and tell him to come down with his drawing? It is better to see everyone in stages, I believe."

She didn't reveal that it was part of her plan for conserving her energy. She could feel the fatigue starting to grate at her skin slowly, like a zester steals the color from a lime, making it white. She straightened her shoulders. She had faced fatigue before and won, standing in the kitchen for twenty hours on end. This time she would manage it with more care. There was too much at stake. She needed to speak to Jean Luc soon as well.

"Sawyer will be here *tout de suite*, Nanine," Madison said after a moment of studying her, departing from the kitchen with the comforting sound of her high-tops slapping the kitchen floor.

"We have only a short moment alone," Nanine said, walking toward the kitchen table she had eaten at with her staff nearly every single day. Suddenly she realized everything was clean, and she imagined she had Brooke to thank for it. "Come sit with me."

"Good thing we put the table back." Thea sat across from her, her heart in her rich brown eyes. "The others moved it for a project. But that's not important now. Can I get you anything, Nanine?"

"In a moment. I would say Operation Thea has been successful. How do you feel, *ma petite*?"

She touched her hair. "I love my new look. Of course, I blew it all when I had a meltdown after a shoe salesperson told me it was impossible to find shoes for my big feet. But I'm mostly over it now."

Nanine arched her brow. "Are you? A woman's true contentment comes from the inside."

Thea studied her hands. "I know. But it's like Dean said. We're all a work in progress."

"Second Course has moments of great wisdom," Nanine agreed. "You have always been beautiful, Thea. Inside and out. That *is* why Jean Luc has asked you to dinner."

Her mouth parted. "Brooke told you? It's still a little confusing. I mean, I'm me—"

A rude noise erupted from her. "You cannot know how he sees you, but I will tell you. He sees you as I see you. Thea, I have always hoped you two might meet."

Thea seemed to fall back against her chair. "You're kidding!"

She chuckled at the Americanism. "*Jamais.* Now I think I hear Sawyer's footsteps as well as the soft murmur my chandelier gives when he's around."

"What sound does it give when I'm around?"

Smiling, she took her hand. "Like a baby laughing for the first time."

Nanine thought of her granddaughter's laugh and felt her heart wrench.

"I love that," Thea whispered, squeezing her hand.

"Will you give Sawyer and me a few minutes alone before making me a *café crème*?" she asked, breathing deeply to resettle her heart.

"Are you supposed to have coffee?"

Catching her frown, she simply nodded. "It won't kill me, Thea."

First Course grimaced, but she rose from the table as Sawyer entered with an art pad in hand. They shared a look before Thea left. Then Fourth Course came forward and sat down, his quiet professor-like manner ever apparent.

"You should have let us pick you up, Nanine," he began after adjusting his gold-rimmed glasses.

The better to see her, she realized, before gesturing to his art pad. "I hear you have the drawing finished."

His hand tensed before he flipped it open, moving past a number of drawings before he found the one he was looking for. Her breath caught as she regarded his creation, and her chandelier stirred as though a whisper had touched its crystals. The swathes of apricot grabbed her attention, along with the wine-colored drapes and shell-white tablecloths. The seating was enchanting—a combination of booths, banquettes, and individual tables, all arranged in an almost carnival-like dance of invitation.

Her eyes wandered over the individual panels marked by flower-patterned stucco and gold-edged mirrors before feasting on the warm lighting from simple but sumptuous chandeliers and lamppost light stations. It was modern Belle Epoque, the kind of Paris everyone kept tucked in their heart.

Nanine wanted to be there every night. She knew she would not be the only one.

A good restaurant was a magical setting one remembered for special events such as a first kiss or a wedding day. He had drawn such a place.

"It is absolutely perfect, Sawyer," she whispered in French, the language of true emotion. "*This* will be the new Nanine's, and everyone will want to come and eat here. You have outdone yourself, my darling Fourth Course."

He blew out a shallow breath. "You're probably being a little nice to me."

"Never. I love it! *This* is the scene of my rebirth and that of Nanine's. She might be old, but she is timeless. She is still here. Like me." She touched the edges of the paper, needing to feel the texture, the heart of his drawing. "Thank you, *mon cher*."

When she extended her hand to him, he clasped it firmly. "No improvements?" he asked, clearing his throat.

She shook her head in complete confidence. "No. I know my heart. Clearly so do you. Like a great artist does."

He rolled his eyes, but she did not miss the emotion in them.

She was smiling when she heard a shuffling of steps in her kitchen, ones she did not recognize. Her chandelier clanged a warning that spiked fear in her heart. "Someone has entered through the back," she said, rising. "Come and see with me."

He put his hand on her arm. "Let me go."

Wanting to honor his protectiveness, she nodded. But she cocked her ear after he left. Voices raised in French—his and another man's—before they died away. Sawyer appeared again with a foreboding frown on his face, holding a single piece of paper.

Her heart gave a wild pang. Whatever was on that paper had the power to destroy her. Or try. Again.

She took a deep breath. "Please tell me. Spare no detail."

"Nanine," he said in an unusually calm voice, the kind a doctor might use before telling someone a loved one had died. "I'm afraid the man says you sold your entire cave to him and he's come to collect."

"My cave? But that is not—" Gasping, she pressed her hand to her heart. "*Mon Dieu!* Jeremy!"

That cave held the collection of a lifetime. Wine. Brandy. Cognac. *Digestifs.* Rare items. Reserved bottles. From all over France. Some were not made anymore. Combined with her food, her collection was the heart and soul of Nanine's. Her daughter would know that, as much as she would know its material value. Estimated around a hundred thousand euros. But in the frantic screaming in her head, she heard a different word: *Irreplaceable.*

She stood stiffly on shaking legs. She could not take this news sitting down. "What did you tell them?"

He gripped the paper. "I told them you had just returned from the hospital and to come back."

He waited another beat, ramping up her fear. Oh, this was worse than she could have imagined.

"Nanine. He has your signature on the bill of sale and says he's already paid the money. We need to call Jean Luc and find a way to stop this."

But Jean Luc said nothing could be done if they had her signature.

Black spots swam before her eyes as Sawyer shouted her name.

CHAPTER
EIGHTEEN

Jean Luc arrived minutes after Sawyer called him.

Thea watched as he walked swiftly through the back door of the restaurant in another one of his signature pinstriped suits, this one in gray with black stripes. Their eyes met. The chandelier gave a lyrical melody, calmer than her pounding heart.

Reaching her, he kissed her Parisian style before studying her face, his own a composite in severe angles of both beauty and anger. "It is dark news, *mon chou*, but you have made some changes, I see. I adore the hair, and I look forward to telling you how beautiful you are when we are alone—"

"Maybe we should postpone our date," she interrupted in a flash. "I don't feel good about leaving her right now. She almost fainted."

His mouth tightened. "Of course. Come, we can speak more of it after I review this paper."

He took her elbow in a sweetly supportive way, and all she wanted to do was lean into his strength. Thea led him to the staff kitchen table where the others were doing what Nanine most assuredly did not want them to do: fuss. She had a *café crème* in her hand, one Thea had not made, and Brooke was rubbing her back in what was meant to be a comforting motion. Dean flanked her other side, a foreboding scowl on his face. Sawyer was sitting across from them while Madison and Kyle stood against the wall, arms locked against their chests to contain their fury.

Nanine lifted her cup bravely. "I said I needed something stronger, Jean Luc, but I was ignored."

He brought Thea to the empty seat next to Sawyer and got her situated with a gentleness that stopped her breath before crossing to where Nanine was sitting. Dean vacated his seat, and Jean Luc lowered into it—Nanine giving Thea a look before she greeted their guest. "I can understand why. You are only just out of the hospital. Now, let me see what was brought earlier."

Sawyer handed over the paper. "I'm afraid it's pretty straightforward."

"Would you like a café, Jean Luc?" Brooke asked quietly.

"*Oui. S'il vous plaît.*" He drew out some reading glasses— ones Thea couldn't help but think made him appear sad and handsome all at once.

"I'll make it," Thea said, rising from her chair as Brooke didn't seem to want to leave Nanine's side. She understood. She wished she could wave a magic wand and make this all go away. What would they do if the contents of the cave were lost? Nanine's beverage selection was famous. Without it, how would they begin again?

Madison and Kyle followed her to the coffee machine.

"Are you planning on canceling your date with Jean Luc?" Madison demanded in an undertone.

She nodded, her heart in her throat. "I told him it might be better to postpone it."

"Why?" Kyle prodded. "Nanine would want you to go."

"Are you ganging up on me?"

"No, we're looking out for you," Kyle said before Madison could speak. "Thea, all this crap that Nanine is dealing with isn't going to go away quickly. We have confirmation of that now. I—we—don't want you postponing the good stuff."

"You deserve it," Madison added. "It's part of Operation Thea."

She pressed her hand to her mouth, feeling her emotions well up. "Nanine is more important. How can I just leave?"

Kyle put a hand on her arm. "That's why you have to go out with Jean Luc. Thea, we all need a win here."

She blinked at them. "What?"

"Thea, you're our only hope," Madison said, her lips twitching.

"I can't believe you used a *Star Wars* reference," Kyle said, ruefully shaking his head.

"I personally thought it was inspired," Madison said. "But let's get back to Thea."

She glared at them. "How am I supposed to go out with him and not think about Nanine the whole time?"

"He cares about Nanine too," Kyle said, touching her arm again. "And clearly he cares about you. A guy doesn't escort a woman to her seat unless he's interested in her."

"You noticed that too?" Thea asked.

"He was a gentleman." Madison nudged her aside and finished making the coffee. "After that and what Sawyer said, I'm all for him."

She fumbled with the saucer as she handed it off to Madison. "What did Sawyer say?"

"That he went all big brother on Mr. Pinstripes, and Jean Luc passed the test with an A-plus, that's what." Madison passed her the finished coffee. "Now take that coffee into your guy and smile."

"But I want to know more about the test!" she protested.

Kyle snorted. "No way. You'll freak."

"Totally freak," Madison agreed, taking her free arm and leading her back to the kitchen table as Kyle tailed them.

When she placed the café beside Jean Luc, he absently reached for her hand and squeezed it with a quiet *merci* as he continued to study the page. Madison made a gesture like *see* from her perch as Thea rubbed the place where he'd touched her. A few of her other friends shot her knowing looks, which she did her best to ignore.

He drank his coffee, his face betraying nothing. Thea imagined he'd need a good poker face, being a lawyer. All lawyers on TV shows had one, and she imagined that was at least somewhat based on real life.

When he finally finished the document, he put his hands over it, almost as if to cover the ugliness inside. "As I told you, scamming in France is not like it is in America. If someone uses your identity to do something, if they have your signature, it is over. Even electronically, like this one. I have seen it, but I must ask. It is yours, yes?"

Thea watched Nanine's lips tremble before she nodded.

"A cave like yours is worth more than the money they paid," Jean Luc continued. "While we can try and reason with the buyer—and offer to repay them—I cannot know until we speak whether they will part with such a treasure."

"Because the collection itself is priceless," Nanine protested, her throat working with emotion. "Adrienne knew this. Bernard and I toured all over France together to find some of those rare and special producers. But it began earlier, from the first moment I decided to open my restaurant. I knew I had to have the kind of wine that would make critics take notice, and it paid off. We can never replace what was lost. Never! It is like taking part of the soul of this restaurant."

Thea clenched her hands as Nanine's anguish washed through the room.

"I will visit the buyer and do my best." Jean Luc sipped

his café. "My heart aches for you, Nanine. This is a grave injustice."

Nanine's eyes fired. "As you say. I have lived my life with honor. I never imagined this kind of wrong. And from my own blood."

He set his cup down. "Now, I will go and do what I can on this matter. Thea. May I see you for a moment privately?"

Nanine glanced her way. "If I may ask, Jean Luc, where are you taking our dear Thea tonight?"

He glanced Thea's way before answering. "It might be better to postpone. You will want to have your Courses around you."

"Nonsense!" She rose fluidly. "You and Thea will go as you had agreed. I will not have it another way."

"But Nanine—"

"Thea," Nanine interrupted, "it will do my heart well to have you go. I could not bear for you to thwart your happiness because of such tragedy. That would be an injury to my heart as much as yours and Jean Luc's. Please go, *ma petite*."

She nearly slumped. "All right. I'll go, but only because you say it will help your heart."

Nanine nodded crisply. "Excellent. Now, where are you going tonight?"

Jean Luc paused a moment, meeting Thea's eyes, before answering, "Chez Marie."

"One of my favorite places when I venture out for a meal myself," Nanine commented.

"I know," he said with a soft smile. "Thea?"

When he extended his hand to her, she rose and walked over to him. His touch was solid, and she felt emotional as he led her to the back of the kitchen.

"You are all right with Nanine demanding we go out tonight?" he asked, studying her.

She nodded. "I wish this had never happened."

"Me too." He gazed at her softly. "But perhaps she is right.

We can help each other put this horrible matter on the shelf. I would not wish a shadow to cover our first date, but I do not want to wait until it is entirely gone either. How long that might be, one can never know."

They were in for a long haul, Kyle had said earlier. But this was life, she realized. She remembered the *Hard-to-find ingredients* on her recipe card for living the fullest life—self-confidence and courage. This was where they came in. She needed to add hope and faith to that list.

He smiled warmly. "I will pick you up at eight as we agreed, if that is all right."

Paris time. "Perfect."

"*À tout à l'heure, ma chérie*," he said, kissing both her cheeks and walking out through the back door.

She lifted her hand to her face as she walked back to join her friends, only to pull up short.

All five of her roommates were standing in the doorway.

"He *definitely* has my vote after that display," Madison declared.

"Were you there the whole time?" she asked, lowering her hands.

"Yeah," Dean said. "We were worried you might need more convincing. Jean Luc knew we were here, but he didn't look over once. Some guys—myself included—might have balked."

"He passed another test," Brooke said with a sly smile. "Not embarrassed to show affection in front of your friends."

"He's cool." Sawyer brushed his shoulder. "Super cool."

Thea strode forward, her cheeks hot. "I want to know more about this test you gave him, Sawyer. You were very short on details, and so were Madison and Kyle."

"Not on your life, sweetie." He held his hands up and walked backward. "I'm going to distract Nanine with more talk about the renovation."

"Good idea," Kyle said. "Madison, can you help keep her distracted while Jean Luc does his thing?"

"Yeah. We can talk about menu stuff. I have some ideas to run by her. Thea, you joining me until you have to get all dolled up?"

"Speaking of. Who's going to help Thea get ready for her date tonight?" Dean asked, lifting his hand.

Two other hands went up. She'd expected Brooke to volunteer, but not Madison, and based on the looks she saw around the room, she wasn't the only one.

"What?" Madison cocked her hip. "I'm going to toughen Thea up for a night out. First dates make you a wreck if you're totally into the guy. And Thea, you are as gooey as your cinnamon rolls."

"Same's true if you're into the girl, by the way," Dean added, making a crazy face. "Completely nutso. I even got my hair cut to impress a girl."

"Color me surprised." Madison fitted her hands on her hips.

"Thea, consider what I'm about to tell you about the dating part of Operation Thea," Brooke said, tapping her fingernails. "We need to talk a little about the French approach to dating. They do it differently. It's more casual. A getting to know each other, like friends, in the beginning."

"But that's perfect for Thea, right?" Dean looked around at them all. "Serious, but no pressure. Friends chilling."

Thea relaxed. "When you put it that way, it's not as intimidating, is it?"

Brooke waved her hand. "Where's your recipe book? You're going to want to write some of this down."

Sawyer looked at Kyle. "We're in too. We can't let Thea's only impressions about dating, men, and French men come from you three. Tonight is supposed to be one of the best nights of your life as part of Operation Thea."

"I think Nanine should give her input," Thea said cautiously. "She is French, after all."

That made everyone smile, and she realized one of the greatest truths about friendship.

Friends helped each other through the best *and* worst moments in their lives.

CHAPTER
NINETEEN

Hours later, Thea was clutching the small pink purse Brooke had insisted she borrow while waiting for Jean Luc inside the front of the restaurant.

The scent of her perfume was a potent reminder of how big this moment was for her. She'd brought the perfume Nanine had given her for Christmas ten years ago to Paris, not imagining she'd use it. Back home, it had always seemed too extravagant, out of place. But she hadn't been able to ignore the urge. It was Fragonard's *Etoile*, and Nanine had reminded her after she'd put it on that she was more of a star than she knew. The scent was fruity and flowery. Like her. She hoped he would like it.

But not as much as she hoped he would like her shoes. Sure, her dress was beautiful, and she'd loved it from the moment she'd put on what Brooke had called a classic hit in navy with its cap sleeves and tight square-cut bodice with a skirt that fell loosely to mid-calf. Only, all she could think about was her robin's egg blue pumps with the metallic silver heels. A model had worn these shoes for a fashion show! Now she was. Her. Thea Rogers from Nowheresville.

The others were lounging in various states behind her on a

set of new casual dining chairs Brooke had had delivered along with a few bistro tables. Madison had prepared *boeuf bourguignon* for the roommates—her answer to Nanine's request for comfort food—and all of them but Thea had enjoyed it before Nanine retired early.

"I'm so nervous I could get sick," she said, tapping her new shoe on the floor. "I now can understand why some women don't eat on dates."

"That's not the only reason women don't eat," Kyle drawled.

"Right?" Dean added, and they fist-bumped.

Was this another dating item she should write down? She had four pages filled with advice from her friends but was as confused as ever. It didn't help that Sawyer thought Jean Luc might surprise them by not going the classic French casual hangout route as was customary.

Nanine refused to have an opinion, only cautioning Thea to watch and listen to the signals *Jean Luc* was giving her. Not some fictional Frenchman they had in their heads. It was them going on the date—Thea and Jean Luc—after all, and not a couple of prototypes. Thea liked that, but she had to admit she wasn't sure what that meant either.

"Oh, don't go *there*," Brooke said with exasperation. "The French don't have that rule."

"Thea likes to eat." Sawyer smiled at her. "I personally like a woman who enjoys food."

"Tells you something about her," Kyle added. "Usually the women I date don't, and it makes me uncomfortable."

"How about we table old dating stories right now," Madison broke in. "That's the last thing Thea needs to think about. But at least she's already broken in her shoes from all her pacing and foot tapping."

She stopped her nervous gesture immediately and then gasped as Jean Luc parked a sleek silver sports car in front of the restaurant and hit the hazards. He exited in one graceful line, making her heart thump. She watched him walk around the car to the passenger side, from which he pulled out a bouquet of blush-pink roses.

Her heart sighed. Flowers! He'd brought her flowers. In the waning light, she found herself struggling to swallow. He looked gorgeous in another navy pinstriped suit with a shockingly white dress shirt.

"Oh my gosh! He's here!" she murmured.

"Perfectly on time," Brooke said. "Score one for not being casual."

"It's basic courtesy," Sawyer added.

Suddenly everyone was standing behind her, Dean's hand resting casually on her shoulder. "He's got roses for you, Thea."

"Yeah," was all she could manage.

Madison whistled. "So, he's not going casual! Sawyer, you win the bet."

They'd bet on this?

"You know, I never thought I'd like a man in a suit," Madison continued, "but my God can that man wear one."

"*Uh-huh,*" Brooke breathed out, putting her hand on Thea's other shoulder.

"His taste in cars is good too," Dean murmured with an audible sound of pleasure.

"Yeah," Kyle replied. "I might whimper."

"And he can quote Voltaire," Sawyer added. "If I were gay, I'd be into him."

"Me too," Dean agreed, and this time they fist-bumped.

"Stop that." Thea started tapping her shoe again. "You're making me more nervous."

Then Jean Luc looked directly at her through the windows and gave a dashing smile. "Oh, gosh, he's seen us!" she cried as she lurched away from the window.

Dean started laughing. "Let's all duck down and pretend he didn't catch us staring."

"We will not," Brooke said as Dean sunk to his haunches playfully. "We'll be cool."

Madison tipped Dean onto his butt with a gentle shove. "Some of us. Others can act like morons."

Kyle helped Dean up. "Come on, boys. We're about to do another big brother routine."

"*What?*" Thea gasped as they strode toward the door like a unit.

"Oh, let them," Madison said, taking her arm when she started to run after them. "Builds character. Now, you… Take a breath."

"Thea, your face is flaming," Brooke said, fanning it. "Breathe."

"I'm trying!" She put her hands on her ribs. "I feel like I'm wearing a corset all of a sudden."

"Totally normal," Madison said. "In Spanish, people talk about love like it's *locura. Madness.* So true."

"Yeah, but we're in France, so let's drop the madness part," Brooke advised, rubbing Thea's back comfortingly.

"Right!" Madison grinned with a spark of mischief in her eyes. "In France, they talk about *la petite mort.*"

"The little death is an orgasm, you idiot." Brooke swatted at her, but Madison danced back.

Thea was glad to see Madison had lost her badass edge with them, but did she need to talk about orgasms right now? OMG!

"True," Madison said with a laugh. "Okay, I'm stopping now. I think I swallowed one of Dean's teasing pills."

Brooke shot Madison another look. "No, you're starting to remember you can act silly among friends." Then she shifted her attention to Thea. "You're going to be fine. Just breathe and be yourself."

"Hey, Thea!" Dean sang. "Your *suitor* is here."

"I didn't know Dean liked Jane Austen," Thea said with a gulp.

"They're enjoying this way too much." Brooke led her gently toward the kitchen. "Remember deep breaths. And *smile.*"

By the time she entered the kitchen, her heart was pounding in her ears. Then Jean Luc smiled again, and she felt her knees turn soft. Brooke's firm grip brought her back to reality.

"Thea! Jean Luc is in a car club where a group of people share a car to reduce their carbon footprint. It's so cool." Sawyer held out his fist to Jean Luc, who eyed it quizzically before warily bumping it.

She only nodded as her date—her date!—strode over to her and kissed her flaming cheek. "You look beautiful, *chérie.* Your friends took the roses for you and promised to put them in water."

"Kyle's getting a vase right after you leave," Dean quipped, making Madison snort behind her.

"We should go," Thea said in a rush. If they kept teasing her, her cheeks were going to rival the pomegranates Madison had bought earlier.

Jean Luc nodded, his mouth pursed as if trying to hold back laughter. "You all have my number if you need to reach me," he said with a glance over his shoulder to her big brothers.

"We expect her to be back by eleven unless you text us about a change in your plans," Dean said.

Thea's mouth dropped open.

"I'm kidding," Dean added as Kyle punched him lightly.

"Mostly." Madison dug into her pocket. "Here. Take my phone. I got an international plan so you can call us if you need to."

They shared a look, and in that moment, she felt like Madison had become something more than just a friend—another sister. "Thanks."

"Have a great time, kids," Dean called out before Madison turned and glared.

Jean Luc kept Thea's hand and turned to the guys for a final goodbye. "*Merci*. Do not worry. I will take good care of her."

She was aware of everyone staring at them as they exited the kitchen's back door. When they reached the street, he stopped and lifted her hand slowly to his lips. His cologne reached her, something musky and masculine. Heaven would smell like that. "You do look beautiful, Thea."

"Thank you." That corset-feeling was back with a vengeance, one she knew she couldn't blame on the beautiful yellow bra she was wearing underneath. "So do you."

He inclined his head. "If it's all right with you, I'd prefer to speak to you in French tonight. If you would like to speak in English, please do. I know you are getting your feet wet, as you say. But I find I can express the contents of my heart better in French, and that I would very much like to do with you, *chérie*."

The contents of my heart... She went light-headed before snapping back. "Sure! Do whatever makes you happy."

Holy moly. *Thea Rogers, don't wake up!*

He studied her again, smiling. "Your friends are still watching us through the front windows. It is good to have protectors, yes?"

She glanced over her shoulder and watched as Dean ducked until he was out of view, making the others guffaw in laughter so loud she could hear it through the windows. "It's sweet and a little embarrassing."

"Is that why you are blushing so? It is very charming."

He led her to the passenger side of the car and seated her like she used to watch men do to women in movies when she was all alone on a Friday night. Pinch her.

After he shut the door, she fumbled for her seat belt. She had it buckled before he opened his door and gave him a bright smile to cover her bumbling. He immediately smiled back. It was like watching the sun rise in the morning. After he got himself situated, he started driving.

"I heard Nanine was resting already. How was she after I left?"

Her mind took a moment to translate, although he spoke slowly. "You know Nanine," she answered in English. "She's strong. Her only concession to being upset was requesting *boeuf bourguignon* as comfort food."

"The place where we are eating tonight does an excellent one," he said, navigating traffic as he turned left and merged with other cars driving along the Seine before crossing the bridge and driving past the pyramid at the Louvre.

"Sawyer looked up the restaurant," Thea said, fiddling with her hands in her lap. "It's not too far from *Sacré-Cœur*, right?"

"*Oui*," he answered, downshifting as a Fiat shot in front of him. "I think you will like it. Now, why don't you settle back and let your face cool? You can be at ease with me. Thea... I want you to be at ease with me."

So did she, or this date was going to bomb before they even got there. "I'm not...very good at this."

"What's is 'this'?"

"Date stuff." She touched her hair, thinking about how Brooke had snuck in a shot of hair spray before she knew what was happening. Everything felt totally weird. She eyed her new dress and the gorgeous heels. Heels she could walk in. Mostly. She never dressed like this.

Is this how Cinderella had felt?

"I'm sure we will be fine," Jean Luc said, touching her hand briefly. "We're only beginning to know each other. Were you nervous when you first met Nanine and your roommates?"

She remembered how tough Madison had seemed, and how Kyle had looked like the prom king, someone who would never have given her the time of day back home. Sawyer was so smart, she'd feared she wasn't smart enough to talk to him. And Brooke had intimidated her with her elegance. Only Dean had seemed approachable, but mostly because he made her laugh. And Nanine... From the beginning, she'd impressed Thea as the most elegant, confident woman she'd ever met, a woman from another world. "Absolutely! Yes!"

He started laughing. "Then there's nothing to worry about. It is simply how you are with new people. Me, however...when I find someone special, all I can think of is how much I want to know them better. And that, my Thea, is how I feel about you."

She melted into her seat and turned to look at his profile. "I feel like that about you too, Jean Luc. Except when I'm nervous."

"You will have some wine and then you will relax more as we talk." He shot past another car when there was an opening. "Thea, it's going to be a wonderful evening, I promise."

She enjoyed seeing the sights of Paris as they drove through neighborhoods she hadn't seen in ten years. The trip to Montmartre was nearly forty minutes in the evening traffic, but it was filled with the Paris she loved. The narrow streets. The flash of bright window displays. The clusters of people smoking and drinking outside the well-lit cafés.

When they arrived at the restaurant, he found a place to park, impressing her by parallel parking on one of the steep hills the area was famous for. The sun was setting in brilliant colors, turning the slate gray rooftops gold under a violet sky. "I haven't been to this area in forever. It always seemed like such a trek from Saint-Germain."

He took her hand as they crossed the cobbled street, her taking extra care, because the cobblestones were treacherous in heels!

"We do become creatures of habit, don't we? I'll admit to not crossing the Seine as much as I should."

"You're either a right bank or left bank kind of person, right?" she joked and then winced. "Gosh, I told you I wasn't any good at this."

He squeezed her hand as they walked. "Would it help matters if I stumbled on these cobbles and looked like a buffoon?" His eyes were twinkling. "Dean seems to make you laugh when he does such things."

"You couldn't look like a buffoon if lightning struck you. I bet your hair wouldn't even stand up straight and your clothes wouldn't smoke."

"Let us hope no lightning strikes." He playfully shuddered. "I do like this suit."

"So do I," she blurted out, making him smile dazzlingly in the waning light. "I mean, I can't imagine you looking bad in anything you wear. Parisians are incredible that way."

"I am completely Parisian, born and raised," he responded. "But my mother is Italian. Which means style is in my blood. The Italians wear sunglasses like the French wear scarves. And I'm blessed to have both genes. It is as it is."

She nearly moaned despite the fact that there was no arrogance in his tone. "No wonder you look like a male model."

"My mother would disagree," he said with a chuckle.

Was he kidding right now? "Oh, Jean Luc, what *are* you doing with me?"

He halted instantly on the sidewalk, his hands settling on her shoulders as he gazed intently at her. "What *am* I doing? I have told you. I think you are the most naturally beautiful and kind woman I have ever met, one who has a great passion inside her for her work and her friends. Thea, what *are* you doing with me?"

Her mouth parted. He was serious. "I'm with you because the moment I saw you…"

Her diaphragm tightened, strangling her. She took another breath as he watched her, waiting.

"The moment I saw you, my heart started pounding and I felt things I've never felt before. I watched you call out greetings and smile at people, and I just knew in my gut you were a good person. Not only the most handsome man I'd ever seen."

He touched her cheek. "Now that *is* a compliment. My parents will be happy to hear it."

His sincerity gave her the courage to continue. "When I found out Nanine likes you and trusts you—she is a very discriminating woman—somehow it gave me permission to feel this way."

He settled her closer to his body. "And what is it you feel, *chérie*?"

Her throat grew tight and she plucked one of the words she'd written in her recipe book. "Hope."

His blue eyes seemed bluer suddenly. "Yes, that is exactly it. Like everything in the world is possible at a whole new level, and all because of one person you've only just met. I believe they call it falling for someone. In an instant, yes?"

She nodded because there was too much emotion rising in her chest for her to speak. He smiled softly and slowly drew her to his chest. He was warm and strong, and his touch brought that sense of peace she'd had with him before. It was as if a gentle wind had blown all her nerves away. "I didn't expect any of this, Jean Luc. I don't even know what it means."

He tipped her chin up gently. "But that is the magic of love and romance, *chérie*. Come, or I shall break my promise to myself and kiss you on these streets as the sun finally sets."

He was going to *kiss* her? Tonight? But that was huge! Brooke had schooled her on Parisian dating, including how big a first kiss was for the French. Oh, goodness. She felt her heart begin to pound in her ears again. His masculine scent seemed to settle around her as he shifted her tenderly against him. Their eyes held as the awareness between them built. He gave her another soft smile before stepping back.

"Come, the brasserie is not much further," he said, leading her down the street and to the right all the while holding her hand ever so sweetly.

The enchanting aroma coming from Chez Marie reached Thea before they arrived at the restaurant's modest brown door, and it brought out the food lover in her. "I can smell the *boeuf bourguignon* already," she murmured.

The delicate blend of onions and roasted meat flavored with wine was unmistakable.

He smiled as he opened the door for her. The waiter closest to them looked over and beamed at them, coming over immediately. "Ah! Jean Luc," he said, greeting him Parisian style. "We have been expecting you and your lovely guest."

"Please meet the beautiful and talented Thea Rogers, Mathieau," Jean Luc said.

"*Enchanté,*" the older man replied. "Jean Luc mentioned you used to work with Nanine Laurent and are now a famous French baker in the United States."

He did? "Oh, I'm not famous," she protested, stumbling to answer his rapid-fire French.

"She's too modest." Jean Luc put his hand to the small of her back. "Nanine said she single-handedly turned a struggling bakery into the best in her city and attracted quite the following with her bread and croissants."

"Well…" she fumbled when they both looked at her.

"If Nanine says it is so, it is," Mathieau said definitively. "Please send her our best regards for her recovery. We were all shocked at the news. But please, let me show you to your table. I know Marie will come out and speak to you."

Jean Luc nodded and said *bonsoir* to some of the French patrons as they passed them to a typically small table for two at the far end next to the front window. Thea knew Parisians greeted each other in such ways, but it still heartened her to see this side of Jean Luc. She stood aside as Mathieau pulled the table out so she could seat herself on the banquette. Nodding to a woman who was already enjoying an *apéritif*, Thea set her purse down and settled back as the table boxed her in. Ah, Parisian dining.

Jean Luc seated himself in the chair across from her as she glanced around. The restaurant seated thirty to her eye and every table was full except for the two with Reserve signs on the white tablecloths. She heard a smattering of English as well as German and Chinese in addition to French. The décor was typical in its tile floor, mirrors over the red leather banquettes, and small white-covered tables that could be pressed together for larger parties.

The restaurant tradition in Paris had focused on putting the money and emphasis on the food, although of course that was changing. Nanine's restaurant was the perfect example of investing in both.

Jean Luc took the menus Mathieau handed him and asked her if she wanted champagne as an *apéritif*. She almost blurted out that Nanine called her First Course before stopping herself, thank God. She nodded and he ordered with an easy command. It was a sweet gesture, not the kind of possessive ordering some men did in the States, which she'd only seen in the movies.

Right. Because she hadn't even dated all that much.

"So you obviously know this restaurant well," she remarked, reaching for her napkin before stopping. The practice here was to wait until there was food on the table, she reminded herself.

"Marie is also a client." He gave a sexy shrug. "There are not too many women restaurant owners, but Nanine and others have referred me to many of them. Some lawyers do not take their female clients as seriously, I'm afraid. My mother owned her own fashion boutique after she stopped modeling, and the lawyers were not as good to her as they should have been."

Her brain shorted. "Your mother was a model?"

"Yes. I vowed that I would help women like her, and I'm proud to say that nearly forty percent of my clients are small business owners."

Gosh. He was so nice. She almost put her elbows on the table and cradled her face in her hands like a girl with a serious crush. "You're one of the good guys."

He lifted another shoulder. "I do my best in a world and a profession where not everyone tries. I wish it were otherwise."

She thought of her boss' refusal to grant her the vacation she'd rightfully worked for because it didn't suit *him*. "Me too. So, your mother was a model…"

He waved his hand at his face. "She says my good bones come from her, if that's what you mean, although my dad's are just fine." His laugh was almost playful. "I was around the fashion world and had a behind-the-scenes seat. Much of it is very ugly. Now perhaps you understand why I value true beauty, the kind you have, Thea. The kind my parents encouraged me to embody and see in others."

Her heart started to glow again, and she wondered if she could be turning into a firefly. "And your father?"

"He was a firefighter in the second arrondissement beside the salon my mother frequented when she modeled," he continued in French. "They met in the street during the *fête de la musique* one hot June day, as my mother likes to say. He won her over not only with his dancing, but his kindness. He had to cut their time short to put out a fire. She read about him saving children and being a hero in *Le Monde* the next day, something he heartfully protested, saying he was only doing his job. Working in a profession where many flaunt their talent, my mother fell for him in two days. They were married a few months later."

"It sounds like something out of a movie," she said with a sigh. "Do you have siblings?"

"Yes. My sister followed in my father's footsteps and wears her firefighter's uniform with great pride as it's still an emerging profession for women. My brother is a doctor. My mother jokes we all inherited my father's habit of helping people in our professions. What about your family?"

Her warm bubble seemed to pop. "They're farmers, and I don't have any siblings."

His brow knit, perhaps at her tone. She could give him a pat answer, like she had so many times before, but she didn't want to do that tonight. Not with how she already felt about him.

"When I was three, my mother fell from a ladder cleaning out leaves in our gutters—the pipes that carry the rainwater away from the house. She couldn't bring a baby to full-term after that and miscarried three times. They decided to stop trying finally because my mother… It was just too hard. For everyone. Gosh, I wish I had a better story for you, but I wanted to be honest. Your story about your family is so wonderful."

He started to reach for her hand and said, "*Tu as le cafard.*"

Wait! She knew *cafard* from the time Nanine had yelled it out in the kitchen. She yanked her hand and shot up, upsetting the table. Right after shouting it, Nanine had killed a cockroach with a copper pan. "*Where?* Where's the cockroach?"

The room went silent around her. But she was still scanning the table, trying to find it. Mathieau came rushing over, and the woman seated next to them was edging away from her.

"I meant *the blues*," Jean Luc said in English this time, rising as well, murmuring to Mathieau, whose eyes looked like those of a fearful horse. "It's how you say it in French. I didn't think about the translation in English. Please, Thea, sit."

Turning, he faced the gaping patrons. "We had a little translation issue, my friends, for those of you who aren't French. The blues are called a cockroach in our language. I don't know why. But let me be clear. There are *no* cockroaches at Chez Marie. Marie would not allow it."

Thea's face was flaming as she sank back into her chair. "I'm so sorry," she whispered harshly, wincing at the woman next to her, who was shifting back to her usual position.

Mathieau met her eyes, his face tense, and then flew back to the kitchen.

"Oh my God!" she whispered as Jean Luc returned to his seat. "I could have ruined their restaurant."

He took her hand. "No, it's fine," he said in English, thank heaven. "One of my other favorite restaurants has a friendly mouse who likes to race along the wall right as the cheese plates start to come out. The waitstaff tells patrons he's a mascot. Most people don't think anything of it."

"That would *never* happen in the United States. I'm mortified. Oh, Jean Luc, maybe we should go. Or maybe I should talk to people and explain how bad my French is." Although she'd been understanding rather well until now.

"Don't think anything of it, *chérie*. It was a simple misunderstanding. Perhaps it is easier to speak English for a while until your face returns to its normal color."

She nodded with enthusiasm despite her mortification. "Oh yes! Thank you!"

Mathieau appeared with their champagne, popping the cork softly and pouring it out, every muscle rigid. Jean Luc motioned for him to serve the couple next to them a glass as well, and they both gave tight smiles of thanks.

Terrific. They all hated her after her epic blunder.

"Now, you must really shake off these cockroaches, Thea," he said with a cute wink. "Let me tell you about my most embarrassing moments with English. When I flew to New York City one summer as an exchange student, the airline lost my luggage. I asked my host parents where I could buy a slip, which made them frown and act very weird to me, but then they took me to Victoria's Secret, and we finally figured out my mistake."

She put her hand to her mouth, trying not to laugh. "Because a slip in French means a man's underwear. Okay, that's funny but it's not so bad."

"What about this?" He toyed with her hand, smiling ruefully. "My host parents took me to the baptism of their new niece, and when I heard the priest say that now he was going to bless the baby, I ran up to the altar and put myself between the shocked priest and the mother because *blesser* means to hurt in French."

"Oh, no," she nearly moaned.

"Did I mention this baptism had nearly two hundred people in attendance?" He started laughing softly. "You should have seen their faces. Of course it took me years of therapy to laugh about it. I'm joking. I was lucky my host dad was on the New York police force. After it all got sorted out, he said it showed character that I'd wanted to protect her."

Her face was feeling less hot, and she was smiling. It was hard not to smile around him. "You really are a good guy."

He shrugged again, picking up his glass and waiting for her to do the same. "Let us toast to the bravery required to learn and speak another language."

"I'll toast to that," she said, tapping his flute gently.

"So you see," he said after taking a sip, "I completely understand. And I want you to know, you can speak with me. I expect your French will return fully when you begin to trust yourself, but I know that feeling of wanting to speak perfectly. Of not wanting to stumble over your words or look foolish. But you could never look foolish to me, Thea."

Gosh. She was going to melt right here. "All right," she

said softly, wanting to reach for his hand this time and hold it. "I hear you."

He took another sip before saying, "From now on, I'll just say you look sad. *Triste.*"

"Do I still look sad?" she asked, drinking her champagne.

He tilted his head to the side, studying her. "No. Your cheeks are still rosy, but you look amused now. I am glad you could feel humor, even if at my expense."

"I *sympathize*," she said, wanting to assure him. "It's completely different."

She turned her head as a woman called out Jean Luc's name. The short-haired blond woman in the chef's apron was about forty with a face of severe angles. Marie. He stood as they greeted each other, and then she was talking about *cockroaches* in French, slapping him heartily on the back and laughing with gusto. Thank heavens!

Thea tried to smile back as the woman turned to her and gestured for her to stand as well. She kissed both of Thea's cheeks and then grabbed her hands and said she'd almost died of laughter in the kitchen when Mathieau had told her about the incident. Then she asked about Nanine, and Thea stumbled to respond as much from emotion as from speaking French. Marie grabbed her shoulder like they were old friends, sent Jean Luc a knowing look, and then charged back to the kitchen.

Returning to her seat, she stared back at him as he joined her. "She's a *tour de force.*"

She saw the slightest hesitation in him before he said, "A person cannot be a *tour de force.* Perhaps a whirlwind? Is that how you pronounce it in English? I still have trouble with words staring with W."

"Close enough, and look, I made another error." She picked up her champagne and grimaced. "If my roommates were here, someone would probably say we should take a sip every time I do that."

Jean Luc lifted his glass. "I will take two now as I told you my most embarrassing stories, and then I will take one more for mangling the *W* in whirlwind. If we must take a taxi home, then we must."

"Oh, I wasn't thinking about that. Let's forget I mentioned it."

He set his glass aside instantly, as if it were on fire, making her laugh. "Perhaps we should order. Marie is likely going to serve us whatever she pleases, but that is the way I like it. What about you?"

"I'm always happy to have the chef's menu, but I confess that I hope it includes the *boeuf bourguignon*."

"I'll make sure it does, don't worry." Then he sobered. "Thea, I'm glad you told me that sad story about your family. I want very much to know you, and I feel that in telling me so much, you wish the same."

Her new firefly feeling swept through her. "I do. Very much."

"Good. Now, tell me more about what made you come to Paris to study."

"Movies, I guess." She made a face. "We never traveled much with the farm, so that was my gateway. I'd always loved *Sabrina,* and then I watched *Julie and Julia* and *It's Complicated.* One was about a woman finding herself in Paris, and then the other two with Meryl Streep were about going to *Le Cordon Bleu* and making croissants. I'm a huge fan of hers. I've seen everything she's done."

God, she was such a geek, but he was listening intently, so she kept going. "Anyway, it all came together strangely. I started trying to make croissants—which isn't easy on your own—and no one around me knew enough about the technique to teach me. No shock. I was in the Midwest. But I wanted to learn. It became an obsession."

"How so?" he asked in a husky voice.

She paused for a moment, calling to mind how she'd felt.

"There's something captivating about it. The rolling of the dough and the lamination process, how the butter and flour magically create layers. The folding and the refolding of the dough is incredible. It makes hundreds of layers, almost like tree rings. It's like putting all your love and hope and dreams into it. Sometimes I imagine myself folding in my wishes for my customers that day. But if the temperature isn't right, it all gets thrown off and your fingers get buttery when you eat it and the bread isn't flaky. Did you know that?"

"No, I did not. I will boycott any bakery making such a mistake from now on."

His teasing had her smiling. "So I thought... If I could learn to make them, it would be something special about me."

"There can be no denying how special you are, as you speak so passionately about your craft."

The sexy timbre of his voice gave her the shivers. "Making them would set me apart from other bakers. Plus, if I could have the kind of transformation Sabrina had in the movie, well... My life would be made."

"And was it?" he asked, reaching for her hand again.

"Not completely, which is why I'm taking the bull by the horns, so to speak, and going for it all the way this time. I... quit my job to come here. My boss wouldn't let me have time off. So I'm staying here for the foreseeable future. I'll be helping at Nanine's restaurant, and then we'll see. I don't know how to explain it, but in Paris, I feel like I could become who I really want to be. And with my roommates by my side again, I feel like everything is possible. Which it wasn't back home."

He caressed the back of her hand in such a way her breath stopped. "And you have me in your corner as well. You are already blooming, and it's only been a few days. Imagine where you'll be in a month. I recall feeling the same way when I decided to study abroad in New York—also because of movies, by the way."

Her feet were starting to dance under the table. She wasn't just attracted to him. She could all but hear Brooke saying *you have things in common!* "Which ones?" she asked, tangling her fingers with his.

He rubbed his freshly shaven cheeks with his free hand, looking almost abashed. "You'll be amused. When I was a boy, I loved watching *Big* and *Ghostbusters.*"

"I love *Big!*" she cried before realizing the woman next to her was inching away again.

"The piano playing scene is still a favorite. I took lessons as a boy, but playing that way, running around to make the notes, seemed so much more fun, don't you think?"

"Absolutely!"

"Of course, my mother made us all watch *Breakfast at Tiffany's* for the fashion as much as anything. But when I took my first cab ride in Manhattan, there was something special about riding in one of those yellow cabs. I felt like *I* was in a movie too, and for a Parisian, it was a little surprising. But movies transport our very souls, don't they?"

Again, she found herself nodding. "I'm in Paris, aren't I?"

"You being here makes me very happy, *chérie.*" He lifted her hand to his lips and kissed it before setting their joined hands back on the table.

She was going to die from all the romance.

"Do still you like the cinema? I should take you to one of my favorite theaters. *Le Champo.* Do you know it?"

He wanted another date with her? "Of course!" She really needed to modulate her voice better or the woman beside her was going to kill her. "Sawyer used to organize movie watching back in the day."

His smile was suddenly brighter, and time seemed to slow as he simply looked at her. He ran his thumb along the back of her hand, and she felt as if her skin had just been struck by a match.

"Good. Then it's a date. I will see what is playing."

She smiled at him. All she could do was smile. In fact, she was convinced that if someone streaked through the restaurant naked, she wouldn't even notice because she couldn't bear to look away from his face. "I really like being with you, Jean Luc," she said, suddenly shy.

"Me as well, *ma* Thea." He lifted her hand to his lips again, his beautiful blue eyes intent on her face.

My Thea! The endearment was so simple, and yet it struck her to her very core. Her heart began to pound in her ears. *Locura.* Madness. Isn't that what Madison had called it? Yeah, she had that in spades.

By the end of their six-course meal, her jaw was sore from smiling. But she couldn't stop. When he suggested walking a bit after they bid Mathieau and Marie farewell, she didn't hesitate to accept.

"You know," she murmured as they walked hand in hand down the cobbled street, "I think it's past my curfew."

He chuckled softly. "Shall I text your roommates?"

She swung their joined hands, feeling young and carefree. She'd never had a curfew before. There had been no late nights out for her. Farm chores demanded an early start, and so she was expected to go to bed early with her parents. "No."

His face transformed into a captivating grin as the golden light from Paris' lampposts washed over him. "Good. They have been having way too much fun with me. Sawyer especially. But I will continue to let them. For you. And because they remind me of my protective Italian cousins and how my brother and I have been with some of the men my sister has shown interest in."

She matched his stride—he'd shortened it for her in her heels—and laid her head against his bicep for a moment. He was strong and warm, and everything she had ever wanted and more.

This might be the most perfect night of her life, and she never wanted it to end.

When they reached the famous view from the plaza in front of *Sacré-Cœur*, his hands settled on her shoulders from behind as they took it in. "Are you chilled? Would you like my jacket?"

She wished she wasn't burning from his touch because his offer sounded thrilling. "Maybe in a bit. I'm glad we came here. I don't know what it is about the Eiffel Tower, but I never tire of seeing it. And to think it almost never got built."

"And it was almost dismantled after the World's Fair," he added. "I admit to being Parisian here. I don't have the same feelings about it as you might, but I do appreciate it more when I'm with someone special."

He meant her! Her back connected with his body, and she wondered if she'd unconsciously leaned against him. But he didn't move, and it felt so good. Is this where he might kiss her? Then she remembered him saying before dinner that he had promised himself not to. She glanced over her shoulder. His eyes were waiting for her.

"What are you thinking, *ma Thea*?" he asked huskily.

She made herself turn around. The Old Thea might have rules about kisses on first dates, but the Old Thea hadn't gone out with Jean Luc. New and Improved Thea, who had a recipe for *Living Life to the Fullest*, was all for kissing immediately, especially under the magical Parisian sky.

"I was thinking I didn't want to squander this moment." She took a breath. "Would you kiss me, Jean Luc?"

His mouth curved as he lifted his hand to cup her cheek. "With great pleasure, *chérie*."

Then she was holding her breath as his mouth lowered slowly to hers. The first touch of his lips was a shock of heat and electricity, but he kept it gentle, the barest brush of their lips. His other hand settled on the center of her back, and she realized he was waiting for something from her. A sign. Yes, that was it. She tentatively lifted her hand and laid it over his heart, and that was all it took. His lips captured hers, and then she was falling into complete bliss.

When he lifted his head, she opened her eyes and found him gazing down at her. He made no move to release her, which was just fine with her. He shifted his hand from her cheek and caressed her mouth with his thumb in the most erotic way she could have imagined. Her heart pounded in her ears as they watched each other.

At last he smiled, and she felt like she was suddenly the center of his world. Wanting him to feel the same, she laid her head against his chest and closed her eyes. His arms embraced her, and she joined hers around him in response.

The skyline of Paris couldn't tempt her, not even when the people around them gasped at something. All she was aware of was Jean Luc's warm hands caressing the line of her back in the most delicious way and the pounding of his heart against her ear, now steadier and slower than just after they'd kissed.

With a tender squeeze, he released her and took her hand. "Come, *chérie*. Your friends are waiting, I expect."

They didn't speak as he led her back to the car and drove her home. Somehow words weren't needed. She could still feel his arms around her, and she knew she had been changed. The kind of change she'd wanted when she'd first bought her journal.

She settled deeper into her seat and watched the lights of Paris go by. This was her life now. *Her*—Thea Rogers. Her new Fullest Life recipe was coming together finally.

When they arrived at Nanine's, Jean Luc came around to walk her to the door. She took a breath, knowing the night was ending. She spotted a few of her friends' silhouettes in the front window as he helped her out.

They walked slowly around to the back, their steps slower, as if they were both reluctant for the night to end.

"I will let you have your moment with your friends inside," he said, holding her face in both of his hands and kissing her mouth softly. "Thank you for a beautiful evening, *ma Thea.*"

She laid her hands over his. A powerful surge of longing rushed through her, and she realized the full force of her feelings. She didn't only not want the night to end. She didn't want him to leave. "It was one of the best of my life."

He kissed her again, more swiftly this time. "Mine as well. I will call you tomorrow."

With a harsh inhale, he strode away, and she realized he hadn't wanted to leave either. Delighted, she rushed inside and stopped at the sight of all her roommates gathered together in the kitchen.

"You don't have to say a word, Thea," Dean said with a grin as the chandelier's crystals gave a joyous jingle. "It's written all over your face."

Brooke marched forward. "Dean, you might not want to hear details, but I most certainly do."

"Me too!" Sawyer exclaimed. "There's nothing better than a date debriefing. I'll grab more wine."

"I just have one question, Thea." Madison set her hand on her hip. "Did you kiss him?"

Her smile threatened to explode even as her cheeks heated. "Yes. Yes, I did."

Everyone let out a cheer.

CHAPTER
TWENTY

anine gripped her phone as defeat—the bone-crushing kind—nearly brought her to her knees.

"Can you say that again, Jean Luc?" she rasped.

"I have just left our meeting, and I did not think the news could wait. The owner will not void the bill of sale for your cave."

She squeezed her eyes shut to stop the tears. "Offer him more money. Jean Luc, my cave—"

"He says he will not change his mind," Jean Luc responded gently. "Nanine, he knows the value of your cave is beyond a price. I am sorry."

She'd been so afraid these past two weeks, waiting for news. The man who'd bought the cave had been on vacation, which had felt like a cruel joke. "It is the worst news imaginable."

"He was not persuaded by your illness or the betrayal of your family."

"I see." She opened her eyes, her salon blurring from rare tears. "I appreciate you doing your best."

"Please do not thank me. Certainly not for failing you. Nanine, I would speak to Kyle about how to start over with your cave. As I understand it, the Courses will be the new investors for Nanine's, and they will help you rebuild."

How much more fallout would there be from her mistake of trusting Jeremy and her daughter? She feared they did not yet know. Her eyes tracked to one of her favorite photos of Bernard. He was sipping cognac at a coveted winery in the Champagne region that would later define her menu that year. The remaining bottles would now be taken from her. *Oh, Bernard, I am glad you are not here to see this day.*

The sticky vines of doubt entangled her. Was she making another mistake by pursuing her grand vision for relaunching the restaurant? Maybe she should stop. Let go of Nanine's. Yet it wasn't in her to give up—she knew she would die if she did—and over the past weeks, she'd seen something else to encourage her.

The Courses needed this restaurant as much as she did. They were coming alive in a new way, working together on this project, along with her. It was like old times, and yet it was not. Most of them were not happy in all the areas of their lives. She remembered she had been the same at their age—longing for something bigger, something of her own—and that was when she had decided to strike out on her own and open Nanine's. It had changed her life.

This was their chance to strengthen their friendship, one forged ten years ago. It was also their chance to reinvent themselves and rechart the course of their lives. No one made that more evident than Thea right now.

First Course's happiness was like eternal sunshine. She hummed from morning until night and was even heard giggling as she talked about Jean Luc with one of her roommates. They'd met every day since their first dinner. A café at Café Fitzy. A walk along the Seine after the end of their workday, Jean Luc preparing legal papers for Nanine while Thea tested bread recipes.

"I will speak to my Courses, Jean Luc," she managed. "You are right. We will find a way to rebuild."

He gave a quiet murmur before saying, "I will help however you wish as well, Nanine. Only…the owner would like to come for the contents of the cave this week. I told him I would speak with you about the arrangements. Nanine, I wish there was something I could do, but the law…"

She looked over at her computer, which now had new passwords for everything imaginable. According to Dean, Jeremy had used it while she was away, but he could not tell her what he had done. Her bank accounts were okay, thank God. She checked them every day. But her electronic signature had been saved on the computer, something that had made this act so easy. Her fault. Her stupid fault for trusting in a daughter who had not loved her for a long time, one whose hate she could never have imagined. "Let us be done with this horrible moment. Tell him tomorrow. Before lunch."

She would encourage some of the Courses to be away. They need not all join in her agony.

"As you wish. I will be present to oversee the task, if that is all right with you."

He would be by her side as much her friend as her lawyer. "I am glad. Perhaps after you can take Thea away for a walk." Even that thought could not make her smile.

"Perhaps."

He was being discreet, which she appreciated. If he were otherwise, he would not be the man she knew him to be. "I hear you will have another dinner tonight and take in a movie."

"Yes. I never tire of spending time with Thea, but knowing her as you do, I don't have to explain more."

"No, you do not." Surely not everything was wrong in the world if people were still falling in love. "I will perhaps see you later when you arrive to pick Thea up."

"I look forward to it. Again, I am deeply sorry, Nanine."

Her heart took the opportunity to clench and remind her of its pain. She fought a gasp. "As am I. *À tout à l'heure*, Jean Luc."

"*À tout à l'heure*, Nanine."

She laid the phone down. "It never should have happened," she whispered to herself before frowning.

She was not giving in to self-pity. No, that would not do.

"*Nanine.*"

She turned at Brooke's voice. Third Course stood in her doorway with fabric samples. "Madison said you were taking a break."

Laughing haughtily, she shook her head. "No, she ordered me out of my own kitchen, saying I look tired. Bah!"

Brooke worried her lip. "I thought we'd agreed you would only work for an hour at a time and then rest for another hour."

"For a total of three hours of work a day." She rubbed her throbbing forehead. "I am a shadow of my former self."

"You just had a heart attack," Brooke said, coming into her sitting room and taking a seat beside her on the divan.

"Do not remind me," she said sternly. "But I will forgive you since you bring me fabric samples for my restaurant."

Brooke began laying out each sample, the colors a bold contrast against the white velvet cushions. "You were on the phone earlier and looked upset. I know Jean Luc had a meeting about the cave now that the owner is back from vacation. I did not want to upset you—"

"The owner is holding me to the sale."

Brooke cried out, "No!" and then grabbed her hand. Her heart gave an answering knock in her chest.

"I was going to tell you and the others, but then you were here."

Her brow knit. "Is there nothing Jean Luc can do?"

Nanine watched her tense features. "No. Jeremy, it seems, is quite adept at subterfuge. Thinking about what he and my daughter have done is a knife in my back I cannot seem to pull out."

"We'll rebuild your collection," Brooke promised. "All of us. And it's going to be even better than before."

She had her doubts, but then again, mourning hung heavy in the air.

"It's a business expense, and Kyle will know best where to start." She squeezed Nanine's hand. "I've been to his restaurant in Atlanta, and he knows his way around wine and liquor."

She could not continue this conversation. The pain was too great. All the memories of selecting those bottles with Bernard would be gone. When someone ordered something special, she always thought of him with a smile. Later, she was sure she would grieve.

After a moment, she said, "Fine. I will speak to Kyle later. After I have told everyone."

Brooke caressed her arm, her green eyes worried now. "I can't imagine how hard this is. But we love you. Let us help you. You can trust us."

This time she caressed her dear Third Course's face. "I trust all of you with my very life. All right, let us turn to these samples. Brooke, they are exquisite."

They shared a look, and Brooke nodded. "Sawyer has paint samples too. But maybe today isn't the best. You should rest."

Her sigh was heartfelt. "I know you all are worried, but I *will* weather this. How could I not with all of your help?"

"We all owe you so much, Nanine."

"You owe me nothing. Everything between us was done with love then, as it is now. I am happy you've returned, though. All six of you have been unhappy with the state of your lives. Of that, we now share in common. And like my restaurant's renovation—and Thea's transformation—my wish is that you will all find what you have come here searching for. As will I."

That had Brooke's tense features easing. "Thea is a bright spot for all of us, isn't she? Even Madison can't contain her grins when Thea waxes poetic about Jean Luc."

Yes, love would always be right—even when it felt like the sky was falling. "And what about you? Is your heart healed enough that you also can believe in love again?"

She scoffed. "I'm not that brave yet. Maybe someday. But right now, love is something that looks good on other people. Even though Thea and Jean Luc just met, there seems to be something special about their connection. I guess it's not surprising though. Thea isn't the kind of person who loves halfway."

Nanine was the same, but right now all she could think was that her love had landed her in this disaster. If only she'd acted like the businesswoman she'd prided herself on being…

"Nanine, do you think Jean Luc is the same?" Brooke asked quietly. "Part of me still worries about her getting hurt. I thought I knew Adam—until he walked out."

"I trust in Jean Luc, Brooke." Nanine bit the inside of her cheek. "As for Adam, in my humble opinion, he was not the love of your life. I did not feel I could say so back then, but it feels right to do so now."

"Part of me knows it." She lowered her head. "But it still hurts."

Yes, they both knew about hurt. "Of course it does, but as someone who had a mad love affair that ended tragically, I can tell you it *is* possible you will still find your perfect love." She would not think of her daughter just now, what she'd thought was the one gift from that tragedy. "I found Bernard, didn't I? And we had twenty-four beautiful years together."

She tried not to think of what he would say about Adrienne and recent events. He had tried for her sake to believe that Adrienne would change and return, eager to mend their relationship. How wrong she'd been. Adrienne had become her father. Someone capable of lying and stealing and betraying. It made Nanine wonder: was there nothing left of her in her daughter?

"I didn't know Bernard well," Brooke said, picking up the photo she kept on the table behind the couch. "You looked so happy on your wedding day. I want to look like that, Nanine."

"Every bride should." Nanine gazed at the younger version of herself. "I knew the moment I saw him walk into my restaurant wanting a reservation that he was the one for me. Love happens in an instant with some people."

She did not say it yet, but she thought it had been the same for Thea and Jean Luc.

"Maybe some people are luckier than others in love," Brooke said with a sigh.

She could not let that comment rise in the air like dust motes shining in the sunlight—even after the horrible news of the day. "Perhaps you are ready to hear from your Nanine something I have not said before."

Brooke warily met her gaze. "Tell me."

"You did not search your heart enough over Adam." She traced her cheek again to soften the words. "You checked boxes you thought were important for a relationship. But those cannot make up for love that doesn't fill you all the way, *chérie*."

"You're right." She crumpled the velvet fabric in her hand. "Nanine, I'm not sure I ever want to make myself that vulnerable again."

Because her mother had left her, Nanine knew, and those scars would always be there. "And yet, you let your roommates know you fully. And don't forget about me. Brooke, if you can do it with us, you can do it with another. You must search your heart first. If the love is there—for you both—you will be able to trust each other. Because when you truly love someone, you do not ever hurt them knowingly."

Again, she thought of Adrienne, and pain streaked through her chest.

Brooke was quiet for a long moment before saying hoarsely, "So you think my mother meant to hurt me?"

Nanine took her hand, squeezing it firmly. "It is hard to know what is in another's heart, but from what I felt from your mother, she did not have enough love for anyone. Not even herself."

"Maybe that's why I feel so stunted inside. Maybe we're love deficient in my family."

"*Non*," she said emphatically. "You have more love inside you than you know. Much like Thea is discovering. When you decide to heal all the way—and you are on your way—you will bloom as well. Do not laugh, but when you bloom, you will attract your perfect bee."

Brooke raised a haughty eyebrow, looking so French Nanine's heart swelled with pride. "My perfect bee, huh? I can't wait for that. I predict Dean's going to dress up as a honey bee when I tell everyone about this metaphor."

God, how they were grasping for humor. "He would be adorable."

They shared a smile and then turned their heads as Thea said, "Look at what Jean Luc sent," from the doorway. "I ran up to your quarters the moment they arrived to show you."

The bouquet of dahlias in cream and burgundy were as breathtaking as Thea's radiant face. "Love has transformed you, *ma petite*."

"He said they reminded him of me." She hugged them to her chest as she walked toward them. "Me! Can you believe that? It says that here on the card. Do you want to see?"

Brooke managed a laugh. "We don't need proof. Clearly you have a grand romance going on."

"I know!" She sank onto the edge of the divan beside

Brooke, who made room for her. "I just keep pinching myself. I even have a bruise, but then Madison told me to stop it or she'd make me wear boxing gloves. Oh, Nanine, I'm so glad you knew Jean Luc."

Her quiet laughter was something to savor, as was this beautiful moment. "Somehow I feel you two still would have met had he and I not been acquainted."

Her sigh was filled with youthful promise. "Me too. Nanine, I thought you might like some of my flowers for your room."

Nanine let go of Brooke to touch Thea's hand resting on the flowers. "No, my love, the flowers your man gives you are for you and you alone. They carry the warmth of his heart in them, and it would not be right to give them away."

She sobered. "I know he had his meeting about the cave. Have you heard from him?"

Schooling her expression, she made herself answer. "Yes. The owner will not void the sale."

"But that's horrible!" She wrapped her arms around Nanine in comfort. "How could anyone be so cruel after hearing what happened? The others—"

"Will be very upset at the news, I am sure." She removed herself from Thea's embrace before emotion could drown her. "Would you two find everyone and have them come up here?"

They both nodded slowly. "Of course," Brooke said, standing up and taking Thea's hand. "We'll be back shortly."

When they were gone, Nanine inhaled a few deep breaths as the quiet settled around her. She had less of the quiet she'd come to know in these past years, but she wouldn't change hearing the happy rumbles from her Courses below for anything in the world. Only today, there would be more anger and tears in the house.

But then, they must move on…

When nothing could be done, only a fool continued to

waste such energy. They would focus on the renovation and keep busy. Her eyes tracked to the fabric samples. Each was rich in color and texture—exactly as she preferred all things.

If only her relationship with her daughter had been that way. Then she cursed at herself under her breath. She was a fool to think such thoughts. Wasn't it time to follow her advice to Brooke and heal her heart the whole way? She could not change the past, and she could not have a relationship with someone who did not want it. Perhaps someday that would change.

God, but her granddaughter…

That pain was still fresh, and its rawness stopped her breath. Focusing on it would accomplish nothing, however. Was she not practical?

She would tell her Courses the horrible news and then talk to Kyle about how best to create another cave. Her restaurant *would* reopen, better than ever, with an even better cave, as Brooke had said.

She must believe. In herself. And her Courses.

They were her adopted children as much as her investors.

No, investors still didn't sit.

She would call them business partners, she decided.

Inside her chest, something shifted.

CHAPTER
TWENTY-ONE

Madison surveyed her latest tasting dish with a scowl.

Can't you cooperate and give me a win here? The rich sauce only bubbled in response—like her anger. Nanine losing her cave hurt. Something raw had clawed at her throat when Nanine had told them the news earlier.

"How's the alchemy coming?" Kyle asked quietly behind her.

She turned, and they faced each other. His normally golden hue was as leached as a green apple in the prolonged sunlight, and she could hear the hoarse agony he was trying to cover up. "I'm still not pleased with the spices in the *canard aux cerises*. How did your talk with Nanine go about a plan to rebuild her cave?"

He stuffed his hands in his pockets and kicked at the floor. "It was like walking on eggshells. Shit. We can set aside a lofty budget but there's no mistaking the reality. The selections she had in that cave just aren't something you can buy through a liquor distributor. It takes years of dedication and searching—"

"So we find another way." She punched the air. "Hey!

Don't look like that. If you start losing faith, what am I going to do? I've got enough pressure with making this menu perfect—"

"*Madison—*"

"No!" She took a deep breath to dam her own wild emotions, ones reflected in his tortured eyes. "Kyle, we've got to keep it together. There's too much on the line here."

His throat moved in a long line of pain before he nodded. God, his heart was in his eyes. She could take this from everyone else, but not Kyle. He always had an answer. He was the golden boy.

"You're right." He took an audible breath before heading for what remained of Thea's apricot bread. "Damn, I need some of Thea's comfort bread."

Comfort bread couldn't soothe away that kind of rage, but he was trying. She turned back to her dish. Maybe she should threaten *it* with her cleaver.

"What's wrong with it?" he mumbled, still chewing. "You growled like a pissed-off bear."

"I'm missing a layer." She didn't mention her pique that every new bread or *pâtisserie* offering Thea made for the new menu and her trade agreement with her Fairy Godmothers had kicked proverbial ass. Even Madison had moaned a few times, making Thea beam, saying it was high praise from another chef. Right now, Thea seemed to have an extra cooking edge, maybe because of that whole *falling in love* glow. Not that Madison would ever do something so stupid again. The one time she'd let herself fall in love, she'd been a total mess in the kitchen.

"We'll still all devour it like wolves for dinner tonight," Kyle said, coming over and punching her softly in the shoulder. "Okay, maybe not like usual since we're all sick to our stomachs over the news, but still… You've got this, Madison."

She knew he wanted to say more, so she punched him back. "Thanks. Poor Thea made Jean Luc an apple tart for tonight to thank him for the all the flowers. I wonder if they'll be able to eat it after the news."

"Nanine says you celebrate the hardest when you receive bad news, doesn't she? Maybe little sis needs to be reminded of that so she can have fun tonight on her date."

The seriousness of that date had been her earlier obsession before the cave news.

Kyle tapped her skull gently. "I can hear the gears in your mind turning. What's up?"

She gave in to another growl. "I know Thea gave him permission to kiss her on their first date—which is what French guys wait for—but they've been moving at the speed of light, spending every day together. Now she's made him an apple tart, which means he's going to invite her back to *his* place."

He only stared back at her. "So?"

God, how could someone who dressed this well be this clueless? "This is Thea we're talking about. The ultimate good girl. It's way too soon for her to go back to his place. Especially since she must be feeling vulnerable after the news today. I'm not even sure she'd get the implications of going home with him."

His blue eyes turned wary. "You might be right."

"I am right! I know the male species. Kyle, I think we need to visit him and talk to him about his timetable for sex."

His face contorted immediately. "Are you nuts? I'm not talking to another guy about *that*."

She held her ground. "What if he moves too fast with Thea? She's only been with two guys, and both experiences were bad. I asked the other night."

He had the grace to wince. "Shit. I don't want to hear this."

"Good friends *hear* shit like this." She jabbed her finger at him. "We need to have her back. I know firsthand that moving too fast can ruin everything."

She'd made a *dulce de leche* cake for a college freshman as a lovestruck high school junior way, way back in the day. He'd invited her over to his apartment to watch *Scarface*, his favorite movie. That should have been a red flag.

His brows narrowed. "You were crazy for some guy who moved too fast? When?"

She wanted to shove him. "Believe it or not, Kyle, I used to be young and naïve. And young and naïve girls sometime think they're in love with the guys who have all the lines and treat them like queens until they get what they want. Dammit, I wish I'd had a big brother or sister to set guys straight about respecting me."

His jaw locked. "Shit, Madison."

He reached for her. Did he think she wanted comfort? She held up her hand to block him and watched as his hands fell along with his face. Her chest grew tight a little—she hadn't meant to hurt him—but she couldn't go there. "Water under the bridge. But Thea hasn't stepped onto said bridge. Yet. And let me repeat: she's feeling more than her usual vulnerability. Not a good combo."

"Why can't you bring Sawyer or Dean? Or Brooke?"

She'd thought about them all going for solidarity but discarded the idea quickly. She ticked off her reasons with her fingers. "Sawyer will want to talk about the philosophical side of sex. Dean will crack jokes. Brooke is…also a little vulnerable since her breakup. I need someone straightforward who can get to the point and keep things clean. I'll be the bad cop, jaded by love, and you can be the good cop, saying we're just taking care of our nice-girl little sister like family does. Got it?"

He tapped his designer shoe on the floor, so un-Kyle. "All right. But you're *going* to have to cook me something in exchange. That, or you can wash my car."

She snorted. "Really? What about your back? God, you're a camel trader at heart."

"That's a good one." His laugh had her fighting a smile. "But there's no way I'm doing this without some kind of trade, Madison."

Now that was the Kyle she loved. "Deal. But it has to be something I can make in under an hour. I have way too much menu testing to do, and the others will whine if they know you're the only one who gets to eat it."

She broke off as the chandelier's crystals clanged noisily, followed by the sound of someone's footsteps approaching the back kitchen door, which she had open for the breeze. They both went on alert, and they shared a look before hearing, "Kyle!" shouted in a woman's voice in a sugary Southern accent.

He startled at the sound and headed to the back door. "*Paisley?*"

Madison followed and stopped short as his former fiancée stepped into view. The pictures hadn't done her justice, or she'd had her hair freshly blown out before coming to see Kyle. Her stunning blond hair was perfectly dyed, the kind of work only a high-priced salon could pull off, judging by how dark her eyebrows were. And yes, Dean was right about her having a nubile body, which she'd displayed in a formfitting cream dress accentuated by a gold metal link belt that ended mid-thigh. Tan legs only possible through regular tanning appointments led to death-defying stiletto heels, but she stood on them with a confidence mastered by years of torture.

"We meet at last," Madison decided to say since Kyle hadn't closed his mouth yet.

Paisley flicked her a glance. "Excuse me? Who are you? *The kitchen help?* Leave. I want to talk to my fiancé alone."

Bitch. "So you're back to reclaim your money train. Well, *honey,* he doesn't want to be reclaimed."

"First, how dare you talk to me like that." She thrust out a finger with a dagger-edged manicured nail. "Second, Kyle can speak for himself."

"Yes, I can," he said, recovering at last, "and first, I agree with everything Madison said. Second, you've come a long way to give me back my house key. And third, don't talk to one of my best friends like that."

Madison's heart got a little squishy at being called that. She shifted until they were standing shoulder to shoulder together. "Word."

Diva Paisley glanced between them before fixing her sickeningly sweet smile on Kyle. "How can you act like this after everything we shared? Why haven't you answered any of my calls or texts?"

"Because I blocked you, Paisley."

Madison wanted to cheer—this was news—while their rude guest looked momentarily unsure. "Well… Clearly, you're upset."

Understatement of the century, Madison thought, but then the woman leveled him the kind of look only a siren could muster.

"Kyle, I'm here to talk you out of the biggest mistake of your life. I thought you'd see reason earlier, but you can be so stubborn. I had to upend my whole life to fly here—"

"Which I didn't ask you to do."

"There is no way you're not coming back to our home and our life," she finished, grinding her stiletto into the kitchen floor for effect. "I'm saving you from yourself, Kyle, and from these horrible people. You're not thinking straight!"

He stared at her as his mouth twisted. "My mind has never been clearer, Paisley. What I said on the phone stands. I don't plan to rehash it. I told you to move out of my house. Have you?"

He hadn't checked? Madison wanted to smack him.

The first hint of fear flashed in her eyes before her haughty demeanor snapped back into place. "No, because I know you aren't yourself. That woman's heart attack must have made you go crazy."

247

"I don't plan to defend myself," he said harshly. "Or my mental state. Paisley, we're done. You will move out of my house nicely—or I will have the police remove you in front of the neighbors whose opinions you cater. Your choice."

Police sounded like a good option. God knew what she would take or destroy on her way out.

"But you can't..." She gave a mighty huff at the sheer impossibility of it and held out her mega-carat diamond engagement ring. "I have the ring. We have a wedding date. The perfect venue. All our family and friends are coming. I have my life planned, and you're a key player."

God, she was a narcissist and a drama queen. What had Kyle been thinking? She turned to see his next move.

He set his weight, his usually agreeable face stony. "Paisley, I've tried to be nice, but you refuse to listen. Showing up like this is just another attempt to bulldoze me. It stops now."

She stomped hard this time, her obviously fake boobs heaving. "It stops when I say it does, Kyle."

Madison wanted to roll her eyes. She'd seen enough drama mamas in Miami to know this woman was never going to willingly give up. Madison pulled her ace, the one card she was sure would have this woman storming out of here. She only hoped Kyle would forgive her.

"*Paisley,*" she practically sang for effect, bringing the woman's focus to her. "Kyle's trying to be nice. What he didn't want to say was that he got here and saw me again, and that was it. We just couldn't help ourselves. Young love and all that. Paris. You know."

Kyle's neck cracked as he swung his head to look at her. She raised her brows and gave him a smug smile.

"*Right,*" he drew out slowly. "Paisley, nothing happened until after I broke things off with you, but when I saw Madison again..."

Paisley sputtered and gestured in Madison's direction. "But she's ugly and rude. And she's the help! How could you possibly want her and not me? I'm better than her in every way possible."

"Stop right there," Kyle began, but Madison strode to him quickly and stepped on his foot, which shut him up as intended. She smiled at him like she'd seen Thea do with Jean Luc and touched his jaw sweetly. His brow rose again, but then he smiled, a truly spectacular smile that told her they really were the best of friends and he trusted her.

She turned back to Paisley. She knew how to finish this.

"I almost hate to burst your bubble, Paisley, but I *am* better than you at some things." She turned back to Kyle and waggled her brows, telling him to play along. He looked like he was holding in laughter at first—and then she planted her mouth on his and did her best impression of rocking a man's world.

Shock rolled through his body, but it only took him half a second to play along, grabbing her by the waist and showing her Golden Boy knew something about kissing. She let herself go soft and gushy—for authenticity, of course—before she put pressure on his chest with her hand and eased back. His eyes were heated but dancing, and they shared another smile before they turned back to the bitch huffing in Nanine's kitchen.

Paisley was fuming, her fists clenched at her side.

"Seen enough, *honey*?" Madison called in her best drawl.

"Kyle, if you've changed that much, I don't want you. You two deserve each other!"

"We really do," Madison said, letting her hand linger on his chest.

The chandelier's crystals gave another loud clang. Paisley dug into her purse and flung a house key in his direction. He deflected it with a hand so it didn't hit them. Next came her engagement ring. Then he stepped forward, keeping Madison a little behind him in case Paisley chucked anything more. "You'd better leave now. They have police here too."

"You're going to regret this." Her rosy lipstick smeared as she compressed her mouth angrily. "I'm going to tell everyone back home that you're crazy and holed up with a wetback slut in Paris. Your parents will be ashamed of you. No one will want to work with you again. Not even your business partners."

They watched as she strode out in a demonic snit, her heels making bullet-like noises on the floor.

"You were thinking about spending the rest of your life with *that*?" Madison asked as his jaw cracked audibly. "Maybe you really *did* go temporarily nuts. Good thing that's over."

"*Jesus.*"

"Hey, everyone calls you crazy when you don't want them anymore." She gave him a playful shove. "Don't make me play Taylor Swift's 'Shake It Off.'"

He rubbed the back of his neck before turning to look at her. "Dean would love that."

"Maybe it should be your new ringtone. I have 'I Will Survive' and Brooke has 'Best Thing I Never Had.' Join the meaningful ringtones club."

Knowing he needed a moment, she started for the coffee machine. Damn, she could use a café. Check that. Maybe they needed tequila shots. What a fucking day!

"Hey, Madison?" he called softly.

She knew he was going to get all gooey thanking her, but maybe it was better if she let him. She should probably even joke about the kiss.

"Yeah?" she answered.

His blue eyes were steady and bright with warmth, the kind that made her edgy.

"Thanks."

"Sure thing, sweetie." She cocked a hip to break the Hall-mark card spell. "But while this might be a vulnerable time for you, I need to be brutally honest about a few things. One, you really should work on your lip-lock technique. Two, I just saved your hide, so I won't be making you anything in return for going to talk to Jean Luc with me. And three, we will never speak of The Kiss again. Our roomies might freak."

His mouth curved. "I have some responses to that. One, my lip-lock technique is legendary, but yours could use some major refinement. Let me know if you want to practice some more. I'd help you out. What are best friends for, after all?"

She laughed to stop herself from going soft again over the best friend comment.

"Two, we'll call it even on the Jean Luc visit." Then his smile expanded into a grin. "But I really kinda want to see people's faces when we tell them that you kissed me in front of my ex-fiancée to make her leave. It might turn this whole rotten day around."

She stared him down.

"Ah, come on. *Please*."

Her shoulders were shaking now from repressed humor. "All right. We could all use a laugh today. But after we visit Jean Luc. We have the perfect cover. We'll take Thea's tart over. It's not like she'll want to haul it around all night on their date."

He held out his arm, miming a gentleman. "Shall we, Ms. Garcia?"

Okay, she could play along. She hung her apron on a hook on the wall, accepted his arm, and they started for the back door after he picked up Thea's dessert one-handed.

"You do know…" he began as the late afternoon Paris sunshine fell upon them, "that Paisley is the crazy one, right? You are a much better woman than she is. In every way."

God, he really was a nice guy. She patted his arm and told herself not to get gooey like a lava cake. "I know, Kyle."

They grinned at each other like the friends they were and set off for their second theater act of the day.

CHAPTER
TWENTY-TWO

Madison and Kyle had kissed!

Thea was sure her jaw had dropped from that bombshell. They'd asked everyone to gather in the front room for an announcement after they'd returned from delivering her tart to Jean Luc so she wouldn't have to cart it around tonight. Of course, she'd been a little scared by what they wanted to tell everyone after the disaster with the cave, so their kiss confession had knocked her for a loop.

"Damn, I wish I could have seen it," Dean mused, sitting on one of the new chairs in the empty restaurant, in what Thea had started to think of as their *Circle of Friends* arrangement.

"The kiss or the altercation with Diva Paisley?" Madison quipped, sitting next to Kyle. The two had opened a bottle of tequila for anyone wanting shots, and after today, everyone had joined in but her.

"*Both* were epic," Kyle said with a laugh.

Brooke was sitting cross-legged in her chair. "I need more details. *Have* you two really been into each other all these years? Because it is/was technically against the rules. Not that we're not swearing—"

Sawyer raised his hand shyly from his perch. "Yeah, I want to know that too."

"What do you want to know?" Nanine asked from the doorway in French. "I came to check on all of you after our talk earlier, but you seem in good spirits, for which I am thankful."

Thea jumped to her feet. "Madison kissed Kyle to get rid of his ex-fiancée, who threw a hissy fit in your kitchen."

"I see." Nanine's mouth pursed as she walked over and gravely sat in their circle of chairs. Thea settled back down beside her. "How do you feel now, Kyle?"

He poured another tequila shot. "Never better. Do you know the American phrase about dodging a bullet, Nanine?"

She shook her head, and Sawyer muttered something in French before she smiled. "*Oui*. I understand the meaning. You Americans and your violent metaphors. Well, tell me the story."

Kyle launched into it again, this time without Madison's snarky commentary about the Diva Paisley's *fake boobs* heaving. Thea had flushed red at that comment. She'd never met anyone who had implants. At least not that she'd known about.

When Kyle finished and punched Madison gently in the shoulder, saying she'd gone the extra mile with the kiss, Nanine gave them a small smile, which felt like a miracle to Thea after today.

"Fifth Course knew how to make her leave." Nanine and Madison shared a look. "Through puncturing her pride. Well, I am glad that is over. Have you arranged for someone to remove her belongings from your house yet?"

He scratched his jaw. "Madison thinks I should capitalize on her being gone and have my assistant pack up her things and take them over to her parents' house, where she can pick them up when she returns."

"I agree." Then a shadow crossed Nanine's face. "Perhaps

you should have them change the locks. You do not want to let someone like that into your home. Sometimes even those we think we know can harm what we love."

Silence descended. Everyone knew Nanine was thinking of her own family. "Nanine, what do you think about them kissing?" Thea blurted out to change the mood. "Isn't that weird?"

Nanine touched her fingertips to her mouth as she looked at Kyle and Madison. "Was it so strange?"

"*Absolutely!*" Kyle said, prompting Madison to punch him a little less gently. "All these years, she's been wondering—"

"How much of a slobbering idiot you could possibly be," she finished for him with a laugh. "His technique needs work."

Dean whistled. "Cold."

Sawyer grinned. "How was Madison's technique, Kyle?"

He turned and looked at her, considering. "She needs major help. Dean, you up next?"

"*What*?" he asked, pretending to fall off his chair. "No way am I kissing her. No offense, Madison. But you're my friend. Just thinking about it... Ewww!"

Sawyer puckered up. "I'm an excellent teacher, Madison."

"I'd practice with *you*, Kyle," Brooke said, batting her eyelashes at him.

Everyone laughed.

"It is good to laugh, especially on dark days," Nanine said, chuckling quietly. "I am glad you handled such a horrible situation together."

"There was trouble here?" Jean Luc asked urgently from the doorway in English.

Thea jumped up again and then stumbled, forgetting she was wearing the new gorgeous strappy black heels Sawyer had found her. Jean Luc lurched forward to steady her and she found herself breathless as his arms wrapped around her. She was never going to get used to the way he made her feel, but she'd come to view that as a good thing. "Kyle's ex-fiancée showed up and went a little nutso—"

"Psycho is a better word," Dean broke in. "But Madison saved the day by kissing him in front of her and making Diva Paisley finally give up. Oh, to have been a fly on the wall."

Jean Luc's brow knit, and Thea wondered if he knew the fly expression. "I see. I feared something else might have happened."

An uneasy silence descended upon the room again, and Thea patted his back in comfort. She'd texted him after hearing about the cave, and he'd told her he was taking a walk to calm himself before their date, which they'd agreed should go forward. He'd said bad news shouldn't stop a chance for happiness.

She needed to add that to her recipe card.

"So everything is all right now?" he continued, tension still on his face as he regarded everyone.

"Yep," Madison replied, forcing a smile. "Good thing Thea wasn't the one in the kitchen. She might have had to kiss Kyle to make that bitch leave."

"I would never!" she protested.

He only gave a sly smile in Madison's direction. "Don't worry, Thea. Madison is only teasing and reminding me of my Italian cousins. They are a protective lot, especially with those they love."

Madison nodded and grinned. "We all have to go the extra mile for friends and family sometimes. Isn't that right, Jean Luc?"

"*Bien sûr,*" he answered with a raised eyebrow.

"Am I missing something?" Thea asked, looking between them.

"No, *ma chérie,*" Jean Luc said, kissing her cheek softly. "All you should know is that you have the best of friends. It seems there is no limit to what you will do for each other."

"Yeah, like kissing Kyle today." Madison lifted her empty

shot glass. "C'mon, don't hold out on me, Golden Boy. I need more hooch to destroy your cooties."

"In your dreams, Garcia," Kyle replied as he poured her another shot. "You two should go. You have a nice date waiting for you and an apple tart for later."

Jean Luc looked like he was biting the inside of his cheek. "You and Madison were kind to drop it by earlier. The visit was unexpected but most enlightening."

"Now, *that* sounds mysterious," Nanine said, beginning to rise to her feet.

Dean jumped up and helped her, which she brushed off with a frown before crossing to greet Jean Luc Parisian style and then kissing Thea as well. "You two have a wonderful time tonight."

Thea blushed before gesturing to her friends. "Don't say anything important without me, okay? I still don't think Madison and Kyle have answered all our questions."

"And we never shall," Kyle said, lifting his shot glass.

"Oh, come on," Sawyer said, reaching to pour himself a shot. "How long was the kiss? Did it involve tongue?"

Thea blushed to the roots of her hair, but she was apparently the only one who didn't want those kinds of details.

Dean set his elbows on his knees. "Yeah. Spill."

"That is my signal to leave," Nanine said as she left the room.

"Mine as well," Jean Luc said suavely. "Are you ready, *ma Thea*?"

She surveyed her roommates. They were all smiling at her, which made her want to go around and hug each of them, especially after how hard they'd all taken the cave news. "You can keep *those* details to yourself, actually, but promise you'll fill me in on anything important."

"We'll let you know the minute Madison discovers she's pregnant with Kyle's baby," Dean joked.

"Not funny!" Madison laughed and threw the top of the

tequila bottle at Dean. Meanwhile, Kyle leapt out of his chair, acting like he was going to tackle Dean.

"You'd better leave," Brooke called, moving her chair back as they playfully tussled. "Things are about to get rowdy. Have a good time!"

Their eyes held. Earlier, a few of them had cried in each other's arms. Now they were all together, making the best of things. She felt her heart swell as Jean Luc led them through the back of the kitchen.

Dean's yawp reached them. "I love my friends, but they do like to roughhouse. Do Frenchmen do that?"

He cocked his brow. "No. It is more of an American trait. We French are more dignified. Perhaps too much, some might say."

Something crashed as they exited the back door. A chair? "I'm sure they're fine. You should have seen them when we first lived together. Brooke used to say they acted like little boys."

"Indeed." He stopped and faced her in the waning light on the street, his silver suit with black pinstripes almost making him look like a knight in shining armor. "I did not have the chance to greet you properly."

She knew what was coming—a kiss. Every time they met, she could feel the excitement course through her veins as he slowly lowered his head and laid his lips gently on hers. The newness still had her tentatively laying her hand on his chest. She loved feeling the fabric of his fine suits under her fingertips.

As if he'd been waiting for that sign, he pulled her gently to him and took the kiss deeper, savoring her lips as if she were the greatest delicacy. His cologne washed over her as his body heat rose, something she was beginning to recognize. *Heat.* Hers rose when he kissed her as well, and her heart never ceased its pounding.

Time stopped, and she floated on a sea where only the two of them existed.

When he lifted his head, she kept her eyes closed. "Every time, it's like magic."

He caressed her cheek, and she finally forced herself back to earth. His blue eyes were bright and filled with tenderness. "For me as well, *ma Thea*."

He took her hand, and they resumed their stroll to his car, which he'd parked in front of the restaurant. "The fly on the wall comment from Dean had me wondering for a moment if there was a bug problem in the restaurant. But no one seemed concerned, so I did not exclaim wildly."

She nudged him playfully, glad he was determined not to let today dim his mood. "Good thing since it's just another colloquialism."

"*Chérie*, I admit to being puzzled. Does a fly even have ears?"

Happy to be with him, she simply shook her head, knowing she had begun her evening of endless smiles. "I don't know. Does a cockroach ever get sad?"

He shrugged, ever so sexily. "Do you think there are a lot of phrases about insects in various languages?"

"I'll ask Sawyer." A smile stole over her face. "You know, I wish you *had* jumped in fright when Dean mentioned a fly. It would have been so funny."

He waved his hand in the air before opening the passenger door. "There is no comparison between a fly and a cockroach. And your friend Madison could take care of both creatures, I am sure."

He waited until she was comfortable in her seat before carefully closing the door. She sank back against the leather, inhaling his scent. Nothing smelled as good as Jean Luc, she'd decided—not even fresh-baked bread. And that would have been inconceivable to her before.

When he was settled on the driver's side, he looked at her

as he started the engine. "I meant what I said. You have the best of friends. It is heartening to see how you support each other. Loyalty is a rare prize in life."

"You're right," she said, feeling another rush of gratitude for all the changes in her life.

"And yet effective." He navigated down the narrow street before heading to the Latin Quarter past Odeon. "Thank you again for the apple tart. The kindness of it was especially touching today, but we will not speak more than we have of that."

She nodded in agreement. "No, we will celebrate and enjoy ourselves—like Nanine always says to do in such moments."

"*Exactamente,*" he said in French before switching to English for her benefit like usual after the miscommunication on their first date. "When it reached me, I must confess to being struck by its beauty. You truly are a skilled *boulangère.*"

"You haven't tried it yet," she said, feeling her face heat.

"Your sweetness enchants me, but it was not necessary for you to go to the trouble."

"You've been so generous, Jean Luc—"

He made a very French sound. "It is what a man does when he is romancing the woman he cares for."

"Then maybe you should let me romance *you* a little," she blurted out. "Oh gosh. Was that okay to say? I mean, maybe your idea of romance is completely different."

"What could be more romantic than a beautiful apple tart made from your hands? I am honored. I am glad you will share it with me after the cinema. You still are comfortable doing so?"

"Yes. Of course! It's not like we could ask the restaurant to serve it. A bottle of wine is one thing, but an apple tart? We would be asked to leave."

"Perhaps. Perhaps not. It depends on the restaurant. Now tell me about the bread you made today for the menu."

She ran through her thinking about the apricot and walnut bread pairing as they wound around Luxembourg Gardens. A few reckless tourists dashed across the street illegally. Jean Luc lifted a hand and made another Parisian sound as he braked sharply along with the other cars.

"That part of the city hasn't changed," she said as he swung left and pulled into an underground parking lot.

"And it never shall. There is always so much to see, I suppose. People are always looking elsewhere."

"I've been guilty of that a time or two." She watched as he backed into a tight parking spot with complete confidence. "Gosh, it's good to be back. When I was back home, I used to find myself longing to be here. Walking on the streets. Having a café. Talking with my roommates. Wishing there was an alternate universe."

He took her hand after killing the engine. "And now you are back, and all is good in the world."

"Yes. Mostly. I still worry about Nanine. Maybe a little about my future. But it's all going to be fine somehow."

She made sure to smile, although nerves rippled in her stomach. Soon, she would need to find a job. Her landlady back home had found someone to take over her apartment, so she would not have that financial worry, and so far she had very few expenses. Still, she needed to feel the confidence of having her own position—something to make her proud.

"Your future, like your present, will be better than simply fine." He leaned in and kissed her slowly in the darkened car. "We will see to it. You have many on your side, *chérie*. Come. I think you will like the restaurant I chose. I changed our plans last minute after my visit with Madison and Kyle. When I asked what kinds of places you used to enjoy when you lived here before, they mentioned your love for Moroccan cuisine."

"They did? How nice of them. Yes, I love it. The flavors and décor are both incredible. I haven't had Moroccan since leaving Paris, so this will be a treat."

"My thoughts exactly." He exited the car and had to wait as she squeezed out of her side given the proximity of the Renault next to them.

Tucked between two rare bookshops with a first-edition *Great Gatsby* and an illuminated manuscript in the window, the restaurant was a charming neighborhood place run by Hassan and Amina. More clients of Jean Luc's, she discovered, and was immediately enfolded in their friendship with him. They had three children, she learned, and grew their own herbs and vegetables at a nearby community garden.

She was dazzled by the purple and gold floor seating and the traditional Moroccan lanterns hanging from the ceiling. The spices whose fragrance had greeted them—cumin, cinnamon, mint, and ginger—more than stood out in her meal of lamb *tagine*, accompanied by roasted red pepper salad, saffron rice, and freshly baked *khobzi*, a bread she decided to attempt making. After two glasses of red wine and more of Jean Luc's company, she was well sated by the time they arrived at Le Champo.

Thea was reminded again of the difference in the movie experience in France as they sat in the theater to watch an engrossing film about a woman seeking the truth about the disappearance of her teenage son. As the movie started, people stilled, reverent, no one slurping drinks loudly or ruffling popcorn sacks. The focus on the movie pulled her in so deeply she was crying by the end, and Jean Luc pressed a handkerchief into her hands in support.

As they walked back to the car, he put his arm around her. "I would not have suggested the movie if I had known it would make you sad, *ma Thea*. Tonight was supposed to turn around any feelings of tragedy."

"I thought it looked good when you sent me the options. And it was. But that poor woman…"

"Yes, her plight was heartbreaking. We French have a tragic streak when it comes to the arts. It's our way of saying life goes on regardless. Next time I'll take you to a romantic comedy, as I do prefer to hear you laugh."

Then he stopped and took her gently by the shoulders, his face full of beautiful angles in the golden lamplight. "Although you do cry very beautifully, *chérie*. Much like you do everything."

Beautifully…

The way he said the word, so confidently, so genuinely, had her heart warming in her chest. She'd never imagined feeling like this.

This was love.

She'd never had it before, but she didn't doubt that this was true. If she'd known how amazing it felt before, maybe she'd have tried harder to find it. Then again, maybe this was the perfect time with the perfect man. Some ingredients you had to add later or else the whole recipe fell apart.

Wanting to share the feeling with him, she lifted her hand to his jaw. His eyes darkened before he leaned down and kissed her slowly and thoroughly, the kind that made her toes curl.

When he raised his head, she knew exactly what her entry in her Paris journal would be tonight. *To be kissed on the streets of Paris in the lamplight is a thing of magic.*

After walking her back to the car, he brought her hands to his lips and kissed them. "You are still all right to share the apple tart you prepared?"

She rested her head against his strong forearm. "Yes. Very much. I find comfort as well as happiness in your company, and I needed both tonight."

"Me as well."

He navigated the streets back to Saint-Germain and pulled into another hidden garage down a dark alleyway. They emerged onto the street to hear someone playing the piano.

"My neighbor is a classical pianist," he told her as they

paused to listen. "He delights us with his talent—but never past midnight. My apartment is just here."

He entered a code on the wall box a couple of doors down and pushed the heavy wooden door open. The lights flickered on when he hit the interior button, and they made their way to the foot of the stairs. "No elevator, I'm afraid. It's three floors up. Watch your feet. I'll be right behind you."

Watch her feet? She froze at the bottom of the narrow, treacherous stairs Paris was known for. She looked down at her feet and then back up at Jean Luc. Had he noticed how big they were?

Why else would he caution her?

Her cheeks flamed. She wanted to die. On the spot.

His hand urged her gently up the first steps, and she bobbled. He was there to steady her. All she wanted to do was turn around and run away, but he was close behind her, guiding her up.

Climbing stairs in Paris sometimes felt like it took an eternity, and today she thought it would never end.

Every step, she was sure Jean Luc noticed the way her Big Bird feet stuck out on the thin steps. She was a freak, and he had noticed. By the time they reached his floor, she was tense and not feeling like her new self at all.

When she entered his foyer, she tried to gather herself, fighting the urge to press her hands to her hot cheeks.

Jean Luc set his keys down on the narrow bureau and regarded her. "Are you all right, *chérie*?" he asked softly.

She nodded briskly. "Yes. I'm fine. Absolutely fine."

But she wasn't, and the way his brow knit told her he knew it. The silence between them suddenly was rank with awkwardness. "I can take you home if you are not comfortable, you know. We can arrange to share the tart tomorrow. I know a café that would let us enjoy it with a glass of champagne. As you prefer."

He wasn't acting normal either. So formal. Maybe he had

just noticed her feet and no longer found her attractive. Gosh, she'd thought these heels had made them look so nice before. What a fool! Her heart pounded in her ears, and she wanted to cover up one of her feet with the other to hide them. But she couldn't blurt out her shame. No, she would eat the tart quickly and say she needed to get home. Early morning. More bread tasting. Something…

"No, it's better fresh." She made a valiant effort to smile. "Then I should probably get home."

His troubled gaze remained on her for another moment before he nodded. He turned on more lights as they walked down the narrow hallway. Every step echoed in her ears. Her feet sounded huge on his hardwood floors.

Ordinarily, she'd look around with curiosity, but the framed art on the walls might as well be paint splatters, because everything was a blur as she closed in around herself. When the lights on the large chandelier in his main salon came on, Thea knew it would be clanging its distress loudly if it were like Nanine's.

All of the magic between her and Jean Luc had disappeared in an instant, and she was sick to her very soul.

He paused as he turned on a table lamp, his profile in shadow. "I should not have brought you here. I did not wish to say anything, but it appears your friends were right. Perhaps it is too soon."

Her friends?

"What?"

"I did not see," he said in a voice she didn't recognize, lifting his head. "I thought you would know I had no ulterior motivations in making this invitation. I did not bring you back here for that, although I hope in time we will become closer. When you are ready, of course. Tell me I didn't ruin this, Thea."

She stared at him in shock. "I don't understand. You think

I'm upset because you brought me back here? Jean Luc, what are you talking about?"

His brows slammed together. "Perhaps I should say no more."

Crossing to him, she stopped a few feet away. He was upset. *Very upset*—and not about her freakish feet. "I think you'd better say more, because I don't want you to think you've ruined anything. I thought I had."

"No, of course you have not." He sighed gravely. "I should have listened."

"Tell me who we're talking about here. One of my roommates, right?"

He gazed sadly back at her. "Madison and Kyle told me it might be too soon to bring you back to my apartment."

She blinked. "Why?"

He raised a finger to his lips as he studied her. "Thea, they were worried about me making advances on you. They thought I might be trying to get you into my bed too soon."

Her mouth dropped open and she gaped at him before she could answer. "They talked to you about *that*?"

She spun around, her face reddening for a totally different reason. *Of course* they'd talked to him. Innocent Thea who had no experience with men. "Jean Luc, I don't know what to say. I'm so sorry. I can't believe they did that. Actually… Yes, I can. They were trying to protect me. Which is sweet—since no one ever has looked out for me but them. Except that doesn't make you feel better."

His footsteps sounded behind her, and she knew he was standing only a breath away. "Like I said, my Italian cousins would do the same, and truthfully, my brother and I might do something similar for my sister. I *have* gone faster perhaps than is customary, as Madison pointed out, but I did not think you were ready to share my bed yet. Despite how badly I want you."

She put her hands to her burning face at the mention of sex. "Oh my gosh. I'm so out of my depth here."

"It should not be so difficult to speak of such a matter." His hands touched her shoulders briefly before pulling away. "Please face me. Let us talk about this."

About sex? She had no idea how to do that. She'd barely managed to talk to Brooke and Madison without dry heaving when they'd asked about her experience the other night!

"Thea," he said again, his voice soft. "Am I not your friend? Can you not trust me?"

The raw emotion in his voice had her lowering her hands and turning around. She bit her lip as tears filled her eyes. His face was ravaged by concern. "You *are* my friend. And so much more. Only…"

"What, *ma chérie*? Surely we can stand up to this embarrassment together."

She couldn't look him in the eye, so she did the only thing she knew she could do. She closed the distance between them and lowered her forehead to his chest. His arms immediately came around her, gentle and comforting. "Oh, Jean Luc. My roommates were right about me. I'm a stupid girl from a small town who's never dated much or had a lot of…"

"Beaus?"

Oh, her humiliation was complete. "Yes, that. But I meant something else." She scrunched her eyes together. "Lovers. Sex."

"Ah…" His response was ripe with understanding. "Well, I frankly don't see why that is a problem. In fact, I am not surprised. You are discriminating. It is one of the things I already know and respect about you. Thea, it is one of the reasons I care for you as I do."

She had to see his face now. Pulling back enough to look at him, she soaked him in. "What do you mean?"

His smile was soft as he traced her cheek. "I knew you do

266

not give your heart or your body without love. It is better that way. *Chérie*, what do you think is happening between us?"

The endearment stole her breath as much as the way he was gazing at her. His blue eyes were warm and filled with something more, something she'd started to notice over the last week.

"Perhaps I have made another blunder, but I thought for sure we were falling in love. Am I wrong?"

He had his head tilted to the side, his gaze so powerful her heart stopped beating at its intensity. "No."

"Then we can put this awkwardness behind us." He embraced her again. "You now know my thoughts, and I know yours, and we seem to have scaled our earlier awkwardness together."

Then he paused, and she could feel tension return in his hands as he drew back.

"Except… Forgive me. I am a lawyer and think like one. You mentioned that you didn't see anything wrong with me bringing you here to share the apple tart you'd made. So there must have been some other reason for your discomfort."

She winced and looked away from his searching gaze. "You mentioned my feet."

"*Pardon*?"

There was no avoiding it. "You said, 'watch your feet.' At the stairs. I thought you had noticed how big they are. I was mortified."

He blinked. "I do not understand."

Rip the Band-Aid off, Thea. She pointed to her monstrosities. "I have freakishly big feet. I thought you'd noticed and been turned off."

"I was cautioning you to be careful on the stairs," he said urgently. "Did I get the phrase wrong in English? Never mind. I will see for myself."

Walking over to his cell phone, he tapped something in and then swore fluidly in French. "I should have said 'watch your step.' Thea, this was another language error. But obviously it raised some serious issues for you."

A language error? She'd gone completely off the rails over a language error? "Oh my God! I'm so sorry. Here I thought…"

"You were uncomfortable because of your feet?" He stared at them. "How are these a problem for you?"

He was kidding, right? "Look at them."

He gestured to them. "I see nothing wrong. So you have good-sized feet. I have a large nose. Does it make me less attractive to you?" He turned to give her his profile.

"I think your nose is perfect. Like the rest of you."

He gave an indelicate snort. "That is how I feel about you, Thea. You are perfect. Exquisite even. Who says you have big feet?"

She was still reeling from his *perfect* and *exquisite* comments. "Do you want a list? It's been going on since my feet blew up to a size nine in fifth grade."

"Yes," he answered with determination, "give me their names. I will sue them for such hateful insults."

She put her hand to her mouth. "You're really upset about this."

He made a very French gesture in the air. "Of course I am! How dare anyone say such things! It is an outrage. They hurt you. Therefore, they are my enemies."

Her mouth drifted into a smile. "Your enemies? Oh, Jean Luc."

Her heart tumbled over in her chest. She walked over to where he stood fuming. His jaw was locked with tension and his brow line was severe now, much like when he was angry about the wrongs done to Nanine.

"*Ma Thea*," he began, taking her shoulders. "You listen to *me*. Not these hateful people. Anyone who insults another has no honor. They are not worth another moment of your time. I hate hearing they hurt you so. Thea, we must work on you becoming immune to such talk."

She was feeling all warm inside again. "We must work on it, huh?"

He took her hands, his face a portrait of utter seriousness. "Yes. Together. Until such people and such talk means nothing to you."

The strength in his grip was filled with a lifetime of promises. "I think I fell a little more in love with you just now," she said softly.

He snorted. "I would have preferred it to have been because I gave you an extra special gift. One that is priceless. One you will always remember."

She gazed steadily into his eyes now. "You did, Jean Luc. You might have given me one of the best gifts of my life."

"Because I think your feet are perfect?" He snorted again. "*Ma chérie*, I can do so much better than that, I assure you."

Laughter poured out of her. "You are too perfect for words."

"And yet you are laughing at me?" He sobered and sighed. "I had no idea outrage on your behalf would be more impressive than romance. What else can I express outrage about? Has anyone ever dared to question your character?"

Oh, he was so funny. "No. It's really only my feet people make fun of."

He waved another hand. "Only your feet! I could list off a dozen insults that have been leveled at me. Enough to leave you shocked."

She put her hand on the back of his neck, using gentle pressure to lower his head to her. "You will have to make me a list too."

He chuckled at last, inches from her mouth. "That is as it should be, given our relationship. A man and woman together defend each other."

Her very perfect toes curled in her heels, and he hadn't

even kissed her yet. "Our relationship. So does that make you my *copain*?"

"Boyfriend." His wince was humorous. "I know it is how you say it in English, so yes, that is what I am. Although the sentiment is not strong enough for me. I will call you *mon amour*, which leaves no questions."

My love. The strongest endearment a French person used for a romantic partner, or so Brooke had told her. Her floating cloud had appeared at last. "Then you are *mon amour* for me as well."

He kissed her softly on the mouth. "Good. We understand one another. But, frankly, this misunderstanding has brought us closer, I think. For that, I am grateful. Madison and Kyle love you like a sister and acted as staunch protectors, which is why I let them speak to me as they did."

"Are you sure? I imagine you were a little insulted."

He lifted a shoulder. "At first, yes. But Madison made a persuasive argument about the usual reasons men invite women to their homes, and Kyle agreed 'as a guy.' Is this true for most American men? If a man invites you back to his apartment after a date, is it assumed he will try to take you to bed even if you are not ready?" He shook his head in aggravation. "And they say Frenchmen have terrible reputations."

She was back to the land of endless smiles. "Like I said, I don't have much experience."

His kiss was the merest brush of his lips, filled with tenderness. "*Mon amour*, we will take our steps together. We learn more about each other every day. My parents always say the happiest relationships are so."

She pressed her mouth to his this time, and he gave a deep groan. Oh, how she loved hearing him make that sound.

"Here is one thing I know," he said as he lifted his head and smiled at her. "You adore kissing me. Just as I adore kissing you. So…"

She could feel desire race through her when he paused and held her gaze in the soft light.

"Let us see if you enjoy this, *ma Thea*."

He kissed the soft side of her neck, making her close her eyes at the sheer decadence of his touch. "Oh, yes. I like that very much."

His smile was triumphant when he met her gaze. "See. It is that easy. Step by step. Now, *ma chérie*. It *is* getting late, and your roommates *are* very protective. Perhaps we should savor your tart together, and then I shall take you home."

She wasn't ready to leave her floating cloud yet. He was right. Tonight *had* brought them closer. Their honesty had increased the trust and commitment between them, along with their newfound love.

More ingredients for her recipe.

She lifted her mouth to his again and whispered, "In a little while, Jean Luc. In a little while."

CHAPTER
TWENTY-THREE

B rooke winced as Kyle handed out bound copies of
the project management timeline to everyone seated
around the kitchen table.

She was used to graphs and timetables at the magazine, as
deadlines were sacrosanct, but Nanine despised technology.
She eyed Nanine out of the corner of her eye. She hadn't
spoken of the loss of the cave again, as was her way, but her
grief was evident. Her high cheekbones were a little starker,
as were the laugh lines around her mouth. But she'd worn her
long white curly hair in a perfect bun along with her red
lipstick and Chanel No. 5 religiously to signal she meant
business.

Losing the cave was not going to defeat her, and they'd all
rallied together to create concrete steps to move the restaurant's renovation forward.

Still, she made a distressed sound before laying her hands
on top of her copy and regarding Kyle. "Forgive me, Sixth
Course, but is this really necessary?"

"You don't like project management tools like this?"
Dean asked after running his finger across his color-coded
copy like it was a woman's body. "But Nanine, this is the

best out there! I was the one who gave the program to Kyle."

"I miss the old days," Nanine said sadly. "Before computers."

Sawyer raised his hands to the heavens despairingly. "Agreed! Why couldn't the world have just stopped at the height of the Roman empire?"

"I ask myself that every day," Madison said dryly, tapping the table. "All right, I'm not a huge fan of computers either, but I've been a part of a restaurant renovation. They can be a bitch. Sorry, Nanine. I'll rephrase. There are a lot of moving parts."

"*Bitch* in this case works for me," Nanine said, making them laugh again. "But I see your point. Many details. Many players."

"And all color-coded for easy review," Dean said with his usual enthusiasm. "Wait until you see my website design ideas, Nanine. They are going to rock your world."

Brooke refrained from rolling her eyes because Kyle and Dean really were doing a great job managing the process. The two of them had interviewed everyone else in the house, Jean Luc, and some of his restaurant clients to ascertain additional ideas for contractors, restaurant innovations in the front and back of the house, and construction and legal practicalities and pitfalls.

"I'm just glad the electrician finished on time," Brooke said. "I've heard horror stories from people I know here who've hired one."

"You can thank Jean Luc for that," Kyle said. "He called in a favor."

"Oh, he's just the best, isn't he?" Thea exclaimed.

"I'd marry him," Dean joked.

Brooke wouldn't go that far, but she liked the man more every day. In the two weeks since the Apple Tart Incident, as it was now referred to in the house, he'd spent more time in an effort to get to know everyone better. Madison had even shocked everyone by inviting his opinion on her latest attempt to master the *canard aux cerises* recipe. While she'd been impressed with his suggestion of adding star anise to the cherry broth, she still wasn't satisfied with the results.

Still, he'd won Madison over, which was a lot like winning against the Death Star, according to Dean. Their praise had only made Thea float higher.

"He's been vetting our list of contractors and has agreed to work with Kyle to negotiate fees," Dean added. "He's represented by the navy and white pinstripe on the graph. I thought that was rather artistic of me."

"I'll make sure to write it up in my fashion magazine," Brooke shot back.

"Always better to have someone smart and local making the calls," Madison said, "or people might take advantage. I've seen it happen a million times in Miami. Thea, you should bake him another tart. Which I can deliver with Kyle, if you'd like."

Thea blushed. "That's…ah…not necessary."

Nanine attempted to hide her smile but the rest of them were far more open with their amusement. Everyone knew about *that* particular visit.

These days Brooke was mostly relaxed. Thea came home every night from her date happy. So far she hadn't stayed over. Nor had she once asked any of them for advice. But worry still pressed under Brooke's ribs sometimes as she thought about how fast they were moving.

Thea was totally in love with him. But what if he ended up showing other colors, colors Nanine would never have seen? It happened in a romantic relationship as time went on. She didn't want Thea to get hurt. She also knew it wasn't fair to foist her fears on her friend.

"Nanine has decided on the fabric samples," Brooke said, sending Nanine an encouraging smile. "I was going to negotiate directly, but I should involve Jean Luc in the contract, right?"

"He'd be happy to help," Thea chirped. "I can ask him when I meet him for dinner later."

Kyle and Dean shared a look before Kyle said, "All contracts should go through Jean Luc, yes. He's very thorough, and we want all our Ts crossed when it comes to the restaurant."

The elephant of Jeremy and Adrienne weighed heavily in the room before Nanine said, "Would I have chosen him as my lawyer otherwise?"

"Your taste remains exquisite," Dean said, blowing her a kiss to dispel the lingering tension. "Now, let's go over the schedule as it is now."

Dean and Kyle traded off highlighting each task and the person responsible for completing it. Brooke was in charge of delivering everything termed linens. She and Sawyer would work together on fixtures while Sawyer was individually accountable for three artistic touches in the new restaurant: a large painting of the women Nanine had originally mentioned; vines trailing up the walls in strategic points of emphasis in the restaurant; and a hand-painted welcome sign that would be situated outside the front door. Thea and Madison were still working on the menu with Nanine's input. Dean was in charge of all things technology from the website to online reservations, ordering, and inventory systems.

Kyle cleared his throat and announced that in addition to his current project management duties, he had a new item to put to Nanine and the group.

Brooke straightened in her chair along with everyone else.

"Please," Nanine began, "I am eager to hear what you have in mind."

He smiled, his hands on the table, looking very much like the restaurateur he was. "Good. Nanine, I'd like to talk about the budget. We have the renovation budget ready now that all of the contractor bids are in. But I will need a few more things from you. A draft menu and pricing breakdown by dish."

"God, I hate those," Madison muttered under her breath.

"You mean the price point," Nanine said dryly. "It is not something I have broken down in detail. I have always had a general sense."

Dean winced but Kyle kept smiling. "That is why you have us. For that level of detail."

She turned her coffee cup around in her hands, her expression with a touch of pique. "Why is it needed now?"

He picked up another sheet of paper at his right. "For staffing. Nanine, we need to look at that budget too, the old one and your ideas for a new one."

Brooke's heart sank. She was glad he hadn't mentioned the budget for the new cave selection, which was going to take time as well as the finalization of the new menu. Wine and liquor tastings would only commence after they finished tweaking the recipes. Special bottles would take a long-term special plan, which they'd brainstormed with no conclusion yet.

But this conversation on staffing... All of them had been dreading it since they could no longer avoid the obvious. Nanine could not work the hours she used to.

Nanine's mouth twisted. Silence filled the room. A few people looked like they wanted to slide under the table.

"I am still considering staffing," she said crisply.

Brooke had to give Kyle credit. His smile didn't slip. "Perfect. Let me know if you want to discuss anything. I'm here to help."

At last, Nanine sighed, and the tension in the room seemed to lessen with it. "I know you are here to help. All of you. Forgive me if I sound...difficult or ungrateful. These changes are taking some getting used to, and I have old and new considerations to balance."

Brooke didn't envy her there. She loved Nanine's longtime

sous chef, Jacques, but he didn't have the excellence or innovation required to execute Nanine's duties. Which is why he wasn't creating the menu. Madison did have those abilities, and everyone knew it, Nanine included.

But offering the position to Madison or someone like her would require Nanine to step aside as *chef de cuisine* of her own restaurant. What was she to do? Sit in the corner and call out suggestions for the staff who were doing the actual cooking? Only cook for a few hours at a time?

Nanine would never stand for such a schedule, believing too many cooks spoil the broth and consistency was critical.

"I am suddenly very tired." Nanine pushed herself up slowly and waved aside Brooke and Sawyer's instinctive reach to help her.

They had only made her feel worse by coddling her. Lowering her gaze to the kitchen table, Brooke clenched her hands in her lap as Nanine left the kitchen.

The silence was deafening, and all they could hear was the melancholy rumble of the chandelier.

"It's never given a funeral dirge before," Sawyer said quietly. "Not even when they took away her cave."

"I hate that sound," Brooke whispered. "I hate all of this."

Thea put her arm around her. "We all do, and her most of all. But she'll come through, Brooke. With all of us to help her."

"Yes, we'll be here, but it's not going to be easy." Kyle's smile had disappeared when Brooke looked up. "Staffing is a big item. I'm trying not to push, but I imagine it's been on your minds, Thea and Madison. Right?"

Neither one of them said a word, and Brooke wasn't surprised. Thea tried not to talk about her current unemployed status, saying everything would work out. Madison had handled her situation with her usual no-nonsense practicality. After she'd formally submitted her resignation to her old restaurant weeks ago, she'd had a co-worker box up a few keepsakes to ship to her in Paris so she could officially vacate her furnished apartment, which had been rented on a month-to-month basis. She hadn't once implied she assumed she would work at Nanine's when it opened, but her laser focus on the menu showed a commendable sense of devotion.

Brooke had always known her friend had character, but Madison had really gone the extra mile. Tough and jaded she might be, but she was loyal to the core and she put a lot of people before her own needs. Not just Nanine—she'd shown how much she valued her roommates by stepping up for Kyle and trying to protect Thea.

"It impacts you two the most," Dean pressed. "Kyle and I agreed not to push—"

"Then don't," Madison said with an edge in her voice, glaring at him. "She'll come to a decision on what she needs to do about staffing. Thea and I will keep working on the menu with her. That is going well, and Nanine needs the focus as much as the creative drive. Thea, I don't want to speak for you if you feel different. I'm still technically banked on paid vacation, and I have some padding in my bank account."

"And I don't," Thea said, an earlier depression filling her voice, one Brooke had hoped Jean Luc and her return to Paris had banished forever. "Maybe I *should* start looking for a job. Even if it's just to see what's out there. I can't rely on all of you forever."

"And who's going to bake the bread for the new menu?" Madison asked sharply. "I'm less valuable to the new menu than you are. Plus—no offense—my position garners a higher salary. With Jacques still on Nanine's staff, I can't see Nanine's having two sous chefs."

"Unless Nanine steps aside as *chef de cuisine* and puts you in charge of the kitchen, leaving Jacques in his current post." Dean held out his hands as if bracing against her reply. "It's one of the most logical possibilities, Madison."

"And Thea?" Brooke put in. "Where does she fit into the logical possibilities chart in your mind, Kyle? Because I know you've drafted every org chart imaginable."

"While factoring in the past three years of revenue, yes, I have," Kyle told her, rubbing the back of his neck. "I'd cut a few of the *commis de cuisine*—"

"Which was my first job at Nanine's, along with Thea's and Sawyer's," Madison said. "So you cut entry-level positions. What about the *chef de partie*?"

"Nanine currently has two as you know—one for pastry and the other for appetizers." Kyle folded his arms over his chest and sat back. "I would broaden the pastry chef's tasks to include bread."

"So, you'd make it a position for Thea, in other words," Sawyer concluded out loud. "But is that what you want, Thea?"

Everyone turned to Thea, who was biting her lip. "I love bread and pastry, although bread is my first love. Of course, I baked pastry at Snyder's bakery. So it's not like I'm a purist. And you know I'd do anything to help Nanine. This new menu is designed to tempt the Michelin people into giving the restaurant a star. It's been her dream."

"Yes, but is it *your* dream?" Sawyer asked her, pushing his gold-rimmed glasses further up his nose as if trying to see her better. "Also, I don't want to point out the obvious, but the hours would be totally different than what you're used to. You'd go from starting work at three or four in the morning like you used to and ending at nine or ten a.m. to starting before lunch and ending after dinner."

"It's a valid point," Madison said with a nod. "Also, while no one else can bake like you, there are other ways to handle those menu items."

"But you'd still have to hire someone new," Kyle said, "because no one on Nanine's current staff has Thea's skills."

"In the end, this discussion doesn't seem to matter," Dean

interjected, raising his hands slowly again. "Don't kill me, but I'm the guy who funds and mentors businesses on the ideas side. Nanine has to decide what *she* wants. Everything else is just speculative."

"Not true," Sawyer said, shaking his head. "Sorry, I'm about to go philosophical."

"Shocking," Madison said with a smile. "Go ahead, Doc. Let's get brainy."

He rested his elbows on the table and set his face in his hands. "Nanine needs to decide what she wants. That's her right. But Thea, you need to do that too. Leaving your job and moving to Paris was big for you, a way of reclaiming your life. To stray from that is to go back to where you started. Albeit surrounded with great friends. Us."

Brooke couldn't help but smile as he waved to all of their roommates. "He's right. Thea, you have to follow *your* heart and decide what *you* want. Independent of Nanine's decision."

She looked down. "But I'm happy creating new breads for Nanine's new menu," she protested, "and I like working with Madison."

"Before you crack a joke, Dean," Madison said, her golden eyes fiery, "I didn't pay her to say that."

A few people chuckled before Madison looked at Thea. "I like working with you too, Thea, but we both know menu creation isn't day in, day out. I've never worked in a bakery, but Sawyer's right about the schedule being different. It's also never quiet in a restaurant, which you remember from working here at Nanine's."

"It's a grind," Sawyer added. "I was glad it put a roof over my head when I was an exchange student, but I could never handle the pressure long term. So, Thea, it seems you are like Nanine. You need to decide what you want to do with your life career-wise."

Judging by the look on Thea's face, her happy bubble was

beyond gone, so Brooke put an arm around her to cheer her up. "Sounds like you have more writing to do in your recipe journal. Great! You're rocking everything else, from your emerging style to your relationship with Jean Luc. You've got this. Now, how about some more good news?"

She gave everyone a stern look not to say anything more.

"Good news would be great," Thea said in a small voice.

Brooke could barely hear her, and her usual enthusiasm was absent. "I'm writing an article on what Parisians wear while dating, and I was hoping you might help me with it. Although I know you're really busy with the menu planning, so don't worry if it's too much to ask."

As expected, her brown eyes brightened. "Of course I'll help. What can I do?"

Someone pressed their foot on top of hers—Dean, she imagined. He was going to die when she got him alone. Didn't he know she was wearing Louboutins? She kicked him under the table with her free leg and enjoyed his wince.

"Well, I thought you could look over some of the clothes I'm being sent and see what you might be willing to wear on a date with Jean Luc. It would really help me out, Thea."

She knew not to look at any of their other roommates. They all were watching closely.

"Your articles always have photos," Thea blurted out. "I—"

"I would only need a few casual shots," she interrupted, trying to relax. "They'd only feature you from the neck down. Easy peasy."

She was still worrying her lip. "Would you want to take a picture of me and Jean Luc on a date?"

Thea's bubble was returning, like a soap bubble gaining size as a child blew into a wand. "Oh, that would be terrific for my article! Would that be something he'd consider?"

Her smile was nearly radiant now, and Brooke could feel triumph pumping into her veins.

"I can ask him," Thea answered breezily. "I'm seeing him tonight."

They all already knew that, of course, because Thea talked about her outings with Jean Luc every day.

"Great. Thanks for asking him."

"Did you know his mother was a model?"

Again, she nodded. Thea had told everyone that weeks ago. She'd been sure her mouth had dropped open. Imagine his mother being the famous Fabiana, known for her Italian curves and passionate demeanor. Paris really was a small world.

"I'm going to go text him right now." She stood and was three steps to the door leading to their apartments when she stopped and looked over her shoulder. "Are we finished here?"

"Absolutely," Kyle said, standing up. "Go text your boyfriend."

She beamed and hurried out.

Madison lifted her hand to Brooke for a high five, who immediately slapped it. "Nice work. She was running out of clothes from our Fairy Godmother trek. Thea's pride wouldn't let her accept any more handouts, even for a bread trade."

"They're not handouts," Brooke protested. "It's love."

"Never underestimate Brooke," Dean interjected before Madison could fire back.

"Word," she agreed.

He reached for a high five. She gave it to him. "Will you take the labels out of the clothes so she won't know she's wearing luxury brands worth thousands of dollars?"

She hadn't thought of that. "Good point. She might freak."

"Someone had better tell Jean Luc not to say anything," Kyle added. "He's bound to notice. I nominate Sawyer to talk to him."

Sawyer shot him a look. "Just because he and I trade

quotes from French philosophers doesn't mean we're better pals than the rest of you guys. Also, Brooke, maybe you should give Madison some clothes so she and Kyle can go out now that they've kissed."

"My cleaver isn't far away, Sawyer," Madison said with her eerie smile.

"I'd do it for the clothes, Madison," Kyle said with a wink. "And to help Brooke out, of course."

"Go out with Brooke then." Madison grabbed them each by the hand and tried to make them touch before they both jerked back, laughing. "Let's keep on track. Sawyer, will you talk to Jean Luc?"

"Fine, I'll mention it the next time I run into him along the Seine."

"Walking like a good Parisian after lunch so you can sketch in the afternoon light." Dean made a motion of a beating heart. "Ah, *la vie.*"

Madison gave Dean's ear a playful pinch. "How is your *vie* going? Are you missing SoCal?"

"First, San Francisco is not in Southern California," he said, "and two, not at all. I'm happy to be back in Paris working with my few remaining clients remotely and helping Nanine. Being around you guys isn't bad either, but I do hate my bed. My feet hang off the end, and if I have to sleep like this any longer, there might be permanent damage. I need to purchase a new one."

Brooke laughed. "Good luck squeezing a bigger bed into that space. Actually, it's easier to be alone in a small bed. My big bed was feeling too empty in New York."

"Small beds as a cure for no sex life?" Dean shuddered in horror. "I can't get on that train even if I haven't met any ladies I'd like to tangle with yet."

"We've been busy," Madison said with a pointed look. "Plus, Nanine's rules."

"Yeah," Sawyer said. "Still sacred."

They all nodded.

"Any idea how to help Nanine on the staffing?" Brooke asked.

"Just leave her to it." Madison put her hands on her hips. "She knows what needs to be done, and she knows it impacts other people. People she cares about. She'll figure it out."

Brooke knew she was right, but it wasn't in her nature to sit by idly. "So I'll focus on helping Thea then."

"Clothes won't answer the yearnings of her heart," Sawyer pointed out. "Let us heed the words of Voltaire in this moment."

They all groaned.

"*My friend,*" he quoted, "*you see how perishable are the riches of this world; there is nothing solid but virtue.*"

"Which Thea has in spades already," Dean said, giving Sawyer a healthy nudge. "Now she will have the clothes too."

"Philistines!" Sawyer cried out with a grin.

"And what about you, Doc?" Madison asked with her usual spice. "How are you faring with everything?"

"Let me answer with another quote by Voltaire," he said with a scholarly gleam. "*I don't know where I am going, but I am on my way.*"

Brooke took a moment before answering, "At last! A Voltaire quote that speaks to me."

"Yeah," Dean said, rubbing his head like he was as surprised as she was. "Me too."

"Me three," Kyle added darkly.

"I am so not saying 'me four' out loud," Madison finally answered after Sawyer looked her way.

"Voltaire is like Paris," he said as he walked out. "Beautiful, layered, and mysterious. Rather like life."

Yes, life. Brooke just wished it wasn't such a bitch some of the time.

CHAPTER
TWENTY-FOUR

T hea sat at Café Fitzy flipping through her journal. Ten years—more or less—of her hopes, dreams, and longings, all in one book.

What do I really want?

Nanine always said sitting alone in a café brought wisdom, but looking at everything in her journal wasn't helping her.

The conversation with her roommates yesterday had left her deeply unsettled. Not even Brooke showing her a few new outfits for her fashion article had cheered her up, but gosh, they were nice. She had one on today for her picnic with Jean Luc in a couple hours at Luxembourg Gardens, some wide black pants and a gorgeous purple sweater that was so thin it was unlike any she'd ever seen. There were even shoes, gorgeous ones in her size: ballet slippers in lime green. She could keep what she wanted—a total shock! Heck, Brooke's whole idea was so totally nice.

Nice.

She needed to banish that word from her vocabulary. Being nice was what had her staring down at her journal, feeling like she'd been tugged backward in time.

Old Thea hadn't known what she wanted exactly. She'd only known what she didn't want. What was missing from her life.

Suddenly she realized that wasn't a *nice* problem. Being kind was important to her, but being *too nice* was a problem. Sometimes it meant she didn't search for what she really wanted or stand up for herself. That she went along with what someone wanted for her so she wouldn't rock the boat.

Now she had to plumb the depths of herself and ask: what did New Thea really want to do with her life?

She stopped on the last recipe in her book. *Living Life to the Fullest.*

A main ingredient to living her best life was bread. She touched the page where she'd written it down. When she and Madison had resumed working in the kitchen after the roommates meeting, her friend had asked what she'd make if she could only make one thing for the rest of her life. She'd looked down at the walnut and blue cheese dough she'd been kneading. Easy. Bread.

Dean had sat beside her on a break and run her through some of the questions he gave his clients. *Did she prefer to work for herself, with someone else, or with a boss? Did she like to do the marketing, the management, and the books?* His questions had overwhelmed her, especially considering her current lack of finances.

Would she be happy baking bread in a restaurant—or even in someone else's bakery—or would she be more fulfilled doing it on her own by opening her dream bakery?

She hadn't liked her old boss. Hence her decision to quit. But she'd enjoyed working for Nanine and then Patty Snyder.

If Nanine wanted her on her staff, it would give her an opportunity to do two things. Help Nanine, whom she loved —and bake incredible bread and pastry. Nanine wanted a Michelin star, and Thea knew that meant she would get one. Nanine was simply that kind of person. Being on her staff would expand Thea's opportunities, although she felt a little guilty for thinking in those terms.

How could she possibly open her own bakery? Even if she wanted to, she had no money, and she knew nothing about opening a business in France. Everyone said it was *compliqué*.

"Smoke is coming out of your head," Kyle said, sitting down in the empty chair beside her. "Did you pick up smoking when I didn't notice?"

She snapped her journal shut. "You know I didn't."

"I was pulling a Dean and trying to make a joke. Clearly a fail." He ordered a *café crème* when the waiter swept in for his order. "All right. How about we talk about some specifics then? Related to your career."

Perking up, she nodded. "Maybe that would help."

His mouth tipped up. "First, I should tell you that Nanine offered Madison the *chef de cuisine* position before I left to find you."

In her excitement, she bumped the small table, making the half-empty water carafe tip. Kyle deftly righted it before putting a steady hand on her.

"That's wonderful," she said before her heart caught up with her head. "Oh, Nanine."

"Yes, Nanine," Kyle said as he thanked the waiter who'd brought his café. "But she's strong and practical. She's going to retain some of the executive chef duties, which Madison has to be okay with."

"That won't always be easy. Strong personalities. But they'll work it out."

Kyle sipped his café. "Yes, if Madison agrees, which I think she will. Even if her compensation won't be as significant as what she was making in Miami. Paris restaurant salaries are lower than what you can get in the States, I've discovered. But I gave her some time to decide. It's an important decision. As is yours, which is why I'm talking to you and not Nanine. She didn't want you to feel pressured."

Her throat thickened. "I love her so much."

"You haven't even asked if she's making you an offer," Kyle said, pushing his coffee aside. "That's why you're you."

Ugh. "I have a *too nice* problem."

"Sometimes maybe." He put his hand on her shoulder and looked her in the eye. "But career stuff is big. So let's talk turkey. Nanine would like you to come on board as the pastry chef with expanded duties. In bread, of course, your true calling. We had to do a little salary blending using a compensation range for bakers and *chefs de partie,* but I'm a little worried we're still under the salary scale you were on in Des Moines. I was surprised how well-compensated bakers are in your town. Thea, it's better than most bakers make in Paris, but again, there's more demand for the jobs here and the salaries show it. It's an employer's market."

"I know." Her stomach was suddenly in knots. "How much is the offer?"

He told her, and she hoped her wince didn't show on her face. Then he patted her on the arm and muttered a *Yeah.* "Bakers with their own bakeries in Paris make more, of course, but the question is: do you want to own your own shop? Dean wasn't sure you'd thought it all through when you two talked. Don't get angry. We're only trying to help. I know you're in the food industry, but he's a business consultant, and I manage restaurants. Another skill set."

She released a huge breath. "You're right. You know, I've been thrashing over this since yesterday. Kyle, it all seems so big right now. That's why part of me *wants* to take the job and work with Madison and Nanine. It's comfortable and a good way to get my feet wet. My French would get better. Every time I think about applying for a job at a bakery here without fluent French, my tongue gets tied up."

"You should speak French more with Jean Luc," Kyle said with a little nudge. "You know what the French say about learning with your boyfriend."

They said *lover*, and she blushed at the thought. They had not gone there yet, but they were doing more than kissing, which she loved, even if sometimes she still blushed when he opened her shirt and bra and ran his hand up her leg.

"Earth to Thea." Kyle snapped his fingers. "You've got crème brûlée cheeks, and being your big brother, I don't want to imagine what you're thinking."

She sputtered. "Sorry. We were talking about salaries…"

"And jobs." Kyle studied her. "But hasn't your dream always been having your own bakery? I seem to remember that from when you first arrived here in braids for *Le Cordon Bleu*."

"I did not have braids," she protested.

He only smiled. "No, but you did have big dreams like the rest of us. What was your plan in Iowa? Because you might be a nice girl, but you're driven. No one who isn't gets up at three or four o'clock in the morning. There are easier and better paying jobs."

He was right. "I thought some of my favorite clients might invest in my bakery, when the time felt right, which would help me get a loan. They were always asking if I'd ever thought about having my own place."

"I'll bet you even knew what part of town you wanted your bakery in, right?"

She nodded. "A corner location on a big intersection with a good-sized parking lot."

"Good. You have a twinkle in your eye now. So it seems you're getting to your own truth, as Sawyer would say."

"Truth?" She nudged him a little, which wasn't hard since he was sitting beside her Parisian style.

He chuckled. "Maybe I'm becoming more philosophical after I broke off my engagement. You're not the only one looking for reinvention, Thea."

They shared a look. "I'm rooting for you, Kyle."

He kissed her cheek and put an arm around her. "Back at

ya. Nanine asked me to stay on as her restaurant manager, and for now, I plan to. As a part-time, unpaid consultant."

"How angry did she get?"

"I used the argument that I'm staying at her house for free, but in her mind, that doesn't count. We're family."

Her heart warmed. "We are, aren't we? But we can't stay there forever for free. It wouldn't be fair."

"I agree. We're going to have to talk about that at some point. I told her we could renovate the Girls' and Boys' Floors into two separate apartments, and she could make a couple of million easy on each. The Paris real estate market never gets less competitive. With the restaurant and her retiring—she won't share what that looks like with me yet—it's something she needs to consider. But perhaps not now. Too much to handle."

"I never thought of that." She tensed up immediately. If that happened, where was she going to live? Paris was expensive. And if she was paying rent, how was she going to ever save enough to get a bakery going? "I can find another place—"

"Stop! You're going to hyperventilate. I only mentioned it to Nanine because it's my job. And because some of us know we want more space. We're not college kids anymore. But don't worry. You'll always have a place. Okay?"

Not worry? Tell that to her stomach. She couldn't keep living on other people's charity forever. "So what next?"

"You have the offer. You know what the job entails. I've sent you an email with the formal offer. Now, you need to decide what you want."

She paused. Language and money were her greatest concerns. Everything else—Paris, her roommates, Nanine, and Jean Luc—was wonderful. The thing was, did she want to go back to working for someone else? Nanine's offer would be the smart choice, until she got her feet a little bit more planted. But it meant putting off her dream for a while…

Was she okay with that?

Did she even *have* a choice?

"Sometimes talking to someone from home helps clarify things. Because sometimes knowing 'not this' is a big help. That got me here." He put a supportive hand on her arm. "Maybe talking to your parents will help crystalize what you want to do."

She gulped. "You think?"

"Yeah, I do. Seeing Paisley helped me know for sure that leaving was the right thing for me." He pulled his phone out of his jacket and put it on the table. "Use mine. I have unlimited international minutes. Let me show you my password."

"You'd trust me with that?" she gaped.

"Yeah. Now Dean is another matter…"

That made her laugh. "Thank you, Kyle."

"Let me know if you need a shoulder after your call." He tapped his own broad chest. "I'm always here for you, Thea."

"I'm here for you too."

"I know, little sister." He kissed both her cheeks. "By the way, no one's going to pressure you about this. You take all the time you need. We all pinky swore after I talked to Madison."

She couldn't see anyone but Dean hooking pinkies. "You did not."

"Didn't we?" He grinned and stood up. "I have some decisions to make myself, so I'll leave you to your call."

Decisions? Before she could ask him what he meant, he was gone.

She didn't leave the café to call her parents since there were no other patrons around to bother. Better to get it out of the way before her picnic with Jean Luc. On the farm, they rose before dawn, and her mother picked up on the second ring.

"Hello?"

She could imagine her mom standing in her usual outfit of

elastic waist pants and a loose matching shirt cooking breakfast in an old apron handmade from old clothes. Nothing was thrown out in the Rogers household. "Mom, it's Thea."

"Your father and I were wondering when you were going to call since you've been gone about a month, but we know it's expensive. And you know we don't email and do all that fancy computer stuff. Even though it's free and all."

Funny how Thea had just been thinking about how expensive things were in Paris. Was it because she was raised by frugal parents? "Sorry, it's been a whirlwind here."

"You always say so."

Talking to her parents had never been easy, but it reached acute awkwardness over the phone. "Well...how are you?" she asked even though she knew the rote answer.

"The same. Your father would say he never felt better, never had less."

Thea imagined she was one of only one in a million people who knew that phrase came from an old song by Gene Krupa from the late 1930s by the same name. And that fact made her a total freak.

"How is your friend?" her mother asked. "Nanine? And the others?"

"Nanine is out of the hospital and getting back on her feet slowly."

"Once you go in, it's never the same," her mother said with her typical matter-of-factness. "You remember how your grandma went in for a hip replacement, and they told her she'd be better than ever? She walked even worse after."

She closed her eyes. This was what her parents liked to talk about. Who was sick. Who'd died. Who'd gotten married. Who'd had a new baby. Who was in trouble and for what. Impersonal stories that were as dryly delivered as commentary on the weather except they were about real people. That and their emotional reserve had never made them easy to be around. Her father always said it was because they slaughtered animals on the farm. A person who did that couldn't become emotionally attached. But she was their *daughter*. Why couldn't they be warmer with her?

Maybe this was a bad idea. They were too different from her to be able to give her any kind of reasonable career advice.

But she was already on Kyle's phone, so she took a breath and went for it. "Mom, I wanted to let you know that I've been offered a job here. With Nanine at her restaurant."

"Why would you do a crazy thing like that, Thea?" Her mother clucked her tongue. "Your family is here. Your job—a good job, you might recall, despite your lengthy absence—is here. You have your own place and your own money. More than I had at your age. I know you love Paris and your friends, but that's where you go for fun and vacation. Sure, and schooling, but that part of your life is over. You belong here with your own people. Not galivanting around Paris pretending you're something you aren't. Thea, we didn't raise you to be fancy."

Maybe this was what Kyle was talking about, because she didn't want *this:* the refusal to see that "fancy" wasn't a dirty word. That she just wanted to be herself and live her most delicious life. Here, she was the best version of herself. And she *was* with her own people here in Paris.

But none of that mattered in the end, because there was nothing to go back to in Des Moines. "Mom, I don't have a job there anymore. Remember? I—"

"But you do!" her mother shot back. "Fred called here when he couldn't reach you to tell you he was granting your vacation."

"He did what?"

"You heard me, young lady. I told him your phone didn't work all the way over there in Paris."

She shook her head, confused. "Why didn't he email me?"

"How should I know? Maybe he doesn't do it either. Or

maybe he was trying to give you a break from the bakery like you'd wanted."

She doubted it. Fred didn't do anything without an ulterior motive. "What did he tell you exactly, Mother?"

Her sigh was aggrieved. "He said you had a whole bunch of time off coming, and if you needed more, then that was all right. He'd manage. Thea, he said your customers were really missing you, but he'd told them you were in Paris helping a friend and taking some time. Maybe even learning to make something new for the bakery."

She sat back in shock as her pulse shot up to alarming levels. "He told our customers that I'm on *vacation*?" Now she understood the lack of response over her departure from Snyder's. "But that's not right. I quit. After he wouldn't give me—"

"Yes, he explained that you got upset with him, probably because you were worried about your friend being in the hospital. He said it was all a misunderstanding and to tell you when you called. He knew you were angry and thought you'd hear it better from us. Thea, the Snyders are good people. You overreacted."

The rebuke made her face flush. "But why didn't you or Father try and reach me sooner?"

"I couldn't call you either, Thea, because your phone doesn't work." The reproving tone in her mother's voice was gaining strength. "And it's expensive—"

"Still, you could have called the restaurant or Brooke. Collect even. I left those numbers with you in case of emergency."

"There was no emergency here. That's what I'm trying to tell you if you'll just open up your ears and listen. Everything is all right. You have your job. You'll be coming home now that your friend is okay, I guess. Right?"

For a second, she couldn't work any words out of her throat, but she finally managed, "I'll have to get back to you."

"I'll tell your father you called the moment he gets in from milking the cows," she said. "Well, we should probably hang up now. This is costing you money."

She hung her head. "Bye, Mom."

"Stay out of trouble, Thea."

She ended the call and squeezed her eyes shut. No final words of love—not like Nanine had always said to her before they ended a call. Those cherished words *I love you, Thea* had been all the more precious because of how rarely she heard them from anyone else. Her parents only offered her shame.

First things first—she needed to call Fred Snyder.

Thea took a breath and called Fred on his cell phone, a number she knew by heart, in case he wasn't already at the bakery.

He picked up on the third ring. "Hello?"

"Fred, this is Thea."

"Thea! How's Paris? Everyone is missing you here at the bakery, asking about you every day. I told them your old friend had a heart attack and you were going to help out over there for a while. Of course, Jillian is doing her best, but she's not you."

He'd thrown Jillian into her spot? "Fred, Jillian is an apprentice baker. But that's beside the point. I quit after you refused to give me my vacation—"

"That was rash of me, Thea," he said urgently. "Like I told your mother when I called your family. I couldn't reach you on your phone all the way over there. Thea, we need you back here. The bakery isn't the same without you."

Of course it wasn't! He hadn't hired a master baker. He'd put Jillian in an impossible position. "But Fred... I quit."

"Can't we forget about all that?" His voice carried a hint of pleading, something she'd never heard from him before. "Thea, you're the best baker in town. Snyder's needs you! My mother always wanted you to take over. I know I should have treated you better, and I'm really sorry."

She almost dropped her phone. Fred never said he was sorry. *Ever*.

Except he didn't sound contrite—he sounded panicked.

"What can I do here to patch things up?" he continued. "How about a raise? I'd offer more vacation, but that would only make you cross. But I promise you can take some, of course, from time to time. It was thoughtless of me to say otherwise in your time of need."

He was groveling. *Fred Know It All Snyder*. She'd never thought this day would come.

"Thea, did you hear me? Look, I was wrong, all right. We urgently need you back. Sales have tanked since you left. Nothing tastes the same even though we're using your recipes."

Now that made her downright happy. "Recipes alone won't make good bread. Didn't your mother tell you that?"

"Like I said. I was shortsighted, Thea. I didn't appreciate you enough. What more can I do?" Desperation colored his voice like gaudy food coloring in frosting.

"Fred, I—"

"How about a percentage in the bakery?"

"A percentage?" She sat back in shock. That had *never* been on the table, not even with his mother. He had to be kidding. "Fred, it's your family's bakery."

"Look, I know how hard it's going to be to lure another baker of your caliber to Des Moines, especially now that our customers have gotten used to all your fancy French pastries."

The word made her angry. Fancy, was it? And it seemed he *had* looked for someone to replace her. Her skills in French pastry were rare in that part of the world, which was why Patty Snyder had hired her. She'd thought their customer base might like a breath of fresh air to their longstanding menu, which dated back to the 1930s when her father had started the bakery and featured more German, Czech, and

Polish breads common in the Midwest. Patty had been right and then some.

"Fred, I left Des Moines and gave up my apartment. I already have a job offer here—"

"I'll double your salary and give you a ten percent stake in the bakery," he said in a rush. "You'd have full control over the baking and what's sold."

"Fred—"

"Thirty percent? Forty-nine!" he said in a panicked voice. "Please, Thea! If I lose the bakery, I'll have nothing. How will I hold up my head at our next family reunion? That bakery's been ours for generations."

She barely heard any of that. All that echoed in her head was *forty-nine percent.*

Forty-nine percent! She'd practically be half owner.

She'd have her own bakery. Kind of. Maybe Fred would sell her the remaining fifty-one percent after a couple of years. But, regardless, after a couple of years with her new salary, she could open her own bakery.

"Thea, please think it over," Fred pleaded. "Your customers love you! All they talk about every day is when you're coming back and how they can't wait to see you."

Cue the guilt. Only her emotions rose up in her eyes, making them tear. She *did* love and miss her customers.

"Thea, promise me you'll think about it! This is only the beginning of a negotiation. You come back to me after it settles in, and we can talk some more. The more I think about it, the more I know my mother would want it like this. All right?"

She pressed her hand to her diaphragm. "Fred, I don't—"

"Thea, I'll wait for your call."

With that, the line went dead. She set the phone on the table with a clatter. Her hands were shaking.

She looked at them. Fred had just put her dream in them.

Shouldn't she feel happier?

CHAPTER
TWENTY-FIVE

er roommates were staring at her.

Nanine included.

"I don't know where to begin," Thea said, putting her hands on the kitchen table, hoping to anchor herself back in her body. Her mind was still spinning from Fred's insane offer, and she'd almost tripped on the cobblestones coming back home.

"Start with the zinger you said to me two minutes ago when you walked back in," Madison suggested, her arms crossed tightly over her chest. "Your jerk of a boss hasn't told anyone you quit and is still expecting you to go back to work there."

There was a collective gasp around the table before Brooke muttered, "That little shit. Didn't you tell him that you're staying in Paris?"

"Wait! It gets better," Madison interrupted, sitting back in her chair, all attitude. "Tell them the rest, Thea. You called your parents…"

"Right!" She pressed her hand to her forehead, hoping to jog her scrambled brain, and the rest of the story tumbled out.

"What an asshole," Brooke fumed when she finished.

"Fred has never appreciated you, and once again, this is all about him. Guilting you about your customers is the final straw."

"Yeah, that's snake belly low," Sawyer mumbled, making the motion of a snake slithering on the ground.

"Creepy, Sawyer, but apt." Kyle paused. "Still, it *is* a really solid offer, Thea. Double your current salary—which I can guess at since I checked the salary scale for Des Moines—and with a forty-nine percent stake in the business."

"Don't forget the extra vacation," Brooke said ironically. "Assuming he wouldn't lock you back in his bakery tower and never let you out again."

"From serpents to Rapunzel references," Dean said with a grin. "God, I missed you guys. But Kyle is right. Thea, you'd have a whole lot of capital quicker. You could save up seed money to open your own bakery. And you'd be a part owner already, so that makes you more attractive to a bank. Plus, you'll gain extra management experience before being completely on your own."

"But he's a jerk and a liar!" Brooke protested, to which Thea nodded enthusiastically. "The whole reason she quit is because he never gave her the time off that he'd promised her. What's to say he won't go back on his word again?"

Dean stuck his hand in Sawyer's shirt pocket and snuck his handkerchief out, which he raised like a white flag before Sawyer snatched it back.

"Don't shoot the messenger," Dean said. "Not every boss is terrific. In fact, depending on which statistic you look at, about three-fourths of the work force think their boss sucks and that they could do the job better. Money and compensation dull the pain."

Pain! Who wanted pain? She wanted her delicious life.

But Dean was right. That much money could dull everything long enough for her to realize every dream she'd written in her journal.

Except maybe being with Jean Luc.

"Thea, you love baking bread and your customers." Kyle gestured to her. "You're already established there. I'm not saying Fred isn't a total dick, but I think you should consider this offer. You'll have your own bakery faster this way."

"Because while I would love to have you work for me, having your own bakery has always been where your heart lies," Nanine said softly. "So I agree with the boys."

The room went silent as everyone swung their heads in her direction. Her white hair usually seemed at odds with her youthful olive skin, but not today. Harsh lines seemed carved around her mouth and forehead where she was tensed. She didn't move from the wall, and Thea suspected she was using it for strength since she couldn't stand for hours at a time now.

That more than anything made Thea's heart catch. "But Nanine—"

"Shh, *ma petite*," Nanine said quietly. "Those of us who work in the restaurant industry know what it's like. The compensation *is* important, as are the duties. A head baker with a percentage of a successful bakery at your age—and as a woman—is a strong opportunity. Don't you agree, Madison?"

Madison's face was set in stone now. "I do. Women have it harder than anyone in the restaurant business, especially with capital. Thea, it could be yours in the long run. But you could also use the money as a launching point for a new business. Your customers would follow you."

She nodded. Yes, she'd thought all of this. Plus, it didn't have the French challenge she had here. With this setup, she could not fail, and gosh, that removed her from her own personal pressure cooker.

And yet… She would be leaving Paris and all she loved. And Jean Luc—when she had just found him.

Maybe she could go back to Des Moines for just a couple

years. By that time, she'd have quite a bit of money saved, possibly even enough to open a bakery in Paris. Or maybe Fred or someone else would buy her out, especially if she'd trained someone to take over the baking properly.

Maybe Jean Luc would be open to a long-distance relationship? Two years wasn't long… And Fred had promised her more time off.

The thought of leaving Paris and everyone she loved made her want to curl into a ball upstairs though.

"Thea," Nanine called, bringing her attention back to her. "You have spoken with Kyle already, and I know he has told you about the differences in compensation between Paris and your hometown. I also understand Dean has spoken to you about what it would take to run your own bakery. This way you do not need to manage anything yet, and—"

"But Fred—"

"He may be a *con*—" Nanine said with a sly smile. "But those are manageable too."

A few people's jaws dropped to the floor while others gasped before Madison started chuckling.

"I can use a vulgarity when it is needed, but only then," Nanine said, raising a delicate brow. "When we overuse words, they lose their power. But we digress. As I was saying, Fred may not be a great human being, but the bakery was thriving until you left. He has not undermined you or made changes that hurt the business. That is a plus. Kyle?"

He nodded after shaking off the shock they all felt at hearing Nanine swear. "If Fred proposed to give you a percentage, you'll want to ask to see the books. I can help with that. Do you have any idea how much the bakery makes a year?"

She nodded. One of the first assignments she'd been given in the business class she'd had to drop because she was too busy with work was to create a business plan. She'd based it on Snyder's but also other research online.

"These are things to explore, Thea," Nanine said, coming around at last to where she was sitting and touching her cheek. "That you are an excellent baker and a superlative employee is not in question, but you should take a moment to celebrate the acknowledgment. Especially from a man like Fred. I have known many such men in my time in the restaurant business, as I am sure Madison has as well."

"We say *cabrón* in Spanish, Nanine," she cheekily replied, "and I've used it frequently in Miami, not to reduce its power but because there are so many."

Nanine walked over and put her hands gently on Madison's rangy shoulders. "Thea, I would be doing you and myself an injustice not to point out how much better the offer is than the one I can give you."

Sawyer coughed. "I'm about to step into it."

"Which philosopher now?" Dean groaned. "Rousseau?"

He shot him a glance as he pushed up his glasses. "One quote does come to mind. *Happiness: a good bank account, a good cook, and a good digestion.* But that's not what I was going to say. Jesus, this is hard, but I'm going to play devil's advocate."

"Using a quote with happiness and bank accounts might suggest otherwise," Dean shot back.

A mixture of expressions crossed Sawyer's face: a frown, a wince, and then a steely knitting of his brows. "Kyle, I recall us talking about putting in money into Nanine's."

"But I didn't put in money myself!" Thea protested. "You guys covered my share so I could be a part of it. With this offer, I could actually contribute on my own."

"Hang on, let's hold that thought," Sawyer said, waving in her direction. "Isn't our investment going to be structured into a percentage stake in this restaurant? I'm not saying a stake in Nanine's would be worth more than the bakery in Des Moines, but given other Paris advantages—"

"I hadn't broached that with Nanine yet." Kyle cleared his voice.

"And why not?" Nanine asked sharply.

Kyle worried his lip before saying, "Nanine, there are a million ways to structure the kind of investment we've made into your restaurant. This being France, it's a bit complicated, so I thought it best to wait until we have some other items off our plates."

"But if you have given money to it, would you not normally be part owners and take a percentage from the first?" Nanine asked. "Why hasn't Jean Luc mentioned this?"

Kyle cleared his throat. "I haven't talked to him about it yet."

Nanine's face went almost as pale as it had been in the hospital. "Brooke?"

Brooke's eyes shone with unshed tears. "Nanine, it was going to cause you more stress if you thought you didn't technically own Nanine's anymore, so we just…"

"You just…" Nanine's voice was hard.

Kyle looked around the table. "We simply paid for what was needed."

"Like a loan." Nanine made a fist. "Tell me this is like a loan."

Thea couldn't stand any more. "Stop this! It's only hurting her."

"*Ma petite,* I love you as I do all the rest," Nanine said in a rough voice, her gaze on Kyle, "but you will answer me."

Kyle sighed. "We—"

"Nanine," Madison interrupted, "no one was going to take away ownership of your restaurant with you not well. Sawyer, I thought you knew that."

"No one told me anything!" he protested, his mouth twisting. "I remember that we agreed to contribute so Kyle wouldn't have to bring in outside investors for the renovation. And I'm fine with it being a gift. I don't want Nanine not to own Nanine's, dammit!"

A tear spilled over Thea's cheek, and she reached for Dean's and Brooke's hands under the table.

"Well, I am not taking your hard-earned money as a gift!" Nanine stood tall, her mouth trembling. "You have been placating me like a child by pretending to be real investors to spare my feelings. It is too much."

Brooke let her hand go and stood up. "It is not too much! Not after everything you've done for us and meant to us. And if anyone wants me to cover their original amount now that it's understood it's a gift, then I will."

"Oh, shut the hell up, Brooke," Madison said in a hard tone. "Just because Sawyer asked a question, which is the way he's wired, doesn't mean any of us need you to step in with Daddy's money."

"All right, that's it!" Kyle's voice carried over Brooke's outraged gasp. "Everyone loves Nanine and wants to help. Can we please focus on that right now and not tear each other to shreds? I was just telling Thea how great it was that some of us don't fight like we used to, and she thought it meant we'd matured. So let's start acting like adults right now."

Nanine heaved in a shaky breath. "Adults! You claim to be adults? When you offered to invest in the restaurant, I felt privileged to have such investors, such partners—my Courses who care as much about Nanine's as I do—but you've failed to present me with an investment plan. *That* is what adults would do."

Thea pressed her hand to her mouth as the room grew heavy with a dark silence.

"*That* is what I expected of you." Nanine looked off, her tension visible in the planes of her pale face. "If you have any love for me, at least show me the respect of treating me like I am still an adult. Excuse me."

Her rapid footsteps were muffled by the clanging of her famous chandelier.

"Well, that went well," Madison said, tilting her head back.

"Fuck," Dean hissed out.

"Yeah, fuck." Kyle pressed his fingers to his temples. "We were only trying to protect her. Besides, I didn't think anyone would want to take profits from Nanine's when she's in the hole, but I should have asked."

"Hey!" Sawyer shouted. "I wasn't asking because of that. I was only following the logic—"

"We know, Doc," Dean said, ruffling his hair like a brother might.

But he shoved the hand away. "I also want Thea to stay in Paris because it's been great having everyone together again, despite how sucky this moment is."

That choked her up, and everyone grew silent again before Dean said roughly, "Yeah, man, it really has."

Sawyer swore softly. "I would *never* hurt Thea. Or Nanine."

"None of us would," Madison said tersely. "No one is accusing you of anything here, Sawyer. I'm sorry if it sounded that way."

"What about your crack about 'Daddy's money'?" Brooke shot back, her shoulders rigid.

Madison worked her mouth before saying, "I was out of line. Totally. I'm sorry, Brooke."

Kyle waved a hand in the air. "Maybe we're not a lost cause. We can apologize like adults, at least. Ten years ago, shit like this would have simmered for days with no honest resolution."

Thea remembered that well, and she'd often felt like she was in the middle. "I don't ever want it to happen again, okay? Nanine was hurt, and so were a lot of people in here. Me included. Sawyer, I would never want to take a percentage of Nanine's restaurant—even if I had actually contributed the money myself. I thought you'd know that!"

More tears spilled down her face, which she brushed aside.

"Thea, I'm sorry," Sawyer said, his heart in his dark eyes. "I didn't think about the implications. Please don't cry."

Dean leaned over and used the edge of his sleeve to wipe her tears, his own eyes shining brightly with emotion.

"Who is going to talk to Nanine and make this right?" Madison asked.

Kyle sighed heavily. "I'll talk to Jean Luc and come up with some investment structure options. With French law, it could take six months minimum, which I'll need her to understand since she's going to be stubborn about this—"

"She only wants to be treated like an adult," Madison answered, "and this is her restaurant. I'd feel the same way."

"We need to remember this heart attack probably has her thinking about her age and mortality," Brooke added hoarsely. "I know that's how it affected my dad. She needs to believe in something to keep going, and her restaurant is it."

A few others nodded in agreement.

"And us," Thea said, checking the time. "We need to fix this and fast. Kyle, why don't you come to Luxembourg Gardens with me to tell Jean Luc what's going on and get you two started on a solution? We can have our picnic another time."

"But Thea," Brooke protested. "It's your date!"

"This is more important." She stood, feeling a little shaky after the emotional roller coaster of the last hour or so. "If I know Jean Luc at all, he'll agree."

She didn't want to miss their time together, but perhaps it would be a good thing to take a little space to think about everything before discussing it with him.

If only she believed that deep down.

CHAPTER
TWENTY-SIX

Nanine rarely shut her apartment door during the day.

She hoped today would be an exception, but she couldn't bear to have one of her beloved Courses attempt to soothe her. Was her pride hurt along with her heart at her own misfortune? Yes. She knew they meant well. She told herself that as she watered her plants on her small garden terrace. Her geraniums were fading, spent from their original vigor, and all they did was remind her of herself.

Her house phone rang, one she kept more to preserve the memories of Bernard calling her from work than for any practical reason. Sentiment in some cases was allowed, especially with a beloved husband.

Crossing slowly, she was aware of the tightness in her chest. If they knew the stress their discussion had caused, they would feel even worse than she imagined they already did. In trying to spare her pain, they had given it. Another reason she could not tell them.

"*Allô?*" she answered as she sat down on the divan.

"Nanine, it is Jean Luc," he answered in French. "I hear I might owe you an apology for not pressing Kyle and the others for details about their investment in your restaurant, and I will make it up to you in person if you would allow a visit."

She rubbed the space between her breasts, a soothing tactic that helped ease some of the tension in her heart. "I appreciate you calling to say so, but a visit is not needed. On the matter of my Courses' investment—"

"Kyle and I have met only now, and we discussed a few ideas given French law, which he knew would make things *compliqué*," Jean Luc said, interrupting. "In this area, the laws in the United States are somewhat easier, I now understand."

That did not surprise her, but his meeting with Kyle did. Frowning, she said, "But I thought you were having a picnic with Thea today?"

"She thought it better to cancel it so Kyle and I could work on this urgent matter. Nanine, she was very upset. As was Kyle."

Her heart uttered a sharp cry. They were all hurting, and that must stop. "We will fix things, as family does. And you will go out with Thea tonight and speak with her about her other upset. What do you think of her dilemma? It is a difficult one, no?"

"*Pardon?*"

She pressed her lips together. "Alas, she has not had the time to tell you."

"I know about your job offer to her, Nanine. I prepared the employment offer, just as I did with Madison's. As your lawyer, I did not mention anything to her before the offer was presented."

"Of course you did not. You are a man of honor. I only meant… I thought she might have told you about the discussion leading up to our talk of the Courses' investment in my restaurant."

There was silence for a moment before he said, "She did

not get to it in our brief time together before leaving me with Kyle."

"I am sure she will tonight," Nanine hastily answered, wondering if she had been unwittingly indiscreet. He did not know about the offer from her old employer yet.

"Of course."

She toyed with the telephone's crinkled cream cord. "Jean Luc, please tell me if it is not my business. But where do your current affections lie with Thea?"

He chuckled. "You too? I have never been pressed as much about the status of my heart as I have lately. From both your Courses and my own family."

Nanine's hand lowered slowly until it rested on her thigh. She'd known things were progressing, and Thea was on cloud nine, but this... "You have told your family about Thea?"

Another chuckle, this time more vibrant. "Yes, I know it is fast, but the heart knows what it knows. My mother wanted to dash over to your restaurant and meet her the moment I mentioned her. You remember the story of my parents' meeting, do you not? My parents thought it might be like that for me."

"And you believe they are right," Nanine said and then winced. "Stop me, Jean Luc, if this is too personal. You are my friend, but you are also my lawyer."

"But now I am also in love with your First Course and hope to marry her one day. There, is that enough of my intentions? I must admit the tests of Thea's roommates have challenged me to be ruthlessly clear with myself, more so than I've ever been in a relationship. And yet, it is easy to be, as my feelings for Thea are so powerful. Nanine, I always knew how much you loved her. I thought I knew why. But I was wrong."

Her heart seemed to suspend in her very chest as she waited for him to continue.

"Nothing could capture the full essence of Thea. Only

knowing her could do so. I am grateful to you, Nanine, for without our link—"

"You would have met without me, I expect, Jean Luc, as I told Thea." She could feel herself tiring and hoped it did not come through in her voice. "I anxiously await details about your discussion with Kyle. Do not disappoint me, Jean Luc. Either as my lawyer or my friend."

"Never, Nanine. Am I not working through my coveted lunch hour after canceling a *rendezvous* with the woman I love? I will talk to you later."

With that, he clicked off. Nanine lowered the phone to its cradle. She wished she had not asked him so much.

Because now she knew even more clearly how difficult Thea's decision would be. Two people she cared about very much might very well end up heartbroken.

CHAPTER
TWENTY-SEVEN

As Thea arrived at the restaurant where Jean Luc had asked her to meet him, she caught sight of him on the patio. He was sitting at a small table, drinking a glass of champagne with a striking woman.

Thea stopped short on the street at the sight. The woman's long black hair cascaded over her shoulders, resting on her sleek black jacket paired with skinny pants. She looked older than Jean Luc, but she wore her age well like most Frenchwomen.

There was a strange intimacy between them, from the way she had her hand on his sleeve to her knowing smile. He was laughing as he pushed the woman's flute toward her and fitted it in her hand, but she patted his cheek and pushed the flute away.

Who was she?

If Thea had witnessed such a scene a month ago, she would have assumed the worst—that he'd found someone better and more compelling, that he'd moved on—but she didn't believe that anymore. She felt a new confidence.

Except that might not be the case two years from now, if she took Fred's offer. And what if it took longer? Everyone said long-distance relationships were tough, and Des Moines to Paris was a *really* long distance with no direct flights. She and Jean Luc might try hard in the beginning, but could their love stand the test of that many miles between them?

What if he found a woman like this that he felt connected to, whom he could see and touch whenever he wanted? Whom he could speak to in his own language. Why would he wait for someone like her?

Because what would happen if she left Paris? Last time, her newly emerging self was snuffed out, like a fire with not enough oxygen. Back in Nowheresville USA, all she'd had left of her time in Paris was her baker training and her friendships. Would the same thing happen if she returned home? Would Old Thea return, relegating New Thea to nothing but happy memories of what was?

Would Jean Luc want that Thea enough to wait for her? Would he even be able to come visit her? He had his own well-established career here, and he was busy. Besides, she couldn't imagine him in Nowheresville. Even for a visit. She definitely couldn't imagine him trying to live there, which she wouldn't ask of him. Even though she was trying to strike a balance between career and relationship, it seemed like the scales were tipped way to one side. If she accepted the job…

Without him, she'd only have her journal entries and the dried rose she kept in the pages from the bouquet he'd given her on their first date. Assuming she didn't end up putting her recipe journal back in her hope chest like she had the last time she'd returned from Paris.

"Thea!"

She looked up to see that Jean Luc had risen from his seat and was moving toward her briskly. He kissed both of her cheeks before settling his mouth lightly over hers.

"You look beautiful, absolutely beautiful, *chérie*," he said, tracing the bare skin of her shoulder along the seam of her dress. "I adore this dress on you. But I must stop my compliments and immediately apologize."

She frowned as his expression grew tense and looked over at the woman he'd been drinking champagne with. She was still casually seated, watching their every move. Unease filled her. Perhaps there was something untoward about their meeting after all. "Ah...you are with someone else. Do you need to cancel our dinner?"

He made a rude sound. "No. Although I did try and make her leave. I'm afraid my sister ratted me out—that is the right saying in English, right?"

She nodded, totally confused.

"I told her where I was meeting you, and she told my mother when pressed."

Suddenly it all clicked. Her age. Her glorious looks. The black hair. "Oh my gosh," she whispered. "*That's* your mother?"

"Yes." He made an exasperated face which was somehow endearing. "I tried to make her leave, but she is stubborn. Is it too soon to meet her in your mind?"

She looked down at her clutch, desperate to text her roommates on Madison's phone and ask for advice. Because if she were leaving, would it be fair to meet her? She didn't want to hurt anyone's feelings, and she especially didn't want to disappoint his mom. Plus, she was waiting, and it would be so rude if she up and left.

She looked up at Jean Luc, wanting to tell him about everything, but it would take too long and they needed privacy. They were standing in the middle of Paris, for pity's sake. So she said, "Ah...is this something you want?"

He took her face in his hands, his blue eyes blazing. "If I had really wanted her to leave, I would have worked harder. Yes, Thea, I would like you to meet her. You are *mon amour*, after all. But it is your choice, of course."

Old Thea would have mumbled an excuse and skittered

off. New Thea thought about her *Living Life to the Fullest* recipe and decided to trust in the ingredient FAITH that everything would work out, even if it seemed impossible right now. "I'd like to meet her, yes."

"Then come." He took her hand and linked them together just the way she liked. "She *has* promised only to stay for a glass of champagne. One she has yet to drink, of course."

Even grounded by his steady presence, nerves rolled through her like a row of dominoes falling in an endless line. Her breathing turned shallow the closer they came, and when they reached the table, she gripped Jean Luc's hand tightly.

But then the older woman was rising with a smile and kissing her enthusiastically on both cheeks. "So you are Thea! The woman who has finally claimed my dear son's heart. It is wonderful to meet you. I am Fabiana."

The French was delivered in a throaty voice as if coming down a tunnel. "*Enchantée.*"

"We will speak in English, Mama, as Thea and I have had some embarrassing miscommunications in the past," Jean Luc said, seating her in his chair and taking the neighboring stool that rounded out a small table such as theirs. "The last thing we want is for you to throw in some Italian with your French like you sometimes do and confuse everything."

She gave him a teasing glare. "We cannot all be so perfect as you, my love. Isn't he infuriating sometimes? I swear, even when he was only a boy barely able to walk, he corrected my speech."

"Of course I do not remember any of these stories, Thea, so do not believe her."

He laid his hand gently on her thigh under the table, another measure of reassurance to help her through this surprising encounter.

If she went back to Des Moines, she was going to miss such gestures. A lot.

"She will decide what she believes for herself, as a woman

must." Fabiana thanked the waiter as he appeared with a third glass of champagne. "We must toast this meeting. My beloved husband is going to be so jealous when I return home and tell him of our time together."

Thea's mind reeled. The difference between his parents and hers was so stark. She couldn't imagine her parents even wanting to meet Jean Luc—he'd be too fancy and too foreign.

She looked at Jean Luc. He was simply lovely. She squeezed his hand, still on her leg, and smiled for the first time. Despite everything, she was going to be grateful for this moment forever, and she was going to *enjoy* it, particularly if she was never going to see this amazing woman again.

Hoping her accent didn't sound as tongue-tied to them as it did to her own ears, she lifted her glass and said, "*Santé*," with all the love in her heart.

After taking a sip, Fabiana reached out and fingered the material at her shoulder. "Your taste is exquisite, *chérie*. You are wearing—"

"Mama," Jean Luc interrupted dryly, "let us not veer into talk of clothes."

She rolled her exotic eyes. "But fashion is my passion. Ah, it rhymes. You would ask me to stifle *that*? Think carefully or I will not make your favorite pasta for a month."

Grinning, Thea nudged his shoulder. "That sounds like a serious threat, Jean Luc."

"It is, and he knows it." Fabiana reached out and tweaked his cheek. "Is it all right if I compliment her shoes? Thea, Jean Luc told me how some people have spoken of your feet."

Her face flushed immediately, but then she was stopped short by Fabiana twisting in her chair and sticking out her right foot, encased in a strappy silver heel. "After my first fashion show, they called me a swan on top and a booby below. I had on this incredible white one-shoulder dress and electric blue heels, like the booby's feet. It was in all the papers! What size do you wear, Thea? I'm a forty-two—"

"So am I!" she blurted out before realizing other people had turned to stare. "But you're a little taller than I am."

"Not by much, and I adore your shoes!" She tucked her foot back under the table. "Then there are my hands. Look at these. My husband, whom you will meet soon when you come over for dinner—"

"*Mama.*"

"He thinks I am pushy, but it is the Italian mother in me, wanting my boy to be happy." She patted his cheek again, earning a good-natured frown from him. "As I was saying, my husband said my hands were so large because they were meant to fit perfectly into his hands, especially when we dance. We met on a day of dance and music, and I fell for him the moment I stepped into his arms, although seeing his eyes for the first time was like finding a gateway to another world."

The romance of the story delighted her all over again, and this time she understood it. She had felt the same when she'd first seen Jean Luc. "Yes, he told me. It's a lovely story."

"Our courtship was very fast," she said with a sly smile. "Somehow I always knew it would be so with my children. When you meet the person who commands your heart, only an idiot dismisses such a thing. And my son is not an idiot."

"She has said otherwise at times, Thea," Jean Luc responded with a laugh.

"Usually when you've gotten into my lasagna before dinner, my son." She raised her hands to heaven. "Oh, how my family loves to eat, but sometimes they are impatient and I am forced to slap their hands. But you are a baker, so you know what I mean."

"Yes, my roommates act the same way with the bread I make," she responded with a conspiratorial smile.

Fabiana nodded and proceeded to finish off her champagne—impressively, Thea thought—and then laughed as she set the flute down with flourish. "My son said I could only stay for one glass, and now that it is finished, I will go. Or he might not invite me out for an *apéritif* again for a month."

She *liked* this woman. She wished…

Her mother would say *if wishes were horses, beggars would ride*. She hated that saying. Wishing just meant there was hope.

Fabiana rose from her chair elegantly, prompting Jean Luc to do the same. They kissed and embraced with great warmth, and then his mother turned to Thea. "You are delightful, Thea, and someone I hope to meet again very soon."

"I hope so too," she said fervently.

Fabiana touched Thea's face as warmly as she had Jean Luc's. "Have a nice evening, my loves."

After blowing a kiss, she sauntered off and headed down the street with undeniable flair. Thea turned to Jean Luc. "I *love* her."

He took her hand and rubbed it. "So I don't need to take you to the hospital? I promise my sister is going to pay for this."

By his smile, she knew he was joking. "Your mother was wonderful. I didn't expect the connection over our feet."

He laughed. "When I told her about what had happened to you, she ended up sharing some insults she'd endured while modeling and before in school. Things I didn't know about. It was…enlightening."

It also explained why he'd never seen her feet as big. His mother wore the same size. Only she wore her large feet and hands with confidence. Thea was sure she would never have even noticed them if Fabiana hadn't said anything. "I'm glad I met her. For so many reasons."

He brought her hand to his mouth and kissed it. "Me too. For so many reasons as well. Now, *chérie*, when I spoke with Nanine earlier, she mentioned there was something upsetting you. A dilemma."

She squeezed his hand. "Oh, Jean Luc, I don't know where to begin."

"Tell me everything." He kissed her hand again, his eyes steady on hers. "I am half-French and well versed in all matters *compliqué*."

Thea's mouth went dry but she bucked up and told him about the offer. When he only continued to look at her, she wanted to fidget. "*Well*," she drew out, "the compensation my old boss back home is offering is so much more than what Nanine can offer. He's also offering a share of the business."

"And so you would be part owner, which would mean you would realize your dream of owning your own bakery," he concluded matter-of-factly.

She nodded.

"But you would have to leave Paris, when I've just found you." He looked away, his jaw tight. "You would be going back to what you know, where you are comfortable."

"I'm so torn." She touched his face to bring his attention back to her. "Jean Luc, I—"

"You have to follow your dream, Thea," he said with urgency, taking her hands. She could see the torment in his eyes. "Thea, I love you, and in doing so, I need to summon the courage to put your best interests first. You must do what's best for you, and I fear being with me right now would be against that, because all I want to do is take you home and keep you forever."

She gripped him tight. "I was thinking maybe we could date long distance. Like I could come to visit you—"

"How often and for how long?" he asked gently. "You wouldn't be able to leave your work easily, not when you're so passionate—"

"But I—"

"Thea"—he shook his head—"I've never known long distance to work. And the miles are too great between here and there."

She couldn't argue with that.

He caressed her cheek achingly. "So perhaps, *chérie*, it is better if we do not spend the evening together."

Tears filled her eyes. She found she couldn't speak.

He traced one of her tears with the gentlest of fingertips, his own eyes bright with emotion. "Oh, that will slay me— seeing you with 'the cockroach.'"

Neither of them could laugh at the old joke.

He let go of her hand slowly, as if the very act was painful. Standing rigidly, he gently kissed her and whispered, "You know where to find me when you reach your decision."

Alone, she trembled. Cold enveloped her. In the waning light of Paris, she knew heartache and cried softly.

How did one choose between a lifelong dream and the love of a lifetime?

CHAPTER
TWENTY-EIGHT

Kyle decided it was time to call an emergency Operation Thea meeting.

He'd had a sleepless night, thinking about the way she'd looked last night when she returned from her date —woebegone and conflicted. She'd murmured a few details about her conversation with Jean Luc—who had introduced her to his mother!—and then climbed the stairs, saying she wanted to be alone.

There *had* to be a win-win solution.

She and Jean Luc were in love—and even with Kyle's recent breakup clouding his vision, it looked like the real thing. If that wasn't something worth saving, he didn't know what was.

He rolled over and picked up his phone. It would be just after five o'clock in Austin, them being seven hours behind. Squeezing his eyes shut, he gave himself one final chance to ask the question he'd been throwing at himself since Paisley had arrived on his doorstep.

Did he want out of everything he'd built professionally in Austin?

He could keep being a partner in their hospitality

company from Paris, and yet…he'd been wanting a break. An out. Even before he found out about Nanine. Maybe it was time for a fresh start personally and professionally. His heart thudded heavily in his chest, but it was pounding with excitement, not dread, as he considered walking away.

Yeah, he decided. He was ready to do it.

He called Alan and suffered through more questions about Paisley before they turned to Nanine's recovery and his plans for the future. With that opening, he laid out what he wanted: to be bought out so he could start his own hospitality company in Paris. After meeting with Jean Luc today, he knew what it would take, and one of those items was more money.

Being the stand-up guy he was known to be, Kyle even mentioned a couple investors he thought they could bring on in his place. Alan tried to talk him out of it, of course, but by the end, he agreed to both a buyout number and a timetable. Their lawyer would be in touch.

When he ended the call, he was juiced. And that juice crystalized everything that had been swimming in his head. About himself. About his roommates. About his life.

In Paris.

He glanced at the clock again. It was barely one in the morning. The others might still be up. Dean had unusual hours since his clientele was based in San Francisco, and Sawyer liked to read late. Then there was Madison, the eternal night owl, always testing recipes in the late quiet of the kitchen.

Pulling on some faded jeans and an old Texas BBQ sweatshirt from the first restaurant he'd created, he walked into the hallway. Light was visible under his roommates' doors. He tried Sawyer first.

The door cracked open moments later. "What's wrong?" Sawyer asked, his face immediately tense. "Nanine?"

His heart clenched at the very thought. "No, she's fine.

Sorry I scared you. This is something else. You up for an Emergency Operation Thea meeting?"

His face transformed. "Hell, yes. Give me a minute."

Kyle detoured to Dean's door and knocked. This time he was ready when the door opened. Dean had on a white T-shirt and the new Eiffel Tower boxers he'd been so proud to find, his laptop still open on his bed. "Before you ask, Nanine's fine. I'm awake because of Thea. Can you meet now?"

"*Now?*" Dean searched his face. "What did you do?"

He gave in to the urge to laugh. "Maybe it's the craziest thing ever, but right now, it feels fucking great."

"Give me a sec to sign off." Dean took a couple of steps toward his computer before he spun around. "Wait. You didn't make out with Madison again, did you?"

Kyle slammed the door in his face and grinned as Dean's laughter erupted on the other side. Sawyer was laughing in the hallway.

"I'm never going to live that down, am I?" Kyle asked.

"Next time I want to watch," Dean called.

Kyle whacked the back of Dean's head when he reappeared. "Come on. Let's go see if Madison is in the kitchen like usual. Who's going to check on Brooke?"

Kyle raised his brows at Sawyer.

He swore beautifully in French before saying, "Why'd I get the short straw?"

Kyle slapped him on the back. "Because she won't kill you for interrupting her beauty sleep."

"You underestimate her," Sawyer complained.

"Probably," he said as he headed to the stairs. "I still think you're our best bet."

"I agree, Doc," Dean added, "but I'll get your beverage of choice started while you handle the Brookester."

"God, we haven't called her that in years," Kyle said with a laugh. "We need to bring it back."

"I'll be sure to mention that," Sawyer said dryly. "If I'm not down in five minutes, don't bother to look for the body."

He smiled, feeling another boost in spirits. "We'll miss you, if that's worth anything."

Sawyer flipped them the bird as he detoured to the Girls' Floor. Kyle and Dean continued down to the kitchen. The light was on, and the smell of cherries scented the air. Madison was still working on her current nemesis: duck with cherries sauce. For some reason, she hadn't nailed the recipe yet. For the life of him, Kyle couldn't understand why she wasn't satisfied. Every iteration tasted incredible to him. Her response: he wasn't a Michelin judge.

He looked up as they passed Nanine's chandelier, whispering, "Don't you dare give us away."

Oddly, it didn't. Madison was bent over a saucepan on the range when they found her, stirring slowly. He motioned to Dean to stay quiet, not wanting to interrupt. If they ruined her sauce, Sawyer was the one who'd be looking for their bodies.

She muttered something and then suddenly she straightened, her back muscles locking with tension under her black T-shirt. Her head slowly turned, her dark eyes slits as if she were preparing to fight.

"We were trying not to scare you while you cooked," he said quietly, unsettled by seeing her on guard like this. He remembered her saying she'd had a couple of close calls with men, and a fierce protective urge he hadn't realized he was capable of surged up in him.

Dean only held up his hands. "What he said. But man, you've got a sixth sense."

"You two idiots were standing right behind me all creepy-like." She set her spoon aside and turned off the gas burner. "In my neighborhood, it pays to know when some guy is watching."

Before this trip, she'd never mentioned any male harassment. Every time she did, he wanted to hunt down the men who'd hurt her and tear them apart. "Sorry."

"What are you two doing up? You're not dressed for clubbing, although I'd pay to see you wear those shorts out, Dean."

"I called an Emergency Operation Thea meeting," Kyle told her as she wrote down a few notes in her black testing book. "How's the sauce coming?"

"She's my current bitch," Madison said harshly. "Every menu I've ever tested has one dish that gives me fits. But once I nail it, I know it's going to be a standout."

"Can I try?" Dean asked, shuffling over.

"You mean, 'can I eat it?', and the answer is, sure." She handed him a new spoon. "Have at it."

The moment he tasted the sauce he moaned. "How is this not perfect?"

She snorted. "Trust me. When I get it right, you'll be on your knees."

He laughed as he took an exaggerated lick. "My favorite place."

Rolling her eyes but chuckling, she said, "Anyone else coming? Or are we going to represent the group?"

"Sawyer was up." Kyle walked over and pulled some milk out from the cooler. They'd all need some *café noisettes* to keep their minds clear. "He's getting Brooke."

She cringed. "Hope that works out for him."

"It did," Sawyer said as he walked into the kitchen. "I'm alive with no blood loss. Actually, she was still awake, worrying about Thea. She's happy someone is taking the lead."

"The lead, huh?" Kyle started making the *noisettes*. "No pressure, huh?"

Madison stepped up next to him and started helping with the coffees. "She's only our little sister, but your track record is pretty good lately."

"I'm all ears," Brooke said, sailing in wearing a simple cream robe over pale pink pajamas. "And I didn't change or do my face, so you can just suck it up."

"I didn't do my face either," Dean joked, rubbing his hair until it stood out in crazy spikes. "That's me standing in solidarity with you, Brooke."

She walked over and touched his arm. "You're a sweetheart. Love the shorts. All right, Kyle, you called the meeting. Talk."

"After everyone has a *noisette*," he said, passing the next one for Madison to finish with the signature drop of milk that gave the coffee its name. "We're back in Paris, remember? Civilized."

"The veneer is thin for some," Madison said, punching him gently in the arm as they worked together to finish off the last of the coffees.

Somehow that punch—the hallmark of a good friend—as much as the way they'd all gathered together in the middle of the night to help one of their own was what pushed his happiness factor over the edge. He turned around and faced everyone. "You know what? I really love you guys."

Brooke's face contorted. "Oh, no. *You* can't get sentimental. I don't think I can take it."

He waited for someone else to say something, and when they didn't, he decided to go for it. "Tough. I'm about to. It strikes me that the best friends I've ever had are all in this room, save Thea and Nanine. And for once in my life, I'm not going to play it cool. You guys change my life. Every time we're together."

Okay, he had to stop for a breath because Madison was looking away, the glimmer of emotion swimming in her golden eyes. Brooke had a tear falling down her cheek, and Sawyer coughed softly and pressed his fist to his mouth.

"Well, shit, Kyle," Dean said, coming over. "I'm going to have to man hug you after that."

He danced out of reach playfully. "Not in those phallic-looking shorts," he cried, but he let Dean wrap him up like a bear and try to lift him off the ground.

They both laughed, and then Brooke was standing there weepy-like. "You weren't supposed to make me cry."

He grabbed her to his chest and hugged her. Damn, it felt good. Why hadn't he done this before? Because Golden Boy had an image to uphold. Well, he was done being that cool. "Who's next?"

Sawyer rushed him and they clapped each other on the backs. Then everyone stopped as he faced Madison and opened his arms. "Well?"

Fear flickered in her eyes for a moment before she cocked a hip, turning all badass. "What *did* you do, Kyle?"

He didn't have the heart to press her more, so he lowered his arms. "I asked to be bought out of my company tonight. And I'm not bragging when I say that it's going to be a big payout."

"Good for you, man," Dean said, holding out his hand for a shake, which really touched him.

Others echoed the congratulations, but Madison brought it back to earth by saying, "So what does that have to do with this meeting?"

He grinned. "I'm going to try my hand at running a hospitality company here. In Paris. Which I'd like Nanine's to be under, with all of you involved, of course. Thea included."

"I think we'd better sit down," Brooke said with a whoosh of breath, taking her coffee over to their family table tucked in the corner of the kitchen.

When everyone else was seated, he turned a chair around and rested his elbows on it. "Let me back up. I've been asking myself whether I want to keep working remotely for my company. A bitch with what's going on here, sure, yet it would be feasible. But honestly, I don't. At the same time, helping Nanine's restaurant didn't seem like it would be enough in the long term. Then my juices got going as we worked on Nanine's renovation and Thea's dilemma surfaced…"

"Yeah, that," Sawyer said softly.

"She's in love with Jean Luc all the way, and he's just as crazy about her." Kyle knew he was stating the obvious. "On paper, her job in Iowa wins hands down because it gets her to her dream bakery faster. But then she'd have to go home, and having faced that possibility myself, I know what that looks like."

"She'd be miserable," Brooke whispered, tracing the rim of her cup. "You know Thea. She'd go back to her old life. I've been there, and it's a nice place with nice people, but she doesn't fit in. She loves her customers, but she doesn't have close friends. Her parents are emotionally unavailable. And she doesn't date. For once in her life, she's found a great guy! How can she leave that?"

"He's 'The One' for her," Dean added. "We always knew Thea wasn't the kind who'd date a lot. She was the *meet the right guy and settle down* kind of girl."

"And what about her career?" Madison asked. "I know she's in love, but a woman has to take care of herself too. And the offer in Iowa is a huge opportunity even if she has to go back to suckitude for a while. I'm not saying it's an easy decision, but people have to make relationship and career choices all the time. Her dream bakery is a big deal, and I'm sorry, but I can't just get on board with the idea of dropping it because she's found some guy—no matter how great."

Kyle nodded. "But what if it weren't an either-or proposition. What if Thea could have what she wants here?"

Dean snapped his fingers. "You want to open a bakery."

"With your new company," Brooke added, her smile spreading instantly. "With Thea leading it."

"And me managing it like I would with Nanine's place

and others—with Dean's help as a business consultant. Assuming you're planning on staying too."

Dean held out his hand for a fist bump. "I am and I will. I'm tired of my old life too. I've got goose bumps thinking about all the possibilities here. Among friends."

"Hang on." Madison blew out a breath slowly. "Kyle, I'm not saying this isn't a great idea, but have you researched what it takes to run a successful bakery in Paris? Least of all other kinds of restaurants. Nanine's is one thing, but it's *established*. The market here is oversaturated and expensive."

"And yet, even in the French newspapers everyone is talking about how you can't get bread like you used to," Kyle argued. "Or good food even. Madison, you know as well as I do the old adage: there's always a good reason not to open a restaurant."

"And yet it's not a challenge to take lightly," Madison said, lifting her cup and drinking. "But you know I'll help in any way I can although I don't know the landscape here like I do in Miami."

"Maybe we should open a place in Miami together," Kyle said off the cuff. "It's a hot market—"

"You're crazy," Madison said, laughing. "Down boy! Paris is enough to wrap your hands around right now. Sawyer, you've been quiet. Since you're the soul of reason—"

"Yeah, Sawyer." Kyle faced him head-on. "Shoot, Doc."

He looked down at his *noisette*. "I'm thinking it all through. My first thought is that Kyle doesn't do anything that won't succeed—even if he has suddenly turned into a hugger and sentimentalist."

"Thank you." He gave a little bow. "It's all your Rousseau quotes."

"Funny. I also want to expand on what he said about people complaining about finding good bread." Sawyer lifted a shoulder. "The internet is riddled with articles saying the Paris restaurant scene is old and tired and has lost its edge."

"Please don't ever say that around Nanine," Brooke said hoarsely. "It's what her daughter accused her of."

"Give me some credit," Sawyer said, pushing up his glasses. "I've been visiting a lot of restaurants to see what kind of decorations they have as part of my research for Nanine's. That means I've also sampled their menus. Honestly, I think there are ways to shake things up, and with the right location, concept, menu, and staff, I think you could hit big. There might be a lot of restaurants here, but I still think there are ways to stand out. Art seems to be one, by the way."

Kyle went on alert. If Doc continued to help their group with his art concepts, perhaps it would build his confidence as an artist. "We'd want your help on that, Sawyer."

"I want to agree," Dean chimed in after Sawyer gave a crisp nod. "But I'd like to sink my teeth into more data and research."

"Consider it one of your first tasks," Kyle said, continuing to watch Madison, whose brows were still knit. "I want Nanine's restaurant to be the first under my new company. Once I talk this over with her, of course. Jean Luc gave me the information I need to figure out the best structuring for our deal. Given our earlier disagreement, I think this is how she'd want it. That makes all of you—my best friends and roommates—investors in my new company. So welcome aboard."

"So... You're opening Thea's dream bakery?" Brooke asked. "Because I want to invest in that too."

"Yeah, I might have to shuffle around my contribution to Nanine's," Sawyer said, "because I want to help Thea too."

"Yeah." Dean was grinning. "Me too! Kyle, I love this! And I have all these ideas. I mean, do you remember the one kind of food we used to bemoan not being able to find in Paris?"

"Tex-Mex," Sawyer said with a sigh. "With kick-ass margaritas."

"Parisians aren't Tex-Mex fans, let me remind you," Madison said slowly. "And this was a hot concept in the mid-1990s here, although not good from what I recall."

"Tourists love it," Kyle added, "and if we make it 'the place to eat,' Parisians will come too, especially the younger ones. They like excellence and they like trendy places. But opening a Tex-Mex place would be down the line if we decided it's a good plan."

"Thank God," Madison said, her mouth curving. "I had this horrible image of having to tie you up to stop you from opening three restaurants in Paris. *At the same time*."

"Did you just talk about tying Kyle up?" Dean leaned his elbow on the table and fluttered his eyelids. "Kinky. You guys are getting really hot."

"You're truly sick in the head," Brooke said with a laugh. "Okay, so I'm an investor in your company. Silent? Or do you want me to find you fabric and decorator deals too, like I have for Nanine's renovation?"

He walked over and put his hands on her shoulders. "First, I'd love that, but I've gotten the sense over the past couple of years that you're interested in expanding into interior design. You've always had an eye for it. I'd want you to work with Doc on that."

Her muscles flinched under his hands. "*You listened*."

"Not only is that what successful people do," he said, "it's also what good friends do."

She laid her hands over his. "Sign me up then. And I can help with publicity. Not boasting, but I know people. Models make great guests, especially when they post about places online."

"Especially hot new places created by best friends and roommates." Kyle looked around at each and every person in the room. "Now that's a story people will want to hear."

"We could be the next feel-good restaurant story in Paris," Dean added, holding out his fist to Kyle for another fist bump. "People love the Five Guys story about the dad starting the business with his four sons."

"And now their franchise is global." Kyle nodded. "Madison, I know you still have reservations, but I want you involved. As the *chef de cuisine* of Nanine's, of course, but also as a creative consultant. Your Michelin star experience is invaluable, and you're brilliant at everything."

Her eyes looked suspiciously bright, so he added quickly, "Plus, I need your snarkiness," because the thought of Madison getting a little weepy killed him.

Her mouth curved, but she remained quiet.

Good girl. He liked that she made him work for it, and he knew how to push her over the edge. "I'm going to ask you to do something I know won't be easy for you."

She slowly crossed her arms over her chest, her gaze unflinching.

"Let me ask you something first." Kyle met her dark eyes straight on. "Like Sawyer said earlier: do you believe I'd do anything I thought I could fail at?"

Her mouth tipped to a smile ever so slowly. "Are you not the Golden Boy? Kyle, I know you're a success. I checked out your company in Austin. I have a better sense than probably anyone at this table just how big your buyout must be."

Well, I'll be damned...

"Why didn't I think to do that?" Dean asked, slapping his forehead. "That'll be the first thing I do when we break."

"I'm totally joining you," Sawyer said, high-fiving Dean.

Kyle only smiled at Madison. "Now, my ask. Will you trust me?"

The table fell silent, and Madison studied him like she was going through every memory they had, every detail she knew about him. He fought to keep his smile on his face. Somehow, he knew this was one of the most significant moments of his life.

Finally, she uncrossed her arms and sat back. "Fine."

"Seriously? That's all you've got?" Dean rolled his eyes. "When Jack asked Rose on the *Titanic* if she trusted him, how do you think everyone would have felt if she'd just said, 'Fine'?"

Madison shoved him. "All right. I trust you, Kyle. Feeling like the king of the world now?"

"Pretty damn close."

They finally shared a snarky smile. Knowing he had her trust felt a little like what he imagined winning a Super Bowl would be like.

"Can we go back to you tying Kyle up?" Dean asked with a laugh. "Hey, maybe you should paint that, Sawyer. We can put it in one of our upcoming restaurants. Or clubs. Kyle, we should start a club, the kind we used to dream of when we were first roommates."

Sawyer put his hands in his wild hair. "My brain is going to explode."

"You have the biggest brain out there," Dean continued, "so it would be a real mess. Kyle, I hope you don't mind, but I'm going to get all sentimental too. I really like this. Us. Being back together in Paris. Working together. I've missed you guys."

"Unlikely friends can stay forever friends," Sawyer said in his usual philosophical way.

"I think that *is* the kind of story people want to read about today," Brooke added softly. "I'm really glad to be part of this group. I've…needed it. You guys."

Kyle raised his eyebrow in Madison's direction. "We've all gone there. How about you?"

She stared back at him. "Kyle, didn't I just say I *trusted* you? You want more than *that*?"

He wanted it all. "Another day then."

She arched her brow at him, but he just flashed a Sphinx-like smile.

"I want more, honestly, Madison," Dean interjected, holding out his arms. "Maybe a hug?"

"In your dreams, Dean," Madison shot back, making them laugh. "Now, who's going to talk to Thea?"

He had one more question to ask. "If she agrees to the bakery, would you source the bread for the new menu from her new bakery? And, if so, would you want it to be exclusive to Nanine's?"

"Good question." She tapped her pointed chin. "Of course, Nanine should be consulted. But I think it could be good advertising."

"Cross-promotion works," Dean said with a nod. "And many restaurants have relationships with key bakeries."

"Maybe she can only sell the specialty breads at her place and to Nanine's. Not to another restaurant," Madison added.

Now they were talking. "Sounds like we have a plan," Kyle said. "I'll present my idea to Nanine in the morning, and then all of us can give Thea the news about her other option. Sawyer, is it time to grab the champagne?"

"If not now, when, my friends?" he said with flourish.

"Sawyer, you must have a quote we can use to cap off this moment," Kyle added.

"Yes, but it's not from our friends, Voltaire or Rousseau. This time it's from Thomas Aquinas." He gave a wide smile as he looked around the room. *"There is nothing on this earth more to be prized than true friendship."*

"Oh, I like that," Dean said, crossing to Sawyer. "What else do you have in that crazy brain?"

"I personally think that's overdramatic," Madison said, true to form. "Why friendship and not your health?"

As they continued to banter, Kyle knew he had his answer.

Best friends ruled his world.

CHAPTER
TWENTY-NINE

When Thea checked on her roommates, they were still asleep.

Then again, dawn's rosy light was just covering the gray mansard rooftops of Paris. She'd cried herself to sleep and awoken groggy, not in her usual good humor. The heaviness of her heart made her body feel like it was dragging an overloaded wagon behind it.

Nothing was right.

Not even baking bread would lift her spirits. She had to figure out her plans once and for all. Returning to her room, she grabbed her journal and tucked it into her Tuscan gold handbag. She slipped on her new shoes. One of Brooke's new suggestions—silver-lined navy ballet flats—they made her feet look elegant and graceful.

She had started to feel that way, with her new clothes and new haircut. She even looked different.

But was she really different on the inside?

Nanine would tell her these were the thoughts for a long walk along the Seine before retiring for a *café crème*. When she arrived in the kitchen, however, she noted a trio of empty champagne bottles on the kitchen table. Why hadn't her room-mates included her? Then she realized why. She was Debbie Downer right now. The thought made her too sad to cry.

As she was leaving, the woman she loved so dearly mate-rialized from the cooler holding a vat of fresh figs Madison had ordered yesterday.

"I thought I would make clafoutis to lift our spirits, but perhaps the champagne already helped some," Nanine said with a soft smile. "But not you, it seems. You look as if you did not sleep well, *ma petite*. Your heart is still torn. Perhaps today, you will hear which direction it wishes to go so you may follow it. Because that is the only path to true happiness. Go. I wish you well."

Thea gripped her bag, warring with the questions she wanted to ask. Part of her still wanted Nanine to tell her what to do. Why was she like that? It couldn't only be from growing up with parents who'd always told her what to do. She was an adult now.

Nanine smiled knowingly, her dark eyes filled with a wisdom Thea envied. "You are ready to become a woman, Thea. A real woman knows her heart and follows it. No matter what. Whatever you decide, know I will toast your decision and always love you. For you are in my heart—like the rest of the Courses."

Could her heart cry? Thea was sure it was overflowing with tears. "Thank you, Nanine."

"Thank you, *ma petite*." Her face was filled with a moth-er's love—something Thea had never seen in her own mother. "*À tout à l'heure*."

"*À tout à l'heure*," she managed softly, marveling at how her French sounded better with her hoarse voice.

The sidewalks were easy to navigate at this hour as fewer people were out. The cloudless sky signaled another warm autumn day. When she reached the quay, the world seemed to open, as it always did when she saw the view of the green *bouquinistes* lining the river.

Today she turned left and headed up the street. The knobby plane trees were just beginning to turn yellow and gold, but she wanted the simple peace of the lone willow tree along the Seine. She used to love to sit by that tree when she'd first come to Paris. She'd still been getting to know her room-mates and Nanine and stealing out for some alone time had been her normal. Now being alone was a rarity, something she was usually grateful for. Before her life was mostly silence and loneliness. Now it was filled with chatter, laughter, and connection.

As she walked down the stone steps to the lower path directly along the Seine, she was stricken by the realization that she'd be alone again if she returned home.

At the bottom, the lone willow blew gently in the breeze. A riverboat was making its presence known on the river, parting it with its berth and making waves. Thea nearly admired it. First Course didn't make waves. And that was something she'd wanted to change.

Sitting on the edge of the stone ledge, her feet dangling above the Seine, she pulled out her journal. Flipping through the pages from the beginning, she read her progress from awkward, hopeful, confused Thea to the more confident happy woman she'd started becoming.

She landed on the most important page in her book—the recipe for *Living Life to the Fullest*.

As she read over it, one thing struck her: Des Moines had *none* of the ingredients she needed in order to bake a delicious life. There were no friends, no pep talks, and certainly no Mr. Pinstripes, the man she loved with all her heart.

The only thing she had to look forward to was baking.

What was baking without love? Would her sourdough starter turn putrid, like she felt inside at the thought of going back? Would she have any passion to make her breads rise to their greatest heights, if she had no more wind in her sails?

Would her old dream of owning a bakery (or almost half of one) be worth sacrificing the rest of her newfound happiness?

As she watched, a scrawny white bird landed a foot away from her, pecking the ground for crumbs. In a flash of clarity, she knew who she would become if she went home. Old Thea. With her own bakery, sure, but she'd still be the woman who settled for the crumbs life gave her. Just like when she'd left Paris ten years ago.

She looked down at her recipe.

Recipe for: *Living Life to the Fullest*

Date: NOW

Prep time: ??? Could take up to ten years

Ingredients: Wine with friends, Baking, ~~Mr. Pinstripes???~~ Mr. Pinstripes!!! Lingerie, Honesty, Trust, Communication

Hard-to-find ingredients: Self-confidence, Courage, Hope, Faith, Love (with the perfect people at the perfect time)

Notes: THIS IS HARD! Sometimes a pep talk from friends is all you need to get started, and you won't find happily ever after if you say no to the prince.

Friends help each other through the best *and* worst moments.

Bad news shouldn't stop you from going forward. Just keep mixing the ingredients and add an extra touch of FAITH.

For best results, sometimes you need to let the ingredients proof for a while.

A shaft of sunlight lit up the word FAITH.

Her heart pulsed stronger in her chest, almost like it was

vying for her attention. Hadn't the word come to her before? When she'd met Jean Luc's mother?

In that moment, she understood what Nanine meant about listening to your heart and finally hearing it. Her heart was telling her to stay and find another way for all her dreams to come true. In Paris. With her roommates and Nanine. With Jean Luc.

Faith. Because if someone had told her two months ago that she would transform herself from an ugly duckling to a swan, find the perfect man, and be offered everything she'd ever wanted professionally, she would have thought they were having a joke at her expense. She'd come so far.

Who was to say this was all there was? What if this was just the beginning of things going great for her? Of the foundation for her delicious life? Even if she couldn't see all the steps, rather like the spiral ones in Nanine's home.

Worst case scenario: she'd work at Nanine's. Would she make less money? Yes. But money couldn't buy happiness, and it certainly couldn't give her love. She'd have to ask Sawyer who'd said that.

The willow's ribbon-like leaves rustled in the wind, making her smile. There would be so many other things she could ask Sawyer and the others. And that was only the beginning. She'd be working with Nanine in the kitchen, and also side by side with Madison, whom she got along with in the kitchen better than she could have imagined. Her friend was snarky, yes, but so very focused. She left Thea alone, and she offered suggestions without judgment and listened when Thea had some for her.

Then there was Brooke, the engine of her exterior makeover. Brooke needed to keep healing, and perhaps when she was ready, Thea would be able to help her find a wonderful man like Jean Luc. And Dean, he would be around to tease her and make her laugh. Kyle would support her, personally and professionally, and continue to show her just how much more there was under his own golden boy surface.

Hugging herself, she closed her eyes and lifted her face to the sky, letting the breeze rush over her. She could hear the willow rustling, and the distant cheers from a riverboat passing. When she opened her eyes, she discovered a few early tourists waving from across the river. She didn't know if they were waving at her, but her heart was flying now, and she lifted her hand to wave back.

"You seem to be in good spirits, *mon amour*," she heard a familiar voice say.

She looked over. Jean Luc was standing in front of the willow tree. "Jean Luc!"

"You could not have imagined my surprise when I came down the stairs and found you here." He started toward her, his blue eyes gleaming. "From your smile, your decision is not one that breaks your heart. That gives me great hope."

She carefully pushed off the ground, but his hands were there to help her. She clenched them when she stood, feeling their strength. "I'm staying."

He grabbed her to him. "*Merci au bon Dieu!* For I did not want to live without you."

Then his mouth settled over hers with the kind of desperate agony driven by the heart's knowledge it could be parted from something it so dearly loves. After those first fraught moments, the kiss changed into one of complete tenderness. The final weight left her, and she let herself float as her lips eagerly sought his.

Yes, her heart cried. *This is what I want.*

When he pulled back, he blew out a breath. "I nearly went mad last night, arguing with myself over what to do. I promised to leave you alone to decide because I love you, but I wanted so badly to tell you that I would move heaven and earth to help you have your own bakery here so we could have the time we need for me to ask you the most pressing question in my heart."

She laid both her hands on his chest, wanting to feel the steady beat of his heart, only it was drumming madly like her own. "And what is that?"

"I know we have only just met, but I am my parents' son, after all." He lifted one of her hands to his lips. "We will still do this officially, so I can give you the moment we both would wish for, but Thea... I want to spend the rest of my life with you. Of that I am completely certain."

Her heart seemed to shoot out of her chest and erupt in fireworks. "You do?"

"Yes." He shook his head and laughed. "I even considered moving to Iowa with you. But when I looked on the map, I realized I didn't even know where it was. I thought it was next to Ohio."

Laughter burst from her. "We're two states over, but it's all right now. You don't have to think about it."

He cupped her cheek, his other hand resting on the one she still had over his heart. "But I *was* thinking about it, Thea. Seriously. I always want you to remember that."

She knew she would. Later, she was going to write this moment in her journal so she could always remember the little details. How his black hair had fallen across his strong forehead. How his blue eyes seemed brighter than the emerging blue of the sky. How his face had radiated the kind of love she'd never imagined directed toward herself as he gazed at her like she was his whole world. She'd call the page *Recipe for: Choosing Love*.

"But you'll have to come with me to that state which isn't next to Ohio," she joked, "and meet my parents at some point, so you're not totally out of the woods."

"I don't care."

He hugged her to him fiercely, and the sounds of cheering reached her ears again, making her wonder if people were cheering for them. Paris was a place where love was celebrated.

"Thea, I want to know where you grew up so I can fully understand what led you here. To Paris. To me."

She thought of all the reasons she'd come back—Nanine, her roommates, and herself most of all. Only there had been a wonderful surprise waiting.

She had also come for her happily ever after.

CHAPTER
THIRTY

Had the world ever looked so wonderful?

Everything seemed brighter, from the stone of the bridges and buildings to the cerulean blue sky overhead.

"I really don't want to stop kissing you," she whispered a while later, tucked against Jean Luc's side as both their feet dangled over the stones with the Seine rushing below. "But this news can't wait."

"Do you mind if I text my mother?" He absently played with a tendril of her hair as he caressed her neck with his fingertips in the most alluring of ways. "She's already insisting I bring you to their place for Sunday dinner. I hope you like Italian food, because she's going to cook up a hurricane."

That had her laughing. "It's 'cook up a storm.' Oh, Jean Luc, are we ever going to fully speak the same language?"

He took her hand and pressed it against his heart. "We already do, *mon amour*. Didn't you know? But I have a theory I want to try out. And then we can go and share your news with Nanine and your roommates."

"What is it?" she asked eagerly.

His smile widened. "I want you to feel my heart and look into my eyes. And then I want you to talk to me in French."

Her nerves immediately surged. "What? I don't know how to say everything I want—"

"Yes, you do," he said, holding her gaze. "Tell me what is in your heart."

She took a deep breath, looking at the treasured planes of his face. His black hair was ruffled a little from her hands. He looked handsome and delicious and so dear, she thought her heart might ultimately pop as it continued to expand in her chest.

What was in her heart? She stilled herself and listened. The phrase rose in her mind in beautiful poetry, and she didn't stumble as she said, "*Je veut passer la nuit dans tes bras.*"

I want to spend the night in your arms.

His blue eyes blazed with love and a desire she was becoming more and more used to, a desire she knew would soon make her transformation complete.

"I can imagine no better way to spend my days and nights than with you, my love," he responded in French, "and tonight will only be the beginning. I love you, Thea."

"*Je t'aime,* Jean Luc," she answered in French and hoped she would always remember how she sounded, all husky and sensual, like a woman should sound when she said such things. Like how she'd been wanting to sound.

He kissed her softly, so softly she was sure she'd always remember his touch and the way the breeze blew over them as if in benediction. "See, we are speaking the language of our hearts at last. What could be easier?"

She smiled at him and touched the black curl that had fallen across his forehead. "Any bets on how soon we'll have another 'cockroach' misunderstanding?"

He helped her stand as she tucked her journal under her arm. "Alas, what does it matter? We will laugh together, and that is what my parents say is the cornerstone of a long and happy relationship."

Threading their fingers together, they started for the stairs. The willow seemed to wave its farewell, and Thea took a moment to savor the feeling of ascending the stairs with Jean Luc, hand in hand. Their touch held new promise—the kind that could carry through for a lifetime.

When they reached Nanine's and entered the kitchen, she was surprised to see all her roommates standing there waiting for her in various states of dress.

Brooke leaned back against the prep counter in her couture and grinned. "This is going to be easier than we thought."

Dean, a sight in his Eiffel Tower boxers and a white T-shirt, raised his hands in the air. "I should have made a bet on this. Of course little sister would choose love."

"It's why we love her," Kyle added.

"How do you know what I've chosen?" she asked, trying not to grin.

Madison snorted, already clad in her black apron. "You're holding hands with your beau and your lips are freshly kissed."

"Dead giveaway," Sawyer commented.

She could feel herself blushing. "Well, yes, I can see how it's obvious. And yes, I'm staying. Turns out all my dreams *are* here."

Dean gave a cab-hailing whistle while Sawyer and Brooke let out a cheer. Then suddenly everyone was turning to Kyle with raised eyebrows. She didn't have a clue what to make of that.

"Thea, we're all thrilled you're staying," Kyle began.

"Me most of all," Jean Luc put in, making her beam at him.

"Earth to Thea," Dean called. "Kyle's got something really important to tell you."

"Give her the Cliff Notes version," Madison added, putting her arm around Sawyer's waist.

Suddenly her roommates were all wearing bright smiles. Her heart began to race again. What had they done?

"Thea," Kyle said, "I would like to formally invite you to join a new restaurant group in Paris."

"That's us, sweetie." Dean motioned with his hand to them.

"But how?" she asked, aware of Jean Luc tightening his hand in support.

"You're *in* because you're an investor for Nanine's restaurant," Madison added. "And don't start in about us putting up your share, or I'll take my cleaver to you."

"Are you going to tie her up too?" Dean asked. "Because I have to say, I'd watch that."

"You're sick." Madison smacked him gently. "Kyle, please continue."

"Thank you," he said dryly before crossing the kitchen and standing in front of her. "Our restaurant group would like to back a prized baker newly returned to Paris in opening her very own bakery. Know anyone by that description?"

Her brain went silent as the shock hit. *What? But... I don't understand.*

"We believe in you, Thea," Kyle said, "and we want you to stay in Paris, living your dream."

"It's what Paris is for, after all," Sawyer put in, pushing up his gold spectacles and grinning.

"But I can't afford—"

"That's what investors are for," Brooke said, making her look over. "And we're yours."

"Would I be able to join in this investment?" Jean Luc asked. "I have a very personal stake in its future head baker."

"Sure," Kyle said with the nod. "Why not? But only as a silent member. Our core management will be a roommates-only group, I'm afraid."

Suddenly it was too much. She let go of Jean Luc's hand to hold her own cheeks. "I can't believe this! I get to stay in Paris with you guys and Jean Luc and have my full dream. You guys are too much."

"Hey." Kyle lifted her chin. "It's what best friends do."

Tears swarmed her eyes, and she knew she was going to lose it. But that was Old Thea. New Thea wanted…to pop the champagne.

"This is why you were drinking champagne without me. Well, no more. Sawyer! Grab the bubbly."

He gave a little bow. "You got it. But I want to go on record and say that if Jean Luc invests in Thea's bakery with us, then that makes him one of our bros."

Both Madison and Dean burst into laughter before they both coughed to cover it. Thea couldn't blame them. She was grinning as she turned to her future fiancé. "I agree. You're one of the bros now. An honorary member of the Paris roommates."

His mouth curved. "I can live with that. Bro."

Hearing his accent as he said the word 'bro' had them all dissolving into laughter, her most of all.

"What is the hilarity about?" Nanine asked. "I heard it all the way up the stairs to my apartment."

"Tell her the news, Thea," Brooke said softly.

Her diaphragm clenched, but then she saw the beautiful smile spreading across Nanine's face as she got closer. Then she was reaching for Thea's hands. "You have decided."

"I have." She could feel the tears gather in her eyes. "My best friends are going to help me achieve my dream of opening my own bakery. Here. In Paris."

The touch of her hand on Thea's cheek was filled with love. "Then all is right with the world, *ma petite*, for I believe this is where you belong."

Belong. Yes. She'd been seeking that her whole life, and

here, in this city and with these unlikely friends, she had found it.

"What about the breads for your new menu?" she asked softly.

"We have some ideas about that," Madison responded, coming over and putting a hand on her shoulder. "Dean thinks you could bake them at your place and sell them at your bakery, but exclusively source them to Nanine's restaurant."

"Seriously good cross-promotion for her restaurant and your bakery, Thea," Dean chimed in. "And wait until you see the ideas I came up with this morning for your online ordering. It's wicked."

Kyle shot him a look before saying, "There are a lot of details to work out yet. Location. Menu. For starts. But don't worry. We'll be with you each and every step of the way. And I know Jean Luc has us covered on the French law side. If he agrees to be our lawyer."

"I am at your service," he said with a courtly bow.

Everyone's support had her wanting to cheer. "Guys, I just don't know what to say."

"Thanks?" Dean suggested before Brooke elbowed him.

Thea didn't feel like thanks was enough as she looked at her roommates. Then her heart whispered something to her, and she realized what she could do. "I know what I want to call my bakery." Just saying it made her feel like she was a single red balloon rising in the Parisian sky.

"*Already?*" Dean asked. "But that's a huge—"

Another elbow, this time from Madison, cut him off. "Tell us, Thea."

She looked back at Jean Luc and smiled before going over to confer with him on the proper way to say it. Nodding, she gave her full attention to her friends. "I'm going to call it *Le Meilleur des Amis*."

"The Best of Friends," Sawyer translated as Dean clutched

his heart and Brooke made an approving sound. "That reminds me of a quote by—"

"No, Sawyer," Madison interrupted, flashing her a grin. "No quotes. Thea Rogers, the new head baker of a soon-to-be opening Paris bakery, wants champagne."

"*Maintenant*," Nanine added with a laugh.

When he didn't move, Kyle took him by the shoulders and pointed him in the right direction. "Yeah, Sawyer. Like now."

"I'll grab the flutes," Brooke called out. "Dean, come help me."

He pointed to himself before saying. "Right. Madison, we need supervision. You know us crazy kids."

"Madison," Nanine said, touching her arm. "I will help you in your observation."

They shot her a grin before they shuffled out, leaving her and Jean Luc alone.

"So, I am a *bro* to all of your friends." His mouth was twitching with humor. "Perhaps you will explain to me what that fully means."

She kissed him softly and then put her hand on his chest. "I will, but first, do you have a pen?"

"But of course." He frowned as he reached into his jacket and pulled one out.

She beamed her thanks as she took it. Then she opened her journal. "I just need to write this recipe down while it's in my head. I had another in mind but—"

Comprehension lightened his expression. "Ah."

She wedged the book against her torso and opened to a new page. She smiled as she felt him come up behind her, leaning over her shoulder to see what she was doing.

"You're going to like this recipe," she told him as she started writing. "In fact, I think you're going to want it daily."

Recipe for: *Thea Rogers' Happily Ever After*
Date: For the rest of her life

Prep time: Forever

Ingredients: My Paris roommates, Nanine, Bread, and especially *mon amour* Jean Luc

Hard-to-find ingredients: NONE

Notes: Love changes everything, and those who love you help make your dreams come true.

Pairs perfectly with a lifetime of kisses under the Parisian sky.

EPILOGUE

Dean surveyed the business cards he'd had printed.

Kyle might want to debate fonts and official names, but he was the dreamer of the lot, wasn't he? And somehow doing this solo had felt right even if keeping a secret from his roommates was hard. Plus, what better way to celebrate Thea and Jean Luc's recent engagement?

The announcement had come just two weeks after Thea had told them she was staying. The young couple had been inseparable. Thea might have blushed the first few mornings she'd come back to Nanine's after a night at Jean Luc's, but she'd gotten over it quickly. Which wasn't to say he hadn't teased her a little to see her blush. No one wanted their little sister to stop doing *that*.

"What are you doing?"

He spun around at Madison's voice, tucking the box containing the business cards behind his back. "Nothing! Jeez, can't a guy go out for a simple errand without running into someone he knows?"

"You know how it is," she countered, striking her badass

pose while wearing all black on Rue Saint-Germain. "This is *our* neighborhood."

Yeah, and it felt pretty damn great. "So are you heading over to Jean Luc's parents' place for the party?"

She looked down and gestured to her outfit of a black sweater, black skirt, and black boots. "Are you implying I'm not dressed up enough?"

He stopped a snarky comeback in its tracks. This was one area he knew not to tease Madison about, especially after she'd confessed during Drink and Divulge a few weeks ago that she wore black to disguise the size of her tits, not to make a fashion statement like Brooke did. "Not at all. You look lovely."

She cocked her hip. "You're full of shit. But I know that I made an effort. I'm even wearing the perfume Nanine bought me for Christmas."

He leaned in closer and sniffed. "*Quelques Fleurs Royale*, right?"

"Yep, although it doesn't make me feel more like a princess. Just an idiot. I hate dressing up like a girl, but I don't want to embarrass Thea. Now let's talk about your skulking behavior right before the party. Is that a present for the engaged couple you're hiding behind your back? Because if it is, I'll kill you if you don't let me go in on it. I didn't know we needed to bring a present. I figured we weren't doing presents until Thea turns thirty in two weeks."

He could feel the need to confess rising in him. "There's no present needed today." He made a face. "Or at least I hope not. This is something else."

She gave a soft but shrill whistle. "Sounds mysterious. What are you up to, Dean?"

"You'll see." He kept an eye on her. "Are you going to try to frisk me? Because that could be hot."

"Not even in your dreams." She chuckled darkly, so dark it raised the hairs on his arms under his suit. "Don't worry,

I'm harmless today. *Today* is a lovey-dovey kind of day. We'll drink and toast our little sister and her happiness. No one deserves it more."

He could hear the edge in her voice. "You ever wonder…"

"*About?*"

"Yourself." He stepped in the street with her so they could pass a loitering couple window-shopping. "You know. The whole love thing."

Her sudden silence had to do with more than them evading the dog shit on the sidewalk. "You mean the forever kind of love? I haven't seen much evidence it exists."

"Until now," Dean added cautiously. "With Thea and Jean Luc."

"Until now," she agreed. "You reading French poetry with Sawyer at night or something?"

He made himself laugh. "Or something. Maybe it's being back in Paris. This is the city of love, where everything seems possible. Don't you ever wonder if it's in the cards for you?"

He glanced over to see the wariness rise in and then depart from her eyes. "Not really. Seems stupid to dream about something that might never happen. Better to take life as it comes. Even in Paris."

He wasn't wired that way. "Maybe it's the dreamer in me."

"For sure." She nudged him softly in the side. "We seem to put up with you pretty well. I mean, even though you, Kyle, and Sawyer are still sharing the Boys' Floor, no one's thrown you out the window yet."

"We have to figure out new arrangements soon." He nearly whimpered. "I'm going to have to go to a chiropractor if I sleep in that bed any longer."

She laughed. "Yeah, my back aches too, but I blame it on working on my feet all day. Job hazard."

"You still think Nanine's will open before Thanksgiving?"

It was what they'd been aiming for, but Kyle had been mute on the prospect.

"Yeah. Or I'm going to take my cleaver to our contractor."

There was the Madison he loved. "Nanine seems stronger and happier. The more time passes, the more it feels like there's nothing more to worry about from her daughter and son-in-law."

"My gut tells me we're not out of the woods yet. Like I said, we take it one day at a time. Whatever happens, we're going to handle it. Nanine's will return better than ever. You wait and see."

He'd already bought a very prized bottle of Krug for that day. "Shit. I need to make a reservation for opening night when it's announced. Remind me."

She only laughed. When they arrived at the address, he grinned upon seeing Brooke and Sawyer out front. "Hey! You two causing trouble already? Don't make me call the *gendarmes*."

"You shouldn't joke about that with someone who's half-Black," Sawyer called back.

"Sorry." And he was. That shit was scary. "Bad joke."

"You're an idiot," Brooke said, looking fashion-ready in a slinky white asymmetrical suit with a pink bolero wrap. "We're waiting for Kyle. He was running late. Some errand."

"Sounds familiar," Madison said, nudging him.

"Nanine is already inside." Sawyer pointed up the building. "If you listen, you can hear the laughter from the party already. Sounds like this could be fun."

"It's Thea's engagement party," Brooke said. "We'll make it fun if it lulls, but from what Thea's told us about Jean Luc's Italian mother, she's going to be a blast. I mean, I looked up old fashion articles about her. She got into trouble for speaking her mind."

"Then we're going to get along great," Madison added, cracking her knuckles. "Ah. Here's Golden Boy now."

Dean turned to see Kyle striding down the street in a navy suit with a snappy silk tie fashioned like a cravat. He looked over at Sawyer, who was wearing a velvet jacket over a tuxedo shirt with black pants. "Am I underdressed? I didn't think I needed a tie."

"You lived in San Francisco, Dean," Brooke said. "You guys don't even have business casual as a concept. You're *always* underdressed. But you can wear my bolero if it makes you feel better."

Sawyer laughed. "I'm just glad he didn't show up in his new Notre Dame Quasimodo boxers."

Kyle rolled up in time to join in. "Another thing to be grateful for today for sure. So, I have something to tell you. As investors."

They all turned and gave him their full attention. "What?" Brooke asked.

"A place is coming up for sale today on Rue Bonaparte right down the street from Fitzy's." He grinned. "I think we should take Thea to see it after the party—"

"And if she likes it, put in an offer immediately," Madison finished. "Good work."

"I told you we needed to chill," Kyle said with a pointed glance in Dean's direction. "Finding the right place is critical. The other places we looked at didn't feel right, and Thea agreed."

Reluctantly, he thought, because she was impatient to get going. "Fine. What can I say? I sometimes rush."

"Word," Sawyer said, rocking back on his heels.

"So, Dean has a secret." Madison shot him a look. "I caught him, and he's been all mysterious."

"Shit, Madison." He could feel the cards burning a hole in his jacket pocket, where he'd palmed them earlier. "I was going to do this later."

"Go get Thea," Brooke said, pushing Sawyer toward the door. "Tell her I have a wardrobe issue and need help."

Kyle turned at her in shock. "She's going to buy that?"

Brooke grinned at them. "She's really embraced fashion."

"I can't wait to see the look on her face when she realizes you've been cutting the tags out of couture," Madison said with a shudder. "She's going to be mortified."

"Jean Luc thinks we can pull it off for a little while longer." She leaned in conspiratorially. "He didn't use the Cartier box when he proposed on purpose."

"Taking it out of your jacket pocket is less pretentious, I think," Sawyer reasoned.

"Are you still here?" Brooke shooed him. "Go!"

He held up his hands. "Why me?"

"Because you and Jean Luc are bros now, and he will let you steal his *fiancée* from his side during their engagement party," Brooke added with her usual logic.

"Got it." He punched the call button for the apartment and moments later was opening the door.

"You also sent him because he won't get distracted by a drink or small talk." Madison settled herself against the wall of the building.

"True," she agreed.

And Brooke's logic was as sound as usual, because Sawyer appeared with Thea a few minutes later. "What happened to your outfit, Brooke?" Thea asked, looking more beautiful than ever.

Her dress was a ruched cream number that made her curves look tantalizing. Not to Dean, of course, but a guy could appreciate the effect. She had on strappy heels in red, which signified her new fire for life, and her hair was pulled back in a fancy Art Deco clip, also from Brooke. But it was the look on her face that made her a real knockout— if he had to put it to words, he'd say she looked like she had her head in the clouds and was loving every minute of it.

He knew from personal experience that he did his best

work with his head in the clouds. Which his roommates were about to behold.

"You look beautiful, sweetie," Dean said, crossing to her and kissing her cheek. "So, the reason you're out here is because of me. Not Brooke."

"*You* have a wardrobe emergency?"

"Oh, little sister." He simply had to kiss the top of her head after that. "No, I got caught earlier with something. A present for all of you. Thea, I was going to do this *after* your engagement party. I'm going on record saying that right now."

She leaned her head against his shoulder and looked up, her eyes bright as stars. "I'm starting to like presents, and if it's a present for all of us, why would we wait?"

"Yeah, Dean," Madison said with her usual snarkiness. "Show us the goods."

"If Thea wasn't here, what I wouldn't say." He pulled out the small box of cards. "Don't kill me, Kyle."

"Why would I?" But Kyle immediately straightened, his eyes zeroing in on the box.

"You should open it." Dean stepped back after handing it over.

"Encouraging," Kyle said as he opened the top. "You stepping back and all. These look like business cards."

"Duh," Madison said, coming closer. "Pull one out and show us what it says."

Kyle parted the stack and yanked one out, staring at it. His face blanched. "Holy shit."

Not a great start. "It's only a starting point. Hence the small batch. You know me. I get an idea in my head."

"Let me see." Brooke snatched it from Kyle's grip. "Oh, my God!"

Strike two.

"Gimme." Madison grabbed the box from Kyle and plucked one out. And said nothing. *Nothing.*

Dean was starting to wish the street would open up, and he could fall into the Paris catacombs below. Only that was scary. There was some bad shit down there.

"Dean, I can't believe you did this!" Thea exclaimed when Brooke handed her the card.

Her smile amped up to the beaming variety, but that was Thea. She'd recently exclaimed how cute the rats in Paris were.

Sawyer took the box Madison handed him along with the card and studied it like it was an original copy of the French constitution or something. Then he looked up and said, "Dude! You're the best."

He pointed at himself before he realized what he was doing. "Yeah?"

Kyle's mouth twitched before it broke into a full smile. "You nailed it, Dean. I couldn't have done it better."

"The name? The font?" He was stuttering.

"Everything." Kyle clapped him on the back. "Come on. We have an engagement to celebrate."

He stood in shock as everyone hugged him. Even Madison. "*Seriously?* You hug me now?"

"You did real good, Dean," Kyle called over his shoulder. "I can't wait to see what else you cook up in Paris with us."

"Be sure to show Nanine when you get upstairs," Thea said softly, kissing his cheek. "The name will slay her."

He stared down at the business card. The name had seemed so obvious to him.

The Paris Roommates Group

Hadn't it all started with them?

"Dean!" Madison called. "Thea says Jean Luc has a gorgeous cousin you might like, per our earlier conversation."

He looked up and smiled.

Romance.

Reinvention.

The Paris roommates were back and better than ever.

"Coming!"

———

If you liked The Paris Roommates, make Ava's day and leave a review.

———

Want to spend more time in Paris? Hang out with Dean in the next Paris Roommates novel! Read on for a little tease…

THE PARIS ROOMMATES: DEAN

Some bigwig *everyone* listens to recently said, "we've entered the age of the death of dreamers."

Talk about depressing.

So where does a person go to keep their dreams alive?

Paris—the city built by dreamers—where dreams aren't just supported and celebrated.

They're a way of life.

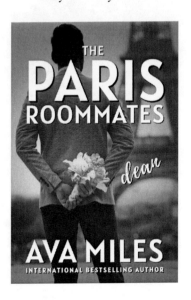

Dream a little with Dean in the next Paris Roommates novel!

STAY IN PARIS...

WITH DARE VALLEY MEETS PARIS!

Mix one genius billionaire, a dedicated baker, and the city of lights. Add a dash of spice and it's the perfect recipe for love.

She turned away from the bread proofing on the counter to face him. Taking a deep breath, she said, "I'm going to Paris with you."

The intensity in his gaze was magnetic. "I know."

She picked up the towel she'd covered the bowl so her hands could hold something. With the scent of cinnamon and bread baking around her, all she could do was lean against the counter with her hand on her heart, wondering what would happen in Paris—and eager to find out.

Get Dare Valley Meets Paris!

BRING PARIS HOME TO YOU!

Do you have a craving to bake some of your own French bread or another delightful treat?

Check out Ava's cookbook, Home Baked Happiness, and treat yourself to some home-cooked love. Oh là là!

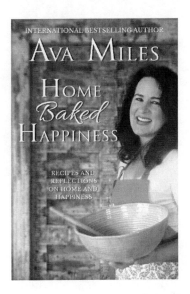

ABOUT THE AUTHOR

Millions of readers have discovered International Bestselling Author Ava Miles and her powerful fiction and non-fiction books about love, happiness, and transformation. Her novels have received praise and accolades from *USA Today*, *Publisher's Weekly*, and *Women's World Magazine* in addition to being chosen as Best Books of the Year and Top Editor's picks. Translated into multiple languages, Ava's strongest praise comes directly from her readers, who call her books and characters unforgettable.

Ava is a former chef, worked as a long-time conflict expert rebuilding warzones to foster peaceful and prosperous communities, and has helped people live their best life as a life coach, energy healer, and self-help expert. She is never happier than when she's formulating skin care and wellness products, gardening, or creating a new work of art. Hanging with her friends and loved ones is pretty great too.

After years of residing in the States, she decided to follow her dream of living in Europe. She recently finished a magical stint in Ireland where she was inspired to write her acclaimed Unexpected Prince Charming series. Now, she's splitting her time between Paris and Provence, learning to speak French, immersing herself in cooking *à la provençal*, and planning more page-turning novels for readers to binge.

Visit Ava on social media:

facebook.com/AuthorAvaMiles

twitter.com/authoravamiles

instagram.com/avamiles

bookbub.com/authors/ava-miles

pinterest.com/authoravamiles

DON'T FORGET...

SIGN UP FOR AVA'S NEWSLETTER.

More great books? Check.
Fun facts? Check.
Recipes? Check.
General frivolity? DOUBLE CHECK.

https://avamiles.com/newsletter/